EVANESCENT
LOVE

EVANESCENT
LOVE

LAMENTATIONS OF A LOSER.

A novel

ION MANTA

EVANESCENT LOVE
LAMENTATIONS OF A LOSER.

iUniverse books may be ordered through booksellers or by contacting:

iUniverse
1663 Liberty Drive
Bloomington, IN 47403
www.iuniverse.com
1-800-Authors (1-800-288-4677)

ISBN: 978-1-4917-4852-7 (sc)
ISBN: 978-1-4917-4853-4 (e)

Library of Congress Control Number: 2014917297

Printed in the United States of America.

iUniverse rev. date: 10/07/2014

DEPARTURE

Every now and again wanderlust may flood the heart.

It so happened for Didonna and I to catch this fever together. One early summer Saturday morning we woke up ready to roll, begin a cross-country trip by car from Gaithersburg, Maryland, to Los Angeles, California, and back. Coincidentally, seven, eight months after the fall of the Iron Curtain, adventure permeated the atmosphere all over the world.

*

I like to brag Didonna has been for some years my girlfriend, a tall lithe and rather voluptuous diva. As often before, she enthusiastically prepared for the trip by getting even better looking than nature made her from start. The previous night she bleached her naturally red hair to platinum blond. Her choice didn't necessarily brush against my principles-- neither did her age of nearly fifty diminish my feelings. Maturity could be an asset in the female arsenal of charms, I mused often. The appearance of crow's feet around a lady's eyes may be marks of character, not unlike some cracks in the walls of a great old castle. Isn't an ancient grand fort nobler than a brand new pretty little country house? Oh yes, I certainly say so, and in my eyes the dame

1

looked rather the castle than the cute *home sweet home*. Defying the years, her irises had retained the azure blue of sunny autumnal skies much better than the rose-petal its vivid redness after wilting to somber, duller and darker shades.

The question is was I still green? Oh no, other than in my longings. But let me return to the dame, about myself more later on.

The tip of her delicately outlined nose pointed upward in a funny insolent fashion above sensuous lips, between high cheekbones, and under perfectly browed arches were attributes of a perfectly pale physiognomy, often switching from seductive to joking or pouting, not unlike a crazy April day. In spite of this rhapsodic fluency she succeeded in appearing level, exuding the kind of light agreeable cheekiness of the negligently elegant by birth. Her quick-witted, vivacious, but seldom annoying temperament I valued more than some acquaintances of mine, rather inclined to mistake the same for superficiality. I could never acquiesce, thinking to have fathomed in her spirit a most authentic love for adventure, a passion we equally shared. She seldom rejected a new experience no matter how insane it seemed. Oh-yes, my girlfriend, dream woman, eternal female, charming lady, irresistible temptress Circe, cool Athena, beautiful Aphrodite, all separate and one in the role as my last illusion in life, your alto voice still rings crystalline, echoing in my heart as a primeval call possibly to last for as long as I live. Where are you now, when I am about to chase your shadows, and set to print my alternating regrets, unresolved rage, petty misgivings, ridiculous envy or just helpless melancholy? Has your time forever gone?

*

A confirmed and reconfirmed good-for-nothing fellow of rather smallish stature, topped by a bespectacled lunar oval face, ostentatiously framed between a slowly graying goatee, and under hair parted in the middle in bad imitation of *George Enesco* --meant to dim the luster of much too melancholy amber eyes--, I seldom passed for a man's man amongst peers, even less as a worthy catch for a respectable lady. Although frequently accused of aloofness, the few good friends I preserved still confess to being amused by my twisted thinking, awkward abruptness, and obviously maladroit showmanship.

In my self-examining retrospect, the love for Didonna looked like a singular respite from the past, otherwise punctuated by two abjectly failed marriages and several sordid one-night-stands. As in her eyes I am afraid our shack-up might have gained only little more importance than an interlude of totally wasted time. Although plunged head first in the affair following the unofficial separation from wife, many say I cohabitated with the dame in sin. Whether true or not, I owe a debt of gratitude to fate for having bestowed upon my life this female's delightful company, even if for a limited time only. I counted daily my blessings in her bed. Something is better than nothing!

From beginning to end, our friendship lasted amazingly long --many a harried years on and off, in spite of predictions to the contrary. But why keep book on the life of a man longing to discover his proverbial *soul mate* for eternity? Why indeed?

Then it should be little surprising how lucky I felt for having enjoyed the lady's graces even as the latecomer in her life. The more I weigh my story, it becomes crystal clear how slim chances fate might have allotted earlier to a worthless life for hitching my puny sentimental wagon to her overwhelming force, when she must have been ten times prettier, surrounded by real men, not by half baked intellectual weirdoes, or cheaters as myself. Having met later in life I am inclined to see our shack-up as a double-edged sword, once with gratitude for having known her at all, and second, with the frustration for never to partake in her maiden purity. On the day our tale is to become history by way of this script, I will probably still confess to feeling unmistakable fits of jealous rage against all the males who melted away in her embrace before me.

*

In the baptismal certificate I figure as Doru Constantin Corbea, a somewhat pretentious name for a Romanian, although a fairly good reason for my friends to endear me simply as Dorel, a nickname I will generally use perhaps too often in the narration.

The reader should have guessed by now I am at best pretending to write in English, since American only through naturalization. This is not unusual, as most Romanians – the saying goes - fancy to being poets. True to this belief, and for other foggier reasons, initially intended to render my memoir into vaudeville, possibly with justice in view of its pettiness. Mercifully for the musical aficionados, the task proved too difficult for a guy lacking either the discipline, or the least bit of musical or dramatic talent. Moreover, the idea struck not only as highly ridiculous, but unconvincingly amusing as well. But because it kept nagging I resorted to prose, to narrate a banal story of love and betrayal, over imposed on segments of a grand cross-country trip, adorned by mementoes of daily life. Eventually my story proved harder to pen then imagined by a naturally lazy character. Consequently, I beg the reader to be magnanimous, and forgive the literary liberties taken, and compromises made for this end. Amen.

*

Our cross-country jut commenced at Didonna's home in Gaithersburg, Maryland. My car, a small white tinniest hatchback masquerading as a roadster, but actually a modest Honda CRX I nicknamed in jest Bucephalos. Although a two-sitter, it possessed a cabin roomy enough to accommodate a couple comfortably, luggage and all the accoutrements.

As most inexperienced travelers, we piled in the vehicle a few useful and too many useless items. The portable cooler --purchased *on sale* a couple days earlier, belonged to the first category --proved unquestionably a good investment, for serving vital needs during the long voyage, unlike the excess clothing, I say a little facetiously in hind sight, stuffed mostly in my friend's luggage.

The first lesson learned became self-evident soon after departure, namely that for feeling reasonably well during any longer journey, one should take along nothing beside bare necessities. But, as most folk, we carried on our backs heavier knapsacks than needed for enjoying a free and easy life. Fortunately, the automobile – wonderful invention of modernity – alleviated our discomfort by not minding the superfluous load, unlike us condemned to drag the full weight of it in-and-out of cheap motels or hotels at nights.

It did not take a lot to learn as well that in the good old USA, two persons in order to eat, drink and overnight need not more than the combined daily average of Social Security retirement benefits, approximately sufficient for covering visits to national landmarks, occasionally enjoying delicious ice cream deserts, cold beer habitually after or before meals, and other unessential, but equally delectable pleasures.

Chewing on these trivial factoids through lively chit-chat, we figured quickly why so many retirees populate the American highways and by-ways in diverse recreational vehicles, as truly modern nomads moving East to West, or North to South, as the depths of their pockets allowed.

This sort of thrifty living the euphemistically so-called senior citizens practice could be supplanted as well by several other pecuniary advantages, offered at government-subsidized facilities set up across the States along better-known routes and sites of tourist interest. Without exaggerating too much, a couple of *old-timers* might survive acceptably even on as much as the low-to-medium pension's daily sum, and enjoy life without ever succumbing to boredom, a feat almost unavoidable for seniors attached to more conventional, sedentary styles of living. Constantly on the move, the same couple could bag a diversity of events never to be experienced by watching the *dumb-tube*, as most retired folk end up doing routinely anyway. No wonder then that based on their combined monthly average of retirement benefits, so many couples prefer spending life on the road, a fairly more agreeable alternative than staying put. Unfortunately, the same cannot be said for those afflicted by disease, or other incapacitating handicaps. How wonderful to be in good health!

But I digressed-- so let me revert to my sordid story, which I do not promise at all to follow to the end faithfully. On the contrary, I will take advantage of any opportunity, and take all the liberties for interrupting the free flow of narration with my pertinent or less pertinent observations. Again, I must implore the reader to forgive my literary bumbling in advance. Please bear with me patiently.

*

For departure Mother Nature blessed the day with wonderful weather. The morning had started on a rather cool note, a definite privilege not only for the traveler, but also for all residents of The Nations Capital during the often torrid, humidity-saturated summers. In the crisp morning air we enjoyed the trip's first few hours with the windows drawn up tight.

The cheapskate in me didn't even consider the option of air-conditioning, as I bought the car in February. 'What about the increased gas consumption?' Some of my wiser friends warned that in the absence of this modern gismo, any trip could turn fast and furiously unpleasant during the hot season. 'Yes, this is true', I admitted, but did I listen? No, not at all, and through time-tested maneuverings of logic –a tactic so dear to politicians-- I turned the argument into a question: 'My friends, wouldn't it be appropriate to experience the southern summer days in a fashion closer to reality than in the false but expensive comfort of an air-conditioned automobile?'

Dear reader, you might have figured by now who I am, what I stand for!

The hour and a half to Richmond passed without a hitch, traffic on interstate highway-95 less busy than usually.

"How lucky can we be,"—my girlfriend quipped sparkling, but I retorted:

"Just smart, dear, just smart. Why do you think I insisted on leaving so early, almost at dawn?"

"Of course, of course, you must be always right. How could I forget? Please, forgive me, your highness."

7

Ion Manta

This was the way our dialogue frequently evolved, at the surface confrontational, while on a deeper level masking on purpose a mutually felt trust and love, carefully avoiding to be seen as cheap sentimentality At least, this is what **I** believed.

Romanians allegedly don't subscribe to the somewhat false sounding pretense of Anglo-Saxon linguistic niceties exchanged between lovers-- *oh my sweet pumpkin, honey-bunny, lovey-dovey, sugar candy, and so on.* No, definitely not, my friend and I were dead set against this type of syrupiness, too. Our linguistic intricacies by having roots sunk in the opposite, much courser un-food-like soil --that I am not about to touch-- might easily offend the more sensitive English language speakers' ears, perhaps less attuned for the rather intimate forms of endearment, mostly epithets – I dare say — abundant in other Eastern European tongues as well. This assertion I advance reluctantly, very much aware that Shakespeare's language is richer than most. This is fact. But –I repeat-- this harsher way of interfacing among Romanians is less about words, and more about the tone. Tones make the music, our saying goes.

As I chewed on these dicey thoughts, the city of Richmond disappeared behind us on the right.

"Isn't it interesting," I went on with my chatter, "that no matter how often we passed this way, we never entered the capital of Virginia?"

"Then why don't we do it now?"

"Forget it. You know we must be in Atlanta by evening, and there is a long way ahead of us."

"So why not make an exception? After all aren't we the owners, creators of our plan? Why not alter it at least a little tiny bit? What do you say, buddy? Can't we show some spontaneity?"

8

"Yes, of course we might, but right on the first morning? The present exception could turn fast into habit next, and our trip will never end in time, won't you agree?"

"Then what was your remark for, just to entice me for no reason?"

"On the contrary, I just wanted to emphasize how strange some trajectories or objectives in life can be. How often we bypass things in haste, never bothering to find out more about them! Don't we do the same with acquaintances? Often by gossiping only about their obvious defects and gross attributes, we seldom dig in to deeper levels. Wouldn't our world be better off if we did? Now, you see, there you have it. I just discovered why so many apparently familiar places, or people exist truly only outside of our destinies. Is my assertion valid, or what? I know, I know my reasoning must sound weird, especially out of the mouth of the inveterate determinist as myself. You know what I mean."

"There you go again. What kind of sissy-fussy convoluted thinking is this? Can't you ever relax, and stop turning everything into meaningless philosophical riddles? Who cares about philosophy anyway? I certainly don't, especially this minute, when I want to enjoy the adventure for its own sake? Better tell me are you ready for a snack?"

"Not yet, not yet. Let's wait until we'll hit Interstate-85, and fill our pie holes once out of this heavy traffic."

The highway became busy indeed. I had to focus my attention entirely on the road, suddenly filled with huge, heavy eighteen-wheelers, threateningly hemming us in on all sides. The cabin fell mute.

*

Interstate Highway-95 I think begins in Montreal, Canada, and ends way down in Miami, Florida. As one of the important and well-known North-South, South-North thruways on the Eastern shore (all odd-numbered roads follow these directions), route-95 is rarely devoid of heavy traffic. Gigantic rigs flow fast both directions, noisily belching thick black smoke, defiantly speeding as if to annoy or terrorize the humble, and not so humble drivers of smaller vehicles.

Our delightful pleasure enjoyed until now, the newly found freedom of dashing ahead unhindered diminished abruptly, replaced by a strangely menacing apprehension and tacit, subconscious premonition of imminently possible doom. The feeling poured ice water on our youthful enthusiasm, temporarily dampening the lust for adventure as well.

Fortunately, the ordinary human soul is much more resilient than the momentary setbacks brought on by chance-adversities. We adjusted as well to the nerve-racking pressure of heavy traffic fast, as most drivers do. In tune with the majority of red-blooded Americans, we accepted and adapted to these conditions with stoicism, docility and indifference, knowing that without trucks this huge country -- the US of A -- could not distribute the food and merchandise needed for gratifying the population's seemingly infinite appetite and demand. Why not endure then with a token of equanimity the little extra stress and nuisance to this end?

*

On the eastern loop of Richmond's beltway, the traveler has to endure the unexpected irritation of repetitive highway tolls, coming up at every two or three miles. At each tollbooth drivers must obediently fork over two quarters or more, fees supposedly collected for the road's upkeep. These tolls added up quickly to about three dollars, not a big deal -- one might say – when placed in proper perspective.

"Oh boy, oh boy, considering the six thousand miles still lying ahead of us, the accumulated expense could easily add up to astronomical figures – particularly for a cheapskate like myself. Frankly, I failed to plan for this."

"Wow, what a bold self-criticism! Man, sometimes you amaze me."

No one then should hold against me the sigh of relief I exhaled a few miles later, when the large, green, phosphorescent board came in sight, to indicate the exit to route- 85, leading straight to Atlanta.

Whether my friend felt the same I don't know, and didn't bother to ask. I am almost sure no such worries crossed her pretty golden head. She was much smarter than that.

By now the thin morning haze dissipated entirely, the sun shone incessantly, inundating the landscape with a whitish powdery shimmering light. As marvelous this was to look at through the windshield, the atmosphere inside the cabin slowly overheated to unbearable levels, to become suffocating enough to render life unpleasant. Willy-nilly, windows had to be rolled down, and us get acquainted with the moisture-filled hot air the American South is so famous for. All of a sudden, we had fallen into a sort of sunny hell on earth, beautiful for the eye, but quite hard on the body's overtaxed cooling radiator. Isn't life often equally harsh as it is sweet?

*

North Carolina's border came soon in view without other setbacks.

On the Virginia side, nothing out of the ordinary catches the travelers' fancy along the road, although the state is well known for historical attractions and splendid landscapes. But subtle changes become noticeable by penetrating gradually deeper in the south, the vegetation grows more luxuriant, while the State's occasionally eroded soils shift colors to deeper and rustier tones along the shoulders of smooth, well-maintained highways. Among the low, sparse, thorny bushes, new species of flowers impress their reddish green-orange-yellow hues on receptive retinas. Along with the flora, several localities went by, none worth the price of a halt within the scope of a transcontinental trajectory. Even if commonplace, it must be noted that Virginia -- a state of great import for the birth and history of the United States --has plenty of places and landmarks to deserve more than a short visit.

Nonetheless a stopover intervened, but only after crossing the borderline to North Carolina. Here we felt compelled to pay a short visit to the tourist information center, of the type generally found at entrances into States along main routes. Our resolution thus came naturally to overlook none in the future, and for obviously good reasons.

At these information centers serving also as rest areas, the weary road roller-trotter can find out about various tourist attractions in the State, about the ways to reach them, and much-much more. Oftener than not the tourist could get here so-called *vouchers* and *coupons,* advertising discounts for restaurants and lodgings, offers lower priced than those of brand-name hotel-or-motel-chains, even for fast food establishments.

Most tourist centers might be seen as veritable business cards of the States. The quality of amenities, facilities or services, including the buildings' architecture - elegant, sophisticated or mediocre, at times even barely noticeable - can say a lot about the particular state's level of socio-economic development. These establishments, besides their obvious usefulness, could be counted as so many blessings for the ordinary visitor, who may drop in for refreshments -- Coca Cola, Pepsi, ice-cream, sandwiches, chewing gum or candy -, or for the curiosity seekers an incredible source of knick-knacks and souvenirs. Even the hobo wanderer with thinner pockets may find solace here, cold water in the fountains, and clean toilet facilities, all free of charge.

But an advice for the novice! Try to visit the centers during business hours, between nine o'clock in the morning and five in the afternoon. At all other times, with few exceptions, the centers are closed, a fact we found somewhat deficient, if not outright ridiculous. Question: what is the ordinary traveler to do, visit the State only within limits of the customary working schedule? Yes indeed. It is exactly what's expected. For those arriving late the subtext might simply and politely suggest: 'While sorry for the inconvenience, you are now on your own, manage as you can.' On the brighter side, the toilets are available twenty-four hours straight. And that, my friends, is a fact not at all negligible for anyone in need of urgent relief.

As for us Lady Luck smiled on. Since the information center was open for business, we stepped right in the pleasantly cool, air-conditioned atmosphere, contrasted heaven-like to the muggy heat outdoors. All furnishings, even the armchairs and sofas covered by cheap imitation leather impressed as so many gifts showered down directly from Paradise. Everything glistened civilized, clean and efficiently organized. Suddenly, life shined promising, worthy to be lived in spite of the cold, a bit tacky PVC, sticking unpleasantly to the skin of bare limbs. But why bother with petty observations? The amenity had been obviously designed to please.

Soon my friend's eagle eyes discovered the prospects and brochures, displayed on the shelves everywhere. She went hawk-like straight for them, and picked up a pile of appreciable size. Later, during the trip, she took upon herself the task of sorting through the advertised attractions, and select the most interesting in her judgment. I readily entrusted her with the task, guessing she enjoyed the rummaging. Why not please your partner in love?

*

It was nearly two o'clock in the afternoon when the splendiferous, air-conditioned heaven of the center got left behind, as the temperature outside must have climbed a few degrees even higher—to judge by the shimmer of light seen through the windows. Good guess. Barely seconds out, the white blinding light combined viciously with humidity in one relentless sizzle, North Carolina's merciless sun smacked us right in the face. Instinctively, we reached for sunglasses. Fortunately, on my head a wide brimmed hat recently purchased in a *Banana Republic* store—of the type hunters in African Savannah customarily sport--, while my poor companion, distinctly vainer, had to contend only with the protection of her flaming blond hair. Sincerely worried about the epidermal damage the merciless sun could cause her, but careful as well not to offend, I broached the subject gingerly.

"Hey, what about a hat, or at least a shield over the forehead? Wouldn't it become nicely your pretty face, so defenselessly naked under this murderous sun?"

"Oh yes, of course it would, but unfortunately…--well, I forgot to include a cap among my things."

"Then something must be done as soon as possible, right?"

"Oh, big-daddy, don't you worry, my visage is less sensitive than you think. Under the car's protection I will survive just fine."

"I certainly hope so. But be forewarned this is not the mellow sun of Romania."

"Come on now, the sun is the sun, here in the States, or back in the Old Country. Why scare me like this?"

"Well, I don't know, you'll find out soon enough."

My warning proved prophetic.

*

Back on the road, refreshed and reinvigorated, we watched silently as the numerous, never heard-of small villages and towns --time forgot under the baking sun-- receded silently into the past. In the Carolinas speed restrictions being less severe than in Maryland, I noticed with satisfaction the speedometer needle rise to the mark of seventy-five-miles per hour, occasionally even higher. Ah, the exhilaration of speeding!

Mostly small, rarely larger houses became visible only for seconds in the rush amid increasingly luxuriant vegetation-- flower gardens alternated with well manicured lawns, all peacefully and incessantly streaming on the left and right, not unlike images in a silent motion picture, an eerily reassuring flow of things and events receding into the immediate past. Our minds sank in a strangely remote vacuum, to a sort of alert contemplation quite impossible to express by words alone. Some events can be only lived. This dreamy state must have lasted for a good long time. Only later, much later, long after having returned to the cruder senses of material banality, when our contemplative vacuity retreated in the rearview mirror as in a reversed motion picture, only then one aspect hit in earnest, to bring forth a strange discovery.

"Where have all the people gone? There is not a soul, not a single man, woman or child anywhere in sight," I exclaimed in loud wonder.

But my companion remained mute-- no one seemed alive beside me. Only Bucephalos bolted indifferently through the landscape of this green, fantastic, luxuriant planet of ours, around this neck of the woods absolutely void of humans.

"Hey, where are the folks, the inhabitants of these beautiful homes? What could they be doing, how could they live like this, why and where are they hiding?

"What, what did you say? Who knows, maybe people are at work, in schools, or went shopping or--"

"All of them, my dear? All of them at the same time?"

She looked perplexed, as if confronted by an utterly absurd, unanswerable question.

"I tell you where they've all gone. Some must be at work, others in schools, or shopping, as you said. But I bet many are cooped up inside their homes, sheltered in safety, separated from the oppressive heat outdoors. They could very well be watching TV, constantly switching channels with their remote controls, attempting to catch two-three shows simultaneously between the ads squeezed in ever so often-- they might obsessively navigate the waters of infinite virtual realities noisy, boisterous talk-show-hosts, anchor men and women relentlessly tell and re-tell, conveying the day's news, or equally titillating gossipy stories-- then they might be watching preferred movie stars acting in fast-paced flicks or soap operas, quarrelling, shooting, kissing, avenging, forgiving, or often making openly passionate love, to the saturation point of even the most resilient, so-called couch potatoes. Eventually, tired by the onslaught of the infinite dizzyingly fast paced images and tales, the same viewers, suddenly thirsty and hungry under the assault of food commercials, could switch to strategically scheduled cooking shows, to end up at over-stacked refrigerators, enjoy a bite or two, and become the indifferent, thoroughly numbed Americans, growing increasingly obese and ill-fit, more than possibly anywhere else in the world. This is what I think we are faced with here."

Didonna could very well have answered the above, had I not decided to speak before her. So she chose only to turn on me a slightly bewildered gaze, showing the sort of pity usually reserved for people not completely at home up there, in the pumpkin-like bud grown out of our necks.

"Don't you give me this look, I am not crazy, well not completely loony. Better try to answer why is it so hard for these folk I described to switch off their infernal devices called TV sets? Why can't they pay attention to more important things in life, such as reading books, pursuing hobbies, or just falling into sweet, innocent reveries? I tell you why. As things have turned out now a days, too many poor souls can't sleep well enough during nights, and precisely due to this constant deprivation they routinely succumb to a state of hypnotic daytime slumber in front of their sets. That's why, I tell you. Just take one simple, superficial look at the shelves of any drug store, and observe how well stacked those are with the constantly advertised sleeping pills. I rest my case, in the hope you can see my point."

"Point well taken, dear philosopher, but then let me ask whether all Americans are like that in your opinion? Really all of them?"

"Of course not all, but far too many appear to me asleep within their own minds, too many live in a dreamlike virtual word."

"And you, *Dorel the Magnificent*, is it your task to whisk them out of it, aye?"

"No, far from it. I am hardly qualified for the feat because I find myself quite often similarly asleep among them. The disease is so conveniently contagious. Moreover, I even confess to nurturing for these modern men and women a secret admiration, for their ability to function reasonably well in such an extreme environment as America is in general, insanely competitive, climatically harsh, and geographically overbearing. The United States may be exceptional indeed, equally sublime and hard country to live in. For this very reason, and not only, I perceive the American so-called Perfect Union rather as a unique historical experiment in living and self-governance, totally unlike the old-type national countries persist in the classic sense elsewhere. The New World seems a lot more international than the Old World. Did I hit the nail on the head, or what?"

"Come on, stop the bull--, and better pay attention to driving." The advise came just in the nick of time as I, lost in the verve of argument, begun veering slightly off the straight line, to cross negligently over lane-markings. Luckily, Bucephalos was at the time the sole automobile on the wide-open road.

"Okay, pretty face, I will shut my mouth, but first let me finish. In spite of things said, I confess to having a deep admiration and respect vis-à-vis the American people for their steadfast and tenacious adherence to the most romantic idea, of ceaselessly trying to conquer everything on the planet, a task they embarked on from the very beginning by the huge expansion across a continent, so mercilessly crushed under this seemingly infinite sky. For the same reason I pity them as well."

"Fine, fine, I get it. Regardless, you must accept United States is a free country, one of the freest of all. Come on, be honest."

"Hm…yes, of course," I moaned in apparent defeat, and let silence fell over the cabin.

The only sound aside my muted thoughts appeared the hiss of the wind, superimposed on the soft purr of Bucephalos's well-tuned engine.

*

Several miles later, the landscape showed off the first time through the delicate nuances of the violet-pinkish inflorescences of Crepe Myrtle --a sublime creation of God, or natural wonder the South is famous for— take your pick-- as if to please the human eye's constant craving for beauty. At this point the reader is asked to overlook my ignorance, had I confused this shrub in the distance with the Wisteria, another flowery marvel typical for the American South. As for Bougainvilleas none yet impressed on our retinas. Be that as it may, we both felt equally grateful for the existence of these natural splendors, even if seen from the fast moving perspective of sixty-to-seventy miles per hour. Obviously, my girlfriend and I enjoyed a lot more in common beside our just expressed petty disagreements.

*

The farther we ventured from home time diminished in significance. What a delight not to be tied to routines!

Moving as we did, in apparently aimless fashion just straight ahead, deeper and deeper into the South, another quite trivial sensation gained the upper hand, following an intense growl in my gut asking for nourishment. Vulgarly, hunger hit again.

The ham and cheese sandwiches thoughtfully packed in the morning had been efficiently wolfed down perhaps too soon. The almost empty cooler, save a few cans of Coca-Cola and Mountain

Dew, offered little solace. But has it been really surprising for the stomach to demand its dues in the wake of so many hours on the road? I turned to my companion for help.

"I am famished."

"Oh brother, didn't you just eat?"

"I am sorry, but that was before noon, and now is past three o'clock, you see."

"Well, the only thing I can offer you is a cold drink. Want more than that better think getting off the highway. As for me just started on a diet, I am unwilling to break it on the first day. Do not count on me, buddy. I can't afford to be hungry now."

What a fine day to begin a diet! But, tactfully smart, I kept the thought to myself.

Soon after this terse exchange, I was surprised to hear her again, all but forgotten what she just said.

"Look, the next town to come up is Charlotte, thirty-to-forty miles ahead. Maybe we pause there, and have lunch? You can resist a little more, can't you?"

"Of course I can." and to emphasize my statement I pushed, as they say, *pedal to metal*.

There wasn't any plan to include a halt in Charlotte, a city in South Carolina, not far to the border with North Carolina. But the idea seemed attractive, and eventually proved useful too. Our stopover in Charlotte turned out to be the first unplanned event of real tourist significance. (I wondered often whether the name could be the same as that sadly celebrated by the well-known tune?)

But as yet all was only a distant proposition. Having not much else to do, we engaged in a meaningless controversy on whether it was advisable to disrespect a well-conceived plan right from the very start. On the other side of the coin our debate might have had the unexpected benefit of killing some time. That it obviously did, although neither of us came off any smarter because of it. All the same, the city of Charlotte made its appearance quicker than expected, proving once more the relativity of time, easily bendable even by sheer nonsense.

Catching sight of the large phosphorescent green traffic board indicating the first entrance in the city, our chitchat came abruptly to a halt. My charming interlocutor had to return to her role as navigator.

The deserted streets of Charlotte greeted sizzling, nearly broiling under the oppressively hot sun. By sheer chance we entered the city's poorer section, populated mostly by black folk. The scene, like in many large American municipalities, looked depressing enough here as well. Along several streets, houses and businesses appeared dilapidated under the baked-over patina of misery, not precisely of material nature, but rather akin to atmospherics. I say this perfectly aware that the world at large is filled by a lot worse, incredibly more sordid, poverty stricken places than The United States is. But can this fact alone suffice for considering American slums excusable? I timidly dare say no.

The numerous plywood-covered show-windows and doors, alternating with those behind heavy metallic grillages, the red-brick-walls smeared by graffiti on top of graffiti, the spit-out blackened chewing-gum-spots uniformly distributed on the pavement, the lighter variety of garbage moving in the wind —paper shreds, cigarette boxes, discarded wrappings—, or solids-- broken glass shards, crumpled aluminum cans, even automobile parts, worn tires, rusty mufflers, and who knows what else--, in no way could impress pleasantly on the visitor's memory.

Gazing silently at the desolation, a strange thought struck my mind.

"Tell me, dear, how come there are so few visual artists to notice the beauty in these decaying façades --once upon a time of distinctive elegance--, even today in degradation exuding the serene charm, let's say, as in many Maurice Utrillo's primitive Parisian cityscapes? If some validity can be attached to my opinion, why have I not heard the name of that artist mentioned in the media?"

Before my bewildered friend could figure the answer, another question burst off my foul mouth to prevent it.

"What artist would find the courage to work in this environment? None I dare say. Why is that? Because this slum emanates, as most do, a distinct although undefined, possibly exaggerated sense of danger. I say exaggerated because, even according to the darkest statistics, the menace associated within slums is less prevalent than it appears. Simply said, in popular perception these poverty afflicted urban areas might be deemed scarier than objectively justified."

"Right, so what?"

"So what, so what? Don't dismiss me like this. Isn't this the other side of the coin, of the proverbial American way of life? Don't all paradoxes intersect, whereby beauty, ugliness, danger and safety become part of the huge multifaceted tale of Americana? Oh, stupid me"—I slapped my forehead--, "how come I forgot the graffiti? Isn't graffiti on the walls art too?" My question came off louder than intended, and in lieu of an answer I've got from my lovely companion only a perplexed but quite telling look.

"Come on, buddy, you can be such a bore, too much of a smart-Alec!"

The first street – named in inadvertent irony *Main Street*— retreated in silence. As it did, another diametrically opposite vista came to fore almost without any gradation: elegant constructions, amid well planned and manicured gardens, betraying the somewhat belabored, unmistakable postmodern efforts of mixing eclectically the old with the new. The sight wiped off nearly instantly the earlier uncomfortable, murky impressions. Lo and behold, America revealed another aspect of its boast, just as paradoxical.

Not a living soul anywhere here either, an eerie void lending these marvelous architectural creations a somber air of melancholy.

"What's the use of beautifying if there are no eyes present to enjoy it?" Then I spit off the well-worn adage, *could the noise of a tree crashing in the forest be real in the absence of ears to hear it?*"

"Hey, smart guy, do I have to remind you that we are *actually* present here and now?"

"Oh, don't be ridiculous, even if, literally speaking, you're right."

Lo and behold, our aimless wandering led into an actual residential neighborhood. Rows and rows of detached houses, townhouses, apartment buildings, all wonderfully monotonous, clean-cut and of predictable appearance, alternated as anywhere in contemporary American suburbia. This type of developments are almost regularly set in the midst of green lawns, generous parking lots, alongside deviously twisted streets, designed on purpose for slowing down vehicular traffic, allegedly for protecting seldom seen children.

Naturally, my silent comment should have been instinctively opposed by an immediate virtual accusation. I almost heard my friend branding me as the unabashed alien, uncorrectable facetious character. As to prove my suspicion, she asked out of the blue.

"Tell me was life in Romania better?"

She hit spot on. Nonetheless, I retorted, filled by indignation.

"How can you compare the two? How can you be so unfair to both countries? Doesn't America deserve a better term of comparison, and Romania a lesser one?"

"Oh, there you go again with your twisted logic. I feel good in this country, for me it's all that counts."

I didn't answer, but wondered.

'Could I've been really that much off the mark? Is cold objectivity so bad? But is there any objectivity at all?' I fell silent, even in the mind.

Meandering for almost an hour or so aimlessly lost in meditation through this seemingly abandoned town, we found at last what we were looking for in the first place, a large shopping mall, strategically and pragmatically erected in the middle of a huge parking lot, thoroughly void of vegetation. Not one tree, bush, flower or patch of grass as far as the eye could see. Nothing. Just the great expanse of the lot's freshly paved black asphalt, incredibly overheated under the merciless sun, enclosed a huge circle all around, the proportionally sized mall building smack in the middle.

Locking carefully all the car-doors had to be only common sense advice, as the luggage in the cabin clearly visible was open to temptation. Although windows got rolled up and doors secured tight, a finger's width of space for ventilation had to be left open, even if reluctantly. Otherwise the brutally incandescent afternoon sun would fast render the interior into a veritable oven, possibly hot enough even for baking the pizza we so much craved. Did we have a better choice? Only God knew. On the other hand, what's worse, to let the luggage overheat or, perhaps, end up without it? Then again, isn't sinful to tempt?

As we emerged, the afternoon sizzle suddenly hit in the face with the force of Saharan sun-hell, adding another notch to the equally hot radiation emanating off the freshly laid down black asphalt. The feeling was not unlike stepping inside a smelter furnace. Lucky me, the hat protected my head. Unfortunately, my girlfriend's porcelain face, shaded only by a few rebellious locks of platinum blond hair, suddenly appeared on the verge of bursting in flames. Something had to be done urgently, or we both were doomed to regrets soon. Among the extra junk in Bucephalos's trunk I found an old, raggedy, motor-oil-soaked cap, used more than a few times under the car.

"Here, cover your mane. For now! We will surely find a more decent solution inside the mall"

A short and not too happy glance later cast in my direction, she accepted the dirty cap, although not without grumbling. Still, her acceptance had been tantamount to a miracle. Redheads are famous for their thin, sensitive complexions, and my truly fair friend, guilty on both accounts, seemed well aware of the peril. Therefore, duty bound to appease, I chose to make light of her indignity.

"When you can't have a horse, a donkey will do. Even infamous Richard the hunchback knew as much. And don't forget, he was king."

"Yeah, I know."

Once again, this is to suggest how torrid that afternoon was, insufferably hot. But, Lady Luck didn't part with us altogether. Covering the distance to the entrance we reckoned to take about thirty-to-forty seconds. Perilous as this interval appeared, the trip looked survivable all the same. And so it turned out to be, although barely, by the time we reached the entrance, the heat of the asphalt almost penetrated through the thin soles of our sandals.

The welcome inside a mall never felt so friendly.

The cool air greeted two deserving mortals in heavenly fashion. Long live to air-conditioning! In the wake of the hell endured outside, life felt good again. So much so that we nearly forgot why we came in the first place. Ah yes, to grab a bite, and guzzle down –possibly-- a few gallons of ice-cold sodas.

Inside the mall, crisscrossing *streets* meandered between well-known varieties of colorful, tastefully arranged shops. But for the moment, the temptation for browsing had to be postponed. Unbelievably, my usually lively mate appeared indifferent too, as we marched past by the attractive well-lit show windows.

'This is a big deal, indeed' I surprised myself musing. 'The heat really got to her.'

At the far end, about a dozen white tables and chairs arranged under colorful umbrellas looked momentarily more inviting than all the merchandise shops gleefully offered. Thankfully, no sun threatened here to incinerate the arrangement.

"What purpose may umbrellas serve in this place?" I wondered aloud. "Okay, I know I am a sissy-fussy, difficult guy to please."

Of truly import however was a simple fact-- wherever tables and chairs are placed together food and drinks might be served as well. This elementary reasoning proved absolutely correct. True to expectation, as we turned the corner, the sight of the familiar line of fast food establishments --minimum six—closed in the space of a wide semicircle around the center. Among these the well-known *Baskin & Robins* gained our attention right away, in all the beauty of its 31 flavors.

"Look, over there we might combine satisfying hunger and quenching thirst in one deliciously cool affair. What do you say?"

My proposal met with a tacit nod of approval almost quicker than I said it. My gal adored ice cream.

"You probably know the United States is famous not only for the goodness of ice cream, but for the large number of its varieties."

"Sure. Everybody knows this."

"But I heard somewhere the same said about Leningrad (now Sanct-Petersburg) in Russia, Milan, Rome and Naples in Italy, or Brussels in Belgium."

"So what?"

"Well then, why not treat these rumors with a little suspicion?"

"Okay, okay, why am I not surprised? Out with it!

"Ice cream might be delicious anywhere, especially some of the more popular varieties. But I tell you preparing this frozen delicacy is not rocket science. In fact, this sweet and cool concoction requires nothing more than a mixture of properly chilled natural ingredients. Having said as much, I still can't believe that 31 varieties of ice cream could be served at one and the same place anywhere else on the planet. No way, I can vouch for that. Sorry. Only Americans can be simultaneously so inventive and frivolous, as to come up with such an esoteric number.

"Wow, I am impressed."

A cute teenaged girl served us two cups of ice cream in a jiffy. I don't remember what kind. Does it really matter? At that instant, the satisfying joy of filling stomachs with equally edible and refreshingly cooling concoctions seemed good enough. The absolutely enormous portions appeared well worth the price, and could have easily substituted for meals, more so when chased by heavenly Coca-Cola. Oh how easy the simplest joys can be! And this happened in spite of Didonna's dieting, melted down to nothing as fast as the delicious ice cream in her mouth. What a pity! I could barely hold back a smile.

Then it was time for looking around a bit. After all, isn't discovery the principal aim of adventure?

The mall looked familiar, simple, elegant, efficient. A number of gift shops, a few small boutiques, two jewelers, three large department stores, one tobacconist, and a line of vendors aligned in the middle of walkways crossing at the central point. One particular store captured my attention more than others.

In the show window an incredible assortment of luxurious fur-coats protected five slender, porcelain-skinned, eternally frozen female mannequins imported from some imaginary, brutally cold *Siberian* winter. The woman in my friend couldn't resist, and lingered over them, desirously focusing on these *haute couture* creations, absolutely useless in the local climate.

"Come on, the last thing you need now is a fur coat."

"Oh you unimaginative dummy of a man! The soul of a lady will forever and ever dream about furs and diamonds, regardless how useless these are."

"Listen dear, what you presently need is a cheep canvas hat. Remember the heat outdoors?"

"How prosaic!"

As always, all imaginable and unimaginable merchandise available in the stores, except the damned, much needed hat. Could this often-recurring situation reflect some unwritten law of human existence? Had Providence destined humanity for everlasting biblical hardship and suffering, or was the present happenstance just the manifestation of Murphy's well-known law? Who knows? I certainly don't. Consequently, I resolved to suspend the question indefinitely, not uttering it on purpose for shielding myself from my friend's sharp tongue, always ready for a swift crack of the whip.

Since returning to the road was of paramount importance, I restrained pondering aloud about silly questions possibly to cause delays. A long way still lay ahead on that day.

Predictably, the air in the vehicle overheated to nearly 130 degrees F, making almost impossible to jump right in. Windows had to be rolled down, doors kept ajar for a while, to allow the space inside become livable again. For an instant I surprised myself musing on whether it could have been better had I opted for air conditioning at the time of purchasing the car. Thankfully, thoughts are silent, otherwise my companion wouldn't have left my niggardliness uncommented during the few minutes wait for Bucephalos to become a little more hospitable.

On the way out of the city, chance guided our path through an old, unbelievably superb residential neighborhood. The architectural glory of the old South unfolded in full splendor. In the bluish shade cast by huge dark green patriarchal oaks—adorned with heavy whitish hanging moss as phantasmagoric angel hair strands—lined the wide streets on both sides alongside incredibly motionless ancient colonial houses, to testify in muted unison to a grander past, even if one built mainly on slavery. But what fool can think about past injustices in moments of explosive rapture? Not even a nitpicker as myself.

Like with most common folk, the time-tested exhilarating beauty caught our fancy uninfluenced by the suffering that produced it. How often is the onlooker awed at the magnificent sight of the Cheops (Khufu) Pyramid, to think about the poor workers who allegedly perished building it? Is it not rather normal for this sort of raw sensory perception to induce the most authentic esthetic bliss, while pushing aside any negative considerations? A truly objective evaluation of the sublime set in proper context almost never strikes the mind as the first impression. Objectivity is icy, emotionally silly-dumb. For a few minutes, the power of unfiltered beauty touched our hearts too.

My, my, what a splendiferous elegance these ornate massive mansions might have emanated once upon a time with their white columns rising silently at the entrances enclosing wide-screened verandas and supporting structures, erected in the middle of generous courtyards filled with a variety of exotic flowers --such as the majestically rose-violet inflorescence of the Wisteria shrub! During those spiritually enraptured heartbeats we could hardly imagine anything more beautifully melancholic than the deep tranquility the motionless frozen-in-time post-card-like images created. Right there and then, for a short eternity we experienced together that form of pure self-forgetfulness and bliss most human souls may only long for.

The neighborhood spread over quite a large area, several blocks long and wide. Not a single person anywhere in sight here either, with the possible exception of ghosts lingering on from a long-forgotten past, probably haunting the place in the warm breeze; gentle ladies and gentlemen sipping sweet julep while exchanging velvety soothing words, echoed softly through delicately ornate porches. Then I came aloud, almost rhetorically:

"Could it be we have inadvertently wandered straight into a bewitched, time-forgotten, magnificently silky fairy tale?"

Another couple of minutes, and Charlotte vanished behind in a haze, burrowed between memory's folds at the rhythm of an old sad tune; *"Sweet Charlotte, Sweet Charlotte..."* –a melody that allowed --correctly or not-- the images caught on the retinas to re-enter the proper past tense.

Under the dwindling spell of these picture cards engraved in memory, time passed fast, and I --true to my nature-- attempted to place our experience under the logical loupe of meaningless analysis, just to prove another paradox how often evil deeds could end up centuries later as splendidly unexpected outcomes. "Isn't Lucipher so deceptively beautiful?" I asked, to which my conterpart lashed out with a sharp admonishing putdown.

"Just shut up and drive. Don't tempt God's wrath with your worthless intellectual nonsense."

*

Six o'clock in the evening. The day's heat slowly relented to give way to more bearable atmospherics. Driving, too, became less of a chore. Or was it simply the resilient super human organism that gets eventually used to even the most trying hardships? Is it not the same quality that helps man survive war, the worst possible kind of collective insanity and misery? Sometimes even Nature can be kinder than her children!

*

On a clear sundown Atlanta greets the visitor with a grandiose show of lights. Like a translucent coat of paint, the amber rays –stuck luminously to the three or four monumental arches bridging over the city's beltway at the intersection with route-65 --turned the site to a fantastic esthetic experience, to an authentic visual thrill. But at the speed of seventy miles per hour, the pleasure is by definition short lived, to fade in memory soon after left behind for a six-lane expressway leading straight to the city's heart. High noise-retention walls hemmed in the road on both sides, to hide large brick-shaped industrial plants, a variety of workshops and warehouses, frequently adorned with well-lit advertising boards above roofs sharply silhouetted against the phosphorescent sky. The strange contrast between the drab constructions and the colorful advertisements --for Coca Cola, or for the famous Copper-tan-brand of suntan lotion smeared on a beautiful young lady's healthy hinny clad only in a tiny bikini half-pulled down by a little insolent dog –ads not atypically exhibited at the outskirts of other large American cities as well.

"If I may say it these trivial displays of unabashed sensuality exude a curiously unifying esthetic quality that is apparent for me in spite of their preprogrammed variety, what do you think?" My lover's repost emerged as a snapping turtle's bite.

"Of course, for you these ads must be by definition attractive, particularly when hitting the eye with shapes of lush, healthy, sexy and almost naked women. Oh man! Have I hit the nail right on the head, my *darling virile stud,* or what? Pardon the pun."

"Come now and be serious. You know this is not what I meant."

"Sure I know it had been only another innocent little observation, right?"

Abstaining from adding insult to injury, she then cast in my face quite a wide ironic grin, coupled with a reassuring touch of her hand placed gently on my thigh as if to say: 'Don't you worry, buddy, I understand all right what drives the *homo sapiens* male. You are precisely such a specimen... and love you for it." But then, her gaze turned back to the unfolding scene, as she suddenly exclaimed-- all said totally forgotten.

"Just take a look up there! Now this is what I really call beautiful."

Straight ahead, floating above the horizon, the sight of Atlanta's skyline came alive scintillating, the line of skyscrapers in full glory beckoning the traveler twice, once with the bounced off scattered rays of the setting sun, and second, with the light emitted out of their very own sources --a strange mixture indeed as the awe-inspiringly picture projected on the background of an eerily phosphorescent sky.

Unfortunately, as we arrived at the feet of these giants of aluminum, steel, glass-and reinforced concrete, the gradually increasing darkness almost obliterated the jewel-like splendor, turned it soon to the banal reality of any large metropolis. Thereafter little of the majestic picture persisted, except the luminosity of the heavens, the eternally expanding, undying light born out of the original darkness at the beginning of Creation. Although the uniquely spectacular American cityscape could impress the puny antlike human spectator at all times, it truly shines in royal splendor during the night more than in daylight. This whole array of fairytale-like pointed crystalline cones, transparent cupolas, glass pyramids, well-polished metallic cubes, the radiating white or blue light-darts, spread over large suspended terraces delineated by bright red incandescent neon snakes must attract the onlooker's gaze against will.

For the hypothetical alien space traveler intent to landing on planet Earth it would be advisable to make the approach at night. Only then might this cosmic visitor truly be convinced to have descended in the middle of an advanced civilization.

Didonna and I, although overwhelmed, reduced to essential awe and the need to respond with emotion, proved unable to utter but a few banal words: "What a grand sight!" We kissed, squeezed hands childishly, as if the mutual manifestation of love could compensate somehow for the inability of properly expressing our admiration verbally.

But eventually, in spite of our exhilarated enthusiasm, we had to admit to a bit of down-to-earth defeat, meandering left and right throughout this magnificent place, we got lost in earnest. Not yet in possession of the city's map, the only thing left was to aimlessly crisscross the well-lit streets of downtown again and again in the dim hope of stumbling across a hotel. What a naïve course of action!

For people of modest condition –be they immigrants or native citizens –seldom is advisable to look for lodgings at *Hilton, Marriott, Ramada or Sheraton* hotels. These grand hospitality firms are mostly reserved for the pleasure of businessmen, or the unquestionably well to do. For common folk the alternative is to seek refuge in several smaller or larger, clean and perfectly comfortable motels. This is the American way, appropriate solutions for all citizens.

Terminally exhausted by the unexpected super-saturation with modern splendor, and the hopeless wandering through unknown city blocks this late in the evening, the revelation downed at last that we'd better turn around, back to the suburbs, to find there the solution adequate for our pockets. Said and done. The wear and tear accumulated during the long day's trip added an extra oomph to our decision.

Almost at the end of our way back on the same highway we drove in, the rather large, high-placed well-lit sign, advertising the *Days Inn* motel chain came at last in view. The text underneath spelled out in smaller letters and numerals the price, 49 dollars per night for a single room. What a lucky break!

"This seems as good of a deal as it gets. Why not check it out?"

"Sure dear, let's spend the night here." Once tuned to the same wavelength, the decision ensued instantly. 'How wonderful' I smiled to myself.

Without much ado our search seemed concluded. Easier said than done. Getting off the highway, then finding the entrance to destination proved more complicated than simply obeying street signs. It took at least three circles around the block before we finally stumbled onto the reception hall. In retrospect, the minute we succeeded the task appeared ridiculously obvious, and our bumbling roundabout the building somewhat idiotic. But we took solace in that even the most seasoned globetrotters faced with the unexpected turns and re-turns within an unfamiliar location might admit to this sort of confusion.

Once again experience had proven how much easier it is to reach a goal in hindsight than in fact. Regardless, our purported *superior* reasoning faculties for discerning most elementary objectives proves often more daunting than looks at first. Fortunately, Lady Luck must have taken pity on us again, but evidently not before letting her subjects wander blindly a bit, and only thereafter pointing ironically to the right, simple way, as if to humble on purpose. How often people notice luck's contribution to the success of their actions? Quite seldom I dare say.

The *Days Inn* motel, larger than all we've seen before, resembled a military compound rather than a civilian establishment, considering the area it covered, the huge parking lot, and the Olympic-size swimming pool, placed right smack in the middle. The fairytale-like blue water of this small artificial lake appeared as an inviting oasis, beckoning the visitor with unbelievably transparent angelic lights shooting to the surface off its depths.

"What a wonderful dip for me here!" I mumbled not softly enough.

"I can hardly wait to see that."

At the reception desk, courteous personnel, mostly Afro-American young women and men garbed in the motel's rusty colored uniform tried with a modicum of elementary courtesy to accommodate more people than we expected to see.

Atlanta is known for its large black community, which produced or nurtured many famous cultural and political personalities-- Martin Luther King Jr., Ray Charles and Andrew Young, to name a few. Besides these figure whites as well. Margaret Mitchell has been a famous daughter of this city too, so it's no accident that she staged her *Gone with the Wind* in the South, where the rhythm of life even today keeps a pace noticeably slower than up North. Indeed, people in hot climates seemingly do not feel the need to hurry as much, they may afford the time even for a few more nice words than is customary for welcoming visitors elsewhere. Why rush? After all the end of the world is not yet in sight!

Ahead of us, a couple of Londoners --betrayed by their unmistakable Cockney accent-- tried in vain to explain a murkier point to a pretty receptionist, for the equal frustration of both parties. Although each side purportedly spoke English, the conversation failed to reach mutual comprehension. What a funny scene!

Getting quickly bored by the tenuous situation, my attention wandered off, to focus instead on a bunch of tourist brochures, spread out on the low coffee table, semi circled by armchairs across a muted TV set's moving images. I picked up a few, and passed them on to my friend. Meanwhile the issue with the British tourists having found a solution, and it was our turn at the registry.

Plenty of rooms available, although none at the low rate advertised. We misinterpreted the sign by ignoring the **"and up"**, following the **49** dollars stated. But as we opted for a double bed--... oh, well-- the higher price had to be graciously accepted.

A warning to the unadvised! Please read ads carefully and thoroughly. But then again, in God's name tell me, dear reader, how to achieve this out of a speeding car?

All in all, the offer acceptable enough, we paid for the night, receipted the keys, jumped in the car, and drove off to locate the room. It happened to be on the third floor of a building across the pool.

The day's heat relented little well past sunset. The humidity and the attending thick smog continued undiminished even in the absence of the day's orb merciless shine above. My shirt stuck to skin, and so did Didonna's blouse to her back. A warm scent of dampness mixed with slightly pungent exhaust fumes filled the air, to cut down a bit the clarity of the pool's lagoon-like blue water splendor.

Like it or not, the luggage had to be dragged in and up all the same. It's common wisdom I remembered again that offering the smallest temptation for the wicked prowlers of the night --in parking lots or elsewhere—is deemed sinful. This rendered emptying the vehicle mandatory with or without the side dish of rumbled dissatisfaction. The task took wholly ten minutes. Only thereafter could our drained bodies crash in the cool room, in the armchairs by the window, the pile of luggage hastily dumped unopened on the carpet right by the entrance.

"Well, so much for that." I said, got up, and headed straight to the mini-bar. Without hesitation I uncapped a bottle of beer. "You want some too?"

"I do, but please pour the beer for me in a glass."

Women pay attention to such minor idiosyncrasies. So I obliged without a hiss, and extracted one flimsy plastic cup off the several wrapped in cellophane by the empty aluminum container poorly trying to imitate a wine cooler, all on the chest of drawers. To judge by my companion's barely restrained smirk of approval, I knew my gesture had been appreciated.

"Hey, cheers!" and touched silently my bottle to the plastic glass in her hand. Polycarbonate does not sound anything like crystal. In spite of the uber-prosaic toast, the beer tasted so refreshingly good we practically inhaled it. Oh marvelously delicious amber-yellow liquid, how welcome *thee art* on a hot summer night!

Deeply satisfied, my stare for a while vacuously steady on the empty bottle, and then I commenced peeling my clothes off slowly, one by one, my sweat-soaked shirt, followed at long last by the trousers, to let the velvety cool air in the room caress the skin all over my shamelessly exposed body.

My mistress watched in silence, but the fleeting glimmer in her eyes showed the readiness to do the same while suggesting, 'my friend, you have no modesty at all.

'Could she be right? Do I feel no shame whatsoever under her gaze? No I don't. Why should a couple in love feel immodest at the sight of each other's nakedness? The Romanians are not Puritans' I argued silently Then again, maybe I was subconsciously aiming at a different target, at teasingly cajoling, provoking my friend to erotic action. 'So what! What if I did? Is it so wrong being the initiating agent? Isn't this part and parcel of the game males and females instinctively are playing before mating? Aren't all mammalians exhibiting the same type of behavior in a great number of beautifully ritualistic ways? Perhaps not all the animal within us is evil.'

The questions quickly found the answer in my woman's reaction, a little bit muted, tastefully and properly delayed, as well-bred ladies should do it. Yet her response had been unambiguous. First she unbuttoned slowly, very, very slowly her blouse, then came the zipper's turn, which once pulled down in the back let the skirt slip off along her long shapely legs, to find rest on the carpet by the sandaled feet. Then the process had to be suspended for effect, at least for another brief interval. The panty and the bra stayed on continuing to hide the essential difference between her and myself, between the prowling male and the oh-so-innocently tempting female. My, my, how strangely luring these flimsy silky white textile surfaces reflected in my eyes. 'Well, well, are we ever ready to reveal everything at once? Why give away the well-known secret in one straight shot? You know, dear friend' --she seemed coyly to suggest--, 'a little mystery before the final curtain drop must be preserved. Isn't a little suspense always welcome before the act?'

I understood the game well, all its necessarily provocative nature, regardless how subtle, or how impudent my behavior that elicited it. I also knew that in spite of all the *macho talk,* preferably the woman is expected to exercise control in this delicate human playacting. Whatever man's simpler ego stupidly demands is it not deemed to meet with gratification in the end anyway? Why then rush the pace of this beautiful, simultaneously naughty and innocent play?

This time I didn't. Instead tempered my desire by watching the quintessential woman in awe, more lustfully than ever. Although the day's trip had surely worn down my mate as much as it did me, I found an irresistible charm in her promisingly reserved, delaying little strategy. The message in her eyes became at once glaringly clear. 'If you want more than what you see come and get it.'

This is the game. It could be played in endless delaying variations that might bring the participants precisely to the opposite, precipitated conclusion, to the lightening explosion of the flesh overwhelmed in passionately violent embrace, occasionally pushed rather prematurely to the same, but forever-surprising sensual outcome. How imaginative could the female be! Compared to her the male is just a simple zygotic moron.

And, true to this inherited dumb nature of mine, I committed that evening's fatal error, of casting a furtive passion-killing glance at my watch. It showed only eight o'clock. The night was young, other things had to be done first. Obviously, the thought showed up on my face, forcing upon the scene a deflating change of venue.

"Cool it sweetie, for now at least. Please. A cold shower, and we'll see what else may be accomplished tonight. Let's take a rain check. Be a good girl, okay?"

The promising beginning of spontaneous eroticism stopped dead on its track.

Under the shower's cold, invigorating spray the day's weariness washed away fast in a ritual of always-miraculous purification. Clad in the motel's immaculate bathrobe, I rejoined Didonna back in the room. To my pleasant surprise she had prepared a snack, a bottle of beer on the side, this time off our own meek supply from the portable cooler. At the age of fifty or so, the stomach may offer man pleasures seldom appreciated at twenty. As my time ticked away as anyone's, I too became ever more aware of this prosaic fact.

The tasty morsels slid down fast in the gut, helped by small talk as well. Another bottle of beer I polished alone, once Didonna vanished in the bathroom. She re-emerged wrapped in the fluffy bathrobe completely refreshed, as I did before her. With her hair wet she looked as a kitten just in from the rain. During such fleeting moments I realized how pretty she still was in spite of her years.

A lady's beauty can be elusive, hard to define, living mostly in the beholder's eyes. But, if one is to catch it before the benefit of make-up magic, then judging it might be an easier, less subjective task. Gosh, how I cherished the privilege of witnessing the purity of these rare moments.

Before taking to the road again, the cups of strong Turkish coffee, slurped down beforehand, might have added a little extra impetus to our recovery. The portable electric hot plate packed in the luggage proved its worth for the first time, to be reconfirmed again and again later during the trip as well. What a delightfully perfect match between a cup of hot aromatic coffee and a fine cigarette! Hey you, brave health warriors dead-set against smoking, forgive me for blurting out my exclamation so incorrectly loud!

Clad in fresh light summer garments, we took to the highway anew, eager to revisit downtown, this time intending to inspect it more carefully. In the car the same oppressive heat and humidity became fast palpable only minutes later.

*

According to locals, summer in Atlanta is torrid day and night, the atmosphere over saturated with suffocating moisture, reminding the nostrils of some wet laundry just pulled out of boiling water. This old Southern city Scarlet O'Hara made famous in her tragic story has evolved into a sophisticated modern metropolis, an industrial, commercial and business center, as well as an important transportation hub. Hospitable restaurants, fancy bars, noisy discos could be seen and heard everywhere on the streets, populated mostly by Afro-American youngsters, but not only. A variety of other groups jaywalked brazenly across streets, to the annoyance of impatient, horn-tooting drivers. Music, the heavily syncopated, rhythmic sounds of the latest so-called *rap* tunes flooded out of several sources, discos, cars, or the boom boxes muscular young black lads carried with well feigned aplomb on their broad shoulders.

Overwhelmed to the point of sheer amazement, for a time we kept simply circling around aimlessly, combing through this cheerfully noisy and inviting urban environment.

"How about a drink in one of these inviting bars?"

"Sure, dear, why not? How nice of you!"

Easier said than done. Yet finding a parking spot on the street proved impossible, on the other hand, to pay seven dollars for an hour in a lot did not seem a reasonable alternative either. Moreover, what could a middle-aged couple seek amongst these super energetic youngsters? Probably less than nothing!

By twelve midnight, safely back in the cuddling safety of the motel-room's comfort, we had no reason for regrets. Stretched out under the cool, immaculate, properly starched sheets, our weary bodies soon immersed in sweet feather-light forgetfulness. My friend fumbled a minute with the remote control in the hope of finding a good flick on the local TV channels, but as the choice had been the same bland and noisy shows as elsewhere in America, she finally gave up.

A click and a white flash later, the dark void spotted by greenish and purple floating shapes swallowed the room. As I turned to my right, a sweet electric shudder shook my body head-to-toe. My girlfriend's moist lips gently touched the skin on my back. Unable and unwilling to resist, I turned around to face the unmistakable call. The womanly flesh received as the warmest shelter of forgetful bliss. The always-vulnerable male took refuge in the feminine abode, to rediscover temporarily the eternal womb-- a smidgen of reassurance the added bonus.

SUNNY HIGHWAYS

In the morning, the appetite for new, unfettered adventures chased away yesterday's fatigue. Following six hundred miles of driving, and a day rich in events, we could be forgiven for sleeping a little late. But no such thing happened. At seven o'clock sharp, our eyes popped wide open. An impetuous sort of *Reisenfieber* had taken over body, soul and spirit. Through a slit in the drapery the sun found a way in, casting strangely vivid light bands over the room's disarray, as the familiar noise of early morning activity outside filtered in too.

It was a sweet awakening, soft comfortable lingering between the sheets. Then something unexpected happened. Didonna placed a soft kiss on my neck, signaling her willingness to spark a spontaneous sensual encounter. She gave away her love freely and quietly, without much of a warm-up preamble. I honored her carnal and emotional homage in similar silence, absolutely overwhelmed, abandoned in her passionate clutch, buried under a sudden avalanche of joy. Before I made the dame's acquaintance, as much as I desired her, I never knew, then or later, how to elicit or be prepared for it in earnest, to respond in kind to sensual generosity. Contrasted with spontaneous gifts of physical love, I could often convey in response only the performance of a wretchedly awkward cheater, the selfish act of a profiteer.

Although my memory fails to recall a tortured childhood –so dear to modern psychiatry--, I still hunger figuring out what lurks behind my stupid awkwardness, behind my inability to express feelings unhindered. In spite of reviewing all evidence in light of the latest mumbo-jumbo fads-- according to which events like the divorce of parents, or the poor relation with an autocratic stepfather could wreck a child's personality for life--, I've never been able to understand my inclination to melancholy and daydreaming that caused the empathetic response to a partner come off my lips always a bit too late. Although not lucky to enjoy the caring warmth of a clear-cut mother-to-child relationship, I have been fortunate enough to escape the negative consequences of a broken marriage thanks to my unquestionably stern but heroic grandmother, who raised me with unconditional love, inexhaustible devotion and trust. On the other side of the coin --often wondered—whether this sort of stern, at times even harsh love could have somehow inhibited my emotional development? Could this *tough love* really be responsible for my innate timidity, for the inability to express openly sentiments at the right time, as for instance on that morning, when faced by my concubine's uninhibited offering of love? Perhaps. What must be confessed, though, is how vividly I recall to this day the heartfelt intensity of passion, my eagerness to express devotion unrestrained in spite of my unconvincingly spoken words, on that occasion rather akin to irony than authentic emotions. She complained about this awkwardness of mine more than a few times, saying that my mutterings of confessed love reverberated incredibly false in her ears, regardless of the circumstance.

Then what in-the-name-of-God motivated my insistence of mumbling false, unctuously sweet babbling more than often during, or in the afterglow of our lovemaking? Wouldn't have been wiser to refrain altogether, and be rather more careful in committing to words the slightly lashing overtones my self-deprecating tongue naturally reverberated with? I don't know. But, with passing of time, I have learned anyway how women are like cats that recognize feigned sentiments instinctively for not to be fooled by half-baked, inhibited or badly expressed feelings popping off insecure boyfriends. No place can be safe enough for a man to hide from the infallible female intuition. In this sense my mistress wasn't the exception, she amply and repeatedly proved her quite uncanny *sixth sense*. For this reason alone, I resolved for the most part to remain mute during our romantic sessions, in spite of the intensely tempestuous passion welling up unexpressed in my heaving chest. At long last, I came to accept this frustration, convinced that only silence could provide the minimally acceptable refuge from becoming ridiculous when tempted to confess my love verbally.

Maybe this self-enforced restraint was the real reason so many women considered me aloof, even cold. Only God knows. Fortunately, Didonna, quick-witted as she was, probably more aware of my hidden handicap than previous girlfriends, could see through the maze, and finally accept my love as given, imperfect, but void of false sounding small talk. For this understanding --although barely effective in alleviating my ineptitude-- I felt for her nothing less than an infinite degree of gratitude.

Once the act completed, including the minutes of abandon in her deliciously sweet embrace, that morning lovemaking made me feel weirdly returned to adolescence, to the time mysteries of flesh confront a boy for the first time, then again, and again, and again in the same, unchanging way nearly to the end of life.

My little she-devil jumped off the bed, put on my unbuttoned shirt in lieu of her robe, and quickly disappeared in the bathroom, leaving imprinted on my retina indelible flashes of her curvaceous silhouette. Certainly an expert in acting at once the lover and mother, she often successfully combined the two, the possessiveness and passionate female impulses superimposed over slightly incestuous motherly feelings. Oh, what better motivates man's eternal longing for the nostalgic return in the universal womb?

An hour later, we landed back on the streets of downtown Atlanta.

*

During daylight, the American city loses some luster. Although the fantastic skyscrapers retain their erect greatness, in the sun's glare those huge glass and steel structures become rather some arrogant exclamation marks than statements of objective achievements, as if to juxtapose the definitely clashing purposes of man and nature. Likewise, as the tall edifices brag ostentatiously about opulent luxury, the lower abodes beg more modestly for small change in the name of sheer, unpolished, decaying poverty, in the vertical dimension unbelievable metaphors reach for the stars, in the horizontal, misery peddles its petty wares, in the dizzying heights precious stones sparkle in the sky, at the bottom the wind blows discarded garbage and foul smelling exhaust smoke. This mixture of aseptic splendor and sordid ugliness the majestic sun bakes in one and the same pie shaped to the inorganic geometry of indolent neglect and disorder is a strange duet of ingredients indeed. Absolute poverty –as for instance, in Bangladesh-- is unheard of in this realm, nonetheless, the incredibly proud elegance of the upper body garment shines in glaring contrast to the modest worn-out foot ware.

Not very far off downtown, in the older neighborhoods history's memory brings back echoes of a not-so-distant past's colonial lifestyle, and the well-mimicked, but definitely provincial atmosphere of the Old World's architecture and ambiance.

Saved from the demolisher's modernizing wrecking ball by brave historically conscious groups of citizen, the old buildings survive only under countless coats of white, red, black, gray or off-beige paint, smeared on the walls with the desperate intention of hiding a sort of pettiness, apparent for the keener observer in contrast to the towering glass and polished, metallic elegance of colossuses nearby. But it is not this weird mixture of old and new the best illustration of eclecticism in post modernisms? Is this not precisely a contributing factor for the modern American urban environment to grow so sophisticatedly uniform, almost monotone? Atlanta makes no exception.

This might be exactly why the streets of older, humbler quarters exhibit more architectural cohesiveness under the unifying thick shade of secular trees. Here the row houses look natural, in spite of fresh tar patches on the asphalt, infinite spots of discarded chewing gum, cigarette buts or even -- yes, yes-- various rusty automobile parts, everything cast off negligently under the sun, to be picked up by public garbage collection that, in turn, carefully avoids performing its task properly, perhaps waiting, or even hoping for the rubbish to self destruct.

On these streets people may be seen as well-- old men and women simply clad, walking slowly, or momentarily pausing to watch noisy playful youngsters in baggy short pants and t-shirts, and shod in the mandatory sneakers, as they bounce basket balls on the hot pavement. These folk clearly prefer the good old outdoors, although seldom appear to be acting in purposeful concert, each pedestrian enveloped in his or her own solitude, the majority peaceful, perhaps less dangerous for the inadvertently lost alien intruder than the fear mongering media lets it known. This civility is valid even in the poorest neighborhoods. The same impression can be rather easily suggested for the euphemistically so-called *good locations* as well, once the absence of people or potholes, dirty patches, rubbishes, or other telling details of poorer *hoods* get ignored. Both types of cityscapes offer the visitor equally eerie surrealist sights, probably better suited to the world of dreams than to palpable reality.

Notwithstanding the paradoxes typical for the quintessential American city, Atlanta -- ravaged by the vengeance and wrath of General William Tecumseh Sherman's Yankee troops during the nineteen-century Civil War - has risen from its ashes to become a truly modern municipality, capable of challenging any great urban world metropolis in all respects. More than that, the city can deservedly boast about its cherished historical town, whereby the tranquil and hospitable colonial atmospherics had been carefully recreated, and maintained to any discriminating tourist's esthetic satisfaction.

*

"As for myself, I prefer the authenticity of smaller towns up north, such as Gettysburg in Pennsylvania, or Williamsburg in Virginia, less opulent, but more original, and realistic through their historic appeal. What do you think?"

"Oh boy, only you can come up with such bizarre ideas. Instead of enjoying the here and the now, you constantly cheapen it by contrasting everything to randomly selected past impressions. You deserve my pity."

"Pity or not, that's who I am."

"I know, and I ask myself why in the name of the Lord I love you?"

"I love you too, darling, but fail to see what's so pitiful in expressing an opinion."

In lieu of response she just shrugged in exasperation, leaving me a bit miffed, since I itched for a little more in-depth-debate on the subject.

Following this exchange, the only smart thing might have been to forget it, and search instead for a convenient way out of town-- I wished to hit the open road before the day became exceedingly hot.

Nonetheless, I went on in my silly talkative mood.

"For me leaving a place behind appears often easier than arriving to it. At departure the only thing paramount to remember is one general direction –for us presently southward. Were I to make a wrong turn it will be easy to correct. This way seldom could even a serious error delay any trip for too long."

What I didn't confess how in the meantime I secretly prayed Lady Luck for guidance, to prevent my ending up ridiculously back at the starting point. This had happened to me more than once. All the same, experience taught me that when faithful to a single direction, the right way would eventually show up. With this in mind, I pushed resolutely forward toward route-65, the only one I retained off the map. And lo and behold, lucky me, it soon came up, pointed out loudly on the large, phosphorescent-green board popped up ahead.

"See, what did I tell you?"

I spoke too soon. A minute later, coming to a bifurcation, I had to make a quick choice. Apparently, only one branch of the highway led to route-65. But which of the two was it? Faithful to Yogi Berra's advise I took the fork straight through without hesitation, before having the time to read the explanation provided in smaller print. Less than a hundred yards later my grave error became glaringly clear, as I glimpsed in passing another sign above the road parallel to ours, pointing tauntingly to the truly desired direction.

Why do I always have to select going left, and not right? Why? Why? Why? Unable to come up with a good answer to a senseless question, I felt suddenly sufficiently enraged, as to channel my moronic ire against my companion, in a futile attempt to blame her for my mistake. Isn't the tactic often wonderfully convenient? To scapegoat is only human!

To my excuse I came to my senses fast enough the minute I saw she had no intention to reproach me a thing, not electing to play along the blame-shifting game. She seemed honestly worried only about the consequences of our wrong turn. I swallowed quickly my wounded pride and abstained from any further comment, resigned to fate, relaxed, prepared to make a little light of the situation as a way out of both anger and the *faux pas* at the first opportunity. Consequently, my mood changed in a heartbeat. Did we enjoy the vacation, or what? If so, why not blame my stupidity on the deficiencies of the American highway system? The cop-out felt mighty good, it conveniently opened the door out of my frustration, and turned the nefarious affair into a new, unexpected potential adventure. Isn't it amazingly wonderful to assign blame totally outside of us? Damned be the accursed human nature! Wisely thus we accepted the unplanned change cheerfully, liked it or not.

Atlanta disappeared behind in a haze, in the memory of a dream dissolved in the strong morning light. Having to face the changed itinerary, we got off the highway at the first opportunity, to end up in a shopping center --a huge grocery store smack in the middle. So far so good! Our mishap turned exactly to what we needed, as our supply of beverage and nourishment got almost exhausted. Other than that, a new unforeseen necessity arose, that of a good suntan lotion, for treating the suddenly painful burns the merciless southern sun inflicted on Didonna's right, and on my left arm. The effect of yesterday's searing rays showed up belatedly on our epidermal surface exposed through the car's side windows. It never occurred to either of us the alternative of wearing long sleeves. It was summer, what the hell!

Inside the store, well supplied with everything imaginable, only white folk. Not a single black soul anywhere. The same American story-- blacks concentrated within a city ghetto, and whites in the suburbia. Oh, well!

We bought the much-wanted items, a roll of cheesecloth on top of it; to be moistened and placed on the burnt arms as improvised compresses. The suntan lotion alone --we surmised in pain—couldn't by itself offer enough protection for the blistered skin, suddenly sensitive even to the plain bright light of fluorescent tubes inside the store. And outside, not a single cloud spotted the sky on that brilliant July morning.

Back on the road, my pretty copilot engrossed herself in studying the map. Her delicately long fingers tipped by red polished nails searched skillfully amongst the several alternatives. She presented them for my inspection one by one, although reading any proved almost impossible, as I had to pay attention to the road. But what if I could have the time to read? What purpose should have served? The Georgian countryside was as utterly unfamiliar to me as to my companion. Obviously, we had to get off the highway again, to get oriented. We did just that.

The spot selected for another hopefully short halt happened to be in front of another little shop, this time a *mom-and-pop* outfit, a combination of general store and fast food restaurant, welcoming and familiar, the type lately touted in the media all too frequently to being less and less noticeable amid the proliferating contemporary commercial behemoths. Be that as it may, here might have been possibly the best place to re-setting our future course. How often in life (or history for that matter) fateful decisions weren't made in apparently insignificant, improbable locations? What would Waterloo be without Napoleon, or Gettysburg without Lincoln?

"Listen dear, why not follow this nice little country road we are on now? Please do me the favor-- it must be so much more beautiful this way than running like rabbits on the boring highway."

Lo and behold, we resolved in one common breath to forgo the beaten path, and drive, instead of the four-lane highway, on the two-lane road, invitingly open ahead of us the minute out of the lot. Indeed, how luring the alternative seemed compared to the drab expressway with its crazy traffic, how seductively the country road beckoned with shady old trees, and the atmosphere vaguely perfumed by flowers of the field? Miraculously and spontaneously, the adventure turned to a feast, equally for eyes and nostrils.

The intention to drive straight ahead for at least five miles, and then, after having passed through the village, eventually to re-enter the highway at the other end sounded wonderfully promising, more so as the cool tranquility of an enchanting rural world invaded the cabin of Bucephalos.

"Thank you, you will not regret the delay." She leaned over and planted a tiny innocent smooch on my cheek. I loved it, and acquiesced in silence by painting on my mug the sort of smirk worthy of the proudest tomcats.

The good feeling however was not to last long-- only twenty minutes or so later, the all too familiar uncertainty returned full force. The next expected crossing with the highway, so clearly indicated on the map, failed to materialize. Ten more minutes of blind rolling forward, and at an altogether different intersection, our error became clear at last.

"Somehow we have missed an exit."

"Yeah, I guess you're right."

The new choice had been either turning back, or finding another *happy* solution. Out came the map again. Fortunately, a good alternative solution became evident immediately, as the country road seemed to rejoin the same main throughway indirectly a little later on. What a pleasant outcome! Isn't sometimes preferable to enjoy the dummy's good fortune than suffer the clever man's failure? Although a bit apprehensive in the wake of our latest *smart* misadventure, my mood continued optimistic enough to drive on unconcerned. Time barely passed eleven o'clock before noon. The day was still young.

Then the road changed again without warning, to turn to a simple narrower pathway, meandering amongst modest houses and gardens, not unlike many I've seen throughout the Romanian countryside, for instance, in Transylvania. I itched to point this out the resemblance

"Look at these pretty kitchen gardens, and the tinny houses behind them, don't they remind you of other familiar places?"

"I don't know. What other places?"

"Transylvanian villages, of course. Is it not obvious?"

"Hmm. Maybe. Indeed, I can see a bit of similarity, but the style and size of these Georgian houses is quite another story."

"Oh well, this is obvious. Of course, this village could be quite different in other respects as well. But I was thinking in terms of general atmospherics rather than making a strict comparison. Don't these southern hamlets emanate a certain, unquestionably tranquil rural charm, very much like villages in Transylvania?"

"Maybe... in a stretched sort of way they do indeed."

In the courtyards people (what a miracle!), men dressed in t-shirts and blue jeans, folk preoccupied with daily chores. The oncoming traffic, sparse as it was, consisted of mostly pick-up trucks, a few of them strangely elevated on huge tires, above some cabins the controversial confederate flag flapping in the wind. This immediately brought to my mind the well known *Hazard County*, the famous TV sit-com of the seventies, and I wouldn't have been that much surprised to see *General Lee*, the supped-up Dodge Charger muscle car, and the two main characters greeting us from the front seats.

"You see how deceptively innocent this quaint little village looks like, almost as the truest embodiment of peacefulness, and faith in the Good Lord on Earth.

"Why you say deceptively, isn't this village truly peaceful?"

"Who knows? Within this splendidly simple serene sleepy village might be still lurking the ugly white specter of a visceral menace, not so very long ago attributed to the so-called *Ku-Klux-Klan*?"

"Oh boy, come on now. Stop being silly."

"No, no, I am serious. The devil can dwell often quite comfortably within the most decent looking remotest little villages, in the hearts of many God-fearing, decent but oh-so narrow-minded folk. Have you ever seen the peacefulness and harmony of a typical Teutonic village?"

"Sorry, smart guy, your analogy is total utter nonsense."

"Nonsense or not, stranger things happened in history, and America is not the exception. While on the surface She can look so wonderfully peaceful, violence may deviously still germinate just a little under the benign surface, for anyone willing to take a peek under it. Fortunately, or unfortunately —depending on the vantage point-- for us, along with the majority of distant and lucky people the effects of this sort of evil could be almost totally ignored. And that's what we exactly do now with shameless abandon, in the mold of all good-hearted, habitually indifferent people. Does this mean or indicate that the level of racism is statistically dead in either color's direction? What's then the meaning of the euphemistically so-called *bad areas,* routinely identified by real estate agents in most urban areas? Why are some neighborhoods considered that bad? This factoid may hide some rather unpleasant aspects, perhaps quite telling in this sense."

"Yes, professor Corbea. May I advance a slightly different opinion? Probably not, yet I still must say it, you are a quite bore sometimes."

And with this the subject drew fortunately to a close. Compelled to admit that for tourists like us, just passing through this splendidly idyllic countryside --or, for that matter, through any other pastoral area anywhere in the world -- the beauty of a place might strike as obvious, and to glimpse under its darker layers would require some additional analytic pondering, which we, conveniently, neglected doing. As humans tend to pacify their conscience with relative ease, we did the same, and tacitly accepted the idea of how little the individual could achieve in the interest of changing the world for the better. As all ordinary folk we preferred living complacently in the comfortable present, inclined to notice only the brighter sides of life. Is this really a fault, or simply another necessary survival aspect of the human soul? Who can tell? I certainly cannot.

Half an hour later, the much-desired highway came at last in view, to take us on its smooth surface to the next destination. Cheered up by our belated victory, I pushed reinvigorated *pedal-to-metal,* until the needle of the speedometer climbed steadily in the vicinity of eighty-miles-an-hour mark. On the perfectly flat whitish-gray, clean-swept endless concrete carpet runner, thrown over this vast geographical expanse of land, we sped along nearly alone. Soon, Bucephalos carried us across the border into the great State of Alabama.

*

In 1955, in Alabama's capital city of Montgomery, Martin Luther King Jr. and Rosa Park contributed enormously to organizing the by now famous historic bus-boycott that pushed them to the forefront of the fight for equal civil and voting rights in America. But as our plan didn't call for a stopover, we left the city behind without a detour through it.

"Maybe we ought to have paused in Montgomery for a few minutes."

"No, a few minutes wouldn't have sufficed. Don't forget we have fallen behind schedule as it is. Too bad proud town of Montgomery! There'll be always another time for you."

"Yeah, you're right, perhaps some other time."

Instead, we halted at the first information center that came along the road. Why cut through a state without gaining some knowledge about its attractions?

It is probably little known to foreigners that it were the Spanish explorers who came around here first -- Hernando De Sotto among them—, that the French established settlements initially, that Andrew Jackson defeated the Creek Confederacy at Horse Shoe Bend in 1814, that the State seceded from the Union in 1861, and other morsels of information ordinary travelers unfortunately often forget right after leaving the place behind. Isn't this a pity? *Sic transit gloria mundi!*

From this point on, the road turned monotonous, the heat up to nearly unbearable levels. The shirt stuck to my back in spite of the strong draft blowing through the open windows. What a foul icky feeling! Could this have been the reason we went by a great number of smaller localities in silence, without even taking note of their names? Perhaps. None seemed sufficiently interesting to merit even a short stop. Please accept our apologies, people of Alabama.

Although the sun shot down its rays hotter than ever, the moisture-saturated air promised rain. Near the horizon, in a murky haze, the outline of low gray hills, barely noticeable in the mist, vaguely asserted their presence in the distance under whirling volumes of dark clouds. A dramatically ominous tempest promised to dim the sunlight any minute, without lessening at all the landscape's almost boring expanse, the interstate highway-65 sliced in two equal halves. Frightful lightening flashes, ear-shattering thunderbolts ensued in fast sequence, lashes of rain soon drummed on the metallic back of brave Bucephalos, and then it was all over, as we fortunately caught only the storm's tail end. But then, the sky didn't turn blue, clouds persisted under it milky gray.

Around one o'clock in the after noon, the first pangs of hunger pinched the stomachs anew. Hastily we veered in the first come-up rest area, to buy gas, and have lunch. The hills melted in the distance, replaced by unending, slightly undulating green fields, uniformly covered by dense shrubbery. Within the rest area, to the left, the gas station perched atop a small bulge of land, a fast-food-place-- a souvenir shop attached to it. As Bucephalos' tires rolled on with the familiar grinding rumble up the gravel-covered ramp, I looked for a spot to park, possibly in the shade. No such luck.

Aside a bunch of thorny bushes vaguely hemming the place in, not one tree on the lot. Eventually, I parked in a spot visible through the eatery's wide windows. The place looked drab, almost forlorn. The few people, some at the pumps, some inside, locals or travelers as ourselves acted boringly uninteresting, and properly blended in the environment, except a young woman struggling to hold a baby from falling off one of her arms.

The fascinating appearance nearly compelled paying attention to her movements. The eatery's wide windows offered the perfect vantage for my secret ogling. On top of a bright red *miniskirt* a white t-shirt rather emphasized than hid her sensuality, the in-your- face protruded fleshy bust, nicely rounded hips, long shapely legs, red polished toes at the end of delicate, well-cared feet shoed in almost nonexistent sandals completed the picture. To judge by the license plate of her new-looking black Mercedes, she seemed out of town. 'What the hell could this young pretty, strikingly provocative woman and her baby be doing in this petty hodge-podge place, obviously unaccompanied, unnoticed, unaided by anyone? Where could she be heading?' I wondered. Then I noticed Didonna watched her too, and this spelled possible trouble.

Knowing better, I refrained asking for her opinion. I've learned long ago how inopportune is to open a conversation with a woman you are with about another female, especially when that *other* is younger, prettier, and to top it, summarily clad. Well, this unusual young female irked my mistress's critical curiosity. I could see the unrestrained acrimonious glimmer in her blue eyes, an attitude as yet unaccompanied by corrosive remarks.

The young mommy, moving awkwardly the baby from one arm to the other, eventually managed to fill the tank of her luxury automobile, and then came in to pay for the gas. For my slight misfortune, after a quick scan around the dining room, she headed straight to our table, and asked matter-of-factly for the permission to sit on the available extra chair. What an unwelcome self-limiting development!

This beautiful little diva, a minute earlier the object of my distant study, by taking the seat next to me made it frustratingly less feasible to continue my inspection freely, without risking to become obtrusive. To avoid meeting her strikingly azure-blue, innocent, but direct gaze, willy-nilly, I was forced --as people in such situations are-- to turn my attention willfully elsewhere, and bury my eyes in the menu at hand. Didonna, perfectly aware of the situation, did the same. What else could we do?

The order of the day the usual ice cream, and for the road two large paper cups of lemonade --more exactly flavored ice shavings called *Italian ice*. Once over our frugal meal, smoking a cigarette appeared just a natural call. The ban of smoking, to be adopted years later in most locals everywhere in the States, did not penetrate yet into this southern roadside service establishment.

Meanwhile, our young female companion kept wolfing down bunches of greasy french-fries, and ketchup off a bag, making sure her baby -- about two years of age --got nourished too. In the process, the little bundle of a boy had his cheeks, chin and nose smeared tomato-red, a side effect he didn't seem to mind as long as his mouth got filled with the tasty tatter slabs. A trusting little fellow he was, I thought the instant his innocent blue eyes fixated somewhat vacuously straight into mine. As often times when faced by a similar situation, in this day and age so easily misinterpreted, I turned my gaze away, following a short-lived acquiescing smile.

"Isn't it strange for this little boy to look me, a perfect stranger, straight in the eye? I wonder what could he find attractive? You know how much I dislike kids, particularly inquisitive babies such as this one," I said in Romanian.

"Don't be ridiculous, he did not register you at all. Then again, you may be a tad more attractive than the french-fry his mother keeps pushing down his pie hole so thoughtlessly, wouldn't you say?"

"Fine sister, fine, be facetious if you like. But let's better finish our repast and be off." Then noticing she did not work yet through her ice, I added with a modicum of irritation. "Come on dear, can't you hurry up a bit?"

"What's wrong with you now, can't you appreciate a joke? Where is your sense of humor?"

Eventually the young mom left the place first without uttering a word, the baby hanging under her left arm as before. We watched through the window as she opened the heavy Mercedes' door with her right hand, leaned inside, and flashed the bottom of her snow-white panties while fastening the baby in the child-seat. Then she drove off, to disappear forever, out of our eyes, though not from memory.

"I guess you liked this innocent little show, didn't you?"

"What show?"

"Gosh! Don't play the dimwit. Please! You know what I mean."

Although I found my girlfriend's lacerating quip a bit tragicomic, as well her malicious comment aimed at the young mother, I left both unanswered in the hope of cutting short the scene to ensue right from the outset. Lucky me, this time I succeeded.

All of a sudden she changed tack, as slurping the last drops off her ice became an inexplicably important preoccupation, while feigning a diffidently forgetful attitude. In response to these annoying new histrionics I had only a self-contained comment: 'How offensively sensitive a middle aged woman may grow, when confronted with an absolutely imagined threat coming from a younger, prettier sister. 'How could such a behavior fit in the natural evolutionary schemes?' I wondered. No response, a new question sprung to mind instead. 'Haven't I left my wife exactly for such an endearing sister, even if not so young? Oh, well--'

Soon it was our turn to leave the premises, but not before my always-nosy girlfriend checked out the souvenir shop, strategically placed between the exit and eatery, the shelves stocked with all sort of run-of-the-mill knick-knacks. To my secret niggardly pleasure, she didn't find anything worthy of purchase.

As the car's engine oil and coolant checked all right, we took back to the road, the air in the open cabin surprisingly breathable in the cross current, a welcome, but unfortunately, quite short-lived respite. Nothing attractive in the landscape, the same milky light-bathed unending thorny fields running backward on either side, sizzling in spite of the sun just barely visible through the thick sticky eerie layer of humid silvery dust.

An hour or so later, the vista changed a last. A luxuriant forest replaced the nearly barren land. In the distance, renewed flashes of lightning, muffled salvoes of thunder threatened the natural tranquility, and our minds suddenly filled with vague, unvoiced pangs of worry.

Who in the United States did not hear about twisters, hurricanes, and other horrible windy traveling disasters, about the so-called tornado alley? On the radio, the annoying static suddenly suppressed all meaningful signals. Was this a bad omen? Perhaps. I turned the receiver off. The cabin fell silent, and the atmosphere charged with a diffuse, heavy, pervasive apprehension. But we pushed on seventy miles an hour, heading directly towards the dark clouds, rising menacingly on the sky ahead. A white little arrow carrying a pair of slightly frightened souls darted willingly deeper and deeper in possible trouble, as attracted by the irresistible force of an impending doom. What other choice did we have? The adventure couldn't pause; it had to go on, whether moving or stationary.

In tense situations time passes nearly unnoticed. Out of this liquid dream-like state I came back to senses only when my loving companion delicately touched the nape of my neck, and begun playing with her fingers in my hair. Soon the pointed little tips circled slowly lower down the spine to waken even more touch-sensitive neurons. Oh pleasure, pleasure, how often comes mixed with danger! My eyes froze, pierced hypnotically ahead in the darkest void of an otherworldly nature.

*

Didonna caught my attention the minute I saw her. Her cousin, for us friend Vartan, brought her along one Sunday-visit to our home. This friend we met ten years or so earlier in Traiskirchen, in the refugee camp in Austria. When squeezing her hand during introduction, I had not the foggiest inkling of the fateful role the woman was to play in our lives in the years to come. However I distinctly remember the vaguely conscious, fleeting sensual exchange between us, when this gal's blue eyes met mine, my strangely warm first impression about her funny hairdo –the rebellious bang covering her forehead in totally un-American fashion for the times. I also recall my barely surreptitious desire a little later, to touching her nicely rounded ivory knees, temptingly showing under the beige corduroy skirt slipped up on her thighs--oh those smooth thighs slightly open for my stealthy peek-a-boo as she sat on the couch. For a heartbeat I felt for the just acquainted lady the sort of fuzzy empathy, reserved mostly for close relatives or love partners, a premonitory impressive glimpse that vanished as fast as it arose. I can swear this interaction happened in spite its brevity, such clairvoyance having visited my perception before, when for a flash I could glimpse in the future of a sentimental togetherness with someone just met.

*

Perhaps this type of foreboding is less strange than it appears, many people confess to have lived through such moments occasionally. This is fact. Sometimes it comes natural for humans to guess the future. Isn't it normal for everyone (aside absolute morons) to foresee the approximate consequences of his or her actions? Aren't those very same possible outcomes denied mostly through complacency, commodity, fear, or lack of willpower? Is it really so rare for a glimpse in the future to turn happiness into sadness instantly, missed opportunities to regrets, misdeeds or procrastinations of the past to present lamentations? How hard and often must destiny keep knocking at the door of life for so many in vain? Too many a folk consistently refuse to hear those knocks. Then why blame fate for feeding its victims in the jaws of failure in the absence of self-control?

*

Our first encounter happened in October, precisely as the dominant colors of vegetation, the infinite reds and yellows intensified the prevailing sentiment of nostalgia for the summer just passed. Following an early but copious dinner, the entire company, the bunch of friends along with Philomela and I went for a leisurely walk in the beautifully sunny and unusually mild afternoon. I don't remember precisely why or how Vartan's cousin and I paired up, lagging somewhat behind the others.

Although hardly an extrovert—but as I said, rather branded as aloof or distant--, with this new female visitor I achieved in a heartbeat the kind of intimacy reserved generally for older friendships. Just minutes in the conversation, and we were talking as a couple long-time familiar to one another, glossing easily over the inhibitions and formalities inherent for people who just met. And when in the heat of discussion I touched for a second or two one of her bare arms, the feel of that cool velvety flesh aroused instantly in my heart the overwhelmingly warm fuzziness, still alive in it today as vividly as was then.

Barely arrived in America she was filled by apprehensions, supplanted by a vaguely self-conscious stage fright-like fever. Working in her first job proved harder than imagined, almost as insufferable as the longing for her two sons left behind in Romania. More than anything she felt worried about the younger son, only six or seven years old. The future appeared to her bleak, as to any thirty-nine-year-old-mother separated of her children. For the single woman out of the homeland's familiarity a totally unknown New World loomed uncertain, to say the least, however promising it might have beckoned before the dissident act. It is hard for anyone to jump in the void without a net, even more so for a middle-aged single female, too often with only a measly chance working in her favor. Many an emigrant met defeat in this exchange of fates. The manual labor this fairly sophisticated lady performed at some small electronics factory --a job Vartan found in the paper-- paid poorly, just barely above minimum wage. To top this, the cousin exacerbated her dissatisfaction by constantly browbeating her into accepting gracefully and patiently whatever life offered, even if that was less than she expected. It is easy to see than why, given the circumstances, the revolt in the poor woman's heart against the status quo of dumb obedience grew daily worse.

As the seasoned immigrant recently naturalized I advised her precisely to the contrary, encouraged her disobedience spot on, and recommended against succumbing to Vartan's advice, against any slavish outlook solely rooted on surviving, instead of thriving in America. Naturally, I asked about her occupation in the old country. Learning that she used to be an illustrator for *Fondul Plastic* --a commercial branch of the Union of Artists in Romania-- the information sparked my enthusiasm, in opposition to my innate skepticism. Having myself dabbled occasionally in the creative arts my, advice veered quickly toward weighing her options on the scale of practicality.

"Forgive my daring an advice, but you ought to seek a job related more or less to your qualification. What's the point of competing on fields best suited for others? Why not try your luck, for instance, in drafting?"

"What do I know about technical arts? Has drafting anything to do with illustrating?"

"More than you think. Drafting and drawing require similar instruments, don't they? Why waste yours, and society's time by working in occupations you had not trained for?"

"This is an angle I never considered."

"It's about time you do. I am sure America prefers to employ people according to their abilities, not let them languish in jobs fit for others."

Later that evening following our stroll, I presented her one of my *how-to-books* on drafting, a trade I have eyed myself for a while, however unsuccessfully.

Shortly thereafter, destiny brought together Didonna with another single Romanian lady, an experienced professional draft-person who revealed her the more esoteric secrets of the craft. Much later, after our paths had merged in our sinful union, one day I dared remind her in passing about my allegedly modest contribution to her successful career. For some murky reasons I still confess to not understand why she felt compelled to adamantly denying the fact, forget altogether the thanks she possibly owed for my help. Her obviously irrational attitude has been puzzling me ever since. Looking back on it, my temptation is to add another complaining note here, but on second thought I won't, as not to offend some present-day sensitivities of the opposite gender. Sorry pretty sisters-folk for my thinking that consistency just might be one of your lesser virtues!

But let me reset the line of my narration-- on that fine afternoon of strolling together way into the onrushing dusk, we touched on a hodge-podge of silly trivial or serious subjects the others fortunately couldn't add their penny's worth of wisdom to, as the distance between us increased beyond earshot. We talked about America, the arts, the past, the present, even about vitamins and trace minerals, about many trivia or fads that made waves at the beginning of the eighties. Briefly, we got acquainted in earnest. Only the chill of the ensuing autumnal evening brought us back to reality, to rejoining society, my wife Philomela, Vartan, and the other couple of good friends.

For a long time thereafter the lady and I didn't see one other. Although Vartan paid his regular visits she had not accompanied him, and I did not muster the courage to ask why. Perhaps I felt already a modicum of subconscious guilt for my behavior to be, as yet predestined to materialize a few years later. My reasoning, some opine, might have been silly, akin to a sort of prevarication. But was it really? Is it possible for a murky premonitory impression to actually betray an impending destiny? Questions, questions!

One evening, in the midst of a conversation unrelated whatsoever to Vartan and his pretty cousin, Philomela strangely changed the subject, to confront me with the following question-statement, a clap of thunder out of absolutely blue skies.

"You like Vartan's cousin a lot, isn't it, my dear hubby?" A strange question indeed, or maybe not so out of whack when the proverbial women's intuition comes to mind!

The second time Didonna and I met had been at Vartan's home, where she still lived as a queasy-permanent guest. In the meantime happily reunited with Alex, her younger son brought over from Romania with help of the State Department, she looked younger, rested, exuding a somewhat more, so to speak, *local* allure. –'How quickly America may change a person, at least on the surface' --I thought.

Little Alex, a somewhat bashful, well-behaved and properly mannered boy, seemed physically almost the exact copy of mother-- blue eyes, reddish-blond hair and un-boyishly sensual lips. Only his fair rose-petal-pink complexion appeared so much smoother than his mother's! Oh well, the little young fellow just turned seven years old.

The new woman exuded a well-justified pride off all her pores, as she constantly surveyed her little progeny with obviously adoring eyes. Altogether reshaped from head to toes, her entire being radiated happiness.

It felt wonderful seeing her again, this time in context of a fine dinner-supper affair Vartan hosted gracefully, although a tad too formally, in tune with his habitually pedantic and hypocritical, petty syrupiness. Perhaps his recent wife of Colombian extraction could have contributed to his artificial style, pushed to the fore in compensation for the poor English she spoke, a lone soul indeed as a neglected minority survivor among the noisy boisterous Romanians. In spite of what they commonly believe whilst boasting openly about their pushy, expansive sort of hospitality, in practice my folk act less accommodating versus their foreign guests' linguistic shortcomings than alleged. Sorry, fellow co-nationals, in my opinion you might be a little bit tinged by shades of xenophobia, not unlike most nations in the Old Word.

Sensing this uneasiness his wife could have endured by being reduced to insignificance in her own home Vartan outdid himself, as he recounted in a heavy accented English even more aseptic jokes than he used to tell in Romanian, while laughing wholeheartedly at each supposedly funny punch line, without ever waiting for his company to do the same.

Philomela and I, thoroughly familiarized with the man's peculiarities back in Traiskirchen-- where he got more than once in minor trouble with fellow refugees, especially females on the account of his exaggerated, pompous behavior—we feigned to be properly amused. Didonna, similarly well acquainted with the oddity of her cousin, also laughed along the rest of us-- forget the Latino lady-host, linguistically pushed deeper and deeper in isolation, contrary to the most elementary dictates of good manners. However sincerely, or just politely, I tried in vain to side with Vartan's considerate efforts to the benefit his spouse, regardless of how ridiculously unsuccessful this might have appeared to others. Later on, when as my girlfriend Didonna confessed about some of her cousin's darker sensual advances she endured in the absence of his wife, I reacted almost incredulously, having to admit once more the difficulty of penetrating a man's inner soul, based solely on a few superficial aspects and facts!

*

Although proper etiquette is expected of civilized people, I must make another observation at this point. Too often within immigrant gatherings of folk speaking various languages simultaneously, the milieu by definition can rarely allow for a fruitful exchange of ideas. In spite of all the fads of multiculturalism blowing lately through the Western World ever more furiously, a language when not shared equally by everyone I believe to rather put a damper on a congregation's hoped-for coherence, on the meaningful discourse attempted within it. Dear reader, please don't feel offended as this is just the opinion of an alien simpleton.

All the same, the speed by which American lifestyle may cast the immigrant in a new mold often borders the miraculous, good or poor English, and all the rest. Then again, could it be that qualities perceived as dully altered in the newly arrived tantamount to significantly less than publicly admitted, or statistically measured? The debate remains open. But as The New World is known to exert presently a great influence on the entire planet, why wouldn't it persist in mesmerizing the souls of hope-filled immigrants as well?

*

Didonna changed in this sense too, and quickly succumbed to the American spell. Her metamorphosis became obvious even to the often-unfocused observer as myself.

She preserved the slender well shaped beautifully proportioned, attractive womanly physical appearance as before, yet something in her demeanor changed, although hard to pinpoint precisely what. Perhaps her new dresses of simpler elegance, better attuned to the latest fashion, might have molded more flatteringly to her curvaceous body, or could've the new hairdo render her visage a little silkier? It's hard for me to pinpoint exactly what caused the change. For sure, though, the dame looked different, radiating a younger and brighter presence than before. Only the ugly, extruding wart above her left eyebrow could have reminded the onlooker of the Old Country, where such blemishes may be viewed less seriously, neither medically or esthetically disturbing. Soon thereafter she took care to correct even that little eyesore, I like to think, after I dared to mention it.

Following dinner, according to a well-established custom, Vartan shot pictures. Interestingly, in one of those I appeared premonition-like smack in the middle of a loveseat, squeezed between Philomela and Didonna --between my spouse soon to fade to oblivion, and the new woman to move in my future. Later on, Philomela will cling obsessively to that fateful picture, for a long time carried in her handbag for anyone willing to see the shot that supposedly heralded the end of her marriage. I wonder whether she still keeps the damned picture handy. I could never convince her to give it up together with the rest of bad memories. Isn't it funny how people enjoy dwelling on past miseries more than looking forward to the promises of renewed happiness?

After that festive evening --memorable as it was—I've seen Vartan's cousin only years later. By then she lived independently in Gaithersburg, in a rental apartment nearer to her job in Virginia. Philomela and I have been invited --if memory serves me right-- to celebrate her son's, as well as her own birthday, both in December, a couple of days past Christmas. A lot of guests honored the festive reunion, many Romanians I didn't know, among them several later arrivals in the U.S.

*

It's hard for me to fathom the reason why refugees almost compulsively flock together as they arrive to these shores, to establish friendships mostly within their own latest cohorts, distinctly isolated from their national fellow veterans. But this is factually correct. Perhaps the phenomenon happens on the account of suspicions, even resentments the newly arrived nourish against their older brethren in the New World, each group considering the other deficient in some respects. While the first echelon frequently displays a disdainful attitude versus the older immigrants for not being up to date on the latest realities in the Old Country, the latter look down on the newly arrived for their glaring naïveté concerning aspects of the American way of life. Oh well!

That night I, as most ordinary persons not a lot different from the rest of the bunch, searched for the familiar, for the company of old acquaintances.

Among these I remember one guy particularly, Mr. Sebastian Zisu, a remarkably intelligent person, a truly agreeable character were he a little less nagging with his never-ending insistence, to the exclusion of almost all other subjects, on the horrible treatment his folk suffered during the last World War.

"Hi, Mr. Corbea, how are things at the Bureau of Standards? Still wasting taxpayer money reading about useless patents published by the Commies? Ha, ha, ha..."

"Hey, Mr. Sebastian, don't knock my work. Somebody has to watch those evildoers too, you know. Why shouldn't I be that lucky guy? At least I speak the language in use today, not to mention a few more besides, unlike our decrepit old-timer reactionaries settled on these shores during the forties and fifties, and presently still shooting the breeze quite well paid at the State Department, or elsewhere in government. You know whom I mean, the after-the-war-generation folk. Those old bastards siphon more taxpayers' money than all of us newcomers combined. I hope we see eye-to-eye on this point."

"Ha, ha, ha, how right you are, although, let's admit that not everybody can be the skilled professionals we are. At least we do some work, not only talk incessantly about cockamamie antediluvian politics. By the way, did you see Mr. Sheldon to ask him for the material I recommended you the last time we met? Or my advice fell on deaf ears the way most of our *newest believers in freedom* ignore everything besides their own interests of getting rich quickly?"

"I don't see what new believers are you talking about?"

"Hey, are you my friend, or what? No need to pretend ignorance."

"Mr. Sebastian, you know how isolated I live from my conationals."

But he waved away my attempt at evasion, and promptly lunched head first in his rant, and obsessive peroration on the subject of thousands-year-long suffering of his folk. I feigned to listen politely to his story, all the while keeping my attention, only God knows why, stealthily focused on Didonna's fluid comings and goings among guests. Like I was forsworn not to miss any little detail in spite of my interlocutor's mercilessly boring bombardment. Then the saving idea hit.

"Listen, forget all the horrible past. Nothing can be done about it anyway. Let's better enjoy the party honoring our beautiful host. Tell me how did you come to know her?"

"Didonna and I got acquainted in Bucharest, at the time wife of my good friend, engineer Micu."

"Is she now officially divorced?"

"Yeah, the couple split apart, and for the dumbest reasons."

"No, really, why do you say that?"

"Oh well, to make a long story short, the lady you see now always wanted to immigrate to the States. This was her obsession. From the outset she married my friend conditionally, forcing him to promise immigrating to America as soon as possible, to join his brother in Los Angeles. But, as he later on reneged on his word, deeming wiser to stay in Romania, this strong-willed woman got really furious over the alleged betrayal, and divorced him immediately. On the other hand, she didn't give up on her dream, and as you see, ended up in America anyway, invited by her cousin Vartan. And then, you know one thing leads to another... she applied for residency."

"Wow, how interesting! By the way, are you married?"

"Yes, I am. My wife is to rejoin me, hopefully sometime in the next six months. Her visa has just been approved."

"Congratulations, and good luck to both of you." Then I raised my glass, but seeing it empty I resorted to the dirtiest sort of evasion. "Please give me a second, for I need a little more encouragement, ha, ha, ha... I'll be back in a jiffy."

And guess what, from the bar I forgot to return. Instead, maneuvering through the crowd of merrily eating and drinking guests, I squeezed my way nearer and nearer to the hostess, who seemed quite amused in the company of a bunch of vivaciously noisy ladies, my wife among them.

"Hi, Mr. Corbea, how are you?" "When can we hope for such a bash at your place? Mrs. Philomela cooks so yummy good!"

"Hey Mr. Doru, you look really dandy today."

"Well, what am I, chopped liver?"

"Ha, ha, ha, you have such a naughty way with words! Aren't you really funny?"

"Indeed, *funny* is my nickname," and on, and so forth, through the crowd, until the distance to my target became nearly negligible

From the outset I must say that observing Didonna's refined demeanor at close range appeared infinitely more fascinating than having to carry a tired conversation with a balding middle-aged man, or exchanging flippant compliments with other men's wives. The easy manner she carried the conversation, always properly adjusted to the situation at hand, her slightly acid humor, beautifully molded to her various interlocutors, won for me the day as well. Besides, from my new vantage point I could stealthily admire her delicately tactful, restrained, but obvious motherly attention directed constantly toward her beloved son Alex. Why couldn't Philomela possess this sort of sophistication in her frustratingly permanent confrontations with Camellia, our daughter? For the sake of brevity, the hostess appeared in my eyes as a serious, but sensually well-charged dame, amply deserving the supportive arm of any equally worthy man. Whether I could be that guy was precisely the question I did not dare ask myself openly. Not yet. After all, haven't I been happily married to Philomela, momentarily more concerned with making herself helpful among the ladies than worrying about her conjugal safety from the same?

Suffice it to say that by the conclusion of the memorable evening I succeeded in charming young Alex off his feet by promising to let him try out my air riffle one day, meanwhile happy to notice the warm rapport created between Philomela and Didonna in the background. Was my subconscious, crab-like sideway moving strategy really so mischievous? At the moment of farewell we parted as newly found friends, promising to see each other more often from then on.

These promises came to fruition soon enough, as the woman became one of regulars at the frequent dinner parties taking place in our townhouse in Damascus. Philomela loved to organize reunions, mostly because she relished performing in the role of the grand dame, especially among people showing appreciation for the abundant culinary delights she always so proudly and gracefully offered. To my pleasant surprise she established a new custom, that of seating our new female guest next to me at the table. Only God knows why married women sometimes resort to such absurd tactical acrobatics, desperately trying to placate the possible enemies, to reveal themselves as usurpers sooner or later anyway. Philomela might have employed the tactic intuitively, brazenly hoping to preempt the outcome, dreaded already deep down in her guts. Can such tortuous approaches spring naturally off the endangered female psyche? Why not?

Unfortunately but predictably, the expected neutralizing outcome of this sort of strategy could end up as just the opposite. Contrary to my often times openly expressed displeasure for Philomela's wasteful dinner bashes in the past, I began gradually to look forward for these, surreptitiously but decisively opting for Didonna's company even if my preference wasn't yet consciously manifested in a glaringly amorous fashion. Soon though, I caught myself longing for the dame's presence in earnest, at the beginning honestly and innocently wishing for nothing more than to cultivate just a simple friendship, as if such a relation between a man and a woman could indeed be feasible in the real world. Quite predictably, the game ratcheted up at each and every time a notch, only to prove once again the near impossibility of having a durable, purely friendly relationship with the opposite sex. Maybe this common wisdom is a natural outcome, for Providence having reserved different roles for men and women on earth than for angels in heaven!

Philomela being often busy in the afternoons at her job of waiting tables, I took the liberty to pay Didonna visits alone, initially, of course, without openly nourishing any untoward, amorously obvious intentions. She neither encouraged nor discouraged my new habit, letting me surmise my company was welcomed the same way as hers in our place without any hidden agenda whatsoever. After all, what's wrong with spending a few hours with a dear friend be that male or female?

One day, during one of Philomela's Sunday parties, when an older friend of ours --down from New York for the weekend-- kissed Didonna jokingly on the neck above her décolletage, I became aware for the first time of the sickly nauseating emotion awoken deep within my gut. The old man's insolent gesture, and attendant overt courtship seemed to me indignantly repulsing, libidinous and crass, absolutely improper. That an attractive lady and an old gentleman as singles had all the rights in the world to engage openly in the flirtation game, and freely evaluate their chances at it, didn't matter for me at all. At that instant my impulse was to brutally smash the old man's head against the wall behind him, not realizing yet how my feelings by now had veered dangerously away from pure friendship to a rather forbidden sort of attraction that is called illicit, surreptitious love.

How many a night following that disturbing event had I not daydreamed for hours on end about the charming lady? How often didn't I pretend to conducting with her *intelligent philosophical* discussions, when in fact my eyes only persisted secretly focused on the curvaceous outlines of her inner thighs way up toward her loins, delineated against the playful sunlight penetrating every now and then through her thin summer dresses? Oh how many a time did I not silently peek at her delicately shaped bare feet and pinky toes, peek-a-booing through the open sandals! Didn't I commit these furtive, lustful voyeuristic acts at every possible opportunity? I certainly did, unabashedly too.

However true this has been, I must confess not to have ever found anything wretchedly sinful about my repressed longings, considering lust as the natural male reaction when faced by the always-novel female physical charms. Some moralistically less forgiving parties might just as well accuse me for not exercising enough restraint, for not asking whether it was legitimate for a married man to nourish sensual desires for a woman other than his wife? But I didn't questions the ethics of such a choice, just followed my impulses. Man, how cavalierly blind can your inner eye be!

*

A whipping crack of lightening and the subsequent rolling thunder returned my attention brutally to the suddenly changed driving conditions, back to the highway. In the same heartbeat Bucephalos got drenched under a deluge of rainwater a truck's humongous tires picked up from the wind-swept asphalt. The water splashed so hard against the windshield as to cause me blink involuntarily. Next thing I became aware of what my mistress just did.

"I wonder if you realize how all truck drivers sitting high above us could have easily watched your performance for free."

"So what, didn't you like it?" she quickly retorted, straightening up to nonchalantly tidy her slightly disheveled hair, her countenance as of the culprit caught in the act of forbidden mischief.

My reflexive glimpse cast straight in her face was long enough to catch the transient mischievous glint lit up in her blue eyes, fixated in mine as innocently as it gets. In lieu of answering, my mug widened to the widest smile only the Cheshire cat could have ever produced. This same smile had taken up all the time left for any further comments. The furiously erupted thunderstorm stopped furthermore my inner wisecracking dead in the tracks. My undivided attention had to focus on the road. It took a little while longer to regain a modicum of confidence in my fate on earth, to afford feeling satisfied at last for what happened, and take note this time of the reassuring, protectively gentle motherly touch alighted on my right thigh, as if to suggest:

"Don't you worry, big boy, everything's just fine."

Today --so many years later— I get often nostalgic about the bliss of togetherness born out of those ephemerally lit-up tenderly thunderous naughty seconds.

So we went on, bravely pushing deeper down South through the heavy downpour. Fortunately, the storm lost its rage as quickly as it erupted. The dark hellish clouds broke asunder as so many rags torn apart to huge strands by invisible, but immensely powerful hands. The sun pierced through the same clouds, illuminating the landscape with a clear purifying amber glow, and the tires kept on singing their high-pitched melody on the wet pavement as if nothing dangerous ever happened.

The windows got lowered in immediate response. Fresh air rushed in, bringing along in the cabin the wonderfully awoken aromas of the field, filling our lungs with incredibly recharged organic and inorganic electrolytes, hearts invigorated by deliciously savage feelings of animal youthfulness, minds swamped with murky memories of bygone primeval eons.

The wet road ahead smoothed out steaming, the white rhythmically broken lines ran far in the graying distance, to pierce straight into the horizon between endless fields. Minutes later, my naughty friend -- her sense of dignity and duty fully restored -- sunk her renewed attention to studying the maps as if nothing untoward happened. Just about time. We were approaching the city of Mobile, Alabama. The green highway indicators kept confirming this repeatedly.

*

The city of Mobile surpassed our expectations as much as Charlotte did in North Carolina. But, taken in the context of a transcontinental trip, this port at the Golf of Mexico would seldom merit more than a few hours of a stopover, at most half a day. What I humbly suggest is that no serious long distance traveler should, in my opinion, spend a full vacation in this town. By the same token, it would be a definite mistake to avoid this jewel of a town altogether. A hugely big error indeed!

At first sight it became clear the city bore the imprint of its French birth certificate. The differences between this French community and an Anglo-Saxon counterpart were immediately noticeable in the architecture of churches, houses, the disposition of streets, by the rather cheerful urban atmospherics as well. This impression will strengthen even more later on in other cities, colonized initially by the French, in New Orleans and Saint Louis, to mention just two.

Mobile -- a French colony settled by Le Moyne de Bienville from 1711 until 1763, then fallen under the British until 1813, thereafter to end up for good in American hands -- today still shows off a lot of its early French imprimatur, particularly evident because the city escaped the ravages of the federal troops during the Civil War. Consequently many of the original architectural features survived intact. The majority of houses older than one hundred and fifty years, built in the most authentic and diverse styles of dignified elegance, are equally worth of marvel as other numerous monuments of historical importance.

Two or three of these grand streets -- Church Street definitely among them--, would make the object of pride in any city anywhere on the globe. Guarded on each side by palm trees, stately giant oaks, flowery magnolias, and smaller shrubbery similarly rich in colors –ranging from the pastel-pink of the Crepe Myrtle to the incredibly velvety pale violet of Wisteria-- the buildings, consisting of a variety of splendid villas and palaces erected on generously wide streets, stood frozen in the mid-day heat, as if waiting for ancient guests to be brought back from a bygone era. Amid tall slender columns, enclosing screened porches with intricately ornate turrets and balconies above, we could almost hear the elegantly uniformed officers, gentlemen in white formal attire, ladies in long evening gowns, colorful characters chatting in subdued tones about who knows what subjects, everyone carefully attentive to preserving their dignified composures through most elaborate mannerisms nonchalantly broadcast in well affected southern charm above very low décolletages, for their counterparts' unsurpassed meridional eloquence and understanding, returned in well measured sentences uttered under white powdery hairpieces. In our fantasy it was unavoidable not to notice the servants as well, even if only barely: black women and men carrying silver trays, serving glasses of lemonade, julep, or other refreshing beverages fashionable at the time.

It is quite hard to understand why Hollywood staged relatively few movies in this splendid setting. The only strident note of clatter in this charming environment was the long line of automobiles parked on the streets, exuding the miserable luster of their metallic simplicity, insolently thrust upon this perfumed, ancient and intriguing *dolce-far-niente*-atmosphere. In spite of this incongruence, modernity's obtrusive interference did not succeed in spoiling altogether the delicious charm of the place. Even the weather seemed to cooperate to this end. As the sun hid temporarily under a few passing clouds the heat subsided, momentarily rendering the event unforgettable, a real memento in our memories to be. Unfortunately, little time remained for additional investigations. We had better stick to the plan, if reaching New Orleans before nightfall remained the goal.

A few hesitations and wanderings through downtown, and we really stumbled on the access to the right route somewhere near the port. This happened to be interstate-10, the highway we were to travel all the way through till the Pacific Coast in California. Often inadvertence could work just fine for the lucky.

*

My watch showed five o'clock in the afternoon when, all of a sudden, pangs of hunger hit us simultaneously with uncanny timing and ferocity, as if to prove once more that loving couples cohabitating for a long time will eventually succumb to synchronization in most respects, even digestively. How prosaic!

This time our appetites called unanimously for pizza.

"Gee, great minds, or true lovers often think in unison, don't they?"

"Of course, sweetheart", she retorted tersely, a vague contended smile on her face, incontrovertibly welcoming my comment.

Good enough, I succeeded to touch one of her soft spots.

Twenty minutes later, the sight of the huge ad for a *Pizza Hut* restaurant came in view, perched high enough on a pole to make it clearly visible for miles. The familiar name elicited right then and there the image and aroma of a fourteen-inch- *pizza supreme* --every possible topping on it—that squeezed all else off the mind, to fill the mouth with saliva in the best Pavlovian fashion.

For the first time during the trip, we found the exit with no difficulty. Did this happen because our traveling skills had turned by now into a well-worn routine, or because hunger makes always for the best possible motivator? Who knows? Anyway, both of us as inexperienced voyagers felt unusually self-confident, quite seasoned maybe just a little bit too soon. But, for the moment, the future looked bright.

"Did the weather cool a bit, or is it just me breathing easier than ever?"

"No, it's not only you. I feel comfortable, too. Take a peek at the sky, the sun seems to have tempered some of its ferocious sizzle."

The heavens got indeed covered, but not by clouds-- a rather strange sort of thin, hazy, silky-grayish-blue varnish dulled everything above and below. Not the slightest breeze moved the treetops. Humidity subsided by a few notches as well.

"I think it's going rain tonight" I said once out of the vehicle.

"Oh no, I bet it won't rain. No way, not tonight."

Just on verge of challenging my companion's baffling certitude, and my thoughts changed course, as we entered the dark empty dinning room, devoid of any soul, either personnel or customers. Although the sign advised to *wait for the hostess in order to be seated,* nobody came to greet us, not even after we rung the bell placed next to the bunch of menus stack-piled high on the lectern-like table. It sure looked like we had to find our way in unaided. And so we went straight to a table by the windows.

"I wonder if anybody will take care of us here, or this is a self-service type deal."

"Let's worry about that later. For now go tidy up, wash hands, and what not. I will do the same on your return. To judge by your mug, I certainly need to brighten up a bit too. In the meantime, I'm sure something shall happen out here too."

The well-bred boy in me obeyed instantly. Then, while my lady took the time at powdering her nose, I immersed into studying the menu. Surprisingly, she returned sooner than expected, followed close behind by the waitress, too, a cute, but somewhat dazed and slightly disheveled looking teenager, overly eager to serve-- all the possible haste and courtesy invested in the effort as if to compensate for her tardiness. Then the order acknowledged twice --one medium-size *pizza supreme,* and two glasses of beer—the little missy disappeared behind the batting kitchen door, leaving us again to our own devices, as before.

"What was this all about?"

"Who knows? The fact is I caught her alone in the bathroom smoking. She quickly put out her cigarette, touched up her face in the mirror as if caught in mischief, telling me in a somewhat excuse-like fashion that the restaurant didn't expect customers this early after lunch."

"Huh, are you sure she's been smoking a cigarette, not something else?"

"What else? How should I know?"

"O-my-god, what world are you living in?"

"What is it you're suggesting? Why must you always be so suspicious? What's wrong with a teenager smoking a cigarette during her break, and in the absence of clientele?"

"Come on don't be naive, don't you really know what's wrong?"

"No, I don't. Anyway, it's not my god-dam business. Is it yours?"

"No, but--"

"Then wait patiently to be served, and forget the rest. May we ever have a good time without worrying about such dumb matters?"

"Okay, okay, let's drink to that, plenty of fresh water in this pitcher." I poured generously in the glasses. But we stopped dead before taking a full sip-- the sensation of the lukewarm liquid on the lips would have turned anyone off.

Water served at room temperature rarely occurs in American restaurants, unlike in Europe, where drinking *aqua frigida* before meals might seems unwelcome at best, and silly at worst. To gulp down a shot of strong liquor yes, but to kill one's appetite with plain water doesn't make much of a sense at all to folk in the Old Word. Then again, as these rules are not chiseled in stone, we came in time to accept the American practice without prejudgment. When in Rome do as the Romans do. Why question customs with senseless reasoning?

Quite a long wait later, the cute little waitress replaced at last the pitcher with the glasses of beer we ordered. Now this tasted a whole lot better. The well-chilled amber liquid quenched thirst in earnest, in spite of its vaguely diluted watery taste-- our fault, as we could have ordered a German brew. On the other hand, it might have been precisely the wateriness of beer added to the cool touch of the shiny vinyl-covered-seats under hot thighs that made the unforeseen stopover indelibly etched in our memory. Why do insignificant details end up often better remembered than important events -- as for instance marriage anniversaries?

As we sat there waiting, slowly our minds receded in aimless thoughts-- children, relatives, friends, pets, all worries and joys forgotten, left far behind at home. For the authentic wanderers we became by then only the present time counted. Constantly on the move appeared nearly natural. Gypsies must be well acquainted with the sensation. Is it not permanent motion the quintessence of life? What else is a road but the interval between two stations, each a new opening for another surprising destination? Isn't this sort of living the best way to freedom and absence of worries? Perhaps nomads are indeed the smartest people on earth!

By the time we finished smoking our cigarettes, pizza landed on the table hot and appetizing. It had been worth the wait. Properly aroused hunger did its best as always. Just the simple act of lustfully biting into a slice of deliciously crusty chewy dough topped with tomato sauce, cheese, pepperoni and a whole assortment of seared vegetables, duly chased by sips of beer, could make for the shortest way to the simple heartfelt happiness on earth. On that hazy mid-day, everything meshed together marvelously during a modest repast in a forlorn *Pizza Hut*, somewhere in Alabama. Can life be much crazier than that?

Pizza, although not classified as genuine gourmet food, has gained all the same a respectable place among the favorite dishes for most people, children included. Along with French fries, hot dogs, hamburgers or --why not-- bean soup with smoked bacon constitute perhaps the basic building bricks of a uniquely satisfying type of nourishment, aptly called comfort foods. It might be quite impossible to survive for long solely on asparagus topped by *Béarnnaise* sauce.

Another smoke at the meal's conclusion, and we showed ready to hit the road again fit and refreshed, but not before asking the waitress for the quickest way to New Orleans. Our next destination seemed less than forty-five minutes away on the same highway we came-- traffic permitting.

Happy Bucephalos moved on the asphalted pavement as a well-waxed sled. Straight ahead the majestic sun penetrated through the haze just above the horizon, gilding the incredibly blue-violet clouds with shining gold and silver. The air filled with pleasantly undefined aromas. My partner has been right, the-morrow promised to be splendid.

In no time whatsoever our wheeled horse rolled on the New Orleans's beltway. The lights just came alive in the city, as the first evening stars began twinkling on the sky in response.

The rather large, luminous firm of the *Days Inn* hotel welcomed the tired traveler with renewed friendly beckoning. Without further ado we exited the highway at the first opportunity. The streets guided to destination, this time, miraculously, no confusing pitfalls on the way. To top this luck, a parking spot freed right as we arrived at the entrance. A good omen I thought, chest properly inflated in self-confidence.

But as the evening's events progressed faster than my initial optimism, the prospect of finding a room promptly diminished soon thereafter. Unlike in Atlanta, the entrance to the hotel appeared locked for good, no reception office anywhere in sight. It's seldom wise to disregard the unexpected. Following an exhausting day at the wheel, the chance of searching for another lodging loomed quite discouraging. To face all of a sudden a new unpleasant setback looked bleak. After circling on foot around the building for a good many times with no result, helplessness set in at last, pride deeply hurt for having to accept the plainest, numbingly disorienting defeat. What to do now? Willy-nilly resigned to fate, we gave up the search, and headed, for lack of anything better, toward the well-lit restaurant by the opposite corner of the parking lot. For the moment, the solution appeared as the sole sensible alternative.

Luck took pity on us again. Less than two steps inside the hallway our glance fell right on the couches surrounding a coffee table, behind them shelves stacked by barely visible pamphlets and magazines. As always, no such details could escape my friend's eagle-sharp sight. And there it happened to be located what we desperately searched for, the hotel's reception desk. Never before had we seen, nor will later find such an unusual arrangement anywhere during our journey. But as the saying goes being alive is tantamount to never stop learning.

The concierge on duty quickly set us up in a room on the fourth floor. The key received fit all doors, including admittance to the pool and the laundry rooms, in the most practical American way. The hotel operated on the principle of self-service, perhaps explaining the reasonable price of only forty-nine dollars per night, no corners cut off comfort, except the liftboy for carrying the luggage upstairs. We had to drag the accursed suitcases and all to the fourth floor on our own power. Thinking ahead of the cold refreshing beer awaiting at the end of the process –to be repeated all subsequent nights-- we set to the task at hand as cheerfully as possible in the given circumstance. Some minor but unavoidable chores, equally unpleasant and badly timed, can often darken ordinary folks' lives. By the same token, why fret about things impossible to change?

Once settled in, washed, refreshed and garbed in new attires, the zest for life poured back in the veins, and we eagerly, but cautiously launched in a small adventure, for the night only around the immediate neighborhood.

Not much worthy of note in this neck of wood. Unlike in most typically American suburbia absent the customary large commercial center, and all the familiar shops, aside some best known fast food places, and a few more elaborate restaurants, all set in clean, neat, well-lit, but perfectly aseptic, non-distinct environment. A brief debate later, we settled for a so-called family-type restaurant (no alcoholic beverages served), a few young families with noisy unruly children sitting scattered across several booths. This unmemorable eatery reminded eerily of the sparkling, surrealist yellow-vacuumed atmosphere Edward Hooper so effectively recreated in many of his famous paintings.

"This joint looks so wonderfully nice under its garb of superficial friendliness, doesn't it? To me is reminding the rather well known cheesy smile '***good***' salesmen grin by baring their teeth, whilst offering their customers only icy hardness in the eyes? *Nice* can be the single most suitable epithet to fit the present scene as well! What a splendidly vague, indiscriminate descriptor! What do you think?"

"Oh my, why don't you shut your vinegar-filled clap for once? Please stop your habitual bitching! You'll find everywhere something to complain about. Let me ask did you like the marginally clean, ramshackle Socialist commerce in the Old Country, or you're rather content to live in these modern, *aseptically* neat places?"

"I don't know. Honestly I don't. It's true life over there in the East could be rough, unclean, often foul smelling, however, in retrospect, after having seen both sides of the coin, this odorless artificiality appears nearly as unattractive in its false glitter, feigned mannerisms, and conventionally imposed artificial respectability. Can you give me at least that much?"

"Then why the hell don't you go back?"

"There is no way back. All returns are barred. You should have learned by now that all roads point only forward. Returning in the past is senseless, and quite illusionary. It's not an option. One can never be at home again in a place no longer there, in one that ceased altogether to exist. Think of the old adage saying *it is impossible to step in the same river twice.*"

"Fine, I can barely figure what you're talking about, but I wouldn't go back even if could. In my dreams America had been always **the Country**, and **She** is exactly, well, almost exactly as I imagined. I bet you ran away from something you didn't like at home, only to find the new reality equally displeasing. You must be constantly chasing utopias. Things are the way they are, and must be compared as such, not against illusionary ideals. You'll never find true happiness, or peace anywhere. I promise you, poor man, the fault sits within yourself, not in the world."

"You really hate me, isn't it?"

"Don't be silly. You're not worthy of anyone's hate. But I often pity you, more so when you feel like showing off your intensely mystifying, bickering side. Wouldn't be easier to let just go?"

"To let go what, to kill off my ideals? That's why I left home? To condemn my hopes for finding an ideal world to hell?"

In the wake of this sour exchange, a curtain of silence fell between us, both in need to meditating a bit upon what had been just said. It is precisely how I pondered silently over Didonna's harshly critical intimations. Must I really let my expectations go to the devil? What about satisfying my incessant curiosity, my innate sense of fairness, constantly gnawing at my very core since the earliest childhood? Am I not duty bound to relentlessly question everything I perceive as incorrect or unjust in this world?

I cast a furtive glance to my pretty mistress. Maybe she's not altogether the understanding soul mate I fancied. But I couldn't read anything on her visage. She simply appeared to enjoy the evening walk, the people, the steady hubbub of the street, the balmy cool air, everything around, as if all seen and experienced for the first time, a happy little girl fallen in a wonderful new world. While taking note of her lighthearted detachment, for a minute couldn't be sure whether she gave a damn about anything serious, even less about what those things might mean for me. For the first time since I met her, she seemed a bit estranged, a distant impenetrable riddle, a being never emotionally available in earnest. Then, as moved by an invisible will, she turned the blue beams of her eyes straight into mine. Reflexively I smiled, and she smiled back. Oh what a warm feeling oozed off this spontaneous exchange! I took her hand she squeezed mine in instant return. We kept walking this way for a long silent dreamlike, timeless interval. No words needed. It felt good simply to keep in step together, absently contemplating the smallest insignificant details of the surrounding universe. Perhaps her advice had some merit. Indeed, I have to let go sometimes.

On the way back to the hotel, we passed alongside the pool, domed in the dark by a lagoon-blue halo, reminding a scene out of the *One Thousand and One Nights* fairy tale. Could all this miraculous luminosity be no more than sheer illusion? Sure it could be not a smidgen more that that. Why is so wrong to believe that? What's the difference between illusion and reality, after all?

Suddenly the light of truth hit. It's all-too personal. On this artfully set stage not a single soul, not one lonely actor present beside us to play a part, and enjoy the sublime beauty. Then the famous question came to mind *whether a tree falling in the forest makes noise in the absence of ears to hear it?* Isn't this a most fascinating question? By the next heartbeat it got answered too, the actors on the stage were our own selves, performing, breathing, alive, united sense-wise in what is common to all folk meshed together in one and the same abstract divine personality. Is there anything humanly more real than what we see, touch, hear, smell or taste?

By nine thirty, stretched out comfortably under covers in front of the TV set's flickering images, we waited to get drowsy, as so many couples in love naturally do, more often than not without resorting to pharmaceuticals. Love is the only answer.

Since no notable news on any channel --just the same old, hundred-fold-rehashed political scandals, the meaningless fights between the two parties, followed by reports on local crimes, sport, and the mandatory trivial events--, my mate switched the set off, then the lamp too, patted the pillow twice, placed her blond head on it, and cuddled me neatly in her embrace for allowing our bodies and souls to melt away in the soft sweet sensations of forgetfulness, abandon and deep, dreamless sleep. Primordial void. True nirvana.

THE BIG EASY

In the morning, refreshed and reinvigorated, we plunged eagerly in the adventure of exploring the crown-jewel-city of Louisiana. No breakfast in the room, not even the hot aromatic Turkish coffee my travel-companion so dutifully prepared by now in a daily routine. Right across the street, a Wendy's restaurant seemed the perfect destination for breaking fast on two fantastic fried eggs, strips of bacon, jam, buttered toast, and unbelievably large cups of classic American hot beverage called coffee, which some *finicky Europeans* might easily consider rather as a soupy ersatz than the veritable brew. On the other hand, won't a donkey do just as well when the need calls for a horse?

Many wonderful things are rumored about New Orleans. This made it hard to contain our impatience, so we cut breakfast reasonably short. Suitably dressed for summer --Didonna in a light vertically striped jumpsuit and pants ending just under the knees, I in shirt and shorts— both showed ready for action. However, even this hastiness couldn't prevent my seeing how the tight jumpsuit outlined my friend's beautifully curvaceous contours, long legs, smooth thighs, cello-like hips and --oh man, how childish can you be-- her delightfully shaped bosom. All the hills and valleys of her body lent their forms to easy guessing, in spite of revealing precious little off the epidermal details, I hoped rightfully reserved for my eyes and touches only. For the inveterate skeptic this hope must have been perhaps one of the few illusions I entertained in a silly optimistic fashion. Realistically speaking, how long can a maladroit guy's luck last with an Aphrodite-like diva he never ever dared to dream of?

"Hey, you look super sexy hot this splendid sunny morning."

"Thanks, dear, but, please, stop lying. Didn't you tell me once how much you dislike women in pants?"

"Well, yes, I did say it, but then again you never figured in my opinion. On your curves everything looks just perfect. Or, perhaps you might think I spread it a little bit too thin?"

"Oh shut up," she lashed back. "You are full of it. Let's better focus on the task at hand, okay?" Obviously, she didn't fall in the trap of my slanted compliment, as pretty women quite predictably do. Yet a barely restrained tiny glint of satisfaction unmistakably reflected in her eyes, virtually contradicting her just spoken words.

Then again, show me the man or woman who dislikes receiving praise.

But she was right I am somewhat prejudicial about women wearing pants. As an old fashioned guy I believe that trousers have not been designed to properly fit female shapes and needs. However true or untrue this might be, I must ask what's so damn desirable in eradicating all differences between the sexes? Wouldn't this superficial equality end up by bringing about a gray, uninteresting world, whereby in spite of the purported democratic gains, both sexes might end up rather as losers than winners? Why should the resulting unisex world be so fantastic, once formal differences between men and women would have been wholly eradicated?

*

Most proud American sisters might be surely and rightfully flummoxed by these views possibly more than the rest of women in the world combined. I bet neither would my mistress have liked my comments. As many proponents of women's liberation, fervently bent on erasing nearly all gender-specifics, for denying everyone, but particularly men, the right to question in the slightest **this undeniably noble ideal** of equality and fairness, she too would have despised me even for suggesting any possible trade-offs to watch for. 'Who do you think you are' she would have asked, 'what kind of poor pathetic dissenter should pose such politically *incorrect* questions?'

Here then is my secret, timid reply: Is there a tiniest chance that such a beautifully egalitarian objective might hide a darker side too, as similarly lofty strivings in the world often did? Maybe the deal could be a bit too dear for everyone, particularly if injudiciously enforced. Why turning women into men, and vice versa—is not allowed some more analysis before being carried to its bitter, senseless end, regardless of consequences? May I meekly ask for that much? Some extremely vocal contemporary sisters would certainly deny me this intolerable liberty. Can this be democratically fair?

Hollywood's myth factory may very well have contributed to this historical development a lot more than is given credit for. This image-forging-cauldron could be partly responsible for creating the modern feminist ideal, the slender, strong, neurotic, bitchy *Cosmopolitan* type woman, equally fantastic between the sheets as successful in dominating her male counterpart in business, a model so many sisters tragically try to emulate almost religiously today. I dare insolently predict that in the coming *brave world* women will neither be respected nor loved if they will persist on proliferating such extreme attitudes. But as they apparently do, the resulting power-deficient, emasculated men might see in their-equal gung-ho sisters, in all respects just natural adversaries or, at best, *business* partners, and seldom some truly organic family members, respected wives, and loving moms. What kind of offspring and environment could such arrangements produce? What kind of a social structure? Take a simple look at these modern egalitarian couples already battling in courts. Is it not obvious how petty men, and how graceless women became in this all too cannibalistic meat grinder? Why should this be called progress? Or is my thinking unforgivably clouded, that of an ordinary, dinosaur-like male chauvinist pig?

I honestly dreaded the idea of confronting my proud mistress with these thoughts. Presently, when political freedom appears turbulently on the march all over the world, expressing such doubts aloud would be more than *unwise,* wouldn't it? In spite of the much-flaunted freedom of speech, one cannot attempt such irreverent, unconventional approaches without risking general opprobrium. A few noisy fanatics proclaim this is precisely how it must be. Please register in this respect my timid, albeit insignificant dissent. Naturally, I will do henceforth my utmost for begging all women to accept my heartfelt apologies, the kind so fashionably welcomed today throughout all the media.

*

Most folk know that in New Orleans the principal tourist objective is The French Quarter, its heart at the *Vieux Carré.* According to statistics, the place attracts in excess of six million visitors yearly from all over the world. The *Old Square* gained fame for its carnival-like atmosphere much beyond and above the pre-lent period. Conveniently, the *Mardi Gras* cheer is alive here day and night all year long. Why is so surprising that we aimed straight toward the city's famous *quarter* from the very start? Much excited by what we learned beforehand, and by the eagerness to confirm expectations, our chitchat within the vehicle suddenly sparkled with enthusiasm.

"Here we are darling, you and I together in the *Big Easy*. Isn't it fantastic to land in this enchanting place we knew only from movies or books?" Overwhelmed by the realization, we turned all of a sudden wild with exhilaration, two teenagers in love, super-enthused, contaminated by the city's atmosphere, real or imagined.

"Oh boy, I am so happy. Let me stamp my approval with a kiss." She leaned over and planted her noisy smooch on my right cheek, as playfully as ever. The little moist touch of lips felt delightfully uplifting, almost as a prize for some unbelievably grand accomplishment. Undeniably, we behaved as kids promised free reign in the candy store, and we plunged into the adventure full force.

It didn't take long to reach the city's modern downtown. Nothing-noteworthy here. The moderately high glass and steel skyscrapers looked as any place else, shimmering slightly in the morning sun. The streets cut ruler-straight between grandiose buildings appeared aseptically clean. But then -- a pleasant surprise—mature trees shaded the sidewalks. Here and there, in the yards of smaller houses left standing between modern giants, even a few palm trees showed off their exotic leafs. Frequently floral arrangements delighted the eye, colorful islands rarely seen in business centers of other large American metropolises. The city promised to be an original. A sense of lush laxity seemed to suffuse the atmosphere, people and all. Could the superlatives have been the result of our overheated imagination? No. Definitely no. Even navigating among these mostly right-angled, crisscrossing streets seemed straightforward, no need of assistance either from passersby, or the map.

Wandering aimlessly just to familiarize with the place, we came face to face with the enormous contour of the well-known Louisiana *Superdome*, rising as a giant concrete mushroom out of the blue. We had never given it a thought, as sport events seldom figured on either Didonna's or my own menu of favorites. This voluminous impact of the colossus --an unquestionable engineering marvel-- loomed massively enough before us to bring about a minor change of plan. It would have been unconscionable to have come this far, and not grant the monument a closer inspection-- moreover, plenty of parking in the vicinity. Three days of continuous driving made for a quick agreement on whether walking had to be the best approach. Following the long period of molding our behinds to the car-seat-shape, going *'per-pedes'* felt refreshing.

The stadium—a humongous exclamation marc in all respects-- covered many acres, each side the length of several blocks. To take in the dome's massive volume, the gigantic grayish bubble pushing for its own right between skyscrapers demanded retreating to some distance away.

For two humble puny human beings stepping in the world of giants, our jaws dropped in speechless awe. Although the admission fee in this technological marvel amounted only to ten dollars, for the occasional sports fans like us even this appeared a bit dear. So we kept our purse string knot tight, satisfied just by a few peeks inside the large hallways, filled by electronic displays glowing red above the ticket windows.

This enormous cave-like hollow hasn't been dedicated exclusively for sports events, but equally for rock-and-roll concerts, and other crowd-pleasing performances as well. We easily imagined the levels sound could reach under the dome, when screaming frenzied teenagers overfilled the tribunes that shook under the reverberating vibrations of mega amplifiers, as famous stars dominated the acoustic space with their hoarse voices, superimposed on the whining electric guitars, and thundering boom of drums. Everything, architecture, performance and the ensuing impression had been conceived here on purpose at a grand scale –admittedly—a bit too large for our taste.

Consequently, we beat the retreat quickly back into the safer past, and to a pace better attuned to our inner world, perhaps obsolete, but rhythmically nearer to what seemed in contrast more intimately human than these impossibly megalomaniac dimensions.

Naturally the next objective in line, following modernity's bragging magnitude of the Superdome, had to be the famous *Vieux Carré*. But finding it proved a bit elusive. It took lots of wrong turns before we literally stumbled on the famous square.

"How is it--I turned a little perplexed and annoyed to my companion --that so few signs point the visitor to such a famous tourist attraction as the French Quarter?"

Although vaguely condoning my outburst by an imperceptible nod, she preferred strategically just to sooth my irritation, in a way not dissimilar to a mother giving comfort to her little rambunctious, but helpless sons-- as women do this naturally.

"Come on, mommy's boy, behave and better pay attention to your driving."

Her admonishment came right in time, and I knew it too. So I conformed, but not without nourishing a smidgen of imperfectly repressed little spite, as whenever my mate got the upper hand over my weakness, nearly always impossible to effectively hide, regardless of my efforts. This time, however, I didn't react with anger. No sir, although I could have, proud to belonging among those incorrigible proverbial Romanian complainers, who gleefully will take advantage of the slightest opportunity to unburden pains by some stridently malicious, totally unrelated divagations. Regardless of how poor the tactic might appear in the eyes of unadvised outsiders at first, I share with my fellow nationals the ability to turning occasionally the overly drab reality a bit more bearable precisely by such tortuous twists of reasoning. Romanians seem to have rendered this absurdity almost to an art. While ruminating on the subjective validity of this seemingly inborn habit, but often objectively helpful in getting over my own absurd frustrations, lo and behold, we rolled triumphantly into the famous *Vieux Carré*.

Tiny as Bucephalos was, not one single free spot large enough to squeeze in among the zillions of cars parked all over the streets as for eternity. This forced to combing the entire neighborhood over and over again repeatedly. Yet the exercise ended up pleasanter than expected. The thrill of taking in the infinitely exotic variety of Hispano-French architectural styles, colors and shapes compensated fully for the difficulty of navigation, as the entire affair turned into a truly moving feast for the eyes.

"Whoever said anything about *Vieux Carré* showing off non-stop its carnival-like colors and moods had been surely right. To fully appreciate this unique charm, one must land here in person."

"My, my, for once you hit it right, the atmosphere this place exudes is hard to describe indeed. Thank You Good God for not granting us a parking spot too soon!"

"Hey, let's not jump over the horse—as Hungarians say. There must be better ways to take in this old city than through the windshield of our brave Bucephalos."

It took quite another while before we could squeeze our stallion into a spot at a street-end, hopefully within legal limits. After feeding the meter with all the coins Didonna found in her purse, and I in my pockets, we showed eager to investigate this marvelous old square at closer range, as two impatient children before a well-anticipated reward.

During the ensuing walk, whenever touching thighs I felt unbelievably proud, overwhelmed by the realization of having at my side a wonderfully alive, supple, sinuously sexy and warm dame. By touching her every now and then I knew I existed. Descartes should very well have said *I touch therefore I exist* instead of *I think*. What a ridiculous idea! Be that as it may, I still looked forward to making contact with those curvaceous hips, but taking care not to push too obviously for it. All the same, I felt singularly thrilling shivers whenever this happened, even if only remotely aware of the silliness of my whim. Floating silently through the crowd in rhythm with my mistress' body-tight red-striped jumpsuit stepping alongside my funny looking short pants, I imagined ourselves at the end of a reversed binocular looking infinitesimally small, fine porcelain toys, a fragile boy and girl run away from home in search of The New World, two entwined souls in *pursuit* of a wonderfully re-invented *happiness*. Not the tiniest atomic particle could have fit in between us I believed then in quiet satisfaction. Our passion for one another, and for America fused as never before. Never before or since had I felt possessed by such a simple joy and deep tranquility. I ached to confess this to the woman stepping alongside, considered her that instant my forever soul mate. And as I took a peek, and saw the luminosity of her aura, I knew words would be superfluous.

On the narrow streets, the slowly moving solid-mass-crowd --made up of all races of the globe-- flowed tumultuously in both directions as two fluvial streams, one up, the other down. On the shaded side various vendors peddled their wares, mostly gaudy tourist souvenirs of Chinese or Hindu provenience, or who knows where else from, but seldom locally made. At another intersection a few portrait-cartoonists -- their artworks exhibited on the sidewalk, Elvis Presley, Dolly Parton, Burt Reynolds, and other celebrity likenesses—awaited eagerly to sketch the less famous mugs of willing passersby in matter of minutes for measly fifteen dollars or so.

As any a respectable tourist we possessed a camera, so it seemed only natural to snap a few shots in this enchanting world buffeting right and left. My pretty friend had to figure in all, either in front of a horse-drawn carriage, or looking up at the forged balcony at the second floor of a flower-framed old house, or standing under the three towers of the ancient catholic church that closed in a plaza crisscrossed by red brick pathways, or leaning against the black fountain in the middle of the same, or posing elsewhere in equally banal postures, surely to become later visual mementos of our journey. On the other two sides of the square plenty of fine restaurants, small boutiques, or coffee and pastry shops lured tourists with deeper pockets to colorful tables and under umbrellas in well-mimicked European style. Inside the premises well worn, blackened floors creaked and screeched under steps in indisputably Old World fashion.

"I bet Camille Pissaro could have been as happy to paint here as in Paris!"

"I don't know much about the guy, but I like what I see. Take as many pictures as you can, and stop wasting time by showing off your wits. Okay? Come on, I want a million pictures in this place."

"Okay, okay, I will do that, although I wish myself to see my own mug in some too."

"Of course, let me show you how."--And without further ado, she peremptorily stopped a young passerby, and asked him to click a few frames with the two of us together.

"You realize the risk you took, don't you? What would you have said had the man run away with my pricey camera? This is America, you know."

"There you go again with your dark suspicions. Didn't you see what a nice, honest looking young fellow he was?"

What could I have said to this, but keep my opinion to myself?

"Oh forget it, the real problem lies elsewhere. By shooting at such furious pace the camera has run out of film."

The extra rolls safely tucked in the luggage couldn't help, but unwilling to waste precious time by fetching some, the only choice left was to purchase another spool in a souvenir shop, and pay double price.

"So what's the problem? Go buy some."

(Today's readers might ask why didn't I possess a digital gismo? First, because it wasn't widely available yet, second, it was very expensive, and third, how could such a preference fit in my conservative—read cheapskate-- personality?)

"I will, but Murphy's Law requires thorough preparedness, or else one must pay the piper, so I—"

"Gosh, why didn't the smart-aleck in you think about this in time? Buy the damned film."

But realizing she spoke with no malice, but just parried in jest, I didn't even bother retorting in kind. Instead changed course diplomatically, for once able to distract her attention to the infinite little knick-knacks glittering on the shelves. Yet, to still add a minimum of alacrity I pointed to the lack of air-conditioning in the shop.

"What a miracle! Tell me sweetie, how can this happen in the Good Old US of A?"

"Hmm! This city obviously goes out of its way to please, but in here the air feels nearly as hot if not hotter than outside. For once I must agree with you." Then she changed tack, quite surprised to see me pay for the roll of film fully with small change.

"Well, well, look at the big spender! This shop will never get rich on your money. No wonder they can't afford cooling the atmosphere."

I confronted the sneer by a vague smile of self-satisfaction, and reminded my friend Benjamin Franklin's advice.

"*A penny saved is a penny earned.* Too bad Old Ben's wisdom is no longer heeded. The day will come when America will pay dearly for its present day profligacy."

"Of course, la-di-dah, la-di-dah, one day America will suffer big time for this sin, I know," she snapped her whip in retort. "But don't you worry, I will never go overboard by spending my pennies needlessly. By the way, I am famished."

"Me too. Let's look for a joint to have a bite."

The place selected happened to be in the shopping mall nearby, built on several levels in the cavernous interior of a former railroad station, a warehouse, port-facility, or something of this sort. Before deciding on the restaurant, we agreed on taking a walk within the premises, just to figure out the building's history. And lo and behold, we discovered the old railroad tracks leading to a blocked-off gate, once cut in the wall at the riverside. Upon further investigations it became self-evident how trains unloaded merchandise directly in the warehouse, some time ago part of the Mississippi port. Within the former facility the upper structure had been removed, although the old blackened iron trusses left on purpose exposed under the roof. Underneath, everything got suitably transformed, the space partitioned for the commercial use of several expensive boutiques, a lot of smaller shops, all anchored around a few larger department stores. Off the mall's four the second level had been strategically reserved for restaurants and fast food establishments.

"This is it, a slightly modified variant of the all-too-famous American Shopping Mall. You've seen one, you've seen them all."

"Why don't you just keep quiet? I happen to like this arrangement a lot more that what passed for shopping centers in the Old Country."

"Sure, sure, there you go again with the dumbest of comparisons, between the number one country in the world and the seventy-fifth at best. A fair appraisal indeed of both, aye?"

Fortunately the argument ceased at this point, as my friend waved my argument aside by pointing to fact a bit uncommon.

"Hey, did you notice how all restaurants in this mall seem to specialize in seafood?"

"In view of the location this might make perfect sense. By the way, are you prepared to try one out?"

Then I almost flipped out, taken aback by the pricey choices on the menus displayed at entrances. But eventually I had to reluctantly relent, as saving time and satisfying hunger gained the upper hand, although the selected establishment appeared inside as expensive as on the outside.

Naturally my friend picked a table by a large window that framed-in spectacularly the murky greenish-brown waters of Old Mississippi river, gently flowing down toward the Golf-- slow ships, barges, oil-tankers, and a lot more smaller vessels on its back. In spite of the slight jolt my thrifty soul endured a minute earlier, the view took my breath away. The scene on the river shimmered in humid haze, brushed over with a dull bluish-green tinge, here and there striped by the bright red of some vessels' float-line above the water.

"Look, look, a paddle boat" she cried out as if had just found a treasure.

Indeed, there it glided past precisely the all too ubiquitous steamer out of a Mark Twain story. Lacking better words to express my awe, I could only exclaim in restrained admiration.

"Take a look at that old contraption, how happily chugs along on the waves of this Grand River!"

The phantom-like ship flowed down soundless, only the low, sad bellowing of its whistle penetrated inside at intervals. Through the thick glass the scene looked rather like a surrealistic kinetic painting than palpable reality. The paddle wheel kept relentlessly swirling the water, leaving behind a long white wake of vanishing foam, as in a slowed silent movie. The ship's two or three decks, the pair of black stacks, and bright red paddles appeared as fragile ghosts, strangely awoken off the past to haunt the evanescent present.

It had to be the waitress to shatter our visual delectation, as it courteously and prosaically materialized out of nowhere, ready to serve after having placed on the table the customary glasses of water and the menus. Once again left to our own devices, out came cigarettes –the antismoking legislation as yet only pending-- and we, perfectly relaxed in the cool atmosphere, engrossed to studying the dinning-selections offered. At times, life can be so uncomplicated!

Louisiana's famous *Cajun* cuisine--a mixture of French, Caribbean and American tastes-- is said to be particularly good in New Orleans, where it's been elevated to an art meshing together the hotness of red pepper and sweet aromas of herbs with an assortment of vegetable garnishing, to go along with meats blackened on the grill.

Didonna opted for prawns and I preferred catfish. Additionally, we ordered a combination plate, tiny deep-fried, bite-size hushpuppies, various vegetables, and tossed salad for both. Our boldness didn't go as far as the *crayfish*, a local sort of crustaceans, for a pair of humble Romanians roaming through America too ugly even to see. Forget swallowing the little suckers looking back at us. We resolved bravely, to give it a try some other time. Perhaps!

It is common sense, and quite pleasant to wash down spicy food with beer, and so we did, eagerly exposing our apprehensive taste buds to exotic delights right at the source. Said and done.

The promptness and courtesy of service equaled the meal's deliciousness.

Less than ten minutes later, oblivious to the world at large, impressed by the combination of the –waitress recommended-- local *Nola Irish Channel Stout* smooth, rich ale, and spicy Cajun food, we acted silly as teenagers, enthused by the show one of the longest river in the world offered freely as it placidly flowed down before our eyes, The Grand Old Mississippi.

All seemed incredible, particularly as no one could have guessed by our looks the Eastern Europeans in us, other than hearing our accents. Fortunately, the Grand River reduced us to mute contemplation. The Old World, along with all its perceived or real complexities receded to a foggy background deeply buried in our consciousness. For an hour or so, we lived liberated and happy in the present tense, two simple human beings stripped of nationality. What fantastic wonders good food and a little alcohol may spark in the soul of a mortal! How easy to forget all suffering and struggles of life when the body gets immersed in the small pleasure of enjoying some tasty morsels, while the eyes get their candy too! In such circumstance everything could appear grand and beautiful to the wise and unwise alike, miraculously part and whole of the same world. But let's not forget the exceptions, namely those few elect individuals constantly yearning for power, possessed by the desire to rule and dominate more than by the pursuit of simple happiness, the very same joys deemed by the above as despicable weaknesses. Why then the admiration for the people ruling us from above the clouds, as all media, pundits, historians and the rest of prevaricators want from us? Don't these wretchedly poor souls deserve rather the pity than our envy? Why history designates them as heroes? Shouldn't these emotionally challenged monsters be properly treated as some handicapped victims, as the damned souls unable to enjoy the curt earthly life without pathologically inflicting pain on their brethren?

Before leaving New Orleans and the above sorry comments behind, my friend had to take the customary tour through the shops in the mall.

"Just let me browse a tiny bit. Come on, we have plenty of time."

And what could a decent man say with his stomach filled by yummy food, and head numbed by a couple ounces of decent alcohol?

"Okay sweetie, do your duty, but be quick. A good walk might burn some beer off my system. Let's go."

"Wow, sometimes you can be a real darling."

"Oh yes?"

The mostly expensive, tastefully exposed merchandise --suited more for viewing than buying—in my eyes looked like elsewhere in the States. Judging by the few customers in the mall, I wondered if any items ever got sold, or just exhibited for simply esthetic reasons, not unlike art pieces in museums.

Satiated at last by merchandise to be had only in dreams, we exited through the doors facing the river, now beautifully bathed in a yellowish haze of light. On the way back to the car --hopefully still there-- we became aware of the city's special character-- always alive, forever in motion, eagerly tempting the visitor with its famous culinary choices, as the local appetizing *"muffas"*, another local specialty luring the hungry into a number of Italian delicatessen shops.

By the square's immediate vicinity, inside an airy but covered market, a line of vendors peddled their exotic and ordinary vegetables --elephant garlic, Chinese eggplant, monstrously large papayas, to name a few. In the next open adjacent building, the largest assortment of hand-stitched leather products, various wood, metal, textile or plastic objects, copper ware, clay pottery and pans, utensils, miniature carvings, pocketknives, purses, imprinted t-shirts, small dolls, or God-knows-what-other knickknacks imported from Hong Kong, or Bombay tempted the passersby.

It was here my fair-skinned friend relented and bought a violet-colored hat, fitted with an oversized sun shield. About time! My redheaded but bleached dame's sensitive translucent complexion hopefully found at last the proper protection from the Southern Sun's murderous rays.

As we paused near a bronze sculptural group-- bringing together life-size tradesmen, a bunch of hogs, and a donkey--, I had to capture on film my pretty mistress leaning against the funny metallic man nearby, his head covered by a top hat. She insisted like a little girl. Then the aroma of coffee struck irresistibly, drawing us in to tasting the local variety of *espresso,* advertised in many a show window. The black tar-like liquid proved well worth the wait in the long quay of people wanting the same.

Seated at last at a small table under an umbrella outdoors, we lit smokes, and after my first sip, I had to say it.

"This is what I call the good life. New Orleans fully deserves the reputation of a truly fun city, its people possess indeed the so-called zest for life top to bottom, know to enjoy living beyond the simplistic thrills of monetary profit. The *Big Easy* is exactly what it wants to be."

"Amen."

But I went on rambling:

"No wonder New Orleans fascinated so many artists. It was this place that prompted Edgar Degas to paint his famous *Cotton Exchange* and this milieu inspired Tennessee Williams to write *A Streetcar Named Desire*, Sherwood Anderson, William Faulkner, Mark Twain, Frances Parkinson Keyes too, had only words of praise for this city, filled by Mediterranean-like grace, whereby siesta is still faithfully practiced, and people afford the time to talk to one another in cafés daytime, or at nights, to absorb the sounds of Jazz and honky-tonk, pervading the humid sticky but, oh so, languorous atmosphere everywhere."

"Sometimes you can almost make sense, my love."

Regretfully, we had to say good-bye to our short stay, as all earthlings must leave behind theirs, either in joy or sorrow. This is life! So long, *Big Easy!*

In July darkness sets in late. Fortunately this meant we returned soon enough to Bucephalos, in spite of the growing sun's fiery globe sliding progressively closer to the horizon. On the windshield, a bright and loud surprise beckoned under the driver's side wiper: a ticket. According to police, the vehicle was parked too near the corner. Moreover, the meter so dutifully and –as it appeared-- senselessly filled by quarters expired. Luckily, the fine was moderate, only ten dollars. All the same, the fact didn't make it more pleasant.

"What do you think, can the state of Louisiana collect this money in Damascus?" the Smart Alec in me asked.

"Why, you think it won't?"

"Well, Maryland is far away, and we are about to leave Louisiana for ever, aren't we? How could I pay the fine even if willing?"

"Then let's go. What are we waiting for?"

*

A month and a half later, my thinking had been proven wrong. The State of Louisiana found my address all right in Maryland, advising to paying up if further complications were to be avoided, such as doubling the fine. I felt disinclined to test the system any further. Long live computers!

Today, when jotting down my story, I consider myself privileged to have visited New Orleans before hurricane Katrina hit in 2005, and apparently has changed the city forever, as the punditry seems to think. Why so often happy memories must be marred by subsequent tragedies?

*

For exiting the city we had two choices, either keep the course on route-10 --the southernmost interstate connecting the coasts from Florida to California-- or follow the local route-90, cutting through the swamps of Mississippi's estuary. The second option had to be more appealing for adventurers, so it became ours even if didn't suit our profile and will exactly. What happened in fact was that, faced all of sudden by two alternatives, we rolled on route-90 inadvertently, as always very much against my wish.

"Shucks, I think the arrow to route-10 unfortunately pointed slightly to the right. Oh well it's too late now. Anyway, show me the driver able to decipher these signs in time out of a fast moving vehicle."

"Why not *ubi* around?"

"Because in this unfamiliar place the maneuver could be even harder than pushing straight ahead, I guess."

"Then go ahead, I don't mind."

"Here we go, dear. Full speed forward!"

I spoke too soon, as the words barely left my lips, and Bucephalos had to slow down to a crawl. The four-lane-highway turned in a two-lane-country-road, congested by barely moving local traffic, mostly beat-up jeeps and pick-up trucks. As Murphy's Law dictates we rode unwillingly but cheerfully straight in a grand new mess, any possibility of reversing to route-10, or pressing ahead at a decent pace denied. Given the facts, passing became not only dangerous, but futile as well. Too often one must play the cards as dealt. Plans had to be readjusted. For the case we'd get tired before finding our way back to route-10, the overnight at some iffy motel in a small village along the new itinerary became almost certain-- dim chance indeed for a better alternative.

"I am afraid our situation just turned into a new adventure. Be prepared!"

"Tell me you' re kidding! The overtones in your warning, as well as the suggestion sounded a bit discouraging. Please turn around!"

"Be my guest. By the way, where is your enthusiasm for America now?"

"Oh man, don't be facetious. You're not fair."

"What's fairness to do with it?"

"Come on, stop acting silly."

In tune with our plans the scenery changed too, and not for the better. Everything visible along the road on both sides wore the sad imprint of utter poverty --material and spiritual alike. A typical sort of industrial decay engulfed by vegetation overgrowth appeared obviously escaped under human control everywhere we looked. The road snaked between rows of abandoned warehouses of corrugated steel or, at regular intervals, under rusty railroad bridges, the paint pealing off the metal as greenish psoriatic scabs on some lepers' skin. Piles and piles of contorted oily metallic rubbish deposited between wet grassy patches asserted their transitory existence before relentlessly sinking in the soft ground, often even in the harder pavement. The air above this amorphous mass hovered musty, fishy and pungent, odors tinged by offensive whiffs of unburned gasoline and bluish exhaust fused in one foul exhale of a cold mellow hell on earth. I said mellow, because lungs got rapidly adapted, as the ugliness turned itself into a sort of weird beauty, evident to us both. It didn't take long to notice the sublime way the sun's slant amber rays clung to the metallic facets and vegetation-contours, combining the disparate elements --natural and artificial-- into one grand metaphor of a poetic reality that turned eternally round and round, dirt to life, and vice versa.

"I tell you life in these parts should be perhaps more authentic, more humane than in the shadow of colossal skyscrapers, doomed sooner or later to the same fate as the picturesque sea of rubbish amidst we navigate now. Agree?

"Of course, dear, but now better stop the nonsense and push on the gas. I want to be out of here as soon as possible. Please do me the favor. Leave philosophizing for later."

Easier said than done. Twenty, thirty minutes later, deeper and deeper in the strange God-forsaken environment, we halted under a bridge to study the map. The attempt, natural as it seemed, eventually proved futile since we couldn't figure anything precise about the location. The only reasonable alternative remained to execute a one-eighty, and find some indicators. For some strange reasons, we elected to move straight ahead, only God knows why as night approached fast, and spending it back in New Orleans appeared wholly unacceptable to either of us. Pushing deeper in the unknown became the only alternative --an inspired decision, as it turned out.

Minutes later, the country road widened, the pavement smoothed under the tires, and we entered a little village, a welcome oasis at the edge of the dark swampy musty world left behind. Suddenly the ember of the majestic burning sun's remaining sliver shone above the western horizon brighter than ever.

Mighty oak trees lined the narrow main street. Under the thick shade of centuries-old dark green giants, a few visible time and weather-beaten houses looked puny. In the village center –name to us for ever unknown -- a few stores, empty show windows, a car-repair shop and a *Seven Eleven* emergency store, the latter the perfect answer to our immediate needs.

Squeezing brave little Bucephalos in the empty parking spot between two bullyboy pick-up trucks felt almost scary. But the beverage supply had to be replenished, some questions about our whereabouts had to be answered. We stepped in. As the store was out of Coca Cola, we accepted Mountain Dew, unbelievably the only alternative available. *'When denied a horse, a donkey will do'* I recalled again the adage. All the same, we inhaled two cans of the super sugary yellow liquid right on the spot, as for a meal went for a couple of ice cream cones. Should it be really so unhealthy satisfying the gut's need like this? I am not sure however the delicious taste of that ice cream still lingers on my tongue. Hunger makes for the best cook!

As for the shortest way back to the main highway nobody seemed able, or willing to provide any useful advice. Two possible explanations-- first, I couldn't be sure whether the folk understood, or bothered to answer my questions, and second, given my strong accent they might have taken me for a veritable alien creature, fallen in their provincial midst directly off a distant, unknown planet. This is precisely how I felt as they innocently shrugged my questions away.

Minutes later, the town and folk melted to nothing more than a vague memory, not unlike a dreamlike flash illuminating the scene during a lazy summer afternoon.

From this point on, the road meandered for endless miles atop a dyke, parallel to a canal filled with murky dark waters flowing slowly under the shade of old, sadly sagging willows. Even the air felt cooler, permeated with thick moldy miasmas. On our bank, not far inland, modest houses showed here and there in the midst of small meadow-like patches and lush greenery, in the yards, boats moored to more or less improvised piers. As elsewhere in the American landscape not a soul visible anywhere. A soft eerie tranquility reigned all over the scene.

On the opposite bank, the dwellings looked anything but modest. Several could have qualified for small palaces, surrounded by large areas of finely mowed grass, to the possible envy of some better golf courses. The water-way seemed to serve as the border line, separating the fat cats on one shore from the less well to do on the other, all arranged the way Providence preordained according to laws of decency, natural necessity, or customs, as apologists of the American way would unabashedly proclaim.

The evening descended slowly, to hide the land under the persistent luminous sky, whilst the last thin band of the incandescent sun disk, a blindingly bright slice of intense orange succeeded here and there to peek through some tree branches.

As the sublime seldom leaves sensitive souls untouched, our conversation turned smoother, calmer, and serene as well, nearly to the point of syrupiness. The signs regularly warning about the dangers of *alligator crossings*—much like *deer crossings* up

North -- might have contributed to this effect too. An encounter with reptiles crawling casually across the road probably seemed to locals here just as natural as it elicited our awe and wonder.

"How would you deem an alligator crossing our path just now? Would that be a good, or a bad omen?"

"Surely I would take it as a bad sign were the reptile black."

Luckily, almighty Providence spared us from finding out whether I had been right or not, as no such terrifying exotic monsters crossed the road in front of us. Not even the tiniest lizard jumped up against brave Bucephalos, although the dike meandered on for another thirty-to-forty minutes alongside the same waterway. Oh well!

By the time we crossed the border into the State of Missouri it was past eight o'clock. The scenery opened up, both land and sky; the water and the bulrush retreated gradually to the left, as on the right the continental landmass got enveloped in the bluish veil of imminent nightfall.

Predictably, the tourist information office closed hours earlier. Nonetheless we inspected it as permitted, mostly on the outside. As always my companion collected pamphlets, and then, after tasted the water at the fountain, and checked out the facilities, we set in motion refreshed, back at last on interstate-10.

An hour later, a short distance before the State of Texas, the dark ink of night covered the landscape so thoroughly that only the white bands on the pavement remained visible in strobe-like fashion, before rapidly vanishing under the speeding car' s belly, and off our mesmerized eyes.

"The effect of these pulsating white lines can be dangerously hypnotic for drivers, often causing distracting reveries. Please keep talking to me."

"Sure, my driving force in life, I'll make sure you'll be alert."

But then, true to her psyche, she didn't. On the contrary, she began playing with her fingers through my hair strands while whispering softly sweet loving words in my ear. Did I protest, as I should have? Nah, I did not complain a penny's worth. Even more, I loved it. Man, how weak can you be!

Slowly everything jumbled up, turned mushy. The white bands sped maddeningly faster under the vehicle, and before long my lover's soft, caressing fingertips raised humongous goose bumps on my acutely sensitized epidermis. Oh boy, how delightfully can pleasure and danger mix every now and then!

*

It happened on a Sunday afternoon Philomela invited Didonna and her son Alex to dine with us. On that nice sunny autumnal day --uniquely colorful in Washington DC and surroundings— fate selected me to greet them in front of the house, where I was tinkering with my car, whether or not as expertly as often proudly and loudly pretended.

Anyway it wasn't hard to drop my activity immediately, and receive the lady with open arms, perhaps a bit more enthusiastically than it should have been proper between a married man and a single woman, even if friends. Under my effusive embrace my chest pressed quite hard against her nicely filled out bosom. She responded in kind, no fuss or reserves, as any unsuspecting friendly member of the opposite sex would naturally do.

I didn't care whether the wife noticed my effusion, whether she was bothered by it at all. She approached the scene with the same kind of exaggerated, supercharged enthusiasm and joy, a behavior I resented and complained about often to no avail.

"Hey sister, you look ravishing. Welcome, and feel at home, *mi casa su casa.* Come my handsome boyfriend Alex, let me give you a kiss too. Dear husband, why don't you part company with your darling vehicle, and take care of this pretty lady instead. I know you'd like that better."

"Okay, okay, I will. Just let me tidy up a bit."

A few minutes later, Didonna and I sat together in the living room, trying hard to strike a conversation. Philomela retreated in the kitchen to take care of her cooking, a skill she seemed always deservedly proud of. While still mulling a little annoyed over her exaggerated welcome, I awkwardly began to say something smart, but realizing in time how senseless my words would sound, I addressed Alex instead.

"Hey little gent, why don't you go down those stairs, take the air riffle off the rack, and try it out in the yard, on the target affixed to the fence? Wouldn't you like to do that?

"Wow", the boy's face lit up, as he looked immediately for mother's approval, "May I?"

"Sure, but be careful not to damage anything."

Once the son dismissed, I turned to the mother.

What would you like to drink?

"I'll have what you have."

"Well then, whiskey and soda it is."

I walked over to the bar counter with a slight knot in my throat. 'I like this woman. She's really nice, I thought, and she seems to like me too.'

It could well be that, prompted by a nascent yet unsuspected guilty conscience, my overheated imagination blew the scene all out of proportion. Yes, this might have been true, but what if it wasn't? Wasn't I a little later with her, and not at home next to Philomela as any faithful husband should be at the side of his wife? This is what I think today, but then I behaved oblivious to such *simplistic* moral dilemmas. Could a man or a woman ever act aware beforehand against the grain of an impending destiny, whether in a good or bad way? It is hard to say. So I will keep on dancing around the idea often, throughout my entire story.

On that afternoon however, I brushed aside the awkward first minutes, and proposed casually to change the thermostat in her car, as I promised some days earlier.

"Why don't we step outside again until my consort finishes her business in the kitchen? Aye, what do you say? Come, take your drink along."

"Alright, if this is what you feel like doing, although I don't want in any way to impose, you know--"

"Forget it, no imposition whatsoever." And out we went, but not before Philomela got informed, and Didonna called her son to help.

Alex, promoted as my assistant, eagerly jumped to the task of handing over my tools, and his mother volunteered to wash my car, perhaps as a *thank-you-gesture* for my taking care of hers. The kid and I took working together seriously. I fell instantly for this blond, fair, alabaster-skinned, blue-eyed boy, enjoyed his naïve questions about cars, formulated in absolutely serious, pretentious manner and words adults find so often amusing.

Then, when I went to my vehicle to fetch a ratchet or something, my female guest's well-rounded derrière, well in relief as she bent down to wash the back window from the inside, stung my eyes. I felt moon-struck. Oh what an intense impression her sensuously revealed loaves left on my eyes peeking under the thin summer dress slipped up on her thighs and hips, to suggest for imagination even more details than it called by definition to hide. In the fortunate absence of the wife's eagle's vision I could linger unhindered on the marvelously rounded forms. How lucky can a guy get!

My instinct told me right there and then the woman must be mine one day, one way or another intimately connected to my life. The sooner it happens the better I thought fleetingly. The idea struck as lightening, though somewhat in semi-conscious fashion. However, on the very same heartbeat the male in me already hatched a secret plot, to act upon as soon as possible.

The opportunity arose fast enough, and I did not hesitate to exploit it. The thermostat once installed it seemed almost natural to take the car for a test-ride. Didonna took the wheel as I sat on the passenger side.

She changed gears skillfully enough to impress any man, reminding how I never succeeded in teaching Philomela to drive a car with a stick shift. Out on the highway, I noticed the delicately lacquered pink fingers of her right hand resting comfortably on the shifter, and became fascinated, almost obsessed by the urge to touch. Without thinking long and hard, I succumbed to the temptation, and placed my hand upon hers squeezing gently, while intently watching for her reaction. Her cutely pointed nose, quivering nostrils, sensuous lips had to betray at least a tiny indication, significant enough to encourage my hope of receiving at least a blue approving glance in return.

No such satisfaction, but she didn't withdraw her hand either. So I kept my eyes affixed on her profile, searing forever in memory the pale pinkish color of her complexion, the straw-yellow shades of hair, the light blue transparency of her gaze trained straight ahead, frozen far in the onrushing space. Although not yet fully aware, I made the first opening move toward a love affair. Incredible as this sounds, I acted impulsively, not exactly sure why. The fact however remains incontrovertible it has been definitely my side that initiated the affair. About her part, if any, never ever seriously tried to find out. For the sake of my affection's indisputable validity in time, her persona has to remain always pure.

*

All of sudden, through the right side-window of speeding Bucephalos, a glaring, orange-red flame's whimsical flicker on the dark distant sky caught my attention. These fiery burning offshoots brought the present brutally back to reality, pushing the past to retreat at seventy miles an hour, and us forward through the overheated air toward Huston, to the immediate future. The flaming emissions of Beaumont refineries tore violently into the night's dark compact cosmic texture. The light these giant torches produced was strong enough to enable a glance at my watch-- five minutes before ten o'clock.

But Huston was still far, about a seventy-mile-drive away. Giving myself to an irresistible urge I stepped on the gas pedal. Bucephalos picked eagerly up on my not-so-subtle prodding, and accelerated fast to ninety miles an hour, a velocity that made the wind rushing past sound as a hurricane. What a pleasant, exhilarating sensation!

Perhaps the barreling asteroid-like through the night after a while caused the moisture-saturated-air feel strangely sensual, at one point making me imagine a beautiful courtesan lazily stretched between satin sheets, as she was about to accept her lover's embrace. Speeding in the dark may often produce lustful impressions in men. My silent companion, as if guessing my thoughts, leaned over and planted subtly one of her usually delicate smooches on my cheek. Some women read men's minds as open books.

This mellow-sweet, dreamy, romantic segment came to end thirty miles or so before Huston, as we drove in the parking lot of a *Quality Inn* motel. Drained nearly to the last drop of our energy as Prairie dogs after a long day of prowling, we accepted with no fuss the last vacancy, the other rooms having been taken just minutes earlier by the load of passengers disembarked off a massive chartered bus that took up five spaces in the parking, next to our little CRX. Lady Luck worked overtime, allowing us once again to spend the night in the middle of nowhere, somewhere not too far from our objective, in a welcoming, clean, air-conditioned room, in spite of the late hour, and all this without having secured a reservation beforehand. Fortune works for the dumb.

The warm water cascading off the showerhead washed rapidly away the exhaustion, the grit and smoke accumulated during the extra long day's motoring. Reinvigorated, slightly numbed by beer, we felt fantastic, capable even of watching the newscast on TV, though not for long. Crashed at last in each other's arms, I didn't realize who turned the set off. Soon *Old Morpheus* stole the light off our eyes, sinking his two prisoners in the pitch-dark waters of forgetfulness. Oh, sleep how sweet can you be!

THE LONE-STAR STATE

It was not the rooster's first crowing to wake us up at dawn. The group of tourists did it instead, as they noisily boarded the bus parked next to Bucephalos the previous night. The powerful Diesel engine fired up for the colorful assembly's departure roared incessantly, filling the air with unpleasant odors of black smoke. Aside this slight nuisance, the day promised to be splendidly sunny and warm. The early morning light filtered milky white in the room through cracks between the curtain folds, bringing in sharp relief the smallest details of objects hidden in the remotest corners the eye otherwise overlooked. Didonna, snatched out of her dream by the clatter and commotion outside, tried to hide her head under the pillow, hands clasped together above, comically indicating the wish to sleep a little longer. Impossible. Finding nothing better for soothing her displeasure, I placed a delicate kiss on her left shoulder, incidentally bared before my always-lustful eyes.

She responded instantly, turned around to take me in her arms, and press her warm body greedily tight against mine as a large soft cuddly feline. Not the smallest surface of my skin could have escaped her touch. The absoluteness of this embrace engulfed body, soul and mind, my thoughts and reactions banished in a strangely unreal remoteness. By the time we came back to senses, the bus, tourists and their attendant agitation had long since vanished, the motel reverted to an eerie silence, seemingly even deeper in contrast to the brilliant brightness of morning prefiguring an unusually hot day. Lazily abandoned in each other's arms for a couple more minutes, we could have easily slid back to new sweet dreams. But the moment slipped, pushed irrevocably away as the urgency of our departure became glaringly clear once again.

Unfortunately, or fortunately, no one had yet discovered the magic of bringing back lost opportunities of the past. My pondering along this theme was however suddenly brought to end by a smidgen of puniest worries. Given the long trip ahead, I wondered whether I didn't push my body lately a bit too hard sensually. Perhaps it was advisable a little more prudence before wasting my energy this way. But realizing the ridiculousness of such worries I wisely pushed off the thought with my next breath, trying instead to guess my love's possible comments, had she seen through my mind.

'Oh dear, can't you ever forget worrying, and enjoy the vacation instead!'

She could have been quite right. All the same, I remained somewhat affected by my musings, and resolved to be stingier at dispensing sensuality in the coming days. Am I as pitiful as it gets? But the cogs under my thick skull kept turning: What if my thought betrayed a small bite of guilt for abandoning Philomela, following twenty years of apparently blissful conjugal existence? Can't really say. However, this sort of, let's say, Teutonic obtuseness combined with a Latin-type prevarication provoked often difficulties in my life. By the same token, I confess not to have ever learned much from such inner wanderings. Or maybe I did, but only unknowingly. Bah!

Nature, obviously stronger than the human will, may easily render mute some pangs of conscience for past wrongdoings, childhood trespasses, broken promises, tasks undone, passions unfulfilled, as so many sins apparently overwritten or misplaced in the dungeons of the subconscious. Deep down in the abyss of psyche, true love may stay for ever buried under piles of rubbish left there by foolishly quarrelsome parents, moronic school teachers, bored benevolent fellow married couples, whose advice gets imparted regularly under the guise of infinitely good intentions. Then how could so many broken hearts in this world genuinely appreciate the virtues of love? But shouldn't my question boomeranged, and asks whether I was capable myself of honest-to-God love at all? Hmm!

A half an hour later, following a plain coffee and croissant breakfast, we rolled on. Soon thereafter we caught the first glimpse of Houston's skyline, which superficially appeared not unlike the New York City of Texas.

Huge advertising boards lined the elevated highway on either sides, business windows cut out crudely off the day's intense blue sky-fabric. Skyscraper summits glistened in the distance, giant stalagmites piercing the heights amid ascending curtains of overheated air. This grand reception brought forward a modicum of good mood, made us feel welcomed in the city. Almost on the verge of bursting to unrestrained laughter, we could barely contain the joy of the wanderlust suddenly exploded in our hearts, rendering the daring vertical freedom ahead into effusive waves of genuine happiness.

Texas is grand, unquestionably so, grander than just *BIG*. Houston, the State's shiny pearl near the Golf, confronts the visitor with another example of the American Dream, even if in a somewhat nascent form. In a country founded on visionary ideals and unrestrained enthusiasm, whereby future achievements hang heavier in balance than the past, the largest city of the second biggest state (after

Alaska) represents just another dimension of the American primary endeavors of innovation, grandeur and hard play. Here, in the steam bath of a harsh subtropical summer, this uniquely creative spirit might easily elicit in the first-time-visitor a gamut of superlatives, loudly confessed by all vistas, beginning with the huge ranches, and the thickest steaks in the world, to end perhaps with the avidest desire for air-conditioning, and the unavoidable collateral power consumption.

Perhaps nowhere in America outside of Texas is this credo more powerful, whereby everything ought to be possible, all within human reach-- most obstacles surmountable. Nowhere is this super-virile dream more incessantly and passionately pursued than in the Lone-Star State. Confident in their invincibility, the enterprising independent spirited Texan men and women believe that nothing can stop them in achieving their goals, even if by means often harsher than morally acceptable elsewhere. This might be the reason Texas sometimes appears to outsiders larger than life, not only on the account of boastful attitudes, but also for the locals' willingness to taking bigger risks than other folk. Isn't it only natural then for *'J.R.'* --the character of the well-known TV series-- to be a proud Houstonian?

Aside that, the Spanish influence still exerts a dominant influence on this part of the American land, where the Anglo's enterprising spirit combines with the Latin preference for the dramatic. Beginning with the wide-brimmed 20-gallon-hats, the cowboy-boots, elsewhere considered a bit ridiculous when paired to business suits, the impossibly sized two-inch-thick steaks served on huge ellipsoid plates, and ending with the skyscrapers rivaling those in Chicago or New York, in Texas the concept of *bigness* must take precedence before all else. This obsession is noticeable in every respect, even in the shape and size of the most defiantly avant-garde skyscrapers downtown, as well as in the unabashedly posh quality of the exclusive River Oaks suburb, with its grand mansions erected for the super rich.

It is said about Texan hospitality to being proverbial, especially when supplanted by a six-shooter-- openly carried on the hip, I might add.

No doubt, the skyscrapers, as well as the villas in the millionaires' district of Houston are real enough, bearing the signatures of world famous architects, such as Philip Johnson and I.M. Pei, or sheltering master pieces of the likes of Jean Dubuffet and Juan Miro, to mention a few of the greatest. These neighborhoods may easily rival in wealth and style some luxurious districts, for instance, of Geneva or Monte Carlo.

In my view, though, this extraordinariness is somewhat lacking-- I can't pinpoint exactly in what way, but it surely didn't impress me as the locals might expect. This time I didn't see my routinely disputatious partner's breath taken away either. I am sorry. Architecture and size alone might not be enough for rivaling New York.

Houston greeted us --coincidentally-- exactly when hosting an important international business congress, purportedly an event of capital importance for the corporate world. Accordingly, the city dressed in holyday garb exuded a festive atmosphere, emphasized as well by the many colors of the participating nations' flags. Long, sleek, black limousines glided along major streets --swept super clean for the occasion--, everything sparkled in the powerful morning light, reemphasizing sharply the precise, geometrical contours of buildings against the vibrant sky.

The city as such was overwhelming enough to cause our jaws drop in awe, but not without some reservations. Unable to hold these locked in my chest any longer, I broke the silence.

"To be perfectly honest, this metropolitan's grandiose promise from a distance loses some luster at closer inspection. Although superficially akin to New York, in reality the city is visibly more provincial and artificial than that, even if built on a grander scale than, let's say, Reston in Virginia, or Columbia in Maryland, both equally modernistic. What do you think?"

"You really want my opinion?

"Don't be ridiculous! Why would I ask?"

"Okay then, in my view this city's architects and builders, awash in oil money, erected these opulently huge constructions in conformity to their ideals and tastes of ordinary businessmen, whose proverbial Texan pride aims ambitiously to rivaling New York or Paris. Instead, in my humble opinion, they created a community more like a huge village than a true city, in spite of skyscrapers, and its inhabitants too often inebriated on the stupefying alcohol of rapid success. Consequently, life here must be by its very nature a far cry from the effervescent cultural, and urban ebullience of a true world metropolis. If you have to know this is exactly what I think. Satisfied?"

"Wow, I am impressed. You hit the nail on the head. Now I know why I love you."

"Fine, I love you too, but cut the crap. Better let me conclude that once over my first impression of awe, this humongous aggregate of bigger-than-life-dreams became in my mind nothing more than a stylishly sterile combination of bedrooms and offices within neighborhoods so precisely demarcated, as to explain in itself the lacking of a more refined, sophisticated general spirit. Yes, these thoughts definitely occurred to me as we crisscrossed downtown. I can barely wait to leave Houston behind as soon as possible."

Hearing my fair friend's verdict, in total confluence with my opinion, yet I had to differ a bit, just for the sake of argument.

"Hey lady, be careful and refrain from hurting too severely the huge, oversized Texan pride, at least as long we'll be here, as your transgression might never be forgiven. I feel guilty enough myself for virtually begging *Restoners* and *Columbians* to forgive me for comparing their wonderfully peaceful, green and forward looking little communities, so fantastically adapted to family living and raising kids, to this barren huge concrete desert. By the same token, let me make it perfectly clear I would advise the tourist to visit Houston for a couple of days anyway. But if they were somehow hurting for time, I would rather urge them to explore San Antonio or Dallas instead, both culturally and urbanely richer." Then to ad oomph to my comments, I added loudly in a tactfully prudent jest, just in case: "Dear and proud Houstonians, please forgive me, and be lenient when judging my transgressions against your humongous pride."

"You must have visited Texas before, right?"

"No I haven't."

"Then how come you dare judge it so brashly based only on a short visit?"

"Is not obvious I am a well read person?"

"Oh, excuse me, sir!"

Now whatever my esthetic opinions and tastes with respect to Houston, I must admit it is unquestionably Texas-sized. Walking and driving through downtown from morning till well past dinnertime, chasing after several tourist objectives the majority of pamphlets pointed to, we ended up famished as wolfs brought to a deplorable exhaustion after a long fruitless prowl. So we faced decision time again, either overnight in the city, take it easy and dine on a wonderful Texas-style steak, to be followed by a walk on the wide well-lit streets at the bottom of canyons between skyscrapers, or take the chance of pushing west, straight into a night-time adventure on the highway. Only God knows why our choice fell on the second alternative. Whether the act of adventure without the benefit of experience versus the expanse of this State was courageous, or simply foolish I am still not sure.

So, instead of the famous steak we grabbed sandwiches at an ordinary *bodega*, made sure to replenish our exhausted supply of beverages, not forgetting to feed Bucephalos as well. Ready to roll, we thought everything should work to our advantage, including the few hours of daylight left. Yet our decision proved quite foolish soon enough, as driving against the setting sun proved a lot less than accommodating for the eyes than expected.

"It still beats driving in the dark, don't you think?" I heard a meekly encouraging well-affected innocent voice.

"Then why not get in my seat for a while? Come be my guest, you never took the wheel since we left home. Didn't you promise to do that occasionally?"

"Don't be ridiculous. You know how little you trust anyone with the reins of Bucephalos."

Rightly spoken. Then again, I never contemplated a twelve-to-fourteen hours daily driving job. This perspective altered my original opinion somewhat, so I would have gladly let my girlfriend take the wheel, at least for a few hours now and then. All the same I saw the wisdom in overruling my dissatisfaction, and to cutting short my complaints, perfectly aware that when a woman refuses a task it is better to leave the issue alone for good, just for saving later troubles.

Obviously, my pretty mistress properly appreciated my gallantry, and promptly expressed her gratitude by planting the usual reward of a tiny kiss on my cheek. The good old tomcat in me accepted the deal with a barely restrained smile of satisfaction painted on my mug. Oh man, how easily can you be cajoled into submission! Isn't love the funniest thing in the universe?

Thirty or so minutes later, an indefinite number of small communities traffic signs announced one after the other got left behind, to register as so many ephemeral glimpses on the radar screen of our attention. Every now and again, a white steeple of a small church lingered on the retinas a bit longer as it pierced the sky above rows of drab looking homes and barns, or the high stack of a decrepit factory towering over similarly run-down industrial buildings and warehouses in the distance. Simply said this segment of our trip became the sheer definition of monotonousness. All things and beings along this road, the insignificant localities together with the dwellers went by not unlike some comets whir by our planet, so near and so distant from our reach at the same time.

As the evening approached, Mother Nature' s thermostat turned the heat down a notch to a more bearable level. Or perhaps we got used to the discomfort, just to prove once more the human being's unique adaptability to any conditions. The enormous quantity of liquids consumed, mostly Coca Cola, might have helped in this sense as well.

"How the hell can we drink, and drink, and not feel the effect?"

"What effect?"

"Oh boy, sometimes you can be so slow. You know what I meant."

"Ah, ah, I get it… I guess perspiration must take care of the job. When traveling with windows down, the wind should help the evaporation process through the pores."

"Yes, this is more like it. In another words our kidneys must be really grateful for having the skin's help, right?"

"Maybe."—Here the dialogue came to an end, but not before I addressed my companion a tiny admonition. --"Listen, you don't have to be caustic. I am aware of my qualities as well as my shortcoming. Okay?"

"Sure dear, I learned this long ago."

"What's this supposed to mean?"

"Nothing really. Nothing more than I said."

I chose to put a stop to pursuing the subject any further, although with some difficulty, in spite of the strong curiosity gnawing within my ribcage for juicier details. I kept mute only to reinforce the new tranquility, invading suddenly from all sides, inside and outside the cabin.

A heavy ink of darkness dripped on the road to cover the scenery, to transform the little distant villages in flickering dots of light, alternating with large bands of deep black nothingness. Only the bright beams of oncoming trucks interrupted the eerie sensation, fortunately, not too often. We tried to pierce the deep space westward mostly alone on the highway stretching as a chalk line straight ahead all the way into the vanishing point. Such conditions may often induce a hypnotic state of meditation in drivers.

A glance to my right, and I noticed my companion gazing intently in the onrushing space, her eyes focused at some imaginary point far ahead in the darkness. Guessing somehow she wasn't asleep, I still elected no to intrude in her solitary retreat, although the moment seemed incredibly intimate, the woman nearer to me than ever before. Perhaps I wasn't quite alone in this large wide-open world. What a comforting thought! The bright white stripes on the asphalt kept rushing against the windshield incessantly as if straight against my very beating heart only to disappear, silent flashes of phantoms relentlessly gobbled up under the car's hungry belly.

*

A half a year of search later and consultations with agents, or discussions with friends, Didonna ended up owning a house, as many immigrants to this great land usually do, simple every day dreamers, calculating investors or daring adventurers alike. Properly elated, she conveyed the news herself during a phone conversation we had one late warm memorable afternoon. Her voice resonated with happy sensual inflections, on that day a hundred fold more pleasantly pitched, betraying an irresistibly infectious exuberance.

While registering the invitation followed by indications to the new address, I felt overwhelmed by this boundless exhilaration, by her sincere willingness to share the joy with me before anyone else. For some reason the favor made me brim with boundless pride.

Without much ado, I decided to pay her a visit right there and then. I could do it easily for Philomela was away, waiting tables in Rehoboth, Delaware, as she usually did during summers. It took me less than twenty minutes to cross the threshold of the said home, a bottle of wine in hand for properly honoring the big event.

Some people, beholden to more traditional values, might argue that I should have brought the lady flowers as a gesture of housewarming, perhaps cake instead of wine. Be that as it may, I confess to have acted always awkward in such situations because of my left-handed nature, or simply for I lacked --so-to-speak—the *proper* upbringing or, who knows why.

As so often, that afternoon my repressed desires gained the better of me for sure, although I might keep forever debating the true reasons of my impulsive decision.

She opened the door to greet me quite casually, probably straight off the kitchen to judge by the apron tied around her waist, yet her face betrayed a great deal of surprise at seeing me so soon following our phone conversation. All the same, I effusively embraced her on the spot, pressing her warm body tightly against mine without hesitation, denying her any time to react otherwise. The skin on her bare arms felt marble cool to my greedy touches, smooth and velvety at the same time. During this effusive, uncontrolled embrace, I tucked my nose behind her ears, in the golden strands of hair that impressed unforgettably on my lips a silky sort of dryness, while strange, vaguely scented whiffs of fresh hay dilated my nostrils. The warm, sweet, slightly pungent aroma her sensually rounded bosom exuded awoke tiny shudders in my body, engendering desires as yet not well processed in the recesses of my conscience. Although a bit confused, new emotions welled up in my heart, so fresh and powerful as to disregard she could have assigned ill will to my actions. Whatever the truth, I tried almost desperately to extend the moment to eternity. But then, noticing the flash of satisfaction barely hidden in her sky-blue eyes as they met mine in a lightening glance, I became aware she saw through my sneaky game, as well as through the gnawing carnal desires camouflaged under my awkwardly acted spontaneity. Also it could well have been for my feelings and thoughts to have amounted to nothing more than the usual products of an overheated imagination. Show me the male capable of unadulterated honesty under similarly taxing emotional challenges.

"Well, well, Mr. Doru, I didn't expect you so soon. But here you are, so come on in," she began in charming tone of voice, while skillfully slipping out of my embrace, and hastily trying to straighten her hairdo, the dress on her body, betraying a bit of agitation in the process, as if caught unawares in her embarrassment.

Then she peremptorily seated me on the couch, and disappeared, back in the kitchen to prepare the Turkish coffee, as Romanians habitually do the first thing for their expected or unexpected guests alike.

Left to my own devices, I began scanning around in this new fashionable suburban townhouse as much as the limited vantage point of the living room afforded.

This type of stylish but practical dwelling –two-or-three-level construction—young professionals frequently prefer in suburbia for being simpler to maintain than the larger detached houses while offering almost as much in space and comfort. Although people of pickier tastes might view modern townhouses as cheaper imitations of the grand city-villas of past ages, these trounce most apartments in many respects, providing all the modern amenities with added degrees of privacy and independence. Although throughout my childhood I have seen better and more elegant constructions of the type, I can still vividly recall the long nights spent in cavernous, hard-to-heat bedrooms during the cold winters of Romania. And when beside these modern comforts even the cheapest homes today are equipped with thermostat-controlled-air-conditioning and heating units, well insulated windows and walls, large flat-screen-TV sets, Hi-Fi receivers and video recorders, stylish sofa- and loveseat-ensembles, more or less tastefully placed in the middle of living rooms covered by wall-to-wall carpeting, then I shouldn't express any regrets for the buildings or furniture left behind in Romania, regardless how intricate or ancient.

A few years of hard work make such modern luxuries affordable to most immigrants in America, an accomplishment not to sneer at in spite of the trade-offs-- the monotonousness of living between wonderful objects, paid for by ceaseless toil, endless loans, tedious commuting, fast eating, short sleeping time, and little else in between.

Then I must ask is the American dream equal to the trouble it entails for its fulfillment? The answer is difficult to figure, and obviously paradoxical. Can a person be truly free when possessing the most wonderful luxuries of the world while not having the time to enjoy them that much? Then again, what's the meaning of such a stupid question? Aren't most folk choosing their aspirations freely, as they see fit?

However meaningless my musings, it did not distract from noticing the joy evident on Didonna's face before she vanished in the kitchen. Thus I let myself swept away by the optimistic '*Fata-Morgana*' of the American way of life, so concretely unfolding before my very eyes that minute. On the other hand, true to my nitpicking nature, I convinced myself soon against all common sense that, when a coin is flipped, the reverse could look less rosy than perceived at first, especially when seen under a merciless magnifying glass. The New World, although rightfully and undeniably defined as the land of limitless opportunities, it does not preclude the existence of some darker sides. America is capable of causing tremendous misery and suffering for a large number of people, pushed down in the gray precipice of despair, insignificance or alienation, as anywhere else in the world.

However pessimistically my thoughts revolved along such philosophically well-beaten paths, when my hostess reemerged with the steaming fragrant Turkish coffee, her happy face helped me in finding the few quite banal words to dissipate the gloom and doom so absurdly arisen in my mind.

"Congratulations, I like your house a lot. It's truly grand."

"Then let me show it to you while the coffee is getting cooled a bit," she caught on to the idea, and after spilling a few drops of dark liquid on the saucers, added in a true Romanian fashion: "Hey, it looks like we' ll have money coming our way. Ha, ha, ha." Indeed, according to an old Romanian superstition, inadvertently spilt coffee could bring a modicum of good luck for the spiller.

Properly cheered up, we left the coffee for later, and started up the stairs, toward the bedrooms on the second floor, the lady of the house leading the way. Willy-nilly, my lower vantage on the way up almost forced me to appreciate the woman's shapely naked calves, moving step by step in a sensuous dance before my eyes. Oh, how beautifully those muscles tensed and relaxed under the smooth curvaceous shapes so alluringly molded under her velvety skin! My senses tickled in response to the muffled sound of slippers on the carpet, and the barely audible rub of thighs under the rather short and tight skirt, all indelibly saved in my mind's hard disk.

Upstairs, the usual arrangement, two smaller and one larger room, the latter called the master bedroom, needless to mention the regular-size bathroom, and built-in closets everywhere, a typical, simple, practical and quite spacious American-style home, not very sturdy, but much envied elsewhere on the globe.

Naturally, nothing had found its proper place as yet except the larger pieces of furniture. Scattered rolled up carpets, boxes of all sizes in disarray all over awaited their destination amid provisory incertitude. But a definitely well tempered visible touch prefigured already a warm, welcoming, intimate environment, the kind only a woman can create.

On the undone queen-size bed the two pillows reminded of her alleged boyfriend a group of sharp-tongued friends spread the gossip about. The thought made my heart skip a beat in green jealousy, to enhance even more my desire to sneak under those sheets so invitingly open before my eyes. Then I caught myself guessing whether she liked to sleep on the right, or on the left side. Come on old boy are you crazy, or what? 'This lady is single and you are married, what the hell is wrong with you?'

But just by invading the sanctuary of the woman I so obviously lusted for struck a definite cord in my heart, a sort of foreboding, a subtle invitation to act bubbled up irresistibly from my libidinous subconscious. Perhaps I should have been better advised, and remembered how adept women could be at second-guessing men's minds, particularly of those perceived vulnerable to their charms. Unfortunately, the warning failed to sound the alarm in my mind. Just a little more perspicacity on my part could have significantly accelerated or, perhaps, forestalled the evolution of events right then. No such thing happened.

The scale in the bathroom, although a common household object, caught my attention as well, making me instantly realize the need of the divorced available woman to stay slim and desirable. Didn't my hostess fit the category?

I often pondered on the secrets of Eve, but right then I would have paid almost any price to peek under my new friend's skull, to find out what exactly made her tick, how did her mind work, whether I figured in her plans at all. That is not to say I didn't know what buttons to press for getting whatever I wanted from the opposite sex. Most men sooner or later learn the art of gaining female favors, although by figuring out only the mechanics they seldom penetrate to their underlying profound mysteries and motivations. Myself never even came close to penetrate that deep. For me the complexity of Eva's soul remained the same unresolved, eternal puzzle. Precisely for this reason, I will always thirst for this apparently unattainable wisdom, in spite of investing almost nothing meaningful to this end. As all ordinary men, I must live with the curse of nurturing the dream in the dark, instead of growing to understanding it in full light and, by way of my ignorance, face the possibility of destroying another person's life together with mine. All the same, discovering the secrets of my gender's opposite often motivated my drives, regardless of how superficially. This same accursed curiosity prompted my actions during that fateful first visit at Didonna's new home.

Once over the inspection upstairs, we descended in the basement that appeared as the ground floor, for the house was built on a slope. Scattered all over as upstairs nothing unpacked as yet, boxes and crates filled with stuff waiting their turn for placement. I caught myself pondering what and how would myself set to the task, as if in my own house. Was it possible for my thinking to have prefigured the impending future? I honestly don't know but on later recriminations I accepted it to have been just that. Had I weighed more carefully all contingencies, maybe I could still have altered our fate altogether—that of Philomela, Didonna and mine, for better or worse. But no such weighing ever occurred.

The back yard, visible through the large window as well as the open back door, extended far down the green grassy meadow bordered by a row of pine trees. The landscaping made the development quite well to resemble a golf course, or perhaps an elegant resort.

American architects and urban planners are quite adept at creating this uniform sort of clean, artificial, superficially enchanting environments made up of simple, repetitive, inexpensive components. These postmodern communities will hardly survive the many centuries as the Old World's charming towns, which still attract millions of tourists, including Americans, otherwise happier to live at home in the present rather than in the past. Europeans may look a bit disdainfully at these Yankee achievements. Who is to say, though, what's better, to build cheaply for the present, or expensively for *eternity,* either way based on the toil and sweat of ordinary people? I can't figure the answer nonetheless feel compelled to ask whether people in the United States are happier than the rest of the world? By living in artificially insulated environments, are Americans spared the dejection and misery of the darker sides of life? Could it be that the people of the New World perhaps discovered an effective shield against the countless blows of disappointment, desperation, and adversity brought on by historic upheavals? Baah! People in the States seem equally buried to the hilt in the quick sands of alienation and existential sorrows as anywhere else on the globe, perhaps even more so in spite of their loudly trumpeted opulence. The Bible must be right man is condemned to eternal toil and sorrow for having committed the original sin. Was it my place to have shared these musings with Didonna on that first visit of mine? I guess not, and fortunately didn't.

On the contrary, I felt quite happy to be back in the living room couch, as the sweet awareness of our knees touching interrupted my mental bickering. And the woman's sensually sparkling voice sounded so gleefully alive in my ears! But then, out of the blue, I had been hit by a jolt of scares, to feel guilty, lost, embarrassed and bashful, all at the same time. To escape off this quirky inner prison became urgently a matter of emotional survival, so I automatically reached for my saving cup of coffee.

"Congratulations are in order, dear lady. The house is wonderful. You surely deserve it. By the way, you brew a mean cup of coffee."

"Oh, thank you. My Armenian grandfather taught me the art of Turkish coffee making. He took refuge in Romania during World Ward I, you know, after the massacre."

The dialogue here came to an awkward halt, for some reason both engrossed in enjoying the hot, dark, fragrant tar-like liquid. I tried hard to find something smart to say, but failed miserably, afraid to hurt possible ethnic sensibilities. Then it dawned on me how lonely a man and a woman can be in their sordidly contemplated, illicit togetherness.

To fill the void of this hard lumpy silence, I cast a glance out through the window. Alex played outside with kids of the neighborhood, a scene as uninteresting as it can be. So my attention reverted back in the room and my gaze fell on Didonna's knees, temptingly showing under the skirt foreshortened by her sitting position. I'd have given just about anything then for a touch, even if for one measly heartbeat! But how could I? Those shapely female protrusions were as yet forbidden territory. Then, as I realized the depth of silence between us turned almost unbearably more awkward, the need to say something, even a tepid banality, became vital. But my mind went blank, as usually in tense situations. Yet I managed to mumble a sentence of sorts, promptly forgotten, lost forever in the vacuum of interrupted, faulty communication.

In spite of this, the tension in some mysterious way relaxed as simply as it arose, and we gradually eased into confessing about our past loves, divorces, children, parents and relatives, adventures, worries and illnesses, about the happier or less fortunate moments of our lives. We disrobed our souls as innocently as children can get naked, oblivious of gender, circumstance or convention. At one point, our particular reasons for defecting Communist Romania came to be confessed as well.

This was how I reconfirmed what I already knew-- why the woman I surreptitiously encircled now divorced her second husband Caius for he did not honor his premarital promise to leave Romania with her at the first opportunity.

"What a tough woman!" I thought fleetingly on learning her story in detail from the horse's mouth.

Naturally, I welcomed her surprising openness, the trust granting me a peak into her past, for learning about flings she had before or after her two divorces. By the same token, however much I appreciated the woman's frankness, what it conveyed displeased me as well. In a strangely irrational way, my pride felt hurt to have been chosen as the last man to learn details about her past intimate life. Why couldn't I have been number one on her list of lovers? Maybe we could have stayed together for good. Suddenly, all those *other* men I never saw or knew grew to mythical proportions, sparking in my heart the most ridiculous pangs of jealousy and jolts of pain. Even today shudders run down my spine, as I remember that night's confession, never to be wiped off my memory.

What prompted the habitually reserved Didonna to open the book of her life this way? Why to me, by then clearly shooting for more than a simple friendship? Could it be she attempted to cast a tiny spell over the entire situation? Or, as the super-sensitive female, she might have possessed instinctively deep enough insights about the male psyche, as to surpass the skills even of best psychiatrists, forget mine? Who can approach such suppositions with absolute certainty? Still my conviction is she played her role that fateful night consciously, or intuitively patterned on a well-conceived plan, most women being a lot more artful hunters than men may ever imagine. How much subtler can our sisters act when faced with the opposite sex!

We sat for a long long time past sunset in the darkened living room, lost in soft, sweet conversation, not unlike two lovebirds about to congress. It was Alex to cut the scene short. He burst in, gave a short greeting and then, without uttering one more word, disappeared promptly in his room upstairs. Regretfully, his appearance caused our come- back to reality, to the need of bringing my visit to an end. Outside I glanced at my watch. It was well past eleven, on the way to midnight.

*

"Did you say something?" came alive softly in the dark cabin my friend's voice.

"No, sleeping beauty, I said nothing. I only wish you keep me company on this monotonous, lonely and dense night on the road. It's easy for me too to fall asleep, and then--... you know what might happen. Why don't **you** take the wheel for a while?"

"Come on man, don't make me drive now. It's so good to watch you at it, and let my mind wonder off into dreaming."

"Then at least try to stay awake, and talk to me every now and again. Anyway, what's there to dream about on this godforsaken road?"

"Well, let's say I dream about us, about our home together, oh... about so many things..."

"Can't you be a little more specific?"

But she didn't oblige, instead engaged in meaningless small talk about the impenetrable night, the immensity of Texas, the humid warmth of summer along the Golf coast, the miraculous scarcity of traffic on the road, and so on and so forth, to almost make me even drowsier.

This suspended state lasted for a long time, to end only as we rolled on the beltway around San Antonio. The density of lights glistening in the distance on the right, the re-emergence of heavier traffic following our lonely run in pitch darkness, indicated the proximity of a large community. The decision to spend the night at the first affordable motel came to a unanimous instant agreement.

The opportunity once again materialized in the shape of a *Days Inn* hotel, advertised by a well-lit sign perched high on a pole, above the building sunk in the dark. Lucky this time, we stumbled on the entranceway without difficulty.

At the reception desk, a lonely, sleepy concierge greeted mechanically, a bored expression on his mug.

"No vacancies" he informed curtly.

What an unpleasant surprise. But at our insistence the man obliged, and inquired at some nearby motels, even if a bit grudgingly. A few dials later, he found indeed a room somewhere downtown, unfortunately an offer we declined on learning the astronomical price. Only one acceptable solution for our thin pockets remained, to take the way back to the road, and drive straight ahead for sixty or so miles till the nearest town. Few choices left for the tired poor hobos at midnight, besides returning on the dark desolate highway.

"So, are you brave enough to roll?

Jolted awake by this hard unexpected alternative, my deadly exhaustion so acutely felt just minutes earlier had to be peremptorily willed aside. Willy-nilly, piercing through the viscously dense monotonous Texas night turned out as the task at hand anew.

"Do we have another choice?"

However unsuccessful the interlude at the *Days Inn*, it had the effect of refreshing my strength and determination. Necessity being the mother of all solutions my loving companion resisted heroically not to fall asleep, careful to preempt all reasons for my complaints. About halfway into our renewed journey, San Antonio and its promise receded to oblivion, reduced to a fleeting, displeasing but insignificant memory.

On the road, the conversation revolved around recurrent trivial subjects lacking any precise contours. Finally my pretty face dared to ask on the meekest voice possible.

"Say, do you honestly want me to take the wheel?"

"Maybe some other time, but thanks for asking," I mumbled at last, following an awkward, ambiguous silence.

"You are welcome. I just wanted to find out how tired you really are. You know I wasn't about to oblige anyway. You figured this much, didn't you?"

"Oh yeah I sure did."

When planning the trip, we decided democratically on alternating turns at the wheel. But now, on hearing the slightly cheeky ironic nuances of my friend's quip I elected to overlook the entire deal. Evidently she wasn't about to honor her promise. Why bother to needlessly debate or dance around it?

As I kept chewing on these thoughts, a strange curtain of silence descended back in the cabin, replacing a number of possibly silly questions, as for instance, about the nature of limitless existential void that suffocates the lonely human soul on planet Earth. Considering the intractability of philosophical dilemmas, perhaps this muted interlude made for a welcome respite. I am not sure. But a while later, as my head turned to my companion, I saw her deeply asleep, head slumped on the chest, body crumpled as a marionette with a broken neck. An endless emotional torrent flooded my heart in pity for the human being's frailty, so acutely evident when unprotected by the shield of well affected attitudes most of us frequently adopt against an universe tailored much too big for our puny size.

A smidgen of a second later my mood changed abruptly, as I became almost equally spiteful, feeling betrayed, utterly abandoned to my own means exactly when the loving care of a supporting fellow wanderer through space I needed more than ever. But having little say about it, my attention turned back on the road, trying in vain to penetrate the dark, soft, mysteriously threatening void, rushing against my eyes from beyond the range of headlights. Then my thoughts fell asleep too.

I must have been driving in this state for an undefined length of time, a few seconds, possibly a couple of minutes, maybe more.

When my senses came at last back to life, I stole a peek to my right again. At seeing my friend's contorted position unchanged, the pity for her reemerged, causing me to adjust her seat as far back as I could reach, to make her rest a bit more comfortable. Following my intervention, she simply rolled her exhausted body to a side, pulled her knees up to chest, all without as much as a whimper.

For a short eternity I felt happy, not sure why. The only thing I remember was an immaterial sort of warmth flooding my body. The silence between us became unbearably heavy and dense, which the ever-pervasive motor's soft purr enhanced even more. Waves of ever-deeper stillness expanded in all directions, outwardly over the veiled landscape, over everything imaginable, beyond the unseen horizon, all coming against my very being at eighty miles an hour or more. Gradually unaware of things and thoughts, of my near lethal exhaustion, my earlier sleepiness turned into a state of generalized numbness. The only thing needed to survive was to never ever stop being in motion. Unawares, I pushed my foot on the gas *to the metal,* watching in mindless abandon as the speedometer's needle rose to the ninety-mile-mark. At this rate of speed falling asleep is almost impossible, and then, lo and behold, my loneliness melted away. The headlights of two trucks vanished quickly in my rear view mirror. 'Well, well', I argued in solitude, 'the police at this late hour must surely be asleep. Why should they risk limbs or life so far out of community?' The thought proved comforting, rendering speed as the only proper solution for deliverance. Then it happened. I became just a moving dot of light-- a minuscule comet rushing through the vast night engaged on a nameless orbit, beyond emotions, reasoning and attachments, the perfectly annihilating, inebriating Nirvana of velocity. All is motion!

*

A few days passed before I paid another visit to Didonna, although it became my habit already to calling her daily. My newfound gregariousness amazed even myself, by nature timid, reserved and suspicious.

Naturally, Philomela had no idea what was about to happen in her absence. As in previous years, she spent much of summer waiting tables in Rehoboth --the traditional weekend relaxation spot for Washingtonians. Better money could be made on the shore than in Washington. As a bonus, in her free time she could enjoy the pleasures of the sun, sand and sea.

I joined her on weekends. She was still my wife. That befriending another woman might spoil my marriage never crossed my mind, the possibility of divorce out of the question. Few people marry contemplating a subsequent separation. Such premeditation or perverse planning never permeated my thinking either. All the same, I began counting the last hours spent Sundays in Rehoboth, just to get home for the nightly conversations with Didonna, of paramount urgency as the weeks went by. My whimsical desire proved progressively stronger than thinking sanely. Aren't humans less rational than imagined? So was I effectively blinded by my just budding love? Or was it only lust?

Gradually, the frequency of my visits increased, to become a daily routine. Evidently, I set on the dangerous path of adultery, however unaware of it in the beginning. For seeing the dame any excuse sufficed, no matter how ridiculous. I went as low as to pleasing Alex, the handsome, friendly fair skinned kid, happy to be taken to motorcycle shows, or engaged in discussions about sport cars. Boys being what they are could easily succumb to such deviously presented temptations.

On the other side of the coin, a single female should be forgiven for accepting the male obviously seeking her favors while friendly to her son too. A mother would do anything to please her little progeny. Why then wonder that the Turkish cups of coffee tasted better and better by every day and week passed in the dame's sweet company?

One day out of the blue, she confessed how unfriendly Alex used to be vis-à-vis all the men attempting to befriend her in the past. This confession could have been a vague indicator, a little telltale sign that my courtship and advances were welcome, that our innocent little friendship might have veered already toward something deeper and more meaningful. Had I been just a bit more careful playing with fire, I could have --or should have-- put on the brakes right then and there. Instead, I preferred to deceive myself, by asking myself in all *purported honesty* what could be so wrong with seeing a friend, even if a pretty woman? It has been precisely this manner the process progressed along the proverbial slippery path, as we both ignored the true nature of our behavior, the unpleasant consequences, soon enough to emerge for every character to be involved in the impending adulterous affair.

The next step along this dangerous path occurred as clockwork one of these nocturnal visits. As always, shoulder-to-shoulder, thigh-to-thigh on the couch, while softly sharing sweet mementoes of our lives, we both got suspended somewhere outside the confines of time. Even as darkness gradually enveloped the room in pleasant semi obscurity, we didn't feel the need to turn on the lights. Our knees continued to touch ever so slightly, but enough for the steady warm stream of sensually charged electrons keep exchanging between our opposite sexual poles ever more furiously. Emboldened by the incredibly inciting warmth the veins injected directly into my heart, an irresistible desire to speak up overwhelmed my entire being. Didonna having already opened the book of her past, why not take my turn at the confessional?

Following the few banal adventures of my youth, I launched straight into the biggest, overly melodramatic love story of my life, stupidly recounted and repeated to all my girlfriends at possibly the most delicate point before bonding in spite of their always openly expressed displeasure. Probably all men cherish a well preserved love-story of this type, tucked away in their emotional closets about a unique and unbelievable *Myozotis Silvatica*, a *Vergissmeinnicht* that happened for me to be my first passion to Adriana, elevated to a standard all future females were to be judged against, to the chagrin of being compared to some unachievable, stupid romantic example another sister served them inadvertently and indirectly from the past. All women aspire to be the magic *number-one*-love in their chosen man's heart, utterly rejecting the second place position in favor of a previous matchless competitor. Could it be perhaps for nature quite impossible for to work otherwise? Who knows?

As if this gaffe of mine had not been bad enough, the need to belatedly self-correct after noticing the evident turn-off caused, I delved even deeper in the idiotically muddy explanations of how badly my bankrupt love affair affected my subsequent well being, handicapped my emotional life, and turned me into the wretched pitiful impotent weakling whenever attempting to connect sentimentally with a new woman.

Whether my justification satisfied or hurt my pretty hostess's vanity as well I can only guess. I remember only how she responded to my insipid excuses with an unusually shrill burst of laughter. In my narrow-mindedness I took this as a lighthearted assurance, believing my story didn't deviate too badly off the norm whereby women see men as birds of the same feathers, all enjoying to freely boast about a supposedly impressive romance, awkwardly dug out of failed adolescent masculine diaries as proof of their boundless capacity to love-- or something like that.

Her ensuing words and lightly patronizing demeanor didn't surprise, on the contrary, melted my timidity away. I can't even begin imagining how other men survive their first fatal love affair, the fact is that my abysmal failure with Adriana forever diminished the confidence in my manliness, to curse me into an inferiority complex, rendering me permanently insecure relative my prowess of satisfying a woman between the sheets. The perception, real or imagined, hunted my love life ever since. Not even my long lasting marriage succeeded in completely erasing this blemish off my psyche. In this ridiculous light, my prospective mistress' encouragement felt wonderfully soothing, in spite of its possible ambivalence.

By then the moon flooded the room with a strange otherworldly glare, dusting all objects with a phosphorescent layer of silvery gold. The same golden dust, evenly distributed on Didonna's pale countenance, made her radiate an irresistibly magnetic energy. Not a single furrow, not the tinniest line blemished her pale face, a mask suddenly frozen in time. Although her eyes lost their precise contours, the gaze shot out of two dark deep holes invited a plunge directly in her very mind, right into her immaterial being, luring irresistibly somewhere at unfathomable depths. I didn't jump in the gaping void only because I feared to unravel the magic, preferring to cover her lips with hot unrestrained kisses, perhaps a cowardly, but safer detour. Instead of checking the queen, in a roundabout way I killed a pawn.

Then my body slowly slid down on the carpet, until kneeling in front of the woman-- my eyes fixed into hers, arms wrapped around her smooth thighs, slowly creeping up toward the warm round bottom sunk in the couch. She put up no resistance, my moves welcome. Her gaze kept following my act slightly transfixed, her lips shaped to a small smile –of the motherly kind-- as her fingers, barely touching, began playing in my hair. Not a single word disturbed the dark tranquility of the room.

Frozen for a long time, each separately fought against our inner contradictory emotions. Our friendship took an abrupt turn onto the bumpy road of a life wrought with some of the most unpleasant complications, to be brought on by the gossip and condemnation of the community we willy-nilly belonged. One step forward, and we were to be exiled to a self-imposed isolation, to drinking the social rejection's bitter brew, administered to all members trespassing the conventional order of things. Yes, intuitively forewarned by the impending consequences of our actions, we hesitated for a tiny suspense, resisted heroically to accede to the terrible lure of mindlessly unleashed sensuality. But as the coin has two sides, we might have chosen only to prolong the enjoyment of the forbidden fruit, infinitely enhanced by withholding one extra heartbeat longer the sweetness and raw power of natural instincts about to erupt. That night we still drank cautiously off the cup of carnal pleasures, frequently more powerful than any psychedelic drug.

As before, it had been Alex who tore asunder our dream-like-textured interlude. He came rumbling down the stairs, heading directly for the fridge. Oh how harshly the glare of suddenly-switched-on-light tore the magic to bits! The moment of bliss slipped away with the speed of a runaway truck. All the emotional heat sweetly nestled in our souls dissipated at the same tick of time, the magic moment degraded to a trivial dialogue on the quantity of Coca Cola cans in the refrigerator. Nothing smarter remained than to leave the scene, and so I did precipitously. Our destiny about to unravel had to wait a few weeks longer.

*

Somewhere in the distance, out of the impenetrable darkness my tired eyes registered some glimmer of lights-- at long last the phantom-like monotony of white bands' dance on the road ahead promised to end with a well deserved, much expected clean comfortable bed. My hopes fired up. But as distances at night may be easily misjudged, the point of deliverance seemed for a long time as remote as ever. And then I almost missed the unlit sign of the motel so desperately needed. Considering the depth of my exhaustion, the error could have been disastrous anytime, tenfold so after midnight. Fortunately, the sign illuminated in the last second was long enough for my slamming the brakes, and cause the tires screech on the dry pavement. The noise snatched my companion out of her slumber.

"Have we arrived?" she asked abruptly, as if to prove she's been awake all the time.

"Let's hope so" I replied curtly, and then struggled out of the car, my tired body badly in need of a stretch. Without wasting precious time, we walked straight to the reception window. Surprise! Only a little hand-written note stuck on the glass inside.

"No vacancy. Please don't disturb."

Beautiful! The news hit as a ton of bricks. What to do next, how to answer the demoralizing sixty-four-thousand-dollar-question that neither of us dared to voice yet? Utterly helpless, we kept starring dumbfounded for a pretty long time at the accursed, tightly shut window. Then it dawned there wasn't any easy way out of the situation, an awareness that gradually over flooded my mind as deadly as poison.

The only viable solution seemed spending the night in the car. Driving on would have been near suicidal, an open invitation to an accident.

Once again in the car's safety, willy-nilly resigned to fate, having nothing smarter to do we scanned the surroundings. At some distance, a large well-lit gas station combined with a small convenience shop – and -hopefully a sandwich counter-- caught our attention. As we approached, the motel, gas station and the store appeared as part and parcel of a truck stop, to attract with magnetic force. Endless lines of massive eighteen-wheelers parked neatly around the perimeter unmistakably confirmed my initial guess.

The parking lot spread over a large area. It took another thirty seconds to find Bucephalos a spot, this time in front of the eatery adjacent to the convenience store. Inside, the few customers, probably truckers, sat on tall stools neatly aligned before the long counter. At one of the four tables a young couple kept talking incessantly, apparently oblivious to anything around them. Both man and woman wore jeans, had long hair, making them almost undistinguishable. We chose the table next to them for we couldn't imagine joining the truckers. Why the precaution? Possibly out of preconceived beliefs, borrowed from motion pictures that often depict truck drivers as mostly rough characters.

The rather buxom waitress, a well padded female in other respects too, dutifully noticed our presence, stopped wisecracking with men at the bar, and swung over to take our order. She behaved matter-of-factly, just minimally polite, showing a well-affected deference, as we obviously didn't fit the mold of her usual clientele.

After promptly serving us two humongous portions of ice cream, and cups of steaming hot coffee, she accepted the tip with a robotic smile, and then quickly returned to her preferred company. We didn't mind her attitude at all, opting wholeheartedly to being left alone.

A few spoonful of ice cream followed by coffee sips worked miraculously to better our outlook. We renewed with hope. On the large map displayed on the wall, a string of communities not far of each other along the highway caught our attention. It seemed feasible reaching the first in less than an hour, and find at last the much desired and well-deserved bed around two o'clock past midnight, we guessed. Good enough! Our earlier gloom dissipated not unlike the smoke of cigarettes in the clear, icy cold air.

Five minutes later, back in the darkness of Texan night, I stepped hard on the gas pedal to force Bucephalos swallow hungrier and hungrier the interrupted white ribbon segments on the highway, running backward among barely visible hills. Reaching the new destination became a life-or-death imperative. Didonna turned on the radio. Nothing came off the ether at that late hour, only static and various electronic disturbances. Civilization, either too far away, or deeply lost in sleep, seemed beyond reach.

"Hey sweetie, why don't you put on a cassette?"

"What would you like?"

"Mozart would be just fine."

Whenever uncertain, lost in space or time, Mozart's harmonies never failed to mold on to my senses as a soothing balm. They still do.

"Goodbye, darling, wake me at the destination," I heard my friend quip right after the machine swallowed the disk. Turning my head to thank her changed my mind, as I saw she lowered the seat back for the unmistakable intention of switching her lights off. It became obvious I was to be left to my own devices, surrounded by the seraphic accords of the well-known *Requiem*, abandoned to the insane run through the immensity of the endless primordial space, mercilessly tucked between myself and the galaxies above. Soon, I felt reduced in size to an insignificantly luminous dot, wandering aimlessly along the Milky Way. 'Is anybody out there to watch over me?' --I wondered.

*

Following the almost fateful evening spent with my new female pursuit in her own living room, this time I gave myself to pondering, as seldom done it in my life before deciding on important matters. But, as most often at such important crossroads, I left tying my fate to a new mate to the whims of chance. True to my character, I hesitated and procrastinated 'Should I jump, or should I refrain?' This question I repeated, and repeated in foolish vainness.

In the end, though, the adventure loomed before me as the personification of temptation itself, promising somehow a great duty-bound fulfillment. I felt entitled to expect at least as much from a prospectively fantastic love affair, equivalent in my mind to nothing less than the *self-evident pursuit of happiness*. The alternative, had I chosen to remain conventionally correct –I argued-- would have been nothing short of dying forlorn, as the abject coward thorn asunder by an unfulfilled destiny, a jailbird punished to eternally insurmountable regrets in a self-imposed cell of petty fears masquerading as decency. Had I acted then based on conventional wisdom, couldn't the adventure end up in unmitigated disaster all the same? Obsessively preoccupied by such gnawing thoughts revolving around thorny choices, for the next couple of weeks I resolved to forget dame Didonna altogether, not to call her at all. She didn't ring me either. At middle age, the smallest sin committed in thoughtless adventurism —I surmised perhaps in flashes of rare wisdom-- might easily render the lives of all implicated parties to irreparable failures.

But, in spite of the unfavorable prospects, I ended up plunging in the adulterous affair with a determination fit only to a sacred mission, totally ignoring the twenty or so years of my marriage. I juxtaposed the new affair against my worn-out, lukewarm union, however comfortable at the level of practicality turned into habit, while arguing in the back of my mind less and less on the side of prudence. Common sense might have advised caution for a man at the crossroads of the proverbial middle age, usually filled to the brim with insecurities. Incredibly though, it was precisely this stark miserable reality that motivated my act, to dare trying my luck one last time, before running out of my virility's steam for good. For once in life, I erred on the side of reckless optimism.

*

The ensuing Saturdays and Sundays I spent with Philomela, in Rehoboth. During this time I resolved to secretly test all aspects of our life together, to analyze what made it good or bad, worthy or unworthy, to be or not be continued under the old, exhausted formula. What I found was a wishy-washy two-decade-old conjugal union the acid of boredom had corroded at its foundation, poking rusty holes in it as November rain does to an old vehicle's body. All the same, our marriage felt rather comfortable, as it provided the illusion of security, so painfully necessary for middle-aged couples, even more so for dislocated immigrant families. Loneliness can have many underlying reasons, and be even more depressing for transplanted individuals than for the natives. On the other hand, as most mortals the two of us lived resigned to a fate turned by self-delusional behavior into second nature, at first barely noticed as significant change, but eventually destined to become an almost invisible sort of hypocrisy. It would have been hard to recall all our disappointments precisely-- the denied ideals, or past expectations deeply woven in the complex mesh of long years lived together within the mutual give and take of causation. As most ordinary folk, we turned a blind eye to the slowly vanishing pair of young beings fallen in love twenty years earlier. And thus, lo and behold, we arrived at the deadliest crossroad Philomela did not seem yet aware of. Unfortunately, it befell me to shatter her complacency.

On that last Sunday at the seashore, I took my farewell with a heavy heart. Unlike her, by then I was fully resolved to take the fateful step, to administer the *coup de grace*, to commit the seriously sinful act of betrayal, the never-before contemplated **adultery**

Although during our marriage I had a few petty fleeting love affairs, all in all seldom more than one-night stands, little escapades with no perceptible consequence whatsoever. But now the outlook loomed significantly different. My impending entanglement with a new woman looked much more like a serious upheaval. The ensuing adulterous affair belonged to a category altogether distinct, akin to an earth-shattering tremor. I felt this in my bones. Oh how easy it had been to peremptorily reject Adriana, my first serious flame in college I forsworn never to forget. How simply I rejected her attempt at rekindling our love a few years later, to laugh off her request to dump Philomela, and marry her instead. Good God, for that dame I was ready to die! But her time had passed. Just as well could not Philomela's time come to end the same way? Any love story must conclude at some point, I reasoned. Or was it that the bells ringing in my ears about Didonna sounded sweeter and more crystalline in middle age than the same in my youth about Adriana?

Who can find a way out of such conundrums honestly, particularly under the gun of an impending decision? All the same, I meticulously and methodically tried weighing the possibilities. What if my dangerous play will end up hurting all the characters implicated? Who will suffer more eventually, Philomela, Didonna, or myself? I asked lamely more than once. Unable to come up with a minimally satisfying answer I hesitated, as the time of reckoning approached ever so fast.

In reality, the dice had been cast already, subconsciously the decision practically taken, determined by the actions to come, not by empty ruminations. By sacrificing my remaining life on the altar of a spent marriage filled by ceaselessly annoying chicanery, I could have still exposed myself to later recriminations, to eternal self-damnation for my cowardliness. Why resign to a marriage soaked in the murky waters of habit? Why persist complacently in a union corroded in the accumulated acrid poison of repressed regrets? Why not accept a fresh love in my life, and sacrifice a marriage no longer working?

Why not shoot for the eventual redemption, and implicitly render all participants possibly happier, or at least more content than before?

So there it loomed before me the big chance of hitting the jackpot at last. Why not act as the winner, for a change? Even if only I alone were to win, wouldn't be better than for all of us to end up as perpetual losers? What's better, to leave behind a wounded solder to die, or allow the few still on the battlefield push on for victory? Conveniently, or perhaps expediently, I didn't ask whether my choices could be somehow morally reprehensible. Just vaguely aware of ethics, I acted compelled by the commandments of nature, ignoring those of men, or Deity.

Off this vantage the unfolding coming events did not appear all that sinister. The atavistic remnants of natural instincts can be overly strong in the so-called modern, civilized man, particularly when embroiled in fast action, whereby nothing counts beside fulfillment of desires. Everyone must be a winner! In a way it felt nearly magnanimous, to be the person to bestow on all implicated in the affair another chance at renewal.

The right of the first occupier –to which Philomela must have subscribed by definition-- I summarily dismissed as obsolete, to curtly and justifiably replace it by the rule of might, enforced by the daring conqueror. Also by fancying myself capable to mercilessly inflicting the painful rupture, I felt wonderfully rejuvenated, the *tough fool* falsely reclaiming the power of his youthful thoughtlessness. At that point, I deemed everything admissible, double-crossing the dictates of tedious morality a duty-bound imperative, in spite of the probable hardship, against all odds and constraints of solid, concrete reality. Nature rewards the brave --I foolishly encouraged myself-- so dear Dorel, go ahead. The future is yours to have. Reach for it. Nature will reward your bravery.

But, frankly speaking, the decision to throw myself stock and barrel in a new woman's embrace happened rather under the impulse of irresistible carnal desire, more so than as the result of clear-cut philosophical deliberations. The latter came only as a meek simplistic amendment to compensate for it, to appease my ever-weaker doubts. However primitive this reasoning, I failed absolutely to weigh in the consequences of an adventure projected beyond the social constraints of marriage. Of this I became only much later aware, but blissfully ignored at the time.

*

Exactly as then, rummaging through my mind I thought about the two of us as we were running deeper and deeper into the night, desperately hoping to find a lodging somewhere in Texas. Under the same sort of starry sky was I speeding, the same way as in the past on a deserted road between Rehoboth and Washington, while weighing the fateful decision whether to plunge or not in the adulterous adventure. As in Delaware, perhaps I ought to have had the advantage of daylight for taking a serious decision, rather than risk the deceptive influence of eerie phantoms, the same night-devils playing tricks on my imagination in the uncanny glare of an evil full moon in Texas. However good the advice seems in hindsight, during those fateful hours I couldn't escape my thoughts, equally madly, obsessively pressing for a desired delivery once more. Is it disgustingly shocking how cavalierly I disregarded all the risks on my way to home years earlier, or the equally undesirable secondary effects all characters involved in the melodrama were to suffer in case of an accident so easy to occur during our run on a dark road toward a badly needed restful night in the middle of nowhere. History has an uncanny way of replicating, particularly so in the light of ever-recurring weaknesses.

*

Later on, emotionally drenched in my bed in Damascus, similarly jumbled notions churned viciously through my mind, to rob the few hours of sleep before daylight penetrated through the blinds, and forced me to my feet for good, in spite of the acute need to compensate for the exhausting drive home completed only a few hours earlier. Lucky me, during summer months, on Mondays work in the office was light. Even so, eight hours behind the desk on that day seemed years long. But, as workdays eventually come to a chronologically predictable end, I was able to knock at foxy Didonna's door unannounced, around six o'clock in the evening, the required bouquet of flowers in hand.

It thought advisable to proceed in this obviously unconventional, perhaps brash manner simply to avoid possible delays. Had her reception been cold, unwelcoming, I could have taken it as a bad omen, and leave after a short courtesy stay. Fortunately, my unexpected show-up didn't seem to disturb the lady at all. On the contrary, I had the distinct impression my arrival had been expected.

Framed by obscurity behind the open door, her face radiated with warm joy. Properly encouraged, I dared reflex-like to plant two little innocent kisses on her cheeks. She eagerly reciprocated. Yet I couldn't guess without being presumptuous about her honest attitude either way, whether she had been naturally friendly, or conveying her own subtle advances. Women's intentions men seldom fathom correctly. What mattered, though, that I had been welcomed nicely, not in the least admonished. Her frank willingness to see me I immediately accepted as a token of intimate familiarity. It was precisely her openness that evening to have irreversibly tipped the balance in her favor.

What precisely came to unfold thereafter I am sure she couldn't have guessed much about, even if projected on the screen of the proverbially powerful female intuition. In retrospect, she too might have admittedly tried the water temperature subconsciously with one of her pretty little metaphoric pinkies, as much as I did. Hypothetically everything is possible. Then again, suspecting such conniving premeditation could be unrealistic on my part, since the whole scheme lacked any telltale precision from the outset. Didonna never ever confessed to having nurtured anytime such untowardly twisted thoughts. On the other hand, whenever two people are about to click emotionally, testing the waters seldom comes from one side only. Common sense clearly demonstrates this point. Shakespeare had been certainly right in saying that love and hate are mutual by definition. It is quite difficult to imagine otherwise. So, whether our minds worked in tandem that evening, or the she-devil on her part was looking only for a naughty, but amicable affair, I couldn't have fathomed in the beginning, regardless of how the relationship eventually evolved. As I said women's motivations prove often quite impenetrable for men.

Minutes later, we were sitting on the couch, sipping carefully, and with obvious pleasure off the hot frothy Turkish coffee the woman knew so well to prepare. As the conversation lagged an awkward silence flooded the room. Not knowing how to break the ice, my gaze fixed on the large curtain-less window, on the pretense of contemplating the outside world. The crimson light of sunset flowed generously in causing things to come alive in the shadows, objects to glow with uniquely strange eerie halos as if nature herself prepared the stage for the hour of destiny to strike.

It befell on Didonna to break the silence, informing neutrally that Alex went out with his newly found friends to play in the neighborhood. My, how much I welcomed this bit of news, although Alex's presence or absence in the overall picture should have raised some questions in my mind before acting on a future union with his mother. It is commonly accepted how jealous a boy can be whenever a strange man comes between him and sweet mommy.

"You know I find it funny how much my Alex likes you. This is unusual as the jealous little boy openly rejected any man I cared to befriend" she said smiling widely even before I concluded my own thoughts on the subject. Wow, what a synchronicity of thinking!

Whether she meant this admission as an encouragement, or a roundabout way of signaling my welcome in her favors, subconsciously or on purpose, I couldn't be sure. But then again, why did she interject the comment? She went on.

"Not long ago when about to strike a friendship with a man I found attractive, had to quit seeing him because of Alex's openly manifested hostility. It's really surprising for me to see him now like you so much."

"Who knows, maybe he…" I began but, on second thought, left my answer tactfully unfinished. Despite this precaution, deep within my soul I loved the woman's comment, however presumptuous her reasons.

As the sun sank behind the horizon and took away its last warm orange rays, everything inside turned bluish-violet at the same time the first sparks of fluorescent bulbs came alive outside. Combined with the sky's phosphorescence this luminous new color transformed the room into an eerily strange abode, and us to silent shadows cast under the spell of *Eros the Arrow-Thrower.*

This is it I thought, as the fateful hour struck midnight in my heart, to change one day to the next, one life to another. Soon thereafter I surreptitiously squeezed my left arm behind the woman's back, reached her opposite shoulder, to draw her torso slowly closer. She yielded without a trace of resistance. As she let her head slowly fall on the couch- back, I saw her visage beaming in otherworldly pallor, an unforgettable mask bathed in the room's iridescent light, the gold of her hair transubstantiated to pure metallic molten silver, the entire picture reminiscent of a fragile seventeen-century French porcelain miniature. 'Oh,' I exclaimed in loud silence, 'what an unforgettable likeness, Madam de Pompadour and Ninon de Lánclos combined!' Her eyes changed too, no longer blue but pitch black in their orbits, whence they radiated intensely the too long repressed, highly charged waves of telluric desire.

I wholeheartedly accepted the invitation body, soul and spirit, and crashed thoughtlessly in the bottomless pit of mutual dissolution, irresistibly abandoned to the nirvana of exploding emotions, whereby everything happens simply, outside of time or doubts.

How long this first kiss of ours lasted I Can't say, perhaps minutes, or even hours. It was Alex – always the little man-- to put an end to our necking, when he broke in the room, accompanied by a friend I vividly remember as a blond vivacious little guy. Engrossed in their own business –forever more important to kids than all else-- they didn't even take note of our presence as they dashed through the living room directly into the kitchen. Our erotic connection brutally shattered, a slightly disheveled Didonna turned on the light, and I stole a glance at my watch.

"Thirty minutes past midnight" I blurted, to which she reacted hastily, all of a sudden the concerned mother promptly replacing the passionate lover she'd been seconds earlier.

"Hey Alex," she yelled, "let me see your mug."

The boy and his friend came in view calmly, obviously not rushing, open cans of Coca Cola in hands.

"Where have you been? It's past midnight. And what's Willy doing here at this late hour? Do his parents know about his whereabouts?"

"Hi mom, I didn't even notice you." And before the stern mother could answer, he continued; "Can Willy spend the night?"

Surprised by the preemptive frontal attack, perhaps still under the spell of the last kiss dissipated in the air, she agreed, although not without a few meaningless, insignificant, powerless counter-arguments or questions mothers are known for posing to their protectively beloved boy-progenies.

"Willy, do your parents know about this?"

"Sure ma'am, I got their permission."

"Okay Alex, Willy may stay, but only on the condition you both go straight to bed. Is this clear?"

"Yes mom."

Although Alex's prompt acquiescence sounded convincing enough, it contained a bit of implied approximation too, relative to an indeterminate time in the future.

As for us cutting the night short became imperative, the spell of sensuality broken. Yet things have changed all the same, the farewell kissing became mandatory, although for the time being gently, furtively, and decently. Then my fair hostess had to ask before shutting the door behind me.

"What are you doing tomorrow? Come and see me. I wish to consult you about some issued with my automobile. Don't worry, you'll receive your cup of coffee, perhaps a little bonus on top too," then she winked.

Women are proverbially adept at finding the right words and tone for as yet unclear situations. The invitation, though straightforward enough, wasn't necessarily tied to opening further new avenues between us. But a feasible alternative had been skillfully presented, just in case. Evolution had probably compensated for women's natural physical vulnerability with skills of diplomacy, weapons they learned to brandish well during past eons in almost any encounter, at any occasion or situation, simultaneously with verbal sophistication and tactical simplicity. This aptitude makes frequently affordable even for the weakest among them to emerge successfully off the worst scenarios.

On the way home, I drove moronically intoxicated, recklessly dancing the car across the lanes. Fortunately, at that late hour police quit patrolling the deserted streets. Decent folk dutifully in bed rested their tired bodies in preparation for the next day's hard hustle. Only a few lonely lunatics wondered aimlessly in the night, some inebriated, a few others of my ilk feverish with the chills of love. God must have been definitely double time on my side for getting me home in one piece, and in my bed without incidents. However, once safely tucked under the sheets, sleep avoided me, no matter how hard I tried. Staring wide-eyed at the dark ceiling, my imagination spilled over, projecting all possible scenarios tied to our unexpectedly complicated future. Sadly, in the morning I had to be at my desk, reading and translating boring texts on some futuristic patents no sane person should be concerned with. As so many less than enterprising persons I condemned myself to work for a living.

*

As the first twinkling of lights appeared in the distance at last, followed shortly by the green, familiar, luminous boards announcing *Junction* --the meeting point of the continent's halves--I reached nearly the end of my physical strength. Fortunately, we arrived at our much-desired objective possibly just a little before my total breakdown.

I pulled overjoyed in the parking lot of a motel simply named '*6*' which, I guess suggests in typically American fashion 24-hours-span of availability, that is from *six in the morning to six of the next day's dawn*. Nobody behind the reception window here either, except the sign *vacancy* clearly visible. Good enough I thought, and rang the bell.

Seconds later, another encouraging sign as the light switched on, and soon the receptionist's sleepy mug showed up in the frame, too.

"A room for the night, yes?" he asked, without waiting for us to speak. Then, taking a quick note of our eager approval, he pushed through the required form to be filled. All happened fast, machine-like charging of my VISA card, receiving the keys, as well as the concise directions to the room's location. Upon finishing, the receptionist retreated, promptly turned off the light and left us to our own means, two grateful souls saved from spending the night under the open sky.

It didn't take a lot to find the room, a rather smallish cubicle, yet equipped with all the essentials-- a clean freshly made bed, a shower stall, a sink and, naturally, the white porcelain crapper. Who needs more than that? – Once again the example of the famous American sense of sheer practicality proved its validity.

Soon the luggage dragged in, and we felt in seventh heaven, however physically spent or drenched in yucky sweat. Yes, yes, our tired bodies could finally go straight to bed. Forget washing, even the customary bottle of beer. But dead I was not, still able to notice for a fleeting heartbeat the whiteness of my concubine's naked body, as it flashed before my eyes before disappearing under the sheets. O well, exhaustion didn't kill my maleness. Who turned the light off I don't remember. An all-pervasive numbness infused our spent limbs instantly, sleep rolled over the tired flesh heavy as a steamroller. The world ceased to exist.

TEXAS, ANOTHER DAY

Everything in The Lone-Star state overwhelms, even the change of night to day.

The morning sun shot sharply through the cracks between the draperies, forcing darkness retreat to the most hidden corners of our small, whitewashed motel room. My sweetheart didn't wake yet. She slept on a side facing the window. Her bare shoulder peeked through golden strands of hair lit up under the fiery assault of the invading early rays, her ear glowed intensely pinkish-red, adding one more note to the angel-like appearance of a sexless being woven of light, an eerie hologram hovering above the bed. Thunderstruck, I keep looking and looking, frozen to the spot as not to scare off the celestial vision. Eventually, no longer able to resist temptation, I planted a delicate kiss on the same fiery glowing ear, and whispered softly.

"Dolly, dolly, it's eleven before noon, you have to get up."

Her answer came whimpering sweet.

"Just a bit longer, let me sleep one tiny minute more, please sweetie. But then she faced me-- her flesh ignited in desire tore asunder the earlier angelic image.

"Come, lover boy," she murmured softly, lips open moist, and I obeyed, abandoned soft in her embrace. But then, recalling last night's drenching exhaustion, and the long journey still ahead, I gently but firmly disentangled off her arms. It was a hard fight against my lust welled up, in spite of my feigning to act as detached as I could. For some murky reason that morning I prevailed, my Germanic side gained the upper hand.

"*Schatz, bei Unz muss Ordnung und Disziplin sein,*" I whispered clearly but lovingly in that deliciously pink ear, using a lingo surely not comprehended.

Aware at the same instant of my somewhat weird behavior, I went on gingerly hotter, as to diminish the offence I might have just committed against my partner's spontaneous gift of love. Yet my effort proved a total waste of time, my worries groundless. Didonna, more mature than I credited her for, was a woman secure in her charms. Her demeanor showed simple and straightforward. Whatever she wanted she took. Only my suspicious mind could resort to such uninspired tricks as the above. Generally I lacked the will to oppose any of her whims forcefully, or charmingly enough, and usually did everything only to stay in her graces. This sorry thought kept nagging a bit, but then, true to my character I forgot the whole deal by the next heartbeat.

Following a simplest breakfast –coffee and buttered bread--, we gathered our things and eagerly hit the road. The weatherman promised another splendid sunny day, as our friendship touched nearly levels of perfection. Nothing alien in the other's personality or behavior. Oh what a wonderful sensation! What a pity for such moments to occur so rarely in a couple's life, and how sad to be aware of these only in the past tense! Wouldn't it be nicer for happiness to redouble at the very realization of its occurrence? What's the use of remembering things lost dead in the past?

How often in midst of the happiest moments couples appear asleep? It has been our story as well on that fantastically bright morning, as we set on the highway daydreaming, utterly unable to recall details of the most immediate past, no matter how hard we tried. The only thing we retained has been a strange banality named Junction, a small community somewhere along the line dividing the American continent. What a pity, perhaps a loss, to never ever find out what the town looked like.

The scenery gradually turned arider and slightly hillier. Randomly dispersed bundles of dry thistle shriveled up under the relentless sun covered the soil as far as the eye could see. A few villages came and went, showing here and there a shack or two surrounded by the seemingly unending yellow-cake-desert only sparsely covered by vegetation. An hour later of running through this wasteland, at an apparently significant crossing, we decided to veer off the main highway, in order to find a grocery store.

Lady Luck acted on our behalf again. Soon, we rolled into a small shopping center, a super-market smack in the middle. Just in time. Badly in need of ice, cold cuts, cheese, bread, tomatoes, fruit, and cold beverages --the absolute prerequisites for bohemian Romanians—we rejoiced.

"Hey Dody, isn't it incredible how much liquid we guzzled down these days, without the need to relieve accordingly?"

"Don't you ever call me Dody, as this reminds me of my former mother-in-law, so please...As far as your question goes liquids must leave our bodies through perspiration, I guess. Didn't you say this before?"

"Probably", I swallowed the put-down, as well as the explanation myself already offered once in the past, which for some annoying reasons slipped my mind.

Fortunately, my pretty companion, seldom given to wasting time by reminding about such petty, prickly trifles, glanced at me sideways, a tiny sparkle in her eyes-- "So let's pour some Coca-Cola down our pipes right now, and forget all the rest."

I gracefully agreed. Two cans of ice-cold, world-famous, brownish liquid, purchased at the vending machines by the entrance, got polished off on the spot.

"O-my-God I exclaimed, this uniquely flavored fluid can be quite a blessing, contrary to its allegedly unhealthy sweetness!"

"At last, you make some sense."

In a hidden corner, several tables and chairs for customers ready to enjoy a quick snack right in the pleasantly air-conditioned business ambiance. Fantastic!

Before we knew it, once finished with our sandwiches and the shopping, it was three o'clock in the afternoon. Time to hit the road, sadly without finding out the name of the town left behind. Too bad! The one person I asked had been either ignorant, or didn't understand my question. He kept smiling at me a bit confused, probably in disbelief even of my existence. So the name of that little community unmarked on the map, as a few others before, had to stick for some reason only anonymously in our minds. Many insignificant things or places, even when pleasant, could pass by without note.

Two-three hours of uninterrupted racing later on the highway, and not arriving anywhere, the vastness of Texas suddenly struck full force. If in the morning the landscape appeared arid, in the afternoon it turned unmistakably desert-like. Cactus bunches replaced thistle bundles as far as the eye could see. These thorny plants knew how to grow in the weirdest shapes and sizes on the dry hillsides, as well as on the parched earth along the highway shoulders. Resilient and strange, smaller and larger vegetal agglomerations awaited patiently under the merciless sun for the welcome gift of a little rain.

"The desert I find quite ugly and unfriendly."

"I don't care much for it either. Go ahead push on the pedal, I won't complain."

It didn't happen often for my even-keeled mistress to nudge me to speeding, so I accepted the suggestion with buoyant pleasure. Bucephalos didn't seem to mind either, responding instantly to my foot's pressure. What an thrill to cut a swath at ninety miles an hour through the overheated air-mass, hovering under the desolate sky and land squeezed under a whitish hazy dome of diffused sun light.

"I wonder why anybody wants to live here."

"Well, you'll be surprised", I began to improvise. "Quite a lot of people live in the desert, and love it too. Look at the traffic on the highway."

"Yeah, mostly Mexicans."

"Oh no, no at all dear, not only Mexicans."

Our conversation hit a snag. Sunk in self-contained meditation until at about five in the afternoon we darted through the overheated space barely feeling alive. Then hunger knocked again, we stopped daydreaming, agreed to look for a place to dine, cool off, and recover some of our strength wasted during this trip through hell. The first opportunity showed up soon at a gas station, a little convenience shop and a modest eatery attached to it. I pulled in abruptly, without asking my companion's opinion. But she didn't complain.

Inside the usual fare, hamburgers, greasy fries, sodas, and *halleluiah*, air-condition! The last thing alone made all else acceptable. Then I noticed my friend's completely disheveled look, a dusty pale-purple layer of grime on her thin-skinned complexion. I don't remember to have ever seen her so beat-down, even as she mustered enough strength to cast her sky blue glance spiked by a bit of reproach directly in my face.

"Promise me your next automobile will have air-conditioning."

"Maybe it will, maybe it will" I began smartly but stopped short, as she poked me in the ribs, and shot new piercing arrows straight between my eyes.

"Not maybe, evil thorp. For sure you will. This is my promise to you."

"Okay, okay," and burst into laughter," but let's face it we couldn't have experienced even half the desert's full force from the comfort of air conditioning."

"Sure smart–Alec, but what about my face? Look at me! Do you really like the raggedy old woman you see?"

'What? You look ravishing,' I was about to retort promptly and properly, but lucky me, a pretty little teenager waitress prevented it inadvertently, as she came to greet and take our order.

"Two cheeseburgers, and Cokes, please." The waitress left, and I said.

"By night-fall we could be in El Paso."

"You better be right, if you want to escape this day alive."

This warning sounded, and my companion got up, and went to the lady's room, as they say, to powder her nose. At her return she looked ninety-nine percent better, almost on par with her naturally charming self. Well, the woman was actually just within the first half of her middle age. The realization made me proud as of my own achievement.

Back on the road, all reserves replenished, spirits refreshed and bodies cooled, the hellish desert-heat had to be bravely faced again. However, my prediction on arriving in El Paso didn't turn out as expected.

To make crossing this wasteland even worse, several miles later, all of a sudden, the car pulled dangerously to the right. Bucephalos suffered a flat tire, a large nail pierced deep through the right rear tire's flesh. Stupidly enough, I tried to pull it out, but then, hearing the ominous hiss, I knew right away it was better to push the nail back in, at least for the time being. Willy-nilly out came the hand pump. Heat or no heat, the flattened tire had to be pumped up to the max in the hope of reaching the next gas station on it. Naturally, the spare might have been the easier alternative, but the skimpy little wheel couldn't work much longer than my solution, while driving on the old tire at full speed I reckoned safer than worrying about a blow out.

Such trifles seldom bothered my pretty friend. A short sigh later, feigning to be helpful she sunk into studying the map, as if nothing unpleasant happened. Should I have construed her behavior as a sign of repressed worries? Maybe. For the occasional psychoanalyst, but even for the professional, phlegmatic behavior is difficult to judge. And my mistress seemed roughly fitting the category, the cool diva personality I admired, although deep in my guts I wished for a little more than a perfunctory interest shown in the matter at hand. In similar situations Philomela behaved infinitely more dramatically, if not outright histrionically at that, often jangling my nerves as well. So what's wrong with me? --I could have asked, but didn't. Not then, not ever, although always eager to vent my frustrations unrestrained. I searched for my friend's eyes, but in her innocently returned gaze nothing provocative. Her calmly disarming tone of voice said it clearly.

"Come on man, don't fret. This is America. I am sure we'll come soon to a shop able fix the damned thing. Wasn't this supposed to be an adventure? Remember? Okay, there you have my opinion if you care to appreciate it!"

Initially, out of her stern look I couldn't fathom immediately the true intent of these words. It took another heartbeat for my noticing the slight girlish hint of apprehension, expressed by her rapidly blinking eyes. This type of obviously theatrical pretending seemed reassuring enough for turning my mood a nanometer happier.

"Don't you worry dear lady, everything will be just fine. I promise."

This way I landed back in the saddle. No matter how old we grow and how repressed our feelings, men and women alike remain essentially forever bound to their basic characters, in my case to showing off a boastful boyishness in spite of having a rabbit's heart. But doesn't it feel good to be the muscular teenage boy again, ready to defend his little girlfriend? How enduringly these boys and girls stay hidden in our hearts, never to grow old, with possible exception of the moronic, or the mentally deranged.

Luckily, the mechanics garage materialized sooner than expected, just across the highway a few miles later. By then I made up my mind to buy two new tires, just to be on the safe side. An expensive alternative, but then again what are credit cards for? *Buy now and pay later*, as the good old American saying goes.

The shop's manager --the only Caucasian amongst the Latino blood surrounding him-- received cordially ready to serve. After having listened carefully to our problem, before answering he scratched his head under his dirty baseball cap. His hesitation had the smell of a bad omen.

"May I see the tire?" he began.

"Of course."

Didonna, a step behind, witnessed the scene without comment, her breath raising goose bumps on my neck. As I turned around to lead the manager to my car, our eyes met, her look seemed perplexed.

"You better go inside, in the cool air. I don't need you out here" I tried to reassure her, and added, "Go in, have a seat, buy yourself a cold drink, a coffee or whatnot, and don't worry your pretty head about a thing."

Adjacent to the reception area there was indeed a waiting room, in it chairs, a low table, and... free coffee for customers. Didonna readily took my advice, and I followed the manager, both facing the hellish heat undaunted.

The man examined the tire expertly, touched it all around the threads with his calloused hands, and then called for his help named Carlos, who promptly confirmed the verdict. He looked up and said reassuringly:

"No problem, boss. Can fix. No necesita buy nueva goma."

Nonetheless, I reiterated my intention to buy a new pair. The manager scratched his head again, then a short pause later.

"Okay. As you wish." Back in the shop, he invited me to have a seat in the waiting room. "Let me see if I have the size in stock."

So I joined my girlfriend, by then well refreshed. Minutes later we were sipping coffee together, while flipping through pages of the colorful magazines spread out in disarray all over the low table. Without taking her eyes off a magazine she said dryly.

"I bet we'll have to wait here for a long time, so why don't you bring in sandwiches, maybe it's a good time for an early dinner in the cool comfort of this room."

What a wise decision. I managed to get to Buchephalos just before having been taken in one of the bays. Ten more minutes, and the manager reappeared, not at all surprised at seeing us munching on our improvised victual, and sipping Coca-Cola.

"The bad news first, sir. We don't have the tires in stock." Then quickly added his reassurance." The good news is we can vulcanize the flat, but need your okay first."

Could I have said no? I had to give my approval, and did it on the spot, figuring there would be plenty of opportunities later on for buying a pair of tires somewhere along the way.

The man receipted my approval by a nod, disappeared, and I returned to our simple repast, the usual bread, cold cuts, feta cheese, tomato, and green pepper. This nomadic lifestyle became almost habitual. 'Gypsies must be right; they certainly know how to set their priorities correctly!' With plenty of time for stuffing tasty morsels in our guts, we kept enjoying life freely in the cool atmosphere. Seconds and minutes ticked away slowly but relentlessly. At four o'clock I went out to check how things progressed. The manager reassured me quickly that Carlos was working on the problem, that he was an expert in rubber vulcanization, and I had nothing to worry about.

"Your car will be ready to roll before you know it, sir, and I guarantee it to your satisfaction."

Armed with this bit of good news about to share with my friend, on the way I peeked through the window separating the workshop, and saw my car high on the lift. Somewhat disappointed, sparked as well by curiosity I decided to confront Carlos directly. The young Latino looked up, waved me away nonchalantly in a renewed reassurance as if not fully comprehending my lingo, and set to back work. To my amazement, I saw him going through the full vulcanization process not by simply plugging the hole, as would be done in Washington DC, but the old, classic way of fusing the rubber layers by heat. This seemed a little odd and worrisome, knowing that a quick rudimentary plugging --without even removing the tire-- in Maryland could run around ten-to-fifteen dollars a pop. So how much would cost such a complex procedure in Texas? But, to my great surprise, I ended up paying only seven dollars for the whole shebang. What a deal! This reminded me again of Timişoara, Romania, whereby this type of vulcanization used to be the standard way of doing the job. America can often surprise the immigrant, I mused. It could be risky to dare definitive pronouncements about her ways in all respects.

This is how I came to realize once more the great contribution the poor Latino, so-called illegal, undocumented refugees bring to the country —a fact many demagogic politicians find yet difficult to accept openly. In the absence of this *hombre Carlos*, the cost of my tire's repair might have easily shot into double digits territory, I presumed.

Impatient to leave behind --for us--another nameless locality, the shop's clock on the wall showed five past thirty minutes, when Bucephalos could finally roll out of the tire shop on its well mended running shoes. We headed back on the highway with renewed élan. By then the heat of day subsided to a more tolerable level. Worrying a little about the patched up tire, for a while I drove cautiously. But soon thereafter, as everything seemed to go well, the need to stepping harder on the gas pedal won the bet.

"We must recover the time wasted," I informed tersely.

"Why do you say that? What's the hurry? Is this a vacation, or what?"

"Yes it is," but rational as her argument seemed, I contradicted it spot on by stepping even more on the acceleration, to cause the car dart ahead soon at a clip of 90 miles an hour.

Minutes later the scenery changed from boringly arid hills to a rocky type desolation, which offered the strangest, most amazing geological formations we've ever seen or imagined. Precariously balanced boulders on boulders of various shapes and sizes, piled unbelievably high into uniquely sculptural ensembles, created naturally the strangest of extraterrestrial landscapes easily to rival even the best of science fiction flicks. We might as well have alighted on the moon or, more realistically, transferred back into savagely turbulent geological upheavals our globe of dirt and water went through eons ago. Duly impressed, an unusually enterprising Didonna took charge of the camera, all the while expelling enthusiastically explosive shrieks at each new rock formation, standing singularly majestic above the rest in this overheated, incredibly stark, but enchanted stony world.

"This is wholly unreal" was all she could muster verbally while busily taking shots after shots.

"You're right I've never seen anything like this anywhere."

Even names of the localities in this part of America sounded exotic-- Sonora, Ozona, David Crockett Monument, Glass Mountains, Balmorhea, Comanchi, just to list a few. A little later, as the day changed slowly into her bluish night gown, these same natural rocky monuments turned into as many phantoms projected against the setting sun, or – even better-- to unfathomable abodes fit for giant poltergeists, ready to frighten the entire world. Eventually, as always the greedy victorious darkness swallowed everything, the mystery vanished behind the impenetrable wall of void, letting no glimmer of light escape, not unlike out of a veritable black hole.

Unable to figure precisely in the dense obscurity the ups and downs of the road through valleys and hills, I thought to have left the mountains altogether behind. Every now and then, acacias in bloom eerily illumined in the headlights, repeatedly confirmed my suspicion again and again. I wondered whether these flowery explosions could be the products of my imagination, but kept the thought to myself, as I realized my friend sunk deep in her own mental meditating abyss.

Aside the light, the vacuum of darkness seemed to have sucked off the cabin all sounds as well. Even the slight engine-whirr melted away, muffled under a velvety blanket of silence. To judge by her unmoving posture, my companion appeared asleep, her soft snoring, associated to a slower rate of breathing soon reconfirmed my suspicion in earnest. Why disturb her? Instead, I allowed myself to sink slowly deeper in my own memories. Until El Paso the way was still long.

*

The next evening following my fateful visit to Didonna, the memory of yesterday's kiss still smoldered hot on my lips. I found her alone, which on its own couldn't mean my arrival had been expected. But sure enough her eyes lit up with delight as they met mine; moreover, she soon served up the customary cups of Turkish coffee, seemingly prepared in advance for my coming. To my pleasure Alex this time didn't show his cute mug at all. I assumed he was out *playing with other kids*, to use his words.

As we sat on the couch shoulder to shoulder, pretending to have forgotten our interrupted romantic encounter of last evening, the conversation revolved around banalities. Then one thing leading to another, Philomela became the subject.

Wanted or not, we had at last to admit to her presence between us as the only person empowered legally and morally to effectively censor our barely budding love affair. Without conclusively clarifying my wife's position and role in the new relationship, we began, nonetheless, to imagine what the future could bring soon for us all. This freshly looming reality became fast self-evident, causing my insisting for a clear-cut resolution right from the outset. Didonna confessed to feeling painfully awkward in her position too, purportedly ashamed to look Philomela directly in the eyes, were our love to become more than a fling. Professing to understand her natural reservations, as the guy caught between the pressure of a newly discovered affection, and the obligations to an old marriage, I opted cowardly but ardently for a secret rather than an openly declared affair. I surmised if nobody knew about our romance no one could get hurt. This ironclad logic didn't impress my pretty counterpart much at all. Her approach came across diametrically opposed, prefigured much simpler than mine. She only wanted to know one thing straight off the bat whom did I want to be with, with her or Philomela? I had to make a clear-cut choice.

From my vantage, the situation appeared a bit more intricate. I lived practically for a lifetime next to Philomela, a span of twenty years--not all that bad. Two decades of alternating joys and sorrows --typical for most marriages—weighed heavily in the balance of my conscience in favor of the status quo. Never before in my conjugal life had I been placed in a position to question our union's validity seriously enough to wish it dissolved, even less to cut it short more or less on a whim, however thunderously. Suddenly I found myself face-to-face with a nearly insoluble dilemma. How to avoid hurting Philomela needlessly, but satisfying my craving for a new woman all the same?

Didonna's solution had been much simpler and straightforward-- either one, or the other, no compromise. This implacability I judged as cruel and selfish, an attitude unfair to me, as well as to my wife. I couldn't comprehend why couldn't all sides strive for happiness at the same time, without anyone getting unnecessarily hurt in the process?

"Why couldn't our spontaneously budding love be altruistic, and overcome some of the patently artificial, obviously narrow-minded, preconceived moral hurdles society so arbitrarily imposes on us?" –I asked.

But the woman *no and no*, held on obstinately to her position, forcing in balance my entire marriage, to weigh all its shortcomings and advantages once and for all. She insisted that only through this sort of honest introspection could I find out whether deep down I still honestly loved Philomela. The dilemma was for me to figure out.

"Only viewed in this light could the choice become rightly ours to pick," she concluded firmly.

Reluctantly, I've been compelled to admit that Philomela and I had been living together for a long time rather out of inertia than based on worthier reasons, and our initial love must have long since turned into the sort of lukewarm, conventional and predictable routine association so many modern couples accept simply out of complacency. True, Philomela possessed an impetuous, temperamental and domineering nature, she too often resorted to nagging, even bitching, defects I tolerated but never acquiesced, particularly as myself had been too often the object. On the good side, though, she was also cuddling in a motherly soothing fashion, always ready to support my endeavors verbally, causing my liver to expand in joy to the degree of sparking sometimes in my for-ever-tortured mind even suspicions about some hidden motivations.

Had I ever brushed over all the incongruence between us on this account, had I resigned to my fate, to thinking that for the complicated, mentally twisted individual of my type life didn't have anything better to offer due to some trivial misalignments? No, I never adopted such an attitude. On the contrary, honestly believed myself reasonably satisfied by dutifully compromising for the sake of our family's endurance. When doubt occasionally raised its ugly head more than usually, I lightheartedly took refuge in some fleeting escapades coming my way incidentally, brief sexual encounters never emotionally taxing, or lasting longer than a few banal hours. After mulling some over these reasons, I heard myself firmly restating my position.

"Look, believe it or not I care about Philomela, and value her friendship. Why break her heart out of the blue, in total disregard of all self-recriminations liable to haunt us later, were I to act as you wish?"

But the dame reacted vehemently, harsher than expected, or I thought fair.

"O how stupid you men can be! Yes, yes, I could honestly admire a husband's respect for his wife, but then again, why do you want my love if you are so pleased by your mate's affection? Isn't this pretty interesting, ha? What then make you ache for my embrace? What are you here for right now? If you love Philomela, why are you so lonely as to want my company at all?"

"How did you figure I feel lonely?"

"Hey, Mr. Doru Constantin Corbea, do I have to repeat my question why are you here with me now? Man, what the hell is it you really want out of this friendship with me? Of course you feel lonely. And now let me tell you something about the wife you pretend to care so much about."

"Alright, adamant woman, enough of this. Let's leave Philomela out of the picture, at least for now. Maybe a few months later you'll see my angle better, and may change your mind."

"Oh no, stubborn man. You started the discussion. We have to finish it now. I can't allow this boil to fester between us, if you want me to be frank. You want me to be honest with you, don't you?"

"Then out with it. Go ahead, empty your bag."

I don't know what made me give myself in to such a selfish, coward retreat, but I did. What the hell did I find still so attractive in this beautiful woman, so openly revealing herself as cruel as a piranha? All her hesitations confessed a minute earlier, about feeling embarrassed to looking Philomela in the eyes, suddenly hit me in the face as having been quite a bit hypocritical. But incredibly, instead of waking up, of coming to my senses, my desire for her grew even more irresistible, an unexplainable force pushed me to do just about anything to get in her graces, to make this no-nonsense female mine, only mine. Why do men and women alike go rather for the *bad* than the *good* in choosing the opposite sex? What is the secret Mother Nature holds in this regard? Stupid question? Maybe. The fact is it was I who invited the woman to speak her mind. And she brazenly did so, her blue gaze innocently fixed into my greens, an imperceptibly mischievous smile lingering on her lips.

"Do you remember the party Philomela gave last year to welcome her former husband visiting from Romania?"

"I do, what about it?"

"Do you also remember her bragging about the beneficial influence you had on their son Dan, present as well?"

"So what? Philomela's babble, her nonstop rattling is almost community-wide recognized. No one takes her seriously."

"Maybe you should."

"How come?"

"Let me tell you then the concluding bragging she offered for the benefit of all present, but mainly for her former husband's ears. '*In this house I am wearing the pants,*' were her exact words. Didn't you hear her proclaim this loudly?

"No. I don't remember, but if she uttered the damned sentence, she didn't mean anything bad. I know her well enough. The boast must have been her strange, roundabout way of paying me a compliment, the triumphant woman reemerging victorious in front of her former husband --a simpleton according to her own admission."

"Really? Do you think the men and women present that night shared your opinion as well? Why can't you see the humiliation she inflicted on you publicly? What sort of a man are you anyway? The entire Romanian community had been talking about the scene for weeks, about the subservient position you must endure in your own house under your wife's hoofs. Listen, you are admittedly a smart man, certainly intelligent enough to comprehend all the arcane books of the world, you excel at explaining the murkiest impractical philosophic theories, but forgive me for saying you know zilch about the intricacies of the female soul."

I stared at the woman dumbfounded. Her recounting echoed unbelievable in my ears, although I must admit it induced slowly my rethinking the whole affair, including the sheer appearance of Philomela's former husband in our house.

Off the blue I remembered Adriana, my high school flame, the woman I was once ready to die for. I adored her so much that even years later when we accidentally met my knees shook like matchsticks. How should Philomela have liked my former girlfriend Adriana paying us a visit one beautiful sunny afternoon? Perhaps Didonna had a point after all. All the same, I chose to deflect her allegations out of hand, justifying Philomela's insensitive words by her innate lack of tact, by her natural inclination to put foot in the mouth.

"Fine, if you want to stay blind so be it. But don't force me to disregard the truth."

"Oh my, the truth, the truth. Who knows what truth is?"

The fact the dame peremptorily tried to push Philomela off the stage did not yet strike me as an altogether unnatural impulse. No Sirree! Don't they all want to have the man they love only for themselves? Females are beautifully selfish. As most men, I appraised my prospective mistress's apparently malevolent inclination as another undeniable indicator of her budding affection for me. Men and women alike, in love often think in such undeniably selfish, cruel manner. Yet my blindness wasn't absolute, considering that I noticed the jealous meanness of the nascent love engendered in Didonna's soul. Any human being would have acted the same way, no matter how decent. On the other side of the coin, was I to notice such things had I been myself deep down truly in love? Such cool objectivity could be quite dubiously ubiquitous. Oh well, who knows? What I knew was how often such intellectual prevarication made pursuing my own happiness difficult. Reason and emotion seldom make for a good common household. Humans are not angels. Then I recalled the way Philomela once nourished the same resentment against Angela, my first nearly forgotten, short-lived marriage partner of a lifetime ago. It looks like nature places everything in balance and perspective, love and hate paradoxically mixed into one emotional knotty jumble.

Still not absolutely certain about the outcome of our budding love affair, but inclined to accept the new desired woman's, and my failings as absurdities of human vanity, as the biologic corollary of all-powerful carnal desires, eventually I decided to let destiny take its course unhampered. Could've this cowardly attitude justify my alleged objectivity just as well missing in action? Perhaps, but as the saying goes in love and war all rules get suspended. It was Didonna's voice that interrupted my tortured musings.

"Listen, Philomela possessed you for a good twenty years. Didn't she have enough? What about me, don't I have the same rights to happiness?"

Her questions snarled my thoughts into a sad conclusion, to a sordid final curtain call. Regardless how hollow these questions sounded even in joking, they reverberated powerfully in my mind ever since, now and again. Have I ever attempted to argue away these strangely awoken echoes out of my conscience? No, no, no, I didn't.

Eventually, the carnal desire proved stronger than all the morally twisted arguments combined.

At this point our discussion ceased, but the bitter aftertaste lingered on far longer in the night. Before returning home to my lonely bed of middle age dissatisfaction, we kissed again more passionately than ever, in spite of the sadness persistent as a bad odor in the background. The will of the all-powerful flesh prevailed, and I couldn't get enough of my new love's incredibly sweet kisses. I could no longer live without her, all of a sudden no longer could accept my old sorry way of life.

During the ten or so minutes of my drive home, my thoughts revolved whirling in a mix of contradictory emotions boiled in the same cauldron of exhilarating joy and pride tempered by an immense sadness, poured topsy-turvy together as into a bottomless void. Isn't **Love** blinding? It sure is. It is, and it is!

*

On my right I saw Didonna crumpled up in the car seat not well suited for sleeping. My hand extended reflex-like to gently touching her hair. Her response ensued as a tiny moaned question:

"Where are we, have we arrived?"

Had I known the destination I would've said 'just a little more patience, old girl. We must wait a bit longer.'—But as it was, I left her question unanswered.

*

Following that night of setting base lines, my visits to Didonna became predictably regular. We met daily, but for a long time without crossing the Rubicon of carnal satisfaction. The worries, possible complications and the unfathomable difficulties looming ahead, kept our friendship safely on the platonic side. However, as the play required, I began gradually to exert increased pressure, bit by bit by every passing day. For a long time she resisted heroically, conditioning her consent to a firm commitment on my part.

"Without your clear option, either for me or for her, I couldn't confront Philomela openly."

But in spite of her stubborn resistance, and to my surprise, the ferocious tigress of a dame didn't appear to have mustered enough strength to reject me altogether spot on. Consciously or unconsciously, neither of us seemed ready yet to cut our chances off for good. Procrastination ruled supreme.

Eventually the hesitation ended up working in my favor. It allowed me to test my patience. For the vacillations to be sorted out, countermanding the dictates of conscience needed time. However by each passing night, my intuition suggested ever more clearly that we'd end up anyway by behaving cruelly, mercilessly unforgiving toward Philomela.

Predestined to loosing the battle against the urge Mother Nature programmed within our genes, in the end we had to play the act of reproduction—although virtually impossible at our ages to producing much of any offspring for the world. The same Mother Nature seldom engages in counting years or real abilities-- she pushes indiscriminately against our better judgment, even when physically long past the capacity of begetting children. Instincts are not hung up on rationality. The nightly passionate kissing sessions did not help either. Slowly but surely our restraint had to weaken, resisting the Divine commandment —*be fruitful and multiply*—became gradually less and less realistic, in spite of its certainly limited probability for us

The last two weekends of August, under the lure of this spell I went as far as to skip my regular visits to Philomela in Rehoboth.

*

In United States the first Monday of September is holiday--Labor Day. Initially established in 1892 in Chicago, to be celebrated annually on May the first everywhere in the world, in America it has been moved in protesting reaction to the end of summer.

Indeed, why should the US of A conform to such a skewed mandate, especially on a day selected as the symbol of anti-Capitalist fight as well? Every freedom loving, down--to-earth, blue-blooded American would naturally cringe, and vote against any such *dubiously* conceived festivity. Consequently, in *America the exceptional*, workers celebrate, or —perhaps-- work in earnest, as nowhere else on the planet. Isn't the God-given prerogative of any country to differ from the rest of the human bunch?

This time, unlike the majority of Washingtonians, I wasn't prepared to enjoy the three days off in Rehoboth, and thus bring the summer vacation to a proper conclusion. These days held a better promise in Gaithersburg.

Had we failed to make love before Philomela's return, the new relationship, willy-nilly should have to come to a screeching halt. In the presence of the wife, I could have hardly continued my evening visits to a female friend without eliciting suspicions, lengthy discussions, or tenuous explanations at home. As the final sticky decision was to occur one way or another, I thought why not avoid the unexpected turns and twists sure to dump buckets of cold water on our sensuality just about to sizzle. So I resolved to apply my clean-cut pressure with renewed vigor even more relentlessly than ever. However crooked or cruel, the decisive step had to occur soon, or never.

With this in mind I leaned harder and harder on Didonna's apparently firm will. Surprisingly, my greater pressure in the beginning only hardened her steely resistance that, in turn, whipped my own desire to frenzy.

On that last fateful Sunday before the holiday, we dined together, the two of us alone. Alex dispatched himself to a friend's house for the night. Everything seemed to work out just fine. As always, once over the meal we sat shoulder to shoulder on the couch, intimately in closer touch than ever, ready to enjoy the usual after dinner coffee and cigarette.

Very soon, we engrossed in passionate kissing. Freed off all inhibitions, my hands searched greedily all over the sweet curves and angles of the welcoming flesh. Yes, she no longer put up any resistance at all. Somehow I slid down on the carpet, at her feet. Bathed in the crimson reflections of sunset, my face came to face with her slightly parted knees, my entire being maddeningly attracted to the luring dark soft void beckoning mysterious under her skirt. Loosing all self-control I plunged into the precipice, desperately trying to obliterate the resurgence of my unrestrained, demanding maleness. As the skin of my chest --revealed under the unbuttoned shirt-- touched her knees that parted gradually more and more in response as a welcoming prelude to accepting a guest in the inner sanctum, I didn't need any additional prodding for squeezing my body in between, while dragging the skirt up the hips until my thirsty lips touched her neck, then the lips, for the eventual climaxing down under in the incendiary union, whence no return is possible. Nothing, not the pain of death could have stopped me from busting in, from casting my searing passion in the abyss of deepest carnal pleasures, delayed for so long.

"Stop, Dorel, stop, we must go up in the bedroom," her hot whisper hissed in my ears, as she jumped to pull me forcefully up the stairs, while hurriedly shedding blouse, skirt and slippers on the way.

I followed zombie-like in her steps, the pinkish bare heels, the sinuous, smooth ivory legs dancing before my intoxicated eyes. Drunk with the pleasure promised between those very thighs I followed mesmerized, clinging on as iron dust to a magnet.

In the bedroom, the large bed, strategically opened and prepared, waited white, fresh and inviting. With her feline passion unchained at last, the woman plunged on the sheet impatiently and I flooded her torso with mine. Suddenly she turned velvety soft, for the sweetest sensual dream of my life come true. Our hands set to work feverishly in pulling off mutually the few vestments still hiding the much-desired areas of until-then forbidden skin. Awkwardly but miraculously, I succeeded to unhook her bra without tearing it apart, and to push her panty down without changing the position of my body weighing down upon hers. She proved better skilled at unbuckling my belt, at peeling off my shirt while forcing my trousers with her bare feet –under-shorts and all-- down my legs. Lo and behold, in fully frontal skin-to-skin contact for the first time, we melted furiously in the hot furnace of embrace. Shaking and shivering, I hurried to destination as the teenager confronted at last with the woman's eternally mysterious secret abode. The pulsating womb swallowed my entire being greedily and thoroughly. Just in time. I couldn't have delayed the culmination of my desire a single heartbeat longer, all reins swept away by the winds of unchained passion. Nothing could have stopped the run-away train barreling down the slopes of carnal union.

"Yes, yes, greedy boy, let go, I must possess you now. Now, now! No more need to delay," her hoarse voice hissed and wheezed hot in my ear. And then, without any further prodding I crashed impetuously, a boulder rolling down over the open velvety-soft, fertile valley to my proud gender's death—man and woman difference temporarily annihilated.

Memory, self-awareness and time itself dissolved to nothingness. Such intervals may be measured objectively by seconds, minutes at most, but as with sleep, or other forms of knockouts, true duration is hard to express other than subjectively. I only remember how I awoke to my senses lying on my back, an incredibly soft-lipped Didonna alongside kissing me gently, whispering sweet gibberish in my ear. She felt sweet and cuddly, the little girl endearingly searching for protection in big daddy's arms.

I kept silent. As always, in the wake of lovemaking --as probably some other men-- I heeded not the advice, neither the urge of returning the well-deserved kindness and love to my new woman's generosity. Although avidly searching for the right words, nothing popped out of my mouth. Unfortunately, expressing emotions comes to me easier through silence than by gushing out foolishly childish utterances. This perhaps is common for the male. Oh, how often and how hard we try not to appear week, or ridiculously sentimental precisely when mellowness is the proper tune to sing! Then again, I must admit Didonna understood my handicap quite well, whenever I tried to compensate by words for my ingrained ineptitude of expressing gratitude, as she promptly admonished.

"For God's name forget it. You sound so unnatural when feigning kindness. I know you love me. Quit acting silly only for the sake of self-imposed fair emotional appearances."

On such occasions I felt a bit humiliated, since believing sincerely in my desire to please, even if poorly expressed. Be that as it may, at the completion of our first carnal embrace my silence should have appeared quite impolite, especially so when glancing at my watch. The thought of guilt at facing Philomela at home pushed all of a sudden other thoughts aside.

"Don't tell me you must go now,"—she began, but I stopped her by covering her lips with mine.

"O-my-love, unfortunately I have to leave. Philomela might be at home already. You know she is still my wife.

"I hope not for long. Promise?"

My answer didn't ensue instantly, but eventually I murmured.

"Okay, okay, I do."

Stretched out in naked shamelessness on the crumpled sheets, she watched me intently as I dressed, a flaccid, sad expression lingering on her visage. But she let me go.

*

We arrived at last in Van Horn --a small town about eighty-to-ninety miles from El Paso-- before the last desperate minute was to strike midnight. As soon as the well-known sign of *Motel 6* came in view we exited the highway without undue trouble. Yesterday's mishap must have taught us a useful lesson. Just as well, because I reached the end of my endurance.

Finally within the four walls of a room--a carbon copy of the other night's-- we tried to relax a bit before hitting the sack. Exchanging a few sweet words as we shared a bottle of beer seemed a natural ending for the hard day and night. However, once nestled safely under covers, sleep delivered a quick knockout punch-- the TV left on, beer unfinished. The hissing set waked us again only at the program's conclusion. Didonna turned it off robot-like without a comment, planted a minuscule kiss on my lips, and mumbled a few unintelligible words, before Father Sleep swept us back in the fluid realm of dreams.

ACCROSS DESERTS

The arid wasteland's daylight filtered in the room milky white.

Slightly unfriendly rays forced our eyes open. But, with the curtains pulled aside, the promise of another splendid day appeared obvious, as the sun fought to emerge victorious off the haze.

"Hey lady, up, up, up! No time to lie in bed forever. Come-on, wake up!"

"Shut up, Dorel. Let me have ten more tiny minutes." Then, in disregard of her request, she sprung off the bed as if nothing said, swallowed a big yawn, and went straight to the bathroom mumbling." Why don't you boil some water for coffee, and set the table for breakfast."

Her words sounded unconvincing, as she never trusted me with the tasks.

"Okay dear, I will do that," but I couldn't finish my sentence, before her voice came alive again, this time clearly, forcefully, with absolute self-awareness.

"Never mind, don't touch anything. I'll be back in a jiffy."

Only God may understand women I thought resigned to fate, after having been practically branded as a *two-left-handed man*. Offended, though, I felt not.

Breakfast consisted of leftovers, cold cuts, cheese, tomatoes and bread, the customary Romanian morning fare. Coffee and the day's first smoke we enjoyed while searching through the channels for the weather report. The meteo-auguries spoke in favor of a sunny day.

At past eight Bucephalos rolled on the highway, as for us, obviously reinvigorated by the good night sleep, the dry landscape in motion appeared strangely more enchanting than the day before. Our path cut a perfectly straight line along the gray asphalt runner, rolled out between rusty-yellow rocky, rhythmically rising and falling hills on both sides. Amid an endless variety of boulders interspersed by small wiry bushes --the preponderant vegetation--, here and there cactuses of spherical, cylindrical, ovoid or disc-like shapes asserted their resilient thorny presence. No artist could ever invent similarly beautiful arrangements with such astonishingly simple components.

"How unbelievably splendid this aridity!" I exclaimed.

"Indeed. Myself too imagined the desert only as boring and monotonous"

Gradually, even for city people like us, quite alien to this stark sort of esthetics, the desert became less uniform than perceived initially-- its sophisticated complexity soon won our enthusiastic admiration as it gradually revealed itself.

"Why are people so eager to pass judgment based mostly on first, superficial impressions?"

My pretty traveling partner didn't bother to answer, as all rhetoric questions properly deserve none.

*

El Paso heralded its presence a few minutes before ten o'clock. The city, though far from being a metropolis in the widely accepted sense, is fairly large nonetheless. The road we happened to approach it led straight to downtown. The usual Texan scenery, this time accented by immediately noticeable Mexican overtones, low building structures erected above arched entrances cut in dusty walls scattered all over vast areas in all imaginable nuances of clay.

"Mexico must be near," I remarked curtly.

The fact became obvious when a hundred yards later the coming huge traffic signs pointed one after the other to *downtown*, and the Rio Grande. And, lo and behold, we found ourselves on a bridge that, willy-nilly forced the inattentive driver across the border. The sign BIENVENIDAS vanished behind us in a jiffy, as well as the point of no return. No customs, no border guards, nothing stopped our wandering over into Mexico.

Realizing the mistake, my friend, instead of getting upset, became giddy, insanely happy at the prospect of visiting a new country inadvertently.

On my part, I began to worry, in tune with my penchant to pessimism. A number of ugly rumors, spread by people who ventured unprepared to Mexico, surfaced instantly in my suspicious mind. I saw us already robbed, trapped in a car accident, involved in dubious money exchanges, or in other nefarious affairs. My worries bubbled up aloud.

"I wonder whether the American automobile insurance is valid in Mexico, or the Maryland identification documents will be acceptable to the Texan border guards on our return."

In response to my dark apprehensions, my foolhardy mistress got amused, laughed in my face outright, and condescendingly qualified my fears as overly exaggerated, best fit to paranoiacs. For her the idea of plunging unwillingly into another country appeared amazingly as the promise of a fantastic adventure. As for me, due to the lightning speed the mishap occurred, my stomach twisted into a knot, my worry-filled mind fretting frantically all over the possible bad outcomes.

"Listen, why don't you keep your glee in check? Please don't pour gasoline over the fire" I demanded somberly. Sensing the situation's gravity through my tone, the prospective danger abruptly downed on her too, and she turned silent, but not before a last, reassuring quip.

"Okay, okay, I will keep my tongue in check. But remember what we did is only an ordinary mistake, not the end of the world."

"I know, I know, still your cooperation is welcome."

Deeper and deeper into Mexico, we rolled slowly ahead on the wide, smoothly paved avenue. Tall-whitewashed trees separated the sidewalks from the roadbed, reminiscent vaguely of Eastern Europe. In the Old Country lines of whitewashed trees hemmed in many roads in the same fashion. The resemblance had the strange becalming effect of encouraging further observations. On both sides small, low, yellowish-white houses brought to mind some Romanian villages along the Danube.

"Is this a coincidence, or what? Look at these modest houses, don't they remind you of Caracal, Corabia or Turnu Măgurele?"

But my somewhat pouting companion, obviously not yet recovered from my previous put-down, hissed back.

"I've never been in those Godforsaken towns along the Danube shore. By the way, what's with you now? Why this sudden revert to philosophizing? Did you forget your worries? How come these dirty puny shacks no longer seem dangerous? Tell me dear what can justify your abrupt change of attitude."

"Oh come on, don't be impossible."

But the dialogue came to a halt as I noticed a somewhat isolated, white shack, a small parking lot on its right hand side, sheltering what looked like an information center. This obvious similarity didn't escape my friend's acute observation either.

"Hey, you need an extra invitation? Drive in!"

"Yes, yes, I will," then happily conformed, secretly plotting to use the occasion for executing a quick *u-turn*, as well as a pretext for changing our soured moods.

Parked in the lot two unoccupied vehicles with American license plates.

"Praise the Lord we have good company here." I felt inexplicably elated, and exhaled a sigh of relief.

But as we stepped out of the vehicle, three dubious looking, mustachioed Mexicans materialized as out of nowhere to surround us. Only God-knew-whence they appeared, as we didn't notice a soul around the lot just a heartbeat earlier.

Cogs in my mind began turning lightening fast, trying to guess the possible reactions expected off these shady characters, had they found out about the large amount of cash in my pockets. The thought, frightening as it was, made me preemptively cocky, stiff, obstinate, even before they addressed us.

"*Senor, necessita cambio dollares?*" --or something like that.

"*Nada dineros, amigo, no habla espagnol, por favor.*"

It was all I could muster off my limited Spanish usage, but to a surprisingly good effect. The men shrugged dumbfounded, then before we knew it disappeared, melting Australian-bushmen-like in the environment.

Inside everything clean, walls whitewashed the same way as on the exterior. We were the sole visitors. 'Then who owned the cars parked in the lot?' I mused, but quickly got distracted by the dry wood-plank-floor's painful screech under our steps, reminding once again of the Old Country. Although not air-conditioned, the atmosphere smelled pleasantly dry, as mud-cake mixed with vaguely putrid aroma of ancient timber. Tourist brochures and pamphlets displayed on simple unvarnished wooden shelves lined the walls. Naturally these couldn't escape my companion's notice. She picked up a bunch.

Returned in the car's safety, I showed eager to drive back toward the American border, but Didonna succeeded in changing my mind again. It took her only a peremptory review of brochures to suggest visiting the Mexican city Ciudad Juarez, nestled on the right side of Rio Grande. My first instinct called for a flat, instant refusal.

"Please, please, why not explore a bit this town, made famous by so many motion pictures? Nothing bad will happen, I promise. Let's have a short detour, and then drive back to Texas. Okay?"

Her voice sweet, gaze enticing and smile so irresistible that I relented, in spite of my wanting first some additional information about the place-- a sort of Mexican extension of El Paso.

"Okay, let's have it your way, but only for a short visit, fifteen minutes at most, then back to America." In the end I had given in thinking my companion might be right-- 'what were our chances for visiting Ciudad Juarez ever again?'

So we rolled in the town proper along, a dusty meandering street, lined with clay-yellow, or *café latté*-colored houses, alternating with various small shops, most barred by metallic doors or shutters. Crowds of modest-looking pedestrians milled on the sidewalks, police cars patrolled up and down constantly.

"Maybe it's crazy, but this much police makes me feel a bit queasy."

The rejoinder ensued instantly shaped as a question.

"Hey, didn't you just tell me how dangerous is for Americans to visit Mexico? Then why not welcome the presence of police?"

"Alright dear, if you are so cocky smart, give me one single reason I can trust these policemen? Don't tell me you haven't heard about the awful corruption in Mexico."

"Oh-my-God, you are always so apt at twisting things around."

Not quite reassured, I kept to myself clamed up, nonetheless flowing with the traffic, in the hope of finding a convenient spot to park, perhaps to investigate a bit the town on foot as well. This proved impossible. Not a single spot open among the many colorfully patched-up, beat-up-cars lined bumper to bumper by the coin-operated meters. Just about to propose returning to the States when, amidst the long line of dusty clay-colored houses, suddenly an unbelievably opulent villa but of distinctly dubious taste came ostentatiously in full view.

Built on a huge lot enclosed on all sides by forged-iron-fence, this mansion of white marble walls supporting a roof of bright red tiles looked like a *hacienda* that —thanks to my preconceived ideas— must have been surely the property of some illicit drug dealer. Deeper in the yard, the perfect mirror of an Olympic-size swimming pool faithfully reflected the blue sky and the midday sun, as it cast its benevolent light on the row of gleaming plaster-statuettes-- the weirdest variety of kitschy angels, nymphs, naiads and other equally semi-fabulous mythological beings frolicking in the huge garden overfilled as well by exotic combinations of flowers and shrubbery.

Reduced speechless by this improbable opulence implanted smack in the midst of poorest of the poor living nearby in what looked like adobe huts, my mind traveled as so often to old Romania. Only there I fancied was the boyar's luxurious manor house similarly surrounded by the picturesque poverty of peasants toiling on his land. Although nobody visible in the yard or by the pool, I could still picture the tough, well groomed and dressed drug merchant, sitting in a chaise-lounge and sipping cold margaritas under an umbrella, the same way I read in literature about the old boyar enjoying *wine-spritzers* in the cool shade of an ancient walnut tree in his garden. Well, so much for the power of culturally ingrained ideas!

*

In retrospect, neither banks of the Rio Grande —El Paso in America, or Ciudad Juarez in Mexico-- qualified as worthy tourist attractions, in spite of their cinematographic fame. Not much to see in these towns. South of the --to me-- ridiculously small **Rio Grande**, Ciudad Juarez looked as dusty yellow and gray as El Paso seemed monotonous and disorganized on the North, I dare say in spite of spending precious little time in either.

*

It was high time to return to the States. Discussing what we've seen, the distance back to the border seemed short. Then, unexpectedly, we found ourselves squeezed in a long line of cars waiting admittance to Texas. Thousands of engines wasted zillions of horsepower, emitting tons of bluish smoke to the already suffocating atmosphere, to make the heat shimmer visibly above the highway's many lanes. For a long, long interval, time promised to stay frozen dead in its track.

But much to our surprise, we pulled faster than expected—less than twenty minutes-- in the narrow lane between the customs booths, suddenly face-to-face with a huge American border official. Causing the uniform stretch tight on his huge body as he bent down to speak, he leaned heavily on the car-door's frame, forehead hid under a wide-brimmed hat, eyes shaded by dark glasses, his entire head almost stuck inside through the window opening

"Sir, what's your birthplace?"

"Timişoara, Romania," came my prompt response. The official turned instantly suspicious.

"What is it you said? May I see some identification?"

I handed over my Maryland driver's license. After examining it carefully on both sides, the man finally returned it, while adopting an authoritative but slightly curmudgeonly tone.

"Next time when I'll ask what's your birthplace you'll say Maryland. Okay?"

"Yes-Sir."--I snapped back replicating his tone, as he moved his gaze to my companion.

"Did the lady see the world first in Maryland, too?"

"Of course."

The man drew back, and waved us summarily in the United States, his attention turned already to the next car in line. Following my short sigh of relief Didonna could hardly restrain a facetious smirk. She earned the right to a victory tour, as in the nineties Americans did not yet need a passport to go in and out of Mexico. My worries proved exaggerated as usually. Consequently, I allowed her gloating in triumph quietly, in spite of considering my cautious behavior fully justified. Is it not better to be safe than sorry?

Back in El Paso, we took immediately westward, on the road leading to New Mexico. Along the way we passed a large jeep, ten or so *illegal* Latinos crammed inside, poor unlucky fellows caught the previous night crossing the Rio Grande. Wrists handcuffed to the railing-bar in the cabin, they huddled tightly squeezed together in misery and despondence. Inadvertently we witnessed one act of the well-known *cop-and-robber* game, going on day and night between *undocumented* immigrants and American law enforcement officials.

This sort of alien influx has been the story forever in the States, so far the apparent winners the migrant workers, their employers and, to a degree, maybe the public at large. Then who should be the losers? Simply said respect for the law, some competing domestic workers and common decency, to list only a few categories. The Rio Grande --as I said less *Grande* than the name makes it sound—could hardly act as a real barrier, as no river or border ever stopped the desperate. Historic experience clearly showed this elsewhere too. The example of German Democratic Republic comes to mind, although the reasons over there might have been quite different, and more complex than to find a scope within the present narrative.

New Mexico *welcomed* us around two o' clock in the afternoon --the voice of its governor stating this in large red letters on the sign at the border crossing. By the welcoming center, a weatherworn hippy or punk-looking couple easily identified themselves by the colorful gypsy-like vestments, equally by their beat-up, psychedelically decorated Volkswagen mini-van. They were probably searching for the same information we did. The sloppily clad female looked slightly more picturesque, although her male companion, sporting a long unkempt beard, heavy boots, a large black hat and numerous intricate tattoos peeking out under his tank top, was almost as spectacular. It may have been as well for the woman to appeal to me naturally more than the man. Having a literally *minimalist* blouse worn over a pair of shinny-ass-blue-jeans -- knees and a bit of bottom visible through cuts in the material, as well as the band of white skin around her waist--, she obviously knew how to coordinate everything with her sky-blue eyes, in order to attract curious looks. For reasons self-evident reasons, I took great care not to share my impression with my mistress who, perhaps true to her gender, paid more attention to the guy, much less to the gal.

"Take a look at this monkey parading his ragged pants, dirty tattoos and stupidly proud face! I can't even begin to imagine how this pretty girl could sleep next to him!" My concubine's voice barely hid her contempt.

For once I agreed, but wisely kept my opinion secret.

"It's only a matter of taste, dear. The gal must surely love the guy."

"Yeah, so it seems. Poor girl. Look at the moron, how openly he ignores her."

"O, don't mind him. This could be just a properly feigned attitude, part of the mandatory macho show-off. He has to be *cool*, if you know what I mean."

"Yes, I certainly do. I also know that you wouldn't dislike being in his place. Have I hit it spot on? I bet you wouldn't refuse getting lucky with the girl tonight."

"Come on, woman, sometimes you can sound absolutely silly."

"Nonsense. All men are the sons of one and the same mother."

To my good fortune she cut her feminine vitriol short right then and there, although her eyes focused on the couple for a while longer in silence. I stepped obediently alongside my companion, took her hand in mine careful not overplay my role, as the self alleged, well-bred boy humbly pretending to swear allegiance to a civiler society.

The young or maybe not so young couple, unaware of being observed, acted totally unconcerned, as they left their van's doors and windows open, unlike us compelled as always to locking the car airtight, maniacally afraid of some improbable thieves.

"How much freer these young folk act compared to us, always obsessively tied down by insignificant material things!"--I muttered softly after slamming the car-door, but my quip had been overheard.

"Don't be ridiculous! You couldn't live as these weirdoes for a second, in spite of your much-touted admiration for them. It's too late for that. I bet the girl with the naked midriff wouldn't give spittle for you. You realize that, don't you? So try to stay calm and reasonable. Okay?"

"What's all this nastiness, sweetie? Have I offended you, or what? Don't you worry I have no intention of becoming a hippy, and I do not like the *gypsy* woman at all. She's not my type. Period."

"Yeah, right."

Lately, my concubine showed more and more outbursts of such petty unwarranted jealousy.

'Was this payback for my not promising firmly to marry her? Didn't she know I had to divorce first? The fact I have shacked up with her meant nothing at all? Who plunged in headfirst? Then again, what did my act prove, love, or simply lust?' I wondered.

"Come, Dorel, this way. Let's sit in that booth by the window, in the smoker section."

She took the lead, to drag me far off the bar and the pair of punks before I could say anything in the matter. Soon and fortunately enough as the crowd obscured the couple, she pretended to forget them altogether, and cut the scene short. I felt grateful.

On the menu's advice, we ordered the breakfast fare still available at lunchtime, for Didonna a mushroom-omelet, for me two fried eggs, grilled steak, and hash-brown potatoes on the side for both. It became by then a custom to complete our meals with ice cream, coffee or Coca-Cola.

It happened to be right there --a few hundred yards within the border area between Texas and New Mexico —to enjoy for the first time in our lives the charm of a diner, a particular sort of Americana. This type of restaurant is nothing more or less than a family type eatery built on purpose to resemble a train's dinning car, only not on wheels-- an establishment somewhere in between a fast food and a full-service deal. Diners must by definition be alcohol free, although some operate for twenty-four hours non-stop, even during times when children can be hardly present. The food served may be classified as traditional American, of better quality than at McDonald's, but less elaborate than offered on a full-fledged restaurant's menu.

Once my friend finished off her omelet, and I my steak, we lit cigarettes, prepared to enjoy the coffee. The need of stomachs satisfied, the time seemed proper for casting a quick look around, and notice the restaurant's decoration, made up entirely of American Indian motives.

Turquoise blues, brownish reds, sandy yellows, sparkling whites cheered up the walls without disturbing the unmistakable sobriety, reflected as well in the cross-beamed ceiling, round brass and glass candelabra hung at the end of rusty iron-chains. Across the hall a souvenir shop peddled local curiosities, dolls, boys and girls in full Indian attire, next to soft moccasins, engraved leather articles, sand-paintings skillfully set between clear glass panes, a large variety of silver-and-turquoise-jewelry, horses, eagles, and other beasts of carved wood, even mini-size totemic poles-- the latter faithful reproductions of the actual ten-feet-pair, topped with spread-winged large eagles, guarding the diner on both sides of the entrance.

"Wow, here is something for you" I exclaimed, but by then my friend's appetite seemed already well wetted for buying souvenirs.

Then, at long last, time came to hit the road again.

Not too far in the distance, on the left-hand side, blue silver powdered mountains beckoned a friendly welcome into this truly enchanting realm, called New Mexico. Although the desert continued uninterrupted from Texas, the scenery on this side of the border appeared picturesque by comparison. Obviously less arid, the desert here sparkled, endless diamantine carpets rolled out before us, right off the indigo-blue sky. One could almost peek into the deep dark cosmic space beyond the sun's shining nuclear orb, to render blind the spectator daring to look at its majesty. Without seeing we felt the stars nearby.

Even the heat, objectively as excessive as ever, seemed mellower, encouraging longer, more frequent halts at rest areas, for taking pictures, either of giant cactuses, or incredibly intricate natural stone formations, challenging in beauty and uniqueness any man-made carvings. Only aliens visiting from outer space could have created monuments of such unbelievable complexity.

Overjoyed by the feverish thirst for newer and newer vistas, we forgot about the dangers liable to attack the unawares behind every rock, cactus or bush, rattling snakes, scorpions, tarantulas or other nightmarish creatures of the desert the unwelcome intruder often inadvertently disturbs. Yes, insanely enthralled by my woman's sensuously bare calves and thighs so temptingly visible under her shorts, I didn't think for a second how attractive that bare skin might have appeared to other odd creatures, hungrier but less sensually inclined. Carelessly, I failed to inform about the risks, and I doubt I ever would, come the next opportunity. Why let fear spoil the fun? Innocent kids, we acted wholly ignorant of the perils lurking under our sandaled feet. Lady Luck must have watched over us fulltime, making sure nothing awful happened. By the same token it may have been a Higher Authority that protected us as always, our welfare having little to do with luck. Let the reader have a pick!

*

Two hours or so later, we rolled in the great State of Arizona. At the border crossing we were forced to a halt, unlike ever in other states. A brown uniformed official inquired whether we carried over fruits from New Mexico. As I said we didn't, he waved us through without further questioning. Only minutes later, pangs of conscience awoke in my chest, as I remembered the slice of melon, the few tomatoes and the orange in the cooler.

"Why did I have to lie? I had nothing to hide. I didn't smuggle fruit to Arizona. I simply forgot about them. Let's eat the fruit left in the cooler now!"

"What? Haven't you just said we didn't have any?"

"Exactly. That's why the need to gobble them up."

"You are not serious, are you?"

"I am."

"O-My-God, you are a crazy. Okay man-- let's have a fruity snack if this makes you happy. I am thirsty anyway."

With my friend's approval secured, the melon, the orange, and tomatoes, too, slid down fast the pie holes. It never felt so good to turn guiltless although I am sure my pretty friend didn't struggle with such nonsense. All the same, her indifference made me happy, very happy, for the subject was dropped for good. 'Why bother with such trivial matters?' I asked mutely before bringing the affair to closure in my mind, too. Soon the Arizona desert came to rescue as well, as it grabbed our attention wholly.

For a long time I have been living under the impression that this state's name resulted from combining the words *arid* and *zone*. But, the truth is numerous geographic names in the US trace their origins back to some Amerindian words. It seems to be the case with Arizona too, although I remain unconvinced, even after having read this somewhere.

Be that as it may, the zone is arid enough, nearly as desert-like as Nevada. The rock formations in these parts surpassed even what we saw in Texas and New Mexico, the Sierra Madre reaching here levels of incredible surrealism. No artist can possibly imagine these indescribably strange *happenings* of random beauty. One has to see in order to accept it as reality. We couldn't stop the *uh-s* and *ah-s* at each newly discovered stone formations, showing off silently their beauty frozen in time under the intensely bright sun, under the same old orb burning hotter than anywhere, although, subjectively speaking, less oppressively than in Texas. The air of Arizona --perhaps the driest on the North American continent—may have rendered the desert somewhat more bearable. Having reached the limit of our endurance in the oppressive humid heat of Louisiana, Missouri and Texas, we welcomed the change.

This segment of road lasted a little less than an hour time, including the halts for shooting pictures. Everything in Arizona looked worthy to record as visual souvenirs. The sights appeared absolutely pristine, undisturbed even by the common scribbling of some semi-civilized folk, customarily attempting to memorialize their pettiness in sentences like *Marry Lou Ramsey and John Luke Danforth kissed here for the first time in 1984,* or *Hillary and Bob had sworn to mutual love on August 15 1977 exactly at two o' clock PM.*

I hope to be forgiven for mentioning the stupid habits of some of our contemporary brethren, compelled to scribble their fickle mementoes to endure at best fifty-to-sixty years, in comparison to the paintings made by supposedly much more primitive men of past ages, whose superb creations still adorn Alta Mira or other caves, even twenty thousand years later. So much for what we call presently progress!

Inside the same breath, let me pin down plainly that some features of the Arizona desert might easily surpass any concrete or virtual human efforts invested in creating the most sophisticated landscaping splendors. For this reason alone, North America I think must figure on the list of any discriminating tourist of any place on the globe.

As for the heat I spoke too soon as it rapidly became quite hard to endure, forcing us again to gulping down from the various chilled beverages in the cooler at an even faster pace than before.

'Indeed, what could have been the survival chances of the poor souls, men condemned by their foes to crossing the desert on foot, as often seen in Westerns?'

"What are you mumbling about, dear?"

"About the godforsaken guys in Westerns, abandoned to die of thirst, subsequently burned to a crisp under the terrible desert sun."

"Oh?"

My pretty companion elected to stay mum on the subject, probably imagining the pains a victim had to suffer, even if from a perspective a bit different than mine. Clearly though, the Western epic suddenly appeared less fantastic to either of us, particularly when viewed through the prism of experience gained in this tough environment on our own skin.

"Hey, take a peek at the sky. Do you see how deep it's blue? Like ink."

"Why do you think this is?"

"Perhaps due to our proximity to it. The road must run in these parts at a higher elevation than it feels," I dared to approximate.

So it was hills and valleys alternated constantly, higher or deeper as in a grand roller coaster. Signs by the roadside warned about the dangers of overheating radiators.

Turn off your air-conditioning, and don't push your car hard up the hills.

I read these signs scornfully, noticing with pride the temperature needle of my little CRX never going even one millimeter higher than usually. Thank you, modern automotive engineers, for producing vehicles seldom in need of refilling with water off these barrels placed at every hundred yards by the road. Our little machine proved safer from evaporation even than the proverbially resilient desert camel. Hurray, hurray for the good choice I made, hip-hip-hurray for advanced automotive technology!

So our fate continued to rest in good hands, unlike the rocks on the hillsides, sentenced to suffering daily ever-larger cracks under the sun's relentlessly pounding rays, following frosty-chilly nights. Fortunately, the caloric overexposure did not make us burst, causing only a near-boil of our own vital juices in constant need to be cooled down by Cokes. Strangely avenged for many a past admonishment my mistress and others gave me on the account of buying a car without air-conditioning, I felt really satisfied for here in the desert the gismo should have been turned off anyway. Why have something unusable when actually needed most?

Luckily, the adventure through this fiery hell lasted only a little over twenty minutes, to bring forth a sigh of relief as we left the unforgettable experience behind. But I had to rub it in anyway.

"See, my love, what would have been the use of air-conditioning in this inferno?"

"Yeah, how right you are! This makes you really happy, isn't it?"

I didn't deem worthy to answer the sarcasm, my attention already distracted by the strangely named localities coming in quick succession after the long stretch of uninhabited hellish land just left behind-- San Simon, Bowie, Dos Cabelas, Willcox, Cochise, or

Dragon, all reminding the mixture of Spanish and English populations settled all over the area initially.

Following a short stop in Wilcox, in order to replenish our seriously diminished cold beverages, I noticed it was nearly five o'clock in the afternoon. Bucephalos had to quicken the pace. And soon enough we rolled on the highway segment cutting through the vicinity of Tucson. Since plans did not call for a detour through the city, its skyline --made up of several skyscrapers hazed bluish in the distance-- disappeared fast on the left. Too bad! Had the city compare in beauty to its beltway, hemmed in on both sides by blooming oleanders unlike anywhere else, it might have been worth a short stopover. On the other hand, beautiful as Tucson might be, we didn't feel too bad by the omission, as it is rather hard to have regrets about places or events not experienced.

Soon after Tucson retreated behind us, the landscape turned less arid, by the same token, without becoming luxuriant either. Cactuses of infinite variety covered the ground far into the horizon. As most people living in temperate climates, until then we've seen cactuses mostly cultivated in pots, having no idea about the huge size these thorny plants could grow in the wild. So by sunset, our jaws dropped in serious awe when seeing the ten-to-twenty, even thirty feet, unimaginably tall cactuses, pushing straight up heliotropically in a so-called forest aptly named the Organ Pipe National Monument.

"Listen, darling, this *forest* reminds me of Alexander Petöfi's poem –*János Vitéz* (John the Brave)—describing some oaks knocking at the canopy of the sky, and flies as big as cows buzzing about the brave man's head. Unbelievably, here in Arizona cactuses could actually grow as tall as poplars in Romania."

These giant, vertically parallel cactuses, with mostly two or three branch-offs, looked rather as so many pipes of a huge church organ. On that day, this large instrument seemed mostly silent and motionless, hissing only slightly as the mellow breeze of the approaching night touched the *tubes* occasionally. We felt compelled to take pictures, taking full advantage of the intense amber sunset-light.

In one of these, Didonna planted herself pretty at the base of an unbelievably tall, thorny living creature. But through the lens she appeared insignificant, our own life petty and small in comparison. The shutter clicked, and my impression vanished as quickly as the scene imprinted on the film's emulsion. What happened during that short duration of time, why the flash of self-awareness emerged in my fleetingly awoken conscience I can't say. Who can decipher the deep mysteries of mind's workings behind the scene? Only one thing, for sure the attendant memory mattered, as it never faded away.

Strangely enough, when reviewing the developed pictures a few days later, my slightly vain mistress reproached the shots' pettiness, for her figure having been barely distinguishable in the environment.

"So this is how puny and insignificant you see me?"

"Oh don't be ridiculous!"— But my attempt at deflecting lacked conviction.

Vanity, vanity! Then the thought bubbled up whether our little adventure merited our countless arguments and exaggerated worries, particularly when projected in the wide canvas of the entire living Universe? Are we really more than the haphazard struggle of two grains of dust barely discernable in its vastness?

Yes, I understood and readily acknowledged my concubine's displeasure, but what could I have done differently? How to treat fairly some sensuously shaped thighs against the majestic beauty of the Organ Cactus Forrest without sacrificing one, or the other? On the other hand, how could the woman I pretended to love accept my dry, objective judgment without complaining? In my struggle to see the situation from both perspectives I faced a dilemma. So I kept my mouth shut, the paradox locked away safely in my heart.

It must have been around eight o'clock, when at a bifurcation we had to choose either to go forward on route-10 or change over to route-8, cutting through the desert toward Yuma. Enchanted by the just discovered beauty of aridity, we decided on the second alternative, avoiding Phoenix for the sake of San Diego. According to some expert advise, crossing any desert in the dark could turn fast into a seriously risky affair. But this is exactly what we did, in spite of all reasonable precautions and warnings.

However I rarely feared nature, on arguments similarly shaky as the subjectivity of my girlfriend's love for the artificial urban environments. Perils, I thought might lurk everywhere, but the fact we finally agreed on something seemed for once reassuring. Doesn't it feel fantastic to find harmony with your beloved half?

The previously jagged forms of relief disappeared behind us, replaced by flatlands at the same time as the fast approaching nightfall poured blue ink over the receding hills' silhouettes, across the entire landscape dotted by only a few barely visible lights in the distance. Before long, our path cut through pitch-black darkness. The strong headlight of brave Bucephalos bore an inverted cone deep into the yellow-bordered road ahead, making the white alternating bands in the middle induce an eerily hallucinogenic effect, as they slid under the car with dizzying speed.

Under such conditions, the slightest driving error could result in an accident, to stick the unfortunate motorist stuck in the sand at least until morning. This was the best-case scenario, since no police or service vehicles adventured deeper than twenty miles in the desert after sunset.

Perfectly aware of hazards, I preferred to keep uncommunicative, gravely mum, but resolute on driving as carefully as possible. Whether my partner sensed these apprehensions I can't say, however this time she didn't fall asleep, helping my staying alert by her incessant chatter. How soothing her meaningless words sounded that night, how sweet her musical voice in my ears, as Bucephalos cut an unending swath of lightening bolts through the increasingly darker and deeper night.

In spite of my determination, less than an hour later, the ensuing exhaustion finally extracted the best of me. At the first rest area about to come up I gave up.

"I must halt a bit here, no matter what. At least for a short while."

"Sure dear, let us have a little rest."

Again we seemed wonderfully tuned on the same wavelength.

In the parking lot not a single soul. All decent people at home safely tucked in bed at that late hour of night.

In the wake of the car's soft purr, the sudden silence of the fathomless, dark, engulfing cosmic space hit hard, weighing heavily on our slightly bewildered souls.

"Wo-ooh-wa-ah-uuh-booh, boooh" —I wailed in jest—"isn't this the best spot for a dialogue with dark lord of hell Beelzebub Himself?"

"Shut up, Dorel. You don't scare me. Don't provoke the devil, as he might be heeding your call." To my amusement, her tone betrayed a tiny bit of alarm.

"You're right. Then let's lay down on the asphalt, and stare at the stars." Before I knew it, she did just that, stretching out quickly at my feet, obviously to prove her courage.

Surprised by the unusual eagerness to cooperate, stupidly enough I followed suit, and stretched out alongside. Neither of us gave the slightest thought about the dangers lurking in the desert, about the fact we had few reasons to fear Satan, and a whole lot more to worry about the equally devilish scorpions, snakes, and other frightening creatures of the night. Remarkably irresponsible, we let our gaze roam free across the sky, among the countless stars shinning bright above in the infinite void as perhaps nowhere else in the world. Only the All Mighty God-protected our souls and bodies.

As for myself I fell prey to a fleeting shudder, to a sensation almost impossible to endure, about the terrible loneliness of the living human individual, just a little speck of dust lost in the immensity of cosmic space! Who are we? Why are we here? Where are we going, whence we came to planet Earth, revolving seemingly forgotten and insignificant somewhere at the periphery of the Milky Way?

No answer from above, either to confirm or reject my questions, nothing came out of the dense darkness, vaguely lit by zillions of stars 360-degrees all around the planet. Only the soft breeze touched my face, as if to alleviate the anxiety the impenetrable black velvet of night awoke in my barely flickering soul. Sensing similar emotions in my sisterly beloved half's heart, I whispered as softly as humanly possible:

"Why must man appeal to religion when lost in perfect loneliness?"

At registering my words she rolled slowly over, to press her gentlest kiss ever on my cheek. I figured instantly what she thus said --and rightly so. Faced by the Infinite Universe, all men and women alike become the same lost little children aching for God's love. And what are kisses, if not the sacred human seal of His Endless Love?

For those few heartbeats I am sure the two of us loved each other deeply, much beyond the transient pleasures of flesh, two ephemerally separated spirits destined to reunite as fitting parts of the uniquely grand, miraculously alive Universe. At that instant, nothing more to ask or to receive, except return the kiss in silence, equally gently. My question had been at last answered, and I am sure my sweetheart's too.

Then, out of this dark velvet of nothingness, I noticed a tiny spot of red light, flickering on and off at a distance, a little above the outline of my friend's body. We were not alone. Another human kin lay stretched out on the asphalt ten-fifteen paces away, drawing rhythmically off a cigarette. This unknown brother or sister must have entertained thoughts similar to ours, I mused. The perceived simultaneity of our existence made me feel a bit less lonely. But only a blink later, Philomela's sad face sneaked surreptitiously in my thoughts.

'Yeah, yeah, she too must be there somewhere, crying her heart out for the right to be together with her half.' My just found happiness tasted suddenly bitter, a foul smelling afterthought, a hard to swallow lump, overheated in the desert atmosphere, stuck in my throat. For the first time since our departure, the sad face of my wife came alive more vividly than ever since our rupture. My heart skipped a minuscule painful beat.

"What's the matter with you? What is it? Tell me, tell me, I heard Didonna out of the blue."

"Oh nothing, dear, absolutely nothing," I muttered softly, and marveled as I withdrew from the face just kissed: "God, the instinct of a woman!"

Minutes of deep silence gained the upper hand as we rested on the warm ground, eyes in the sky. At some point, prompted by a mute signal we returned to Bucephalos in tandem. My suddenly born irrepressible sadness my mistress not only sensed, but countered it too, more loquaciously than ever, succeeding somehow to lend me a strange new reinvigorated will to go on. Down here on Earth self-preservation usually wins all bets.

"Come on, love, cheer up, I am here now, your always adoring woman, ready to make all your dreams come true." Her voice scintillated, inflections so playful, gestures so funny that her unexpected exuberance rubbed off at last-- my mood resettled, not to honest-to-God jubilance, but at least to my everyday cynicism. Good enough!

It was past midnight when we crossed the Arizona-California border to Yuma, a new place, and a new adventure.

It took the better part of an hour to find lodging. Thoroughly drained of energy following the nocturnal pass through the desert, at first completely disoriented in the wide open city, we crisscrossed countless highways winding mostly between closed shopping centers, illumined empty office buildings and deserted parking lots. Finally, as out of nowhere, the well-lit sign of a *Best Western* motel rekindled our hopes. Had we lost a few more minutes in aimless wandering, our bodies might have collapsed in the increasingly unbearable heat, flesh and spirit crushed under the weight of lethal exhaustion. Never before in my life had I been so tired, so wasted. Summer heat felt nowhere so oppressive.

Safely settled in the room, looking out through the large glass patio-door to the aqua blue swimming pool, its lure never ever so uninviting. I pulled the shutters down, to obliterate the view without the tiniest hesitation, or temptation for a quick dip.

"Good," came my friend's approval curtly.

As I turned saw the woman hastily casting off the sweat-soaked blouse, shorts, bra and panties, as if no male present to witness her disrobing. It was obvious she did not advance the slightest sensual innuendo.

In instant imitation I followed in her steps equally shameless. Although together in the shower no romantic thoughts interfered, the female naked body looked nothing more than that, pounds of white flesh voided of sensuality. Mine must have appeared much the same. A bit refreshed by the cold-water stream, we crashed our wet bodies on the sheets, and quickly turned off the lights, within and without.

"Good night, sweetie." She squeezed my hand gently, soon the slowed down breathing betrayed her having instantly fallen asleep.

The gentleness of her reassuring touch should have left a warm impression in my heart. This time it didn't. Instead of properly appreciating the woman's token of affection, my thoughts wandered off to Philomela. I tried in vain to figure what she might be doing alone. Suddenly, her phantom-like pale image loomed sad before my eyes, to persist silently crying for a long, long while in the dark. 'What the hell is happening?' On this perplexing note I wandered off, too, in a dreamless, lead-like sleep.

*

We opened eyes six hours later, two naked bodies in the same position, stretched out on the sheets in the half opened bed.

"Dorel, are you awake?"

"Yes, I am."

"I am famished."

"Me too."

Pushed by an invisible spring my gazelle jumped up first, and commenced her daily protocol of preparing coffee. My gaze followed, this time quite pleased by the sight of her superb, mature nakedness, moving about the room unrestrained. As if seeing her for the first time, I felt the irrepressible urge to touch. Once the water on the burner, she returned in bed, and climbed on top of me, a clear down payment toward a little innocent hanky-panky play.

I delayed my reaction on purpose, perfectly satisfied just to hold her tight.

"What's the matter? Is something wrong?"

"No dear, nothing's wrong."

"Oh?" But she couldn't go on, having to jump up, as the water began gurgling in the pot. Attending to her duties meticulously as always, lucky me, she did not feel like, or forgot to pursue her intent any further.

Quietly I thanked Good God for my luck. During the previous night's interlude on the desert floor, something in my heart must have changed. Yes, I still loved the woman in the room with me, but my passion for her somehow diminished a tad. So much for the male's much-touted emotional stability! I thought in muted self-irony.

Before returning on the turnpike we crisscrossed the streets of Yuma anew, in search of a grocery store for the food and drinks in the cooler had to be replenished. Not much to excite the imagination in this flat vast town scattered in between deserts, except for the gated leisure communities for the retired, artificial oases providing everything modern civilization may offer the old-timers and the younger visitors alike. Alongside many septa- and –octogenarians barely moving their worn bodies under the hot sun, we too found everything needed in a Safeway supermarket.

By the time we parked the sun rose in the sky high enough to heat the air again to unbearable degrees of discomfort.

"Why would anyone want to live in this hell?" I asked, but got answered before my partner could have done it, as we stepped in the almost chilly premises of the super sized grocery store. Modern technology makes today surviving in comfort almost anywhere possible.

True, by the twentieth century's conclusion, science and technology made living possible in the desert not only for the suffering rheumatics, but for healthier people as well. The landscaping all around the hard-edged building, designed in clear-cut postmodern eclectic style, consisted mainly of sparse, but exotic palm trees and tropical flowery arrangements. The only spoiling element, probably on purpose somewhat isolated within this man-made environment, might have been the parking lot, filled to capacity by endless rows of huge gas-guzzlers, ostentatiously opulent Lincoln, Cadillac behemoths, several Mercedes and Beamers among them.

"How insecure must these old-folk feel for needing the succor of such impossibly inefficient cars?"

"Well, this is old age for you."

In agreement once again, we found Yuma depressing, in spite of all the advantages it may provide for some rheumatic senior citizen.

"I wish never to live in this town," my friend quipped in conclusion.

This way receded Yuma back in personal history, to become fast just a faint imprint on our memory banks.

A few minutes, and we crossed the border to California, to White Sands Desert, a vast blinding space stretching westward right off the Yuma city limits. This land seemed more barren than we ever seen before. From facts learned in school, movies or literature in my imagination White Sands came closest to the Sahara Desert. On either sides of the road, the wind built up dunes out of the finest imaginable sand particles, their reflected glare so strong as to force shading the eyes. We reached instinctively for sunglasses. Nothing seemed to disturb this vast sea of dunes, no visible fauna or flora evident in this oven's glowing high and dry heat.

"What a pure bleached inferno! Even grand master Beelzebub might find this repelling!" I uttered involuntarily, to which my companion only bobbed her head.

It took a quarter of an hour of driving for the land to rise ever so slowly, and reach at last the peak forty-five minutes later. At the summit the desert ended abruptly, passing miraculously on the way down into a lush green valley, mile by mile ever more akin in looks and feel to the Italian Riviera than anything else. Lower on the down slopes, red-roofed and white-walled elegant haciendas amid rainbow-colored flowery gardens, exotic light green bushes and dark green cypresses sparkled as only a divinely-inspired Van Gogh-like artist could have brushed on the canvas of a most intense azure-blue sky. Here and there, variously shaped swimming pools reflected their blueness as if to render on purpose the whole picture into a grand impressionist painting.

Suddenly I understood California's attraction, why its lure so irresistible for so many. Our mood changed as well. A super-lively Didonna couldn't hold in check her glee, exclaiming with childish joy, compelled impulsively to emphasize every new picturesque vista verbally.

"Look at that villa, do you see the cypresses by that swimming pool? Oh my, I never ever dreamed for such mix of splendors possible in one and the same place. Good Lord, thousand thanks for granting me admittance in this Paradise."

This unrestrained enthusiasm proved infectious in spite of bombast. True, the sights seemed out of this world, breathtaking indeed, of a quality the traveler expects to find perhaps only in the enchanted lands around the Mediterranean Sea. But then, to my new surprise, my concubine's overplayed effusiveness, her exaggerated behavior became a bit histrionic, not at all suited to her character as I assumed it initially, making me wonder whether I've seen everything about the woman I moved in with so impulsively, to eventually marry. Again and again since our shack-up, a renewed shadow of doubt sneaked surreptitiously in my heart. Another heartbeat, and her words no longer reached me, only a faint echo of a strangely muted, distant background noise persisted in my ears. Why the extra notch down in my heart occurred precisely then, I can't even guess today. Although I doubt it, one day I might fashionably submit myself to an analyst for the explanation. Until then, I can only say that my companion's unrelenting, rhythmically musical chatter had mostly the effect of recalling a past believed long forgotten, namely the fateful night, when I brutally informed Philomela about my decision to leave her for good, for the seemingly irresistible charms of Didonna.

*

The scene happened in the basement laundry room of our townhouse in Damascus.

It must have been well past midnight when, instead of going to bed following our chit-chat over the nightly cups of tee-- enjoyed usually together after Philomela's returning home from work—out of the blue she had been overcome by the urge to do the laundry, accumulated over the week. Perplexed about the unjustified urgency I had to ask.

"What the hell is wrong with you, why not leave the laundry for tomorrow? You really have to do it right now?"

"Yes. Our dirty laundry has to be taken care of right this minute. Tell me, dear husband, how long are you going to prolong your stupid affair with that evil woman? Don't even think to deny it. I am well aware of everything going on between you and that bitch."

She didn't name Didonna, but I guessed right away whom her anger had aimed. Still, disregarding the severity of the admonition, for starters I feigned to feeling a bit offended, the hurt innocent, little-trusted spouse.

"What are you talking about? Are you out of your mind?"

"Come on, Dorel, stop playing this silly game. I have lived long enough with you to learn all your tricks. Okay, I accepted your cheating once or twice with this so-called *friend* of ours. I noticed right from the outset her attitude toward you, as well as your eagerness to getting better acquainted with her --so to speak. But now the time had come to end this foul *friendship* for good. Try for once to walk in my shoes."

Philomela halted, apparently waiting for the effect, while frantically searching for my eyes. Realizing I wasn't going to reply she went on, adopting a faked sarcastically self-reproaching tone.

"Maybe it was my fault to leave you alone for such long periods of time. Trusting you has been truly my mistake. But what's enough is enough. It is high time you end the affair. If you do I promise to forget the whole thing. All right? Please don't try my patience any further."

She started down the stairs, as if signaling the end of our nasty exchange. But I couldn't leave it at that. Philomela's sudden assertiveness, her firmness in dictating what I was supposed to do took me aback at first, but then it irked me furious. I followed her down.

"Hey, woman, how dare you attack and accuse me like this without a shred of evidence? Who do you think I am, your little kid, obedient slave or whatnot?"

She stopped dead, turned and faced me.

"Listen, I am your wife. And don't you forget wives have the express right to question their husbands." Then, she continued her walk.

"No, they don't. Not this way."

At this point we landed in basement.

"Oh yes, exactly so. Be assured dear spouse I could do much worst than this, and you know it. So shut up and put an end to the affair with that blonde whore. Okay? This is the only thing I demand from you, and will not say one more word about it. I promise."

"Well, well, I can't give you the satisfaction just like that. And since you pushed the issue to the point of explosion, I must confess, yes I'm in love with the *blond bitch*. More than that, intend to move in with her. Is this clear? But don't you worry I will not ask for a divorce, fully prepared to fulfill my contractual obligations, except the part concerning affection. Nobody, but nobody in this universe can force me to love you."

"What? What did you say?"

A pause ensued, then I saw the change within Philomela rising up from her guts, the slow evolution from cool reasoning to unrestrained and desperate rage, gradually shaking her body and soul to the core, not unlike the premonitory gurgling of a volcano about to erupt. And then the lava of anger burst open, bitterly bringing forth at last the unavoidable tears and reproaches.

"So, after all we went through together-- leaving the old country, crossing illegally from Czechoslovakia to Austria, cohabiting with the human dredge and dirt in the refugee camp, waiting for months and months for the American visas, then the hard beginning in this country, enduring the humiliation of accepting the worst menial jobs in the world for the sake of our survival, and this is my reward? Then at the end of all this, just simply you confess to no longer loving me?

Oh no, this won't stand. Now, when finally over our worst sacrifices, you simply want to shack up with this shamelessly insolent, clearly trespassing woman? Who do **you** think **I** am? Have you gone totally bonkers, or what?"

"No, Philomela, I am not crazy. I am deadly serious. Why continue like this, the two of us living a lie? But as you say, for the sake of the past, for all we went through together, I am ready to fulfill my conventional obligations as before. This is a contractual matter I must respect. As for the affective part, the ball I toss now in your court. It will be up to you either to accept my proposal, or sue for divorce. Whatever your choice, it'll be all the same for me."

Momentarily unable to register and digest what I said, she just stood there, a long while frozen to the spot, her large dark eyes bored madly in mine. Finally she blinked and whispered, as almost to herself only.

"All this for Madame Didonna, strangely enough for another old bitch. How ridiculous?" She paused briefly. "Man, I wonder what sort of middle age crises must you be going through? Couldn't you have at least selected a woman a bit younger and more attractive? That I might accept easier. But to leave me for an old whore don't you think is way too absurd?"

"It's not about her age at all, and not about my middle age crisis either. Philomela, please understand it so happens I am in love with that *whore* you so deeply despise. Simply said, I fell for her charms in earnest. At long last I found my true soul mate, and for that a human being, any honest character must sacrifice everything as for a most sacred cause. Love has to be always the final objective, any sane being's pursuit for happiness until death. For our relationship to end in flames and ashes I feel honestly sorry, but why betray the salvation of my own soul for anybody in the world? Try to see my point."

Uttering these terrible words, my soon ensuing emotion took the best off me too, against all efforts to keeping it bottled up. All the same, that minute I fervently believed what I said, particularly the part about not betraying my soul.

Thus had I set in motion the final tragic scene. Before able to do anything to forestall it, Philomela hit the ground with a thump, then stretched out on the laundry room's cold concrete floor-- her chest heaved terribly under the freshly inflicted pain, her whole body convulsed by spasms of crying that couldn't erupt fast enough.

That night, a strange new power gained the upper hand over my emotions, deep within my chest the spigot of pity turned off, then toggled on again for a torrent of disgust, instead.

"Come on, for Chris's sake get up. Stop the hysterics for I am not leaving right this minute. Let's go upstairs, sleep on it and discuss the whole thing in the morning under the benefit of daylight. Okay?"

Instead of becalming, my intent at appeasing only aggravated the crisis, and before long the repressed voice of the wounded female broke free through the walls of the heart's prison-- desperate waves of liberated pain echoed between the basement walls as prolonged howls of a wild animal caged for the first time.

Dejectedly helpless, all my compassion died on the spot, mind emptied, the resulting void filled by the triplets of disdain, fear and cruelty. It took less than a heartbeat to make up my mind, for the merciless decision to leave Philomela behind right then--, but not before rubbing some salt in the just rejected wife's freshly inflicted wound, and increase the twitching pain by another cruel notch.

"Fine. If this is all you can say, so be it. I see no use for any further civilized discussions. Good bye."

I dashed upstairs, thrown some clothing items in a handbag, and made my exit slamming the door as hard as I could for the proper dramatic effect. On the deserted streets, drove as a maniac, but couldn't take my mind off the image of Philomela's crumpled wriggling body, a wretched lump of suffering flesh on the cold basement floor.

Ten minutes later I rang the bell at Didonna's.

She opened the door, not much surprised at my arrival. In the bedroom she helped me undress, tucked me in bed as the good nurse, lied at my side, and then pulled my body gently in her arms, in a motherly embrace that broke me down to a soft sob.

"Calm down, dear, everything will be all right. You'll see. Hush my little big boy, hush."

Her world sank straight in my soul pushed instantly into a deep black hole of nothingness. In the morning --a Saturday of early October-- I opened my eyes, still cuddled in Didonna's receiving velvety arms. Her sky-blue gaze calmly meeting mine, just a glint of satisfaction showing through a smile that I took for a sign of gentle love.

"What would your lordship like for breakfast?"

After that awful night, enveloped in a renewed welcome womanly embrace, Philomela's fate miraculously ceased to trouble my thoughts seriously for a long, long time, if at all, in spite of seeing her in person every now and again for practical reasons—firstly to collect the rest of my personal belongings. All the same, for me she and all the past about her practically had died. Yet, each time I saw the old wife following that fateful night in the laundry room, I noticed unwillingly how she appeared to have gained the new bearings of restrained gravity and dignified composure. Only her dark eyes, portals into the human soul, those for-ever-piercing coal-black-eyes seemed shaded by melancholically reproachful spiritual mascara.

THROUGH THE LAND
OF MAKE-BELIEVE

Didonna's chatter surged back to my ears the moment we began rolling down the valley toward San Diego. But her words sounded for the first time strangely insignificant. In spite of the vivacious intonations, sensible and affectionate as always, their sweetness felt artificial, the syllables hollow. Why I can't really figure. But on that first late morning in California, a tiny link broke open in my chain of illicit love. I took a glance, and noticed on her freckled sunbathed visage the zillion tinny lines of aging that for the first time displeased. Man, why fancy yourself as the rational animal? What made me notice the unpleasant details I never seen before?

It was nearly midday as we passed by a string of exotically named localities --Bostonia, El Cajon, La Mesa, Spring Valley, Lemon Grove, and National City—before reaching the southern outskirts of San Diego, the town of Chula Vista. Judging by traffic-density, the appearance of city buses, the beautifully sleek red streetcar running north south on the main street, the elegant stores, modern buildings, and streaming passers-by, it felt like the suburbia of a definitely larger metropolitan area.

Chula Vista --a name for some reason I found onomatopoeically funny-- is at least as large as the rest of San Diego, even if not equally famous or beautiful. In proximity of the border, the town borrowed some Mexican influence that made for a vaguely chaotic appearance, when compared to the urban refinement of downtown proper. Indeed, Chula Vista is the Southernmost American outpost before crossing the border to Mexico, right to the town of Tijuana. But before a bit more exploring we had to find a hotel room for at least two nights, as our planed sojourn called for.

We literally stumbled to a *Best Western* hotel, to find a room quicker than expected. The price, although a little stiff, according to the pretty and polite receptionist, was a very good deal when compared to the competition. Quickly convinced by the young lady, I accepted the offer on the spot, to my friend's instant dismay.

"I see now where you stand. You'd pay any price for something advertised by a pretty lady, isn't it?"

"Come on, dear, your jealousy is silly. The girl knows what she's talking about."

"Yes, ma'am" --came the young missy's eager confirmation--, "ours is the best deal in town."

"See, what did I tell you?"

"Okay, okay, I was joking", put my companion period to the discussion, a shrug and a barely noticeable mocking grimace on her face, which, to my utter dismay, I noticed.

On this unpleasant note I drove Bucephalos to the room's location, mentally prepared for the chore of dragging the luggage in, as usually. Then, once in the room, the same Didonna threw herself out of the blue on the bed, in a shameless, erotically provocative posture and said feigning a little girl's innocence.

"Do you really need my help? What's the hurry? Why not take a little rest, plenty of time for the luggage. Better jump on top of me right now. O-my-love, I'm so badly hungry for you."

"What?" I begun *sotto voice*, but couldn't say more, as my horny gazelle jumped up, and pulled me down over her.

Before I knew it, or had time to protest, she almost tore my shirt off, pulled the trousers down, and all this while slipping out of her few skimpy summer garments, only to savagely launch into the wildest, hottest passionate love feast she ever attempted until then—at least to my benefit. Dumbfounded, half shocked, irrevocably overwhelmed by the contagious eroticism, my body reacted promptly, instantly warmed up to my own absolutely unrestrained response.

This sort of animally unchained love, although thoroughly satisfying for the flesh by its searing temperature alone, seldom heralds an enduring erotic experience, as it often may end up prematurely. It is precisely what happened. Stretched out on my back in abandoned relaxation, body and spirit drained, panting in the wake of the drenching embrace, the only need I felt was to light a cigarette.

Following my naughty accomplice's fast consuming act, obviously tuned to the same wavelength she sprung up lightly as *Bamby*, pulled two sticks out of the pack, lit them, then back on the bed, handed me one. Before nestled again sweetly over my right arm, she planted several soft honey-sweet little kisses on my heaving chest. For several indefinable minutes I saw her and myself elevated to the ninth heaven in true togetherness. Time stopped dead in its track. During this imprecise interval only God knows how long, our love reached the point of perfection, even if oh-so-ephemerally. Sometimes the power of spontaneity can bring forth the short bloom of miraculously exotic flowers!

As the recovering alcoholic from the unexpected gift of a last drink, I noticed *en-passant* how easily can burning flesh erase the doubts and guilt elicited by an adulterous affair, how simple is to forget the worn-out wife for the sake of a new woman rekindling the old fire in the nearly cold hearth. But as all things are bound to pass, the emotional roller coaster reversed course soon, my petty mind returned to the interrupted chores, still waiting undone outside. With renewed self-discipline I reminded this to my still hot concubine, who responded in a strange way only by gently, but hungrily rolling over me again, her hands in feverish search for the uniquely erogenous zones on my body.

"What are you doing? Let us bring the luggage in first." But the she-devil kept whispering, her voice strangely hoarsened, kisses burning on the side of my neck, and steamy breath in my ears.

"Come, old stud, love me again, this time harder than ever. My thirst for you today is unquenchable."

My answer suffocated before it started, her lips invaded in a frenzy of redoubled passion, irresistible for the flesh that, to my dismay, responded promptly in kind. O proud masculine spirit, how feeble your resistance when faced by carnal temptation!

Our renewed erotic session did not come to resolution as quickly as before, lasting infinitely longer, to the point of almost lethal exhaustion. However, lucidity had to return eventually with vengeance, to the attendant crash of self-contemplation in spite of the inertial persistence, of the unwillingness to surrender, for proving material fatigue victorious, vying once more to bring all physical activities to a halt. This happened as well to us at last.

Suddenly scrutinized through the eye of cold, rational objectivity, our recurring scene became tenuously tortured. From the virtual perspective of above the bed, at this point our bodies seemed engaged in an act resembling a struggle rather then the expression of unchained love. It took just a few heartbeats thereafter for me to begin secretly laughing at the sight of the funny-looking, disrobed woman perched atop me, fighting hard to bring two tired bodies to the much desired but, oh, so frustratingly delayed finish. At last my lover's turn to spend herself off occurred in a whimper, her limp, and soft, sweaty body coming to rest on mine as lead. Eagerly welcoming this conclusion I responded instinctively with a thank you note, delivered a gentle kiss, however hesitatingly, on my partner's chin. Why the hesitation one may ask? Because for an instant shorter than a blink, in a shadier corner of the room I glimpsed the large dark saddened eyes of Philomela --one pearly teardrop run down her cheek.

"My, my, what the hell is wrong with me?" I wondered, secretly letting my flattened passion turn to pity, at the same instant aware that my partner's eroticism and words were meant honestly only to please.

"Thank you, thank you dear sweet man. A woman must always express graceful thanks to the man who just filled her emptiness with love. Thank you for lording so kindly over my body, and please accept my honest appreciation for the gift."

It wasn't the first time Didonna expressed herself bombastically in the wake of lovemaking, utterances I never quite knew how to interpret. Is there one lonely man on the planet to penetrate the secrets of the female soul? Perhaps Molier guessed it right in the following approximation: *a woman's ultimate desire and ambition is to achieve the undivided love of a man.*

Gradually, Philomela's image faded, a dark void replaced her phantom with my irresistible wish to disappear forever in the abyss of a dreamless slumber. My counterpart in lovemaking must have felt the same, as she fell asleep even before I did. An hour or so passed for my eyes to reopen, my friend's spent body still softly asleep on my arm, one of her long bare legs heavily, possessively weighing down over my hip.

'Hmm,' I mused, 'too much erotic activity might just as well kill a man.' It has been a fleeting thought, no anger meant against my female partner, the world, or myself. On the contrary, a dumb smile painted on my mug. Love could weigh heavy on the human soul, but the lack of it might be even harder to bear.

"Hey dolly, wake up, wake up," I whispered, trying to extricate my body from under her soft, heavy pin-down.

"Okay, okay, I will," the satisfied woman sniveled cat-like, and cuddled even closer to my chest, mumbling; "Just a little bit more, just a bit more." She turned face brightened up, lips puckered for a kiss as her hand slipped, perhaps involuntarily, gently south on my nap-refreshed body.

"O no, pretty tigress, definitely no. We still have some chores to do."

"You evil little ingrate thorp, you don't deserve my affection." But her tone of voice didn't betray any hurt. To prove it she jumped up, and added; "You're right, I must never again spoil you as I did today. Anyway, I am famished, so you better take us to a good restaurant. I don't feel like setting the table. O-my-love, why won't we eat out today?" and before waiting for my acquiescence, she disappeared in the bathroom. Soon the shower got running.

'Yes, princess, you're right today we deserve to have lunch in town.'

Half an hour later, chores completed, we rolled victorious in sunny San Diego, in my eyes one of the most beautiful city in the United States.

According to records, the place explored and claimed by Spain in 1542 was the site of the first of Fr. Junipero missions and the Presidio fort, nowadays a metropolis grown to more than 800.000 inhabitants, an important cultural, medical, oceanographic center, as well as a resort famous worldwide for its Aquatic Park and for the enormous, unique zoo. The city may be justifiably proud about several other historic sites as well, the famous Cabrillo National Monument among them.

After digesting these factoids, we altered our plans slightly by allotting San Diego a few more days and nights than initially contemplated, to allow for a more leisurely exploration.

Following a delightfully light lunch of mixed salad bathed in a fruity Californian dressing, and topped by strips of grilled chicken-- perhaps the healthiest possible meal we ever tasted, asking nonetheless for the mandatory wash-down of an ameliorating, crisp, refreshing Napa Valley wine-- we launched into the adventure in earnest, for starters just aimlessly cruising along the main streets of downtown, and then along the breathtakingly spectacular coastline.

The first impressions—always the most pregnant-- proved overwhelming. Under the after noon's glassy clear sunlight, the city appeared in permanent bloom, colorful flowery explosions delighting the eyes wherever we cared to look. My more than vivacious companion barely controlled her over-spilling enthusiasm.

"Look at those fantastic red flowers. What are they? Tell me, tell me, do you know their names?"

Fortunately, before I could admit to my ignorance, she aimed her attention elsewhere.

"You see that surreal-looking tree over there? Oh my, what a marvelous town this is. Don't you wish we could live here? Let's move in this paradise. Please! Forget Washington, and all our troubles will vanish. I promise."

"Oh yes, dear girl, I'd move gladly, unfortunately that's quite impossible at the present time, and you know it too well."

"Why must you be always negative? Anything is possible if you honestly want it. Don't you love me? Be daring for once in your life. Divorce the wife, breake away from the past. Can I ask at least this much from you?"

Her outburst left me nearly speechless. Indeed, why not move? Then Philomela's saddened face came alive again, bringing my mind back to stark reality. But, unwilling to spoil my mistress' childishly wild exuberance, I answered softly in my usually guarded way.

"I wish it was so simple. You know the divorce could take a long time before becoming final. Philomela wouldn't agree to let me go just like that. She threw it to my face in just so many words: '*my dear beloved husband, I will never let you go. I wouldn't give that bitch of yours the satisfaction. I swear to this'.*"

"Oh gosh, how mean and selfish! But listen, Philomela won't be able to hold on to your tail indefinitely, if no longer part and parcel of the marriage. She is a woman much like I am. She wouldn't want to live alone forever. Don't you understand this much?"

"I understand quite well, also know a threat when hear it"

"What threat? Can she really be that much of a threat?"

"Oh yes she can. I divorce her, and she would take me for everything."

"And the woman had the gall to call **me** a bitch! Anyway, what's there for you to lose, the mortgage, the other debts? Big deal! Why cling on to those?"

"Look, even by letting everything go I will still have to pay up. You must surely know how divorce works in this country."

"Of course I know, but since we both work may have enough left over to live together a decent life anyway. Hard as divorce may be people survive it. I went myself trough one. Believe me breaking marriage never hindered a strong character from pursuing happiness. People divorce and get married again. The right to love can be reaffirmed again and again, isn't it? Is this not the story of modernity? You do love me, don't you?"

"Sure I do. You know it, but... but… well, this is not the best time or place to discuss the issue."

"Why not?"

"Because divorce is too important not be approached seriously. Deciding on spur of the moment, or on a whim might be quite perilous for us. But I promise to weigh the alternatives once at home again. You will get my definitive answer then. As for now let's enjoy our vacation together, forget all other troubles."

"Frankly, you sort of disappoint me."

A long, heavy silence ensued, as we wandered inadvertently back to the streets of Chula Vista, back to square one, so to speak in all respects.

"Okay dear, so be it", she reemerged first. "I agree to suspend this discussion for now, but here is my warning: I will expect your decision two weeks after we had returned home. Then you will have to tell me whether you want **me**, or **Philomela**. Okay? -- End of discussion. Now let's go to Tijuana."

"What? Why Tijuana? Why now?"

"See the sign over there?"

Indeed, a large traffic across the street sign pointed straight to Mexico.

"Yes, I see the sign. So what?"

"Well, I want to go to Tjuana right now."

Considering the gravity and firmness of her tone, as well as her willingness to postpone the difficult discussion about my purported divorce, I happily obliged.

"Fine. We go to Mexico. But this time we'll leave Bucephalos parked by the hotel."

"I surely hope you don't plan on walking to Tijuana, do you?"

"No, not at all, no need to walk out of the US. See that sleek tram just stopped at the station?"

She turned her head to my pointing, and saw the red city rail car taking on and discharging passengers. Clearly visible on the tram's lit indicator was the destination *end station Tijuana*, the first locality right across the border.

True to my word, once Bucephalos got safely stabled in the parking, we boarded the Siemens-made, ultra sleek streetcar toward the border. The trip proved short and uneventful, the scenery unfolding through the train's large windows rather drab, much the same as other peripheral American industrial areas.

The actual crossing had to be accomplished on foot, through some clanking, noisy revolving metallic gates. Flanked in by streaming crowds, we walked straight ahead to find ourselves before knew it body and soul right in Tijuana proper. Five more minutes, and we mixed in the hustle and bustle of Mexico, together with the flood of mostly American citizens, returning —as I learned a bit later --from work in San Diego, to their homes at the other side of the border. Pushed along in this out-flowing crowd, at one point initiated a conversation with a friendly, clean, geek looking young man.

"Sir, please excuse my asking why so many Americans are headed this afternoon to Mexico? Anything special today?"

"Oh no, not at all. Most folk are returning home. The day for tourists is on Sundays," so the man informed promptly, then asked.

"I detected an accent. May I ask where are you from?"

"We came originally from Romania, but have been living in Washington for over twenty years."

"Well, I see now what's your wonder about. The explanation is that a lot of professionals work in San Diego, but reside in Tijuana's gated communities."

"Gated communities, what's that?"

"Simply said these are luxurious, walled in residential developments, well separated from the poor Mexican neighborhoods. You see rents on this side of the border could be as much as seventy five percent cheaper than in San Diego."

"Ah, I get it."

From this point on the discussion revolved around the theme, to the chagrin of my saddened mistress, whose dream of moving to California had suddenly and unmercifully crushed to bits on the hard rocks of reality. We learned that renting a simple two-bedroom apartment in San Diego could be at least forty percent pricier than in Washington, absolutely unaffordable for our pockets. In Maryland we owned our houses outright, and the monthly mortgage payments amounted for either of us to substantially less than even the cheapest rents in San Diego. On top of it, if moving we had to find new jobs.

Soon after parting with the young Californian, I itched to rub this in under my girlfriend's pretty pointed up nose.

"You see, dolly, there is no way for our kind to live in this town, even if were to earn as much as back home."

"In other words what you tell me is that I might as well forget about marrying you? Is that it?"

"Hey," --I was about to remind the woman furiously of our recently concluded pact, but wised up, and lowered my tone to softer notes: "No. Don't be silly, I didn't mean it like that. Surely I want to marry you, really do, but allow me to give you my definite answer at home. Didn't we agree on that?"

"Fine, fine…" but her tone sounded unconvincing, in spite of the obviously feigned satisfaction. On my part, the efforts to re-directing her attention at enjoying our vacation seemed for a moment equally forgotten. All the same, her sour quips made myself think 'Maybe I should seriously consider cooling down a bit my enthusiasm for another marriage arrangement.'

*

Unlike El Paso, Tijuana's streets were tumultuously overcrowded, a surprising variety of people bustling among interesting, vividly colored buildings, intriguing smells, and above all, flooded by thumping rhythms and sounds. Nearly every other man carried a musical instrument, guitars, violins, saxophones, harmonicas, or what not. The double bass a funny looking skinny individual dressed foot-to-toe in black carried on his back was hard not to notice. Peppery music vibrated in the air, everywhere fast grilled food, diverse artisan articles peddled on street markets amid intense noise, brash haggling and humble begging side by side made for the liveliest urban scene. At first, the reality of this rather smallish, disorderly border town, visited regularly by Americans, seemed simple enough, the town's entire economy geared to the mighty dollar-spending visitors, willingly and freely coming over from the North for mostly short visits.

Aside this, the colorful atmosphere –typical for a third world country bordering the huge developed neighbor-- exuded poverty, seemed chaotic and truly sad, in spite of its exuberant gayety on the surface. My mind involuntarily flew to the long forgotten gypsy-filled slums of Bucharest. But I abstained from comparisons, fully aware that the Romany, a minority embedded within the Romanian people, their folksy diversity had deeper roots in a medieval past than

Mexicans in theirs. Although comparably cheerful, the Romanian and gypsy garb had long since ossified in clean, parallel patterns of endlessly repeated colorful abstract registers, often only superficially as lighthearted as the sombrero or the black star-studded, body-fitting costumes of the mariachi. Whereas Romanian geometric folk art had long past the age of its formative fluidity, in Mexico –as all over the South American continent—the visual interplay appears open for change, still leading to improvisation, whereby artistic innovation is not only possible and desirable, but necessary as well.

*

"You see when our folk contemplate the future, they have to peek in the past, while Mexicans -- probably most Americans-- could project their looks unhindered forward, less burdened by seriously deep sunk roots."

"Hey, why don't you stop talking in riddles? Better tell me where would you rather live, over here looking ahead for the future, or over there stuck in the past?"

Her unexpected, but significantly pertinent question — particularly for immigrants-- struck as a thunderbolt. Not sure whether she intuited correctly my analysis, I felt a bit lost, my wit caught between a rock and a hard place.

"I don't know. This is an awfully difficult question. I need to think a bit before giving you a straight answer."

"Then shut up and enjoy the present. Okay?"

"Perhaps you're right, but tell me, can a man really forget his past?" Out of the blue, Philomela's tortured face surfaced again vividly in my mind.

"That's for you to figure out. What I know is that one day you must decide whether you want to wear the same old comfortable rags, or be the elegant fashionable modern man of today?"

Somehow she touched the right chord. Indeed, I always opted for the impossible, to live simultaneously in the past and the future, a feat as unachievable as having your cake and eating it too or, as in the Romanian folksy, earthy variant—I mellow it hereby on purpose--, *to have your soul in Paradise and body caressed by a beautiful courtesan.*

Willy-nilly, I let myself succumb to the present, and plunge alongside in the shopping adventure of buying Mexican souvenirs the way most decent folk usually do around this colorful place. Wisely or not, I resigned to follow the woman's lead while secretly trying to chase my always-elusive dreams of wishful thinking. Momentarily enthralled by my friend's enthusiasm for the meaningless pleasures of shopping for knick-knacks, I suddenly saw her as desirable as ever. Am I a dead ringer of consistency, or what?

In the same heartbeat, my thoughts changed course again to my habitual angle, "Why, when in love, a man must stick faithfully and scrupulously to a single woman, while freely hating her sisters? Why shouldn't people devote their love and loyalty to the entire world rather than only to a single person forever, and ever *until death do us apart*? Isn't this sort of foresworn exclusiveness a bit morally deficient? Aren't we all brothers and sisters, equally children of God? Why not love the wife and mistress at the same time? Must the latter always be rejected for the benefit of the first? Don't both deserve their fair share of love? Perhaps some of the ancient biblical heroes had been wiser than us in this respect."

The sun about to sink behind the horizon, straight into the perpetually present Pacific Ocean not far beyond the city's low, rundown but colorful buildings, turned even more picturesque on the luminous sky.

"Hey baby, I am thirsty. Let's have a beer, maybe even a snack, and watch the busy street from the terrace up there. What do you say?"

"Gladly, my love, finally a good idea. Let's go."

Said and done. Minute later we sat ready to be served at the only free table my friend's eagle eyes immediately spotted on the terrace. At first, the waitress, a cute young Mexican girl wearing a red bandana pulled down on her forehead, did not pay any attention, allowing us time to relax, to make up our minds in a fashion untypical back in the States. So we went on chitchatting, while quickly surrounded by a bunch of five-to-ten years old urchins, awkwardly trying to peddle their tinny feather-made birds, tactfully placed on the table for our inspection.

"*How mucho pagar por esta?*" I asked in my totally imaginary Spanish.

One of the boys, a cute dark little creature stepped bravely forward, peered straight in my face, his irresistible doe-eyes unflinchingly beg-full in mine. I repeated my question. The boy shrugged his narrow shoulders, and then mutely pushed the little feather-bundle even closer. As I reached in my pockets for change, he snatched the emerging dollar bill with lightening speed almost before I could reveal it, at the same second he repossessed his little bird off the table. Stupid me to believe the bird was for sale! Then, before having time to react, another little man --an exact copy of the previous—took rapidly his turn. This game repeated three of four times, until my pocket ran out of dollar bills. Only the waitress' arrival saved me, as she mercilessly and unceremoniously chased away the burgeoning crowd of little beggars, instantly moved to another corner of the terrace overlooking the busy, colorful street below.

Unable to express in Cervantes' beautiful tongue my wishes for some good eating, and fearful to choose among the allegedly unwholesome, super hot Mexican dishes, I ordered two glasses of *chervesas*. Who didn't hear in the States about *Montezuma's revenge*? Minutes later, the waitress brought four full glasses, two for each. Whether this misunderstanding had been the result of my nonexistent linguistic aptitude, or on the contrary, was the local custom, I do not and will never know. But then again, considering the low price I readily paid the bill, adding an extra generous tip. It was worth it, the beer excellent and properly chilled.

"Well, well, amigo, what happened to your proverbial stinginess?"

Wisely, I let the facetious question slide, but not without a mental note on my friend's ability for occasional pettiness, an ominous new detail added to my recent suspicions about her newly revealed facets of character. Oh well, why must love at first sight be always blind?

Around nine, and a good, vigorous walk later, back at the border point, re-entered the States without undue delays based on our experience in El Paso. By ten o'clock safely and comfortably locked in the room, we crashed exhausted on the cool sheets, prepared to watch TV, bottles of beer in hand, this time off our own stock, imported —according to the label-- directly from Bremen, Germany. Long-live free trade!

Informed about the day's news and the next day's weather, the bed appeared suddenly the most desirable abode for our tired, aching limbs. So when Didonna rolled into my arms asking for love, I almost got mentally scared in spite of my egregiously willing body. Fortunately, the bell so-to-speak saved my behind, both having fallen asleep before anything could have materialized sensually. Oh slumber, how sweet your saving embrace can be!

The one extra day in San Diego we devoted for the city's famous, truly fabulous zoo, to the incredibly beautiful shoreline, and other lesser tourist objectives, natural or artificial landmarks. Simply we planned on enjoying a wonderful time together, successfully feigning to be the happy lovebirds of before, while completely ignoring our recent existential questions, the unavoidable reckoning tacitly postponed for later. More or less, our affected behavior contained a modicum of welcome common sense that afforded the adventure go on as intended, combining relaxation, learning and pleasure. Both of us thought practical to leave problems for a later resolution, to be tackled at home amid the more mundane and boring conditions of everyday life. Why spoil a wonderful vacation by useless quarrels and bitter arguments? Aren't couples known for resorting to this type of evasive strategies all too often?

*

The trip to Los Angeles on route-5, faithfully along the shoreline all the way, offered such incredibly exotic vistas and places of note as to render almost impossible any acts denying full-time enjoyment of this objectively unique visual feast. Literally squeezed between mountains on the right and Pacific Ocean on the left, we committed to memory the towns of Del Mar, Solana Beach, Encinitas, Carlsbad, San Clemente, San Juan Capistrano, and many other equally strange sounding names. Under such enchanting conditions almost any man and woman journeying together must naturally succumb to love, forced to forgetting all mundane troubles, compelled to disregarding dilemmas raised by lousy customs, or false mores of everyday life the devil himself invented for torturing and tormenting the, ah-so-poor human souls. Why can't universal affection blossom free, beautiful and indiscriminate? What kind of mean deity enjoyed placing so many limitations, pitfalls and suffering in its path?

Along the way we halted several times, only twice longer than ten minutes, first at Carlsbad, to gobble up some sandwiches, and second at San Clemente's sunny beach, populated by remarkably blond, buoyantly healthy looking California girls and boys roller-skating on the boardwalk. A visit to Richard Nixon's White House, the unfortunate ill-fated US-president's western immaculate summer retreat, we deemed a must for some murky reason, too.

Most travelers to have cruised along the sunny shore-hugging route-5 might enthusiastically bear witness for California's magnetic lure, equally for the young and the more mature romantic. The same magic quality might explain also the unbelievably optimistic, futuristic, easy-going and –to many *loony*-- philosophical outlook of Californians in general.

The reader shouldn't be surprised by the level of delirious joy reached as we arrived in Los Angeles around five in the evening, equally in love with life and ourselves, inexplicably enthusiastic, prepared for conquering the world undeterred by obstacles, all difficulties forgotten.

But soon enough, the City of Angels, beautiful as it sounds, had dampened our enthusiasm about two hours of aimless wanderings later trough the maze of its vast urban outlying neighborhoods, in search of a decent hotel or motel. Following hours and hours of trials and errors, our patience had to bump against a final limit and succumb to the idea of sheltering body and soul just about anywhere, before the fast descending night might have thrown us totally to the wolfs of the chanciest risks. Coerced by *force-majeur* to accepting whatever shelter available against any cost, urban ugliness, distance to landmarks, or allegedly dubious, perilous hoods, we trusted our fate to Providence, and secondarily, to some quite shady surroundings few God-fearing people wish to ever get familiarized with.

After settling at last in a so-called motel room in this neck of the wood that came our way incidentally, I tried to switch on the air-conditioning, only to turn it off next minute due to the insupportable rattling noise it caused.

"Man, open the windows. The cool evening air outside seems pleasanter than the foul smell in the room."

"I would if I could," I said, trying in vain to pray open the window hopelessly stuck shut.

The linen on the beds appeared in no better condition either. Although fairly clean looking, the sheets and blankets emitted a distinct odor of the cheapest sort of laundry detergent. Didonna turned up a bit her finicky nose, to conclude in quick resignation:

"Oh-well, we have to spend the night here willy-nilly, so let's make the best of it. I am exhausted and you must be too. Why not accept things as they are, and look for something more suitable tomorrow, okay?"

Surprised by my gal's newly found wisdom, I quickly agreed, happy to settle in before the fast encroaching night could render any attempt for further searching quite dangerous in the iffy, run-down neighborhood. Faithful to custom, we dined in the room. My friend obviously didn't mind, as she routinely proceeded to set the table. Following the previous week's exciting adventures, our mood naturally settled on spending a quiet evening reading, watching TV, chatting, or even writing long overdue postcards.

Once over the expertly improvised dinner prepared out of scraps and bits found in the portable cooler --the bottle of good Bremen beer included-- we put on pajamas, laid down alongside one another in bed to watch the news, hopefully followed by a good flick. For ten minutes or so everything went all right, then the TV suddenly started buzzing, and the image flickered wildly, a disturbance impossible to correct in spite of all manipulations and interventions I attempted with the set's controls. Fine! Forced off from watching TV, we settled to writing post cards. Finished with the task around nine o'clock, as the night turned darker and darker beyond the window nothing remained but hit the sack. Just as well, in the morning we had to get up early.

A new tacit agreement to behave as if everything continued in the old path became the norm, both equally feigning to forget the previous day's discussion, as well as my promise to give it an answer later. Consequently, our lovemaking diminished a tad in passion, but without turning totally mechanical, reverting instead to a pattern commonly attributed to rather well seasoned couples with long years of trust and friendship under their belt, to a relation kept warm within mutually confessed affection and meticulously self-imposed inertial enthusiasm. As my mistress often-quipped *sex is by definition better than the lack of it, even when it ends up as no more than a sporty, well-rehearsed play.* Essentially I agreed with this no-nonsense, practical approach.

At the conclusion of our acceptably warm embrace, ready to sweetly fall asleep in each other's arms as during the best of times, the outside world suddenly came alive with jolly good, cheerful, but quite disturbing Mexican music, interspersed with shouts and laughter of young men and women obviously having a heck of a good time. Windows had to be shut tight. The room quickly turned into a suffocating stuffy cave, insupportably filled by the putrid stench, as of a decaying corpse. The air-conditioning turned on in immediate response, a solution to be reversed equally fast as the ensuing rattling noise proved even worse than the musical mayhem filtering in from the outside. Between the foul air and the noise, the latter seemed easier to bear. The window opened again, our bodies condemned to turning and tossing, our mood swung back and forth between laughter and rage until the first crack of dawn. Eventually, it has been the wailing police sirens that chased away the hot-blooded Latino revelers, the ensuing silence allowing at last our drained bodies a couple hours of deadly sleep, nearly to seven in the morning.

"Listen, I can't endure this nightmare much longer? Let's get out of here, and forget the whole thing as fast as possible."

Said and done. Fifteen minutes later after my friend's starkly expressed wish, we rolled out of the godforsaken parking, off the lot decorated by yellow police tape, encircling the alleged scene of an earlier stabbing incident.

"Welcome to America" I quipped, and the rebuttal came as lightening.

"This could happen anywhere in the world."

"True. The question is how often?"

"Oh well… I don't know. I seldom spend time in such awful neighborhoods. But had you invested a little more for a decent hotel, this discussion wouldn't even take place. About that I'm quite sure."

"Nice, very nice, spoken as a red-blooded Yankee. Your reasoning is faultless indeed. As the old Hungarian saying goes *dogs bark, money talks*, isn't it?"

"Why the hell not? Let me quote you a Russian saying in response *better rich and healthy than poor and sick*."

"Fine, I get it, to each according to abilities and luck."

"Boy, have you gone totally bonkers! For God's sake stop picking a fight, and drive out of this misery right now! Let's find the Los Angeles the entire world raves about, to leave forever behind this bad first impression."

I cast a glance at my *Blondie's* pretty face, and noticed the glint of playful mischief in her eyes.

Maybe she's right I could be a bit loony.

"Okay, I will drive alright, but not before you my darling will study the map, the first step any adviser would recommend for the visitor lost in such a huge and widespread community as this City of Angels seems to be."

We reckoned to allot three whole days for the dream factory of the world, the fantasy center of the Universe, and the embodiment of all there is about the art of make-believe. Indeed, Hollywood --a neighborhood of Los Angeles-- is boasting to have more recording and film studios than any other place on the planet.

"By the way, are you aware how many hopes had been born, nourished, and mercilessly smashed to bits in this town, otherwise so famous for its laid-back easygoing life style?"

"Not exactly, but let's find out. Drive us straight to the Walk of Stars. That's precisely the spot I wish to begin our visit with."

*

The chosen few elected to the celluloid Pantheon on the famous Walk of Stars still lure aspiring young gods and goddesses, working in interim as gas-station attendants, waiting tables, flipping hamburgers, or doing other menial jobs, while dreaming of becoming a Humphrey Bogart, Elisabeth Taylor or John Wayne. This almost impossibly ambitious dream of reaching stardom via the small or big screen still seems to obsess the young as forcefully today as in the past. Yes, America changes continuously, but only to stay the same! Keeping up the illusion, make-believe should be one of its biggest secrets.

It is not by chance Los Angeles came to be considered the Mecca of body-cult as well. Jogging in this city must just as naturally complement living in the Fast Lane, as looking youthful is a prerequisite of success. Why then the surprise that in this town holistic wellness, and plastic surgery centers, new diets and fads spring up all the time, to come and go faster than in all the other American cities combined?

*

But in spite of superlatives, I confess to have been unimpressed, a disillusion unhesitatingly expressed as we drove up and down the famously posh Beverly Hills.

The opulence so ostentatiously piled high in this dark sad park reserved for the ultra posh and rich seemed to me a bit repulsive. It was almost impossible to catch a glimpse of the folk living within their mansions behind those seemingly forever-locked gates.

"Why are these people so secretive? What could they be hiding beyond the impenetrable fences? What are they so afraid of?"

"Shut up, man, quit talking like a Communist, and don't spoil this ride. Let me imagine myself a few seconds behind those fences, will you?

Reluctantly, I did shut my mouth, even if taken aback by the eagerness of my female friend's wish for such a life of laziness in a community, to my view, largely rooted on envy, jealousy, misplaced pride, arrogance and vanity. How can a minimally faith-filled Christian spirit aspire to live surrounded by such cardinal sins? How come these loudly professed believers in God bow their heads before Mammon so eagerly? Then it dawned on me whether I ever can offer the woman sitting at my right the sort of life she dreams about? Of course I can't. So why have I paired up with this pretty face I profess to love and cherish? Was she just as phony an ideal as the false dream I smashed my home for?

My mind paused. Philomela's pale face came to the fore slowly, causing me to think in sadness whether I wasn't the same evil Goddamned sinner as everyone else. Yes I surely was. But what exactly were my sins? Hmm... Could it be I fell in love with love itself, and not with the flesh-and-bone living woman sitting on my right? How bad my trespassing may look in the eyes of God? Wasn't He the One Who commanded Adam and Eve to love and multiply? Yes, yes, how true! But did He mean we should love by any means possible, even at the expense of our brothers and sisters? Oh well... questions, questions... On the other hand, what's wrong to love indiscriminately? My ever hunting question returned as a leitmotiv, why is so improper to love all people, male and female at the same time? Bah! Isn't all love similarly valid? Why not?' I kept arguing left and right around and around all facets of my dilemma--'by loving Didonna did I really take anything away from Philomela? Or perhaps I simply committed the sin of lusting, hypocrisy and heresy, fallen in the trap of a particular type of gluttony. Wow! Maybe I did precisely that.'

At this point we were passing by the Pink Palace of Sultan of Brunei.

"Tell me, pretty, would you like to be one of the Sultan's wives?"

"Don't be stupid, and leave me alone? Sometime you can be a real moron. Had I wished to be the wife of a Sultan, or of a similarly rich guy, why would I be here with you now, to answer your idiotic questions? Come on quit acting the fool. I know you can do better than that."

"Excu-u-u-se me! I just tried to convey my feelings, elicited incidentally by the Sultan's splendid abode and surroundings. Do you want to know what a certain gossip author I forgot his name said about Beverly Hills, about Los Angeles in general?"

"No wise guy, I don't know. But let's hear it, come on give it to me straight if you must."

"There is always something so delightfully real about what is phony here, and something so phony about what is real."

"Are you now happy with this off your chest?"

"Yes I am," ensued my snap-back, although in truth I felt pissed, a bitter aftertaste in my mouth. But all vanished in the same heartbeat as my always resourceful kitten leaned over, to plant one of her soft little kisses on my cheek. She used the strategy quite often, to apply the balm of appeasement exactly at the proper time. Predictably, I felt suddenly the happy child mommy just rewarded. So much for my fortitude as the proud, self-respecting male!

The next few hours we crisscrossed Los Angeles aided by the map, a task impossible to ever finish due to the city's inconceivable magnitude.

I vividly remember pondering on this thought as we went through exploring the well-known Sunset Boulevard end-to-end, aiming to conclude the trip somewhere in Malibu Beach. Eventually, it took ninety minutes just to getting there.

An advice for the novice wishing to explore The City of Angels-- let him or her make sure to plan the trip carefully, way ahead of time, no matter how simple the task seems at a first. To anyone not heeding this warning, I will promise only disappointment, a lot of aimless driving, and little to see.

In our case, clearly inexperienced newcomers, what we succeeded in one full day was still plenty to swing by the Chinese theatre, and take a stroll on the famous Walk of Stars. But it had been all we could do, no time for anything else. By seven in the evening we got so damn hopelessly exhausted as to forget everything planned, happy to dine in a Thai restaurant that just came our way. Thereafter, finding a place for the night became again a matter of most acute urgency.

"Forget about the hotel. We'll have plenty of time. Let's go instead to Rodeo Drive. Please do this for my sake, wouldn't you, darling?"

"My pleasure, but must remind you we could end up spending the night in the car, I guess you won't like that."

"There you go again with your pessimism. I wonder what the hell made me shack up with you?"

"Oh?"

"Yeah. Really. You do nothing I want, always afraid of something ridiculously insignificant. I tell you what you might as well do, go back home to your old bitchy Philomela. She is the woman best suited for you. As for the two of us, we don't seem to have much in common."

"Hey, hey, now you're not fair, hitting hard under the belt." Before I could add a little acid to my words, she hastily cut me off.

"Sorry Dorel, I really am. Forgive me, I was only kidding. Believe me it was only my foul mouth speaking. She kissed me repeatedly and childishly, while pleading with obviously affected tone of voice." Come on my love please forget what I said. I meant no harm. Honest. The fact is, though, I want right now to go to Hollywood, see the nightlife, and maybe later, even enjoy a drink in a bar. This would be a nice change of plan, in my opinion, too firmly set. For once please see things my silly feminine way. Okay?"

"Yes, yes, but why not postpone the fun for later, for after we've found a room for the night?"

"To hell with the room. We live only once, and I know the minute we've settled in for the night it will be harder to get out again, tired as we are. You know I am right. Stop being so uptight. Dare be all you can at least once in your life."

Naturally, the woman won the argument, and I drove, even if reluctantly, toward Hollywood as indicated on the map. On the way the conversation halted, myself a bit sulky on the account of her earlier remark. It wasn't easy to forget her outburst, even if intended as a joke. However truly angry I was not, just a bit hurt in my self-esteem. Then my thoughts flew again to Philomela.

*

I remembered her in Traiskirchen refugee camp, how she had to wake up daily at the crack of dawn, to go sorting cookies at the *Blaschke* factory, not unlike Lucile Ball in one her most hilarious series-- less the comedy. I imagined how frantic this must have been for the former opera chorus singer, used to seldom rehearsing before ten in the morning, rarely compelled to do manual work, except in her own kitchen. I also recalled how stoically she endured the hard life, without complaining once about having to provide for the family's welfare -- particularly when compared to me, and my easy job as a *dolmetcher.* My, my, how selflessly she sacrificed her pride for the sweet pleasures Vienna is so famous for, enjoying the cafés on *Kertner Strasse* on weekends, strolling through *Nashmarket* on Sundays, or going to the opera at New Years eve, for the two of us and daughter Camellia to partake in the good life of Austrian *Gemūtlichkeit.*

Involuntarily, I had to compare Philomela's dedication to Didonna's recent bitchy corrosive attitude. A nagging doubt popped up in my mind anew. What if I had been too quick in evaluating her, what if I only imagined her affection as a palliative for my own shortcomings? What if she had ulterior motives? What if the immigrant mature woman wanted a male companion only to help with bringing up of her little handsome progeny? What if my love for the woman was another manifestation of my own middle age crisis? What if subconsciously feeling no longer young, I jumped in the affair to reconfirm my waning manly vigor and naturally diminished power of seduction? What if, what if?

For a long time no answers ensued, my mind stuck in deafening silence. Then it dawned, had I to reconfirm my manhood why didn't I select a younger female? How come I've chosen a lady past her prime as myself? Incapable of an honest answer, I simply dismissed my doubts as simply idiotic. But have I been justified to do so?

*

We arrived in Hollywood shortly after sunset. Streetlights slowly came on slightly buzzing, setting the stage for a romantic nocturnal episode. Wishful thinking-- in fact our first impressions ensued soon less than enthusiastic. Instead of the glamorous, sparkling full-of-life-community we knew from movies and advertising, the town seemed more akin to some banal commercial neighborhoods, say of Baltimore, Philadelphia or New York. Nothing glamorous cut off our breath in Hollywood. The same type of discount outfits offered their cheap kitschy colored wares inside or exposed on the sidewalks, shoes, clothing, knickknacks, nameless watches, luggage galore, sunglasses, or what not, as in most American discount commercial neighborhoods. The mellow evening breeze moved up and down various paper refuse, discarded bags, cups, plates or other contemporary litter of undefined origin, not unlike elsewhere in large cities. Even Didonna, habitually inclined for superlatives about America, painted on her cute mug a clear expression of disappointment. What struck immediately was the mixture of races milling on the sidewalks, Asians, Afros, some Caucasians among them as well, the latter mostly of the kind sporting extensive tattoos on their carelessly hypertrophied muscular or simply just obese bodies.

"For once you were right it could have been more useful searching for a hotel, and having a drink in the lobby, instead of wasting time in this place."

"Let's do an about face right now," I caught quickly on my friend's changed mood and, as I attempted my way out, stumbled instead on Hollywood Avenue, on the Walk of Stars.

All of a sudden, my usually cool-headed sweetheart went literally gaga, as for me, a little less fervently enthusiastic about movie stars, or their names and palms imprinted in cement, I tried to keep to myself, marveling on the innate human need for adulating some type of royalty, even if not of the blue-blooded variety. Indeed, this famous, always densely populated avenue attracts folk from all over the States, from the entire world, prostrated in reverent admiration at this open air pantheon of make-believe stars, for their flickering achievements on celluloid, for their glamorous, often controversial life styles commoners could only dream of. Then I opened my foul mouth on the subject, in spite of my resolve to stay mum.

"Some might find this strange, but precisely here I found the quintessence of the American psyche, the naïve freedom to entertain mostly unachievable dreams, more often than not available only for the very few. America loves to brag about these lofty ideals how anybody in the New World can be anything he or she dreams of, conveniently forgetting that the same goals may be achieved almost anywhere with nearly the same rate of success—all proportions guarded. No, my fellow immigrant girlfriend, not only in America simple folk may become movie stars, presidents, geniuses, or influential persons. Let me tell it to you straight how some tiny minorities achieved greatness and fame over here as in many other lands. This is mostly due the nature of things and mathematical probabilities. Didn't the mediocre painter Hitler, bombastic Mussolini or martial Napoleon rise to power practically from very low stations? Were the Georgian Stalin, the Ukrainian Khrushchev and Brejnew originally rich, or blue-blooded?"

"Yes, but your examples are clearly facetious, because remember the guys you listed were all tyrant thugs, murderous, pathological villains."

"So what? My question was whether these people had reached the pinnacle of power in spite of their low origins, not about their vicious characters. And, you too better remember that I made my point for the benefit of a friend, not at a political rally. All the same, let me change the track a little-- could have all famous musicians, movie actors, directors, scientists, artists, or politicians outside the US been exclusively evil scions of the privileged classes? Just search through the pages of any encyclopedia and see how Israel, England Turkey, Pakistan, India, The Philippines (soon probably other countries as well), allegedly less perfected democracies, elected by now female-presidents or prime-ministers, while in America this goal is to be achieved only from now on? What about that?"

"Come, come, silly boy, shut up, you know this will eventually happen in America too, so stop hitting under the belt and especially the fishing for a gender-based response. Are you a god-dam lefty, or what? You know one had to be a party member to achieve anything back in Communist Romania, male or female."

"This is undeniably true in communist countries only a minority penetrated the ranks of the so-called nomenclature. But let me ask what's the proportion of ordinary people in the States to catapult among the super rich billionaires, or among the truly influent personalities? Comparatively speaking, aren't the large majority of Americans living modest humble lives, toiling for the benefit of the few-selected proverbial *one per- centers* as anywhere on the planet? All proportions guarded, are not similarly narrow minorities dominant across elsewhere on earth, whether belonging to the privileged rich, the well connected, the blue-blooded nobility, or the *worker's vanguard*? This is just a fact nothing to do ideologically either with the left or the right. Isn't this obvious enough for anyone willing to look at the statistic truths straight on? Seen through this lens on what ground can the American system be deemed so *exceptional*? By the way, don't you find the term itself a little troubling, or boastful?"

"Now hold it right there. If you don't like it here, why don't you go back?"

"Go back to where? Oh, oh, I get it *--love it or leave it,* right?"

"Indeed, why not leave? It's your choice. You came on your on accord."

"Maybe I did, but leaving is no longer my choice only. Were I to leave now I would be looked upon as an outcast anywhere on the globe. By the same token, haven't I been lured across the ocean by the promise of exceptionality, that over this side of the ocean everything would be different, fairer, more beautiful and unique? Stupid romantic me forgot that human nature is everywhere the same! Haven't all former great powers ardently believed in their own divinely granted destinies? I vividly remember even my poor fellow Romanians –hardly citizens of a world power-- bragging about their mental superiority, or national prowess. A lot of them professed being proud even of Cheauchescu, for his rising to power from a simple cobbler's apprentice, to become the supreme commander in communist Romania. What's so special when such an improbable climb happens in the west? So you're right indeed, the choice had been mine, my fault as I came on my own accord. But then again, how was I to guess about something practically barred from investigating beforehand?"

"Please don't mind my saying that sometimes you can be an absolute fool, blinded exactly by your admittedly sharp wits. Why must you always spoil all I happen to like about America? Why insist in hurting me this way? I feel free in this country, I love it and, by all means so should you. You make me suspect you weren't a lot unhappier in the Old Country than you are now over here. If you moved across the big pond only to act as the perpetual complainer, no one could do anything for you anywhere. I am sorry dear, but you must be rather sick up there –she pointed to my head. The real problem is **you** suffer from a serious mental disorder. Though, I must agree with you in one respect, a potato is a potato no matter how you twist, peel or cook it. And this applies to you too, buddy. You will be the same dissatisfied customer anywhere on the globe. This is a defect that might be part of your own DNA, my friend. But maybe, just maybe, even you can feel less the ordinary potato in the New World than in the Old. Doesn't the same potato soup taste better in the fresh open air of America? For me it certainly does, and this I firmly belief. For me is all that matters."

"Fine, but don't forget I chose this country as much as you did. You must consider I am here as well, it's only for the sake of facts I stressed that not all-pioneering belongs exclusively to The New World. So think more, and go easy with the preaching!"

"O live me alone with your twisted logic. Please!"

Bewildered, I saw my pretty love in a new light, no longer the seductive charming temptress, but a dour, unforgiving, calculating harpy I never seen before. What exactly happened during the last couple of years, and why to me? Then wondered what if she's right, and I am just a nincompoop, really bumbling idiot? An eerie silence settled in the vehicle on our way out of Hollywood.

In spite of soured moods, the most immediate practical needs had to prevail, the settling of scores to be postponed for the sake of resuming the prosaic search for lodging in a quieter, safer part of Los Angeles, as agreed earlier.

It took the better part of two hours to find this destination at last at a *Quality Inn* hotel --swimming pool and all the amenities included—even if pricier than acceptable until then during our whirl-windy path across so many States. In view of the previous night's unpleasant experience, the one-hundred-dollar rate per night seemed fairly decent. My agreement came forth promptly, even without consulting my companion, once I understood how fast the opportunity could disappear at such a late hour against a reasonable price in Los Angeles, actually in any other large metropolis.

The room, by all benchmarks nice, provided everything tired citizen could welcome at the end of a busy day-- clean beds, a spotless bathroom, air-conditioning, TV, and a little more generous space than in cheaper motels. But, all things considered, these bonus extras I found negligible, hardly justifying the exorbitant price. After all, the typical tourist entertains no plans to moving in for good in a hotel, only to spend a restful night under some roof. This is precisely what I wanted, a clean bed, the essential shower stall, and the TV-set –by now available anyplace, cheaply or dearly. But as it was we paid the premium for not having secured a reservation in advance. Wouldn't most folk accept this for a good enough explanation?

Most certainly my mistress didn't care for such petty justifications, she felt elated, transported in seventh heaven in a heartbeat at the prospect of unexpected luxury, if judging only by the speed her summer vestments got summarily cast off, in preparation to shower in the marble-lined bathtub.

"Come, my love, get out of those dusty rags, let's wash together, for then I'll treat you on this ultra wide bed to the most passionate embrace I ever delighted anybody with. This is a promise. On second thought why not jump on top of me right now?"

"Sure, wicked temptress, I will, but why not have first a dip in the fairytale-blue waters of the swimming pool downstairs? I guess you saw it on the way up."

"Of course I did, little weasel of a man, but you know how afraid I am of any water above the knees. But don't spoil your pleasure as you already did mine, go on have the damned dip alone. I am willing to forget showering together, and to prove it I will prepare a small snack in your absence."

Taking advantage of this spontaneous generosity, I quickly jumped into my trunks, and vanished almost Houdini-like from the room. Perhaps for the first time, I forgot to acknowledge my girlfriend's largess even by a simple *thank you*.

The water in the pool felt as marvelous as it looked. But only a few laps later, the loneliness of the place, amplified even more by the fairy tale-like illumination, made me strangely sad, regretful of not having my woman alongside. 'Perhaps I should have dealt with her a bit more tactfully', I thought. Instead of impressing on her my twisted, but well hidden pangs of conscience induced by my refusal, I'd better lured her to come along, to keep me company, swimming or no swimming. A little compassion and understanding might have gone a long way in alleviating her aqua phobia. It took another half an hour of abandoned soaking in the blue water, as well as in my own moronically remorseful recriminations, before I gave up my selfish pleasure, to return in the room as confused as ever, without even guessing what to expect next.

To my surprise, Didonna showed no signs of any leftover grudge. Buck-naked on the unopened bed --a brochure of Los Angeles in hand-- she greeted me cheerfully, as I stepped in the dimly lit room.

"Be welcome, love. Did you have a nice dip?"

"Indeed I did", and then, without further ado, I tore off my swimming trunk and the slightly wet tank-top only to plunge on top of her, all worries and recent apprehensions summarily pushed off my mind. All happened on the spur of moment, the ensuing love session, exhilarating as if not a single cloud of doubt ever came between us. Oh yes, pure physical love often times obliterates the ghosts of dissension, momentarily bothering the hearts and minds of amorous couples, licit or illicit. Marched lockstep into the shower we washed one another in the afterglow of satisfied intercourse, its sweetness still lingering soft over the stimulated senses.

The plans of the-morrow we discussed in the bar downstairs while nursing deliciously uplifting liquors, my friend an exotic Margarita, I a straight shot of Chivas Regal Scotch whiskey over ice, a little seltzer water on the side. Eventually, we agreed on spending the next day visiting the world-famous Universal Studios.

*

In the morning, although the destination proved easy enough to find, it took a great effort not to effect an instant change of plans. The price for the admission thickets, well in excess of our total daily-allotted expense, shocked as an icy shower. In the end, defeated by the argument of life's shortness, as well as the rarity of the opportunity, we forked over the money with well-feigned childish optimism, hoping for a unique experience. Our expectations got partially fulfilled. However subjective our views, two-three hours later, as we sat down in an outdoor Mexican restaurant strategically located within the compound, I still had to conclude:

"In spite of all the alleged one-of-a-kind attractions, I could have happily lived out my life without adding these to my cultural baggage. In my opinion, none justified the exorbitant price. Agree?"

"Bah, there you go again."

"What's this *there-you-go-again* supposed to mean?"

"Tell me what is exactly you didn't like?"

"Oh, well…it's not what I liked or didn't, only that nothing had been tailored to the taste of the modern cultivated adult I like to think we are. All attractions, even if technologically impressive, seemed rather kitschy, of a quality suited mostly to infants, not grown-ups. In this light wasn't the show a bit pricey?"

"Why do you have to measure everything against cost? Can't you have any fun at all, enjoy the moment for its own sake forgetting altogether about money?"

"Sure I can. A few stunts could amuse even some grown up kids, as for instance the train derailment, or the *Jaw's* shark attack on the lake, spectacular and scary enough to make even my heart skip a few bits. But then again, the show might have been better suited for your Alex a few years ago."

"Why Alex of a few years ago? Is there anything wrong with him now?"

"Please, don't play the innocent blind mother. I am sure you didn't forget about his recent boozing, and smoking more than cigarettes, to ask me now what's wrong with him."

"Why do you think I entrusted you with taking care of him? A growing adolescent boy needs the support of a father figure, won't he? Didn't you promise to be precisely that for him?"

"Haven't I helped him pass the GED test? But tell me how many kids you know had quit school out of the blue in the ninth grade? Alex is a smart boy all right, but maybe, just maybe, a little too smart for his own good. Can't you accept this?"

"I am sure he'll outgrow the phase. You assured me in this sense, too."

"I am no longer so sure. He keeps bad company, trying hard to look the *baddest* among his peers. This must be his way of excelling. Kind of lost my influence over him. The prevailing American punk *culture* beat me to the punch. I am sorry."

"See that's another reason to make our relation official. You know how teenagers badmouth their peers for a mother shacked up with a married man. Didn't you marry Philomela twenty years ago, to become Camellia's official father figure?"

"Hey, don't bring my daughter in discussion. It's not fair. I know how much you dislike her."

"It's true I do resent her more than a little, but am I not justified? How did she repay for the sacrifice you made for her sake? By smoking dope, marrying a bum, and returning from California a total wreck? Nice girl, ha?"

"Once again, why don't you get off her case? She's not your concern."

"Yes dear, she is. You made her my business too. Didn't Philomela and Camellia abuse you long enough? Give Alex and me our chance too."

"What chance? To abuse me?"

"Don't be facetious, and don't twist my words. You know what I meant."

"No I don't, but I know what I heard."

"Okay then, let me be frank, didn't Philomela and her foul-mouth-brat enjoy your kindness for twenty long years? Maybe the time has come for them to be banished, off your back for good. Much as I care they might as well perish from the face of the earth."

"What? This is crazy. I invested a lifetime in them. They became mine. I can't just forget two decades of togetherness, as it never existed. The past is past as well as you will be the future, don't you see? You must have been well aware of this the minute we agreed to join our lives, didn't you?"

A long pause ensued, then her attitude softened.

"Forgive me, Dorel, I didn't mean to hurt your feelings. My mouth runs sometimes afoul, racing ahead of my mind. Of course I had been well aware of the disadvantages when I became your concubine, I told you so at the time. Let's not fret over the matter. Come, let me give you a kiss as proof of my remorse."

As so often, my mistress switched her anger off as easy as it arose, in the obvious attempt to compensate for the vicious meanness of her outburst by turning instantly playful.

For me, however, it was a bit too late. I had to digest her words before able to forgive and forget. Again it occurred to me that maybe, just maybe, I've been a little hasty and impulsive when I shacked up with her seven years earlier. On the other side of the coin, looking forward to ten more days of vacation, to crossing the continent together, I had to proceed carefully. Why spoil the promise of some good times by unnecessary frictions?

"No problem, my fair friend, no problem. My tongue had been often dipped in poison, too." Her kiss wisely accepted, I concluded:

"You'll have my answer for your concerns soon after our return home. I renew now my promise. Until then, let's enjoy our vacation. Okay?"

"Agreed. You are a decent man all right, but not easy to live with. But don't forget I care for you. Please disregard the occasional sharpness of my tongue; my only wish is to be happy together. You know that. So what are we going to do next?"

"Given the late hour, the only sensible thing is returning to the hotel, refresh, and perhaps enjoy a drink in the bar downstairs. Stan Gets is scheduled to be playing tonight, down in the hall."

"Wonderful! Why can't you act always as a gentleman?"

Silence reined in the car all the way through the trip back to the hotel, my companion's obviously tendentious question left cautiously suspended, never answered.

Later that night, when already nursing together a few cocktails, for some totally murky reasons, I rounded the bill by a large tip the cute young pretty Californian waitress accepted with a wide grin. My concubine must have surely noticed my untypical generosity, but abstained from comments. A new strange, carefully tailored wisdom settled over our relationship.

*

Nine years had gone since the fateful day I left Philomela wriggling in pain on the cold basement floor in our home in Damascus. For the first few weeks in the new woman's home I managed to live out of a small suitcase, as one would on a business trip. But then, running out of the necessary daily items, and eager to avoid the needless largess of buying new stuff, the time came for a visit home, to claim my things, eventually to reach a more permanent agreement with my abandoned wife, regarding the state of our blown up marriage.

To my utter disbelieve, in her place I found Camellia whom I knew moved away with hubby Mark to California, the place of her teenager dreams. Shockingly emaciated, looking as an Auschwitz concentration camp escapee at the end of the Big War –her large eyes bulged out dark above the deadly violet mascara, lips rouged black, skin ghastly pale and drum-tight on the cheekbones, hair bleached paper-white, two stick-like arms attached to a sickly flat torso. Only God knew what kind of life she had left behind in California, what kind of abuse had she undergone, what could anyone do to help her out of misery. Oh-my-God, this is why we brought her over to the New World?

She told me in one breath how her husband Mark, arrested repeatedly for the same infraction of selling fake drugs, finally succeeded to piss off even herself, married to him a few years back only to ease him out of prison in Maryland, where he was to serve some time for a similar felony. The judge freed him conditionally on his promise to conduct from that day on a normal domestic life together with Camellia, within the confines of a marriage. Needless to say, Philomela and I frantically opposed this weirdest of an arrangement. However what are the arguments ever to work in the way of thwarting the decision of a young woman in love with a charming handsome bum?

Dully optimistic at the time of our escape from Romania, we envisioned a brighter future for Camellia, for the child considered more adaptable, pliable than her adult parents, already shaped to a different mold in the Old World. Quite a lot of our subsequent marital dissensions flowed off our naïve hopes, off the clashes between our differences in ways of handling the rambunctious kid's integration in the new, free, but perilous society we knew mostly from well-publicized and mythologized stories, circulating unfortunately about the States, particularly in Eastern Europe during the years of so-called *Peoples' Democracies.*

Our Camellia easily veered off the beaten path if only for the sake of winning modicum acceptability among newfound peers, among kids often openly and brazenly expressing the obtuse, visceral disdain for a mate they called *the little Communist intruder* among them. Isn't it interesting that, later on, Didonna's Alex, similarly endowed by slightly higher than average intelligence, but unusually assertive personality, did the same? Could this be a coincidence? Oh how little we figured in equation the meanness of kids everywhere, how often erred in our ignorance on the account of busy work-schedules, because doggedly preoccupied by building the requisite foundation for a better life in The United States, a place so frightfully alien to us in the beginning!

Where are the people, books, magazines, films, or other sources to describe the New World for newcomers in this light? How often stories revolve mostly around the blessings of the *free world*, while revealing precious little about the trade-offs, about the darker secrets and failures the masses of immigrant folk keep clutching to their chest out shame and misplaced pride? How often did the so-called *unbiased media* of Radio Free Europe, or Voice of America placed the critical spotlight on the Capitalist system's shadier aspects, instead of bending the truth toward self-aggrandizing propaganda, especially during the years of the Cold War? To make the story short, Camellia, my stepdaughter, as well as subsequently my virtual stepson Alex, both fell head-first in the alluring traps of life in the less than conventional, fascinatingly fast, illicit lanes. Luckily, however deeply imprisoned in the dungeons of self-effacing illusions about the meaning of liberty, thanks to God both our kids miraculously escaped without being enmeshed by the official justice system that still stamps so many young lives forever with bad records.

*

"What are you doing at home? I knew you were in California? What happened, where is your mother?"

"I don't know. She fetched me from the airport, and then disappeared as fast as she could. I have no idea where she went."

"Did the two of you go through your usual shouting matches?"

"Not initially, but then, as she suggested to take me to a recovery center for addicts... this did it. You know, she's back to her old tricks."

"That is you insulted her again, isn't it?"

"Not that much... anyway less than other times... But tell me pappy Dorel, why aren't you at home. Where the hell have you moved, and why?"

'That's none of your business."

"Oh yes it is. It very much is. Am I no longer part of this family?"

"Please, please, spare me the nonsense, you left on your own accord, didn't you? Better tell me what's on your mind, what are your plans?"

"Nothing. First I will have to file for divorce. Then I'll see. I hope you have nothing against my staying at home until then."

"No dear, stay as long as you wish. I will come to see you every now and again. Maybe we can talk, work something out together. By the way, you need to get in better shape. Nobody will deal with the way you look now. You need mullah?"

"Oh daddy, I knew you understand." She endeared me so only when in need of something."

Then she approached, with a clear intention to kiss and appease.

"I hope you come back to us soon."

"Us???"

"Oh yes, us."

Oh well… We talk about this later, but now I have to gather some things of mine and go. I'll be down in a jiffy"

As I climbed up the stairs to our former conjugal bedroom I noticed deep, ugly poke marks in the walls, totally unlike the nicks of daily wear and tear. Five minutes later, suitcase in hand, I had to ask as matter of fact as possible.

"By the way, sweetheart, do you know anything about the poke marks in the stairwell walls?"

"Yes, I made those. Don't worry-- I will take care of the damage soon. I have some good handyman friends."

"Forget those friends of yours, I will attend to the task myself as soon as I can. But tell me how could you cause such holes with bare knuckles? Are you bonkers?"

"She made me do it. I used a hammer, not my knuckles."

"So this is why your mother moved out, isn't it?"

"I don't know… maybe, I suppose… but believe me I didn't intend to hurt, only to give her a little scare. You know how she's always dead-set against me?"

"For God's sake she's your mother. Can't you ever grow up?"

"I'll try, I promise. Tell me you're not angry."

"Well…" about to express some doubts, I changed my mind, hoping against hope Camellia finally reached the long overdue turning point. "I must repeat, don't touch anything. I will fix the walls in the next couple of weeks. Now I have to go."

"Can you give me a number to reach you?"

"Sorry I can't", and before she could say anything, I stepped out, having enough for one session of insanity.

*

Another surprise awaited us at the hotel eventually turned out as not ours, although an exact copy of it. At the reception desk I asked the stern looking concierge for the key.

"What did you say the number of your room is?"

I gave it.

"The key is missing, you must have taken it earlier."

"That's impossible. We checked the key in the morning, and never returned since."

"May I have your name, sir?"

"Corbea. Doru C. Corbea. D-o-r-u - C -C-o-r-b-e-a."

"I am sorry, no such entry in our records," came the somber answer after the concierge checked his ledger.

"What? That's impossible. We rented the room last evening, our luggage is in there for sure."

"Let me check once more." Another minute, then: "I am sorry again, we don't have you on record. Sir, may I see your receipt, and the credit card used."

"Sure." Irritated under the clerk's suddenly intensified scrutiny, I fumbled a while, before coming up with the damned proof. "Here!"

The clerk's face relaxed to a smile, as he expertly glanced over my bill.

"Sorry, sir, but you came to the wrong address. You see your room is over here –and he politely pointed out the address on my bill. Unfortunately, this is not the same *Quality Inn*. Let me call them up." His earlier ominous demeanor gradually eased, became solicitous, properly tailored to the decorum for dealing with a customer, in the end always right, even when a bit idiotic.

His suspicion alleviated at last, the man politely, patiently and succinctly pointed out the way, this time to the right *Quality Inn* he marked on a map fished off from under the counter. Obviously, we were not his first customers lost in the vast City of Angels.

"Let's go dolly, Stan Gets, and his orchestra must wait for us a little longer."

She followed as sheepishly as had been silent during the entire affair, guardedly careful not to add any of her red-hot-peppery-quips in the soup of my supposedly infallible navigational skills, although perfectly justified to doing so. By strategically not pouring gasoline in the fire, she delicately tried to save my wounded male's proverbial pride. And hurt my pride had been! Oh boy!

Unfortunately, the night's story didn't end at this point. The always-lurking Murphy's Law interfered perfidiously, adding another layer of annoying surprise. To cut it short we arrived at our *Quality Inn* only in the wee hours of morning, the City of Los Angeles having at least fifteen hotels of the same name, all exact clones located at nearly similarly looking streets and intersections. We must have surely visited all the units during our nearly endless nocturnal peregrinations. At the end of the nightmarish adventure, we became almost hysterically happy when learning that concrete reality had not been sucked down for good in the black hole of Heussinger's famous physical uncertainty after all. And what an exhilarating piece of news this was for two poor immigrants, even if dropped in decades earlier from some sleepy provincial towns of Eastern Europe! God be praised!

*

The spaghetti-like-freeway-tangle in the City of Dreams spares few unprepared visitors from this sort of misadventures! The sheer vastness of Los Angeles alone could be overwhelming even for the most seasoned Yankee tourist, once hopelessly and forever lost, frantically searching across eighty-seven suburbs, a fact unfamiliar to most folk on the Atlantic Coast. Forget the European metropolises altogether! Nothing like Los Angeles exists in the Old World anywhere.

Even by New World standards, California's alternative of the Great American Dream, besides marvelously egocentric, absurdly ambitious and impossibly eccentric, could be in your-face-voluptuous as well. Whether this ebullience came as the result of ever changing, effervescent mélange of ethnic minorities I leave for the experts to comment on, although I dare declare *The Big Orange* to be the absolute embodiment of over conspicuous consumption, kitschy vulgarity and obnoxiousness, so often associated by part of the outside world toward the well-advertised, all-pervasive American way of life.

*

It was exactly what we tried to emulate, a poor illicit couple of imported Romanian lovers roaming across the continent in pursuit of personal freedom and happiness, trying to absorb this greeter-than-life-reality, by definition superficial, fast paced, and emotionally distorted, while randomly crisscrossed the city the next two days along its famous boulevards, avenues, and drives of international fame.

Whatever spiritual gains the two of us ended up with as a result could well have been of questionable value, however deeply etched in our memories. Isn't this sort of hodge-podge knowledge and impressions precisely what most occasional tourists derive off the vast grandiose, but often so puny reality we live in?

To illustrate the point let me describe our journey to Santa Monica along the world famous Sunset Boulevard.

Naturally, we set out based on information gained off a map. The distance didn't seem that great, in our estimation doable in less then two or three hours, a lunch break included in the deal. What a hopeless illusion!

"This is a must-do itinerary, sort of mandatory for a tourist worth his salt. It might be simply sinful not to see Santa Monica, Venice Beach, and Marina del Ray when in Los Angeles."

"Then stop the talk, and drive. What are we waiting for?"

My poor dame, by definition ready for adventure, this time her enthusiasm spilled over in earnest. Perhaps the spring like Californian air, or whatnot intoxicated her with the joy of careless easy living, as this might have happened to many other dream chasers before her. How else could the city have grown so impossibly large? Even I, the perpetual sour-piss skeptic, got infected a bit by this microbe of loony optimism.

"Yes dear, here we go" –and soon enough Bucephalos rolled on one of the expressways crisscrossing the city toward the desired direction, hopefully to reach the eastern end of Sunset boulevard in fifteen-to-twenty minutes max. Barely off to a start, and we promptly got ensnarled in the world-famous L. A. -traffic.

This was for appetizers only, the first cold shower pouring mercilessly over our initial enthusiasm. In the end, beside the aggravation, another hour or so piled on top of the fifteen minutes planned at the outset.

"So far so good, what's an hour delay within a life time?" – I quipped, trying to deflate by sarcasm the frustration accumulated in the meantime.

"Okay, Mr. smart guy, I get it life is not all dreams in Los Angeles. You don't have to rub it in. I know it is twelve noon, and we didn't even cut the first slice off the trip."

"Maybe we'll be luckier from now on."

My companion didn't bother to further elaborate.

At the time, just passed by the Chinese Theater on the right hand side, then along Sunset Boulevard for two or three blocks without even realizing how we did it.

"You see Lady Luck smiles again. At least we are heading in the right direction. Another hour and we'll be strolling in Santa Monica."

"Fine, keep driving."

"What the hell is wrong with you lady, what's my offence now?"

"O man, you know how much I wanted to see this place, don't try to spoil my pleasure with your never ending petty remarks. "Can you do me this small favor?" She was about to burst in tears.

"O God, I'll shut my mouth."

I did, but not without pushing down an indigestible lump of bitterness in my guts. 'Where the hell did I err this time?' I wondered as my memory turned again to Philomela, who in similar situations rarely complained, but often went cheerfully along with my sarcastically humorous, harmless comments.

But on Sunset Boulevard our problems just began—to end only the first act of our adventure. An hour and barely five or six blocks later, the traffic slowed to a crawl anew. During the long minutes spent on red after red lights, we tried to keep calm by watching the tumultuous mass of passers-by, mostly employees out for a quick lunch.

"It might be the perfect time to stuff our pie holes as well" came my friend suddenly alive, out of her contemplative moroseness.

"Why not? Let's find a spot to park."

Hope springs eternal! Another forty-five minutes, and humbled in defeat, we finally gave up the quest. One of the many well-known fast-food establishments had to give up on us as well. Too bad! All things considered, just as well we had to be better off by going on hungry, and adding a few measly minutes to our lifespan by skipping on the extra fat, I thought.

"Hey baby, you might have just shaved a fraction of an inch off your waist, and a few notches of bad cholesterol off your blood."

"What? Am I overweight?"

Sensing troubled waters, I instantly switched to the tactic of evasion.

"Oh no, not at all. You are perfect in all physical ways. Aphrodite herself could envy your body, why would I wish to change it? Then again, why spoil perfection by sticking even a tiny millimeter off fat to your bee-like waistline?"

"Oh shut up little devil, before I smack you over the head. Keep driving, my hunger just vanished."

Happy to oblige I did as ordered, well aware of my fair friend's fibbing through her teeth. She seldom said no to a smoothie, or to a soft vanilla ice cream, both on the McDonald menu. About hamburgers she didn't care much, even less than myself. Sorry McDonald, Burger King, Wendy, Roy Rogers, or Jack in a Box!

As all trips must eventually end, so did ours at about three thirty in the afternoon on the Pacific Coast Highway, with stops in Santa Monica, Venice Beach, and Rodeo Drive. Of these Venice Beach appeared the liveliest and most colorful, closest to the image California enjoys in the rest of the world-- sunny beaches, loony libertine behavior, daringly unconventional, borderline-to-nudity attire, generalized but superficial friendliness. Even the short-trouser-clad police officers on bicycles blended in naturally among the skaters and the roller-blade-runners gliding skillfully up and down the crowded boardwalk. At Rodeo Drive my friend nearly lost her head and breath before the show windows of the conspicuously opulent worlds of Gucci, Yves-Saint-Laurent, Versace, Calvin Klein, Dolce y Gabbana, or who knows what other fashion icons, deliciously tempting deep-pocketed customers. So her frenzy proved of short duration, once she glimpsed at the hot peppery prices, barely affordable even to look at. This was definitely not our world.

"Tell me dear, are you still considering a move to sunny California?"

"I don't know, maybe Maryland isn't such bad place for regular folk like us after all."

At this point I cut my comments short, silently wondering about my concubine's miraculous conversion, about what exactly could have triggered her change of mind. Most often is difficult for men to fathom women's true motivations. Probing the issue deeper would have been foolish, tactically unwise, and potentially perilous to my momentary emotional comfort. Thus I swallowed my friend's admission in well-feigned humbleness. *Liberated women* must cherish this sort of political correctness, however false it may sound. At some level their attitude might even make some sense. Aren't all cultural habits and believes the result of repeated conditioning? What the hell do I know!

Our day concluded in Santa Monica, at the table of a cute outdoor Thai restaurant, offering a menu well adapted to local culinary tastes, heavily bent toward *healthy* vegetarianism.

What we have chosen wasn't bad at all, absolutely satisfying to taste buds, although I am not so sure what it's really been, what kind of weeds we ingested along with the spicy stir-fried tofu cubes. What counted was the feeling of warm happiness nestled in our guts afterward, and this I dared to confess out loud:

"This Oriental stir fried *whatnot* tasted real yummy."

"I'm glad you found at last something good to say, beside your usual sarcasm. I loved the dish too."

What a joy to have once again your female accomplice sing in the same musical key. Perhaps there is some future for us together after all. But then, why think so narrowly and selfishly? Can't all folk simultaneously share common happiness in this crazy world? Must by definition individual joy exist only at the expense of another? Why must life be frequently a zero sum game? Sorry, for I seem to repeat myself in this sense.

The rest of night we spent in the hotel room's quiet harmony, found this time around without extra difficulty, although too late for doing much else than watching TV and sipping some excellent Bavarian beer. Even the cobalt blue waves of the swimming pool failed to exert the usual mesmerizing effect on my desires.

Thereafter only one more objective remained on our list for the City of Angels-- a morning visit to the Getty Museum of Art in Malibu. Based on the few days experience of driving through the city, we set out well before rush hour, hoping to reach destination around opening time that was at eleven o'clock. Surprisingly, we succeeded too. What a victory!

The three hours allotted for this undeniably superficial visit --lunch included in the deal-- passed fast enough to afford a few conclusions, among them the promise of returning to the museum for subsequent visits, and reaffirm once again the need of adding the American collections of 19th century impressionist art to those of Europe, only if for obtaining a clear picture of the movement. Although can't confess to being a fervent student of the subject, but from what I've seen, more impressionist masterpieces could have been brought over to The New World during the past hundred years than remained in the Old. Too bad for the local artists, American collectors apparently and regrettably less concerned about the domestic avant-garde of the 20th century, in turn, better represented across the Atlantic Pond. This impression I offered up somewhat rhetorically.

"Why do you think the American art collector is generally inclined to care more about monetary than artistic values?"

"There you go again… with your loony suppositions! I can't even figure what the hell you said. Better push on the gas pedal-- we want to be in Las Vegas before nightfall, don't we?"

Right she was. Crossing the Mohave Desert could be hazardous even under the best conditions. Such is the nature of deserts, love affairs and lottery-- utter unpredictability.

CHASSING *THE FATA MORGANA* OF LAS VEGAS

Before off to a journey it is advisable to plan the itinerary on the map.

It's precisely what we did in order to avoid repeating our previous failures in reaching various destinations. The daylight in mid July being long enough, our choice fell on the four hours or so of driving eastward by perfect visibility-- sun in the back. But we better wasted as little time as possible uselessly meandering through the residential maze in the City of Angels, on the way out to the Mohave Desert. The strategy appeared propitious for getting to Barstow –the midpoint to Las Vegas—a little before five o'clock in the afternoon.

But simplicity may often end up more elusive than initially envisioned. To our chagrin, we had to face a new dilemma early on, so-to-speak out of the blue, whether to push hard forward fast enough to outrun the thunder storm ominously forecasted on the crackling radio receiver, or stay put and await in safety for the weather to clear, but risk arrival in Las Vegas too late for securing an inexpensive room for the night. The usual contradictory dialogue ensued.

"I say it's wiser to wait, even if arriving in Las Vegas late, and risking to spend the night on the streets. Yet this could be a fun-filled mishap in the *city that never sleeps.*"

Naturally, my quintessential maleness, too often inclined toward a *mucho-macho* logic, opted instead for the speedier solution of outrunning the storm, for the moment only a threatening dark band at the bottom of the southwestern sky.

"You see the map shows less than sixty miles to Baker, a town north of the National Mohave Preserve. We can easily reach there in about forty-five minutes time. As speed restrictions get rarely enforced in the desert, I say we drive on. Moreover, the storm is forecasted to follow a path south of the Preserve."

And then, without waiting for my friend's slightest democratic opposition, I opened up the throttle abruptly and widely, letting Bucephalos reach fast ninety miles an hour, all options of a 180-degree-turn practically and instantly rendered impossible. Four-lane highways generally deny such turns-about legally.

The feminine reaction to this machismo, although muted, came down clearly against my decision if to judge only by the way my friend's body suddenly sunk stiffened in the seat, in obvious frustration and barely restrained anger. But she knew it was too late, totally futile to go against my will.

However Bucephalos loved the unrestrained gallop at the exhilarating neck-breaking pace, hopefully faster than the dark storm's furious whirls of sand, raised menacingly right behind our rear ends. Just seconds before the final two or three miles off the Preserve's greenery, the storm nearly caught up with us, fleetingly spraying a few rapping noisy, angry blasts of sandy rain over the barely working windshield wipers. But by then it was all over, the ever-victorious sun pierced through the dark clouds as suddenly and forcefully as the tempest passed on the left, while I gently steered my victorious stallion in the parking lot of the small shelter, by the Preserve's entrance.

I jumped out spring-like to inspect the damages. Except myriad hair-thin scratches around Bucephalos's white muzzle, all else seemed in perfect order. Nothing serious: just a minor blemish simply erasable by a good buffing. Justly elated for once in life, I won the battle against Mighty Mother Nature. The need of sharing my joy, to dotting it at least by a toast with drinks of Coke and puffs of cigarette smoke became overwhelming. I rushed over to the passenger side. Still in sulking mood, my obviously angered lioness waited ready to bite-- the window rolled down for my reception.

"Come on baby, don't be cross, join me for a drink and smoke. Isn't this a wonderful afternoon, or what?"

"Okay sun-of-a–gun, you won the bet this time, but don't ever do it to me again. I might reconsider dealing with you altogether."

Obviously, her anger relented, melted away with the storm, now present on the northern sky the same way it introduced itself above the southern horizon less than a thirty minutes earlier as a menacing dark band. All is fine when ends well.

"What's your preference, *Mountain Dew* or *Coke*?"

Then she and I –drinks and lit cigarettes in hands-- leaned against Bucephalos's fender and gazed back at the desert we just emerged off unscathed. We couldn't believe what we saw.

The same barren expanse so furiously roughed up minutes ago became instantly an honest-to-God paradise-- never-before known exotic-scents invaded our dilating nostrils. The entire field just seconds ago the raging storm so violently swept over by sand and wind exploded in a unbelievably colorful flowery show, to disappear as miraculously in the following ten-to-fifteen minutes, and return to the ever arid looking wasteland.

At the conclusion of this unbelievably fleeting span of the sublime, I opened my arms to draw the somewhat misty-eyed girlfriend tight to my chest in soothing, father-like fashion.

"There is certainly more to life in the desert than it appears at first inspection."

My embrace received a warm welcome, my concubine's body molded softly to mine in loving submission. My heart skipped a beat, maybe there is still a chance for our love to bloom, I thought.

Having no further need to waste precious time by The Preserve, our trip resumed toward the State of Nevada border, which got in sight shortly, followed soon by the expected information center, this time morphed into a miniature gambling station as well.

"What could be more fit to the reputation of this crazy state?"

"Wow, I love it already. How far to Las Vegas from this point?"

"Forty five minutes give or take a few."

Shuffling through the stacks of information brochures my travel-mate dutifully gathered we showed eager to roll on. Then she came to a fantastic discovery; inserted among the pages a three-day voucher for the luxurious *Bally* hotel, against only fifty dollars per night. Whoopee-do, what a deal!

The unexpected gift contributed to a significantly improved mood, portending a much happier sojourn in Las Vegas than two Romanian immigrant bumpkins of our kind could have enjoyed in the overly complicated, widespread City of Angels. Even the gamble of our contorted sinful love affair could now steer, hopefully, toward luckier outcomes. My mistress's scintillating voice came alive, echoing this very thought.

"Listen, can you for once in your life switch off the bitter sarcasm, to allow for some good time as well?"

"Not only can, but I do promise it too."

"Oh dear, why can't you be always reasonable?" She leaned over, planted a gentle, definitely make-up kiss on my earlobe, as her hand squeezed my thigh perilously near to causing my slumbering maleness to wake up.

"Be patient, baby, don't jump the gun. I'm sure we'll have a wonderful three days together in Las Vegas."

"I swear to this, vouch for it body and soul, lover boy. You know what I mean."

She slowly withdrew, and I sensed her gaze asking for mine. I obliged fast enough to catch the most mischievously sweet glint a man would ever want to see in the eyes of his darling gal. A splendidly warm glow filled the cabin for the remainder trip. The good vibes came to end only in the cavernous underground parking of *Hotel Bally*, as we parted company with brave Bucephalos-- at least for a while.

"So far so good. Let's hope for our welcome upstairs will be just as smooth."

"It will, I feel it in my bones. Trust me!"

Why argue with such over spilling optimism? I couldn't, not then or later in the lobby, when one of the prettiest and sexiest imaginable receptionists handed over the magnetic key to our designated room-- all smiles, no superfluous questions asked.

"Las Vegas seems to be doing just about anything to please, to encourage customers gamble by any means possible."

"Listen, we will try our luck too, right?"

"Sure we'll try our luck. What else is this town for, anyway?"

Faced with the childish prospect of bubbliest happiness, show me the man with the heart to deny his beloved mistress such an innocent request?

The room on the fifth floor surpassed all expectations, the one of the Los Angeles *Quality Inn* puny by comparison, not only in size, but opulence as well. One could easily wish for such a place as a permanent residence-- ivory encrusted classic English style furniture, a double bed so large that even the sultan of *The One Thousand and One Nights Tales* would find irresistible, the white marble-tiled bathroom luxurious enough for Queen Salome herself.

How could a simple diva like my friend not loose her head in this frivolous fairytale-like paradise? She shrieked in delight each time another of the unlimited array of pampering amenities caught her attention. To top this was perhaps only the view out of the two large panoramic windows, overlooking the kinetic pink light show of the *Flamingo* hotel and casino across the street.

"Come, my love, let's shower together-- I promise to show you later a heavenly time, to equal these exotic and sinful luxurious surroundings."

And then, before I could catch my breath, she quickly tore off her skimpy clothing articles, then pushed me violently across the bed, savagely removed all I wore, to end up with her buck-naked body piled on top of mine. It took all the willpower to resist the challenge, and not to succumb in defeat to the reopened abyss of a lethally unchained, erotic release anew.

"No, no, please stop this game right now! It's not a good time."

But she hissed and kissed hot syllables in my ear, as her hand slipped between our tightly touching bellies, and then, to my surprise, she conformed, suddenly pushing her needle-sharp nails in so hard between my ribs that I jerked up in pain. With her dug in cruelly like that my passion subsided instantly, and I rolled on my back. Her grip released, and the quick delicate forgive-me-kiss on my chin saved the day. 'O woman!

"Do not worry, I'll make it up to you later. Come on, let's cool passions in the bathroom before I change my mind."

And what could I do, but obey? Never in the wildest dreams have I imagined my naughty sorceress possessed such hidden talents in her arsenal of teasing pleasures mixed with bittersweet suffering she soon demonstrated again under the shower spray, alternating hot and cold, between pain and pleasure, between teasing laughter and affected denials, between maternal soothing or unchained animal fire, however none finalized, even back on the bed's titillating silky sheets. This way we fell asleep. By the time we woke from the deadly slumber following the encounter with Baby-Amour's honey-mead-like temptations, night descended upon the city, strangely enough without the attendant darkness.

On the *strip* anywhere one looked only light, glitter and sparkle, of the kind not even the permanently incandescent nuclear torch of the *Great Ra* could shower down on Earth during the day. Torrents of colorful folk flowed past against each other on the sidewalks as opposing currents inside well-carved riverbeds, in and out of endless lines of famous casinos and hotels, out of long limos or variously decorated taxis, patiently waiting for their turns under blindingly lit canopies at all entrances.

It was true Las Vegas never slept. On the contrary, dedicated to sheer fun the city appeared more alive at night than during daylight hours. Nobody seemed to mind the reversal, us included-- jaws dropped in awe at the great water-and-fire-volcano-show running non-stop by the entrance to the *Mirage*.

"Wow, this is wholly unbelievable. I never dreamed a magic show like this was even possible. You must agree this is America all right."

"True, and all this cascading water in the middle of a dessert. By the way, do you know where the water comes from?"

"Who cares? Please spare me the annoying details. You promised."

So I did conform instantly, as a gentleman had to keep my word. But no one could stop my thinking about how little present-day-Las Vegas resembled its Spanish heritage, the old *Meadows*, the green oasis in the middle of a dessert, originally inhabited by the *Painted Indians'* tribe. It befell the Mormons to fortify the oasis years later, inadvertently creating the foundation for the relatively recent multi-billion dollar pleasure industry, whereby cheap glitter combined with kitschy décor became almost overnight a separate art form, instantly famous all over the world.

"Yes, my love, right you are this could exist only in America. But let me remind you that the true *raison d'être* of Las Vegas is ultimately gambling."

And as good Americans, whether born or imported, we tried our luck too, ten dollars for each of the three days of our sojourn in this *Mecca* of pleasure. Needles to say we promptly lost our bets at each attempt, either at the one-armed bandits, the poker machines, or once even at the roulette table. What did it matter? Happy to be playing together we felt free of worries and cares, two kids locked up a few nights in the candy store of all dreams.

All good things in life are destined sooner or later to pass, so did our mood suddenly change out of the blue on the morning we cruised for the last time along the *strip* on the way out of town. It happened unexpectedly, when rolling past one of those special marriage chapels Las Vegas is famous for.

"You see, beloved man, we could hitch our lives legally together right here on this spot, were it not for your dilly-dallying about cutting Philomela definitely off your life. Wouldn't we be happier to leave Las Vegas as a married couple? What do you think?"

The shocking question cut my breath off. Absolutely unprepared for the unambiguous proposal I kept staring at the woman in utter disbelief, as hit by lightening.

"Hey baby, don't forget I am still married to Philomela. I can't marry you without becoming bigamous. You must know that."

"Yeah, it's precisely what I meant by your dilly-dallying. Be frank, you don't really want to marry me at all. Is that it?

"But your accusation is blatantly unjust. Who has been living shacked up with you all these years?"

"Why then haven't you at least initiated the divorce? By now we could have been free to rebuild our lives, including Philomela hers, don't you see?"

"Why must you bring this up now? I told you Philomela wasn't about to give up her marital rights just to please your and mine whims, as she formulated it. If I remember you agreed to give her time enough to get tired and more rational about the whole thing, right?"

"Well, I am about running out of patience. How much longer have to wait? Don't I have full rights to the man I love the same way she did before me? It's not my fault her marriage didn't work out, or is it?"

"Fine, fine, but haven't I promised you a definite answer the minute we'll get home. Couldn't you wait until then? Why spoil this perfectly pleasant vacation?"

"I'm sorry, my life is more important than this so-called vacation of ours."

"So-called vacation? What the hell happened to you? What about all those signs of affection you gave me lately? Why the big change now?"

"Because I did everything within my power to convince what I can be for you. Now is your turn to reciprocate my generosity. Will you return the favor, or not?"

"In other words your gift of the last few days of love feast had been only part of a grand, cold calculating scheme, wasn't it?"

"Come, come, try not to be childish. You know quite well such gifts can't be faked. I do honestly care for you, but the time has come to show your true face as well. Either you want to spend your life joined to mine, or you don't. Time is not on our side. I am sick of waiting forever. So who's going to be your next significant one, Philomela or I?"

Instinctively, I avoided answering straight on, hoping to formulate my position later as guardedly as possible, deeming totally unfair to have been put on the spot, especially in the light of our earlier agreement.

I stole a glance to my right. Sunk in her seat the woman appeared sulking anew, withdrawn deep within her own seething anger, lips pouted, gaze pointed stubbornly ahead, somewhere in the dashboard gray. For the first time since we met, her opposition loomed paralyzing, icy cold, perhaps even menacing, not unlike a beautifully colored copperhead ready to strike. 'I must play my cards really close to my chest. Be careful Dorel about gambling our three lives – hers, Philomela's and mine—on a haphazard impulse turned suddenly sour.' Then I issued my words out loud firmly measured.

"Listen, dear lady, I must once again appeal to your good judgment, to beg you recall our previous agreement, and allow me to give you my answer as soon as we'll get home. This time I implore you not spoil the week or so still left in our unique adventure across America. Try to be fair for a change. Your time is exactly as precious as mine. You'll see I will not disappoint your wait."

A long super-prolonged pause ensued. Speeding miles after miles on highway-15, beautiful or monotonous sights left behind barely registered in our minds folded inward. Only the sudden chill invading the cabin brought us back to senses. The road crested as we rolled on the high plateau of Utah. The parking lot of the motel and coffee shop that just came up appeared good enough to drive in on the spur of the moment.

"This seems a perfect spot to have lunch, to put on a sweater, or whatever warmer garment we have brought along."

My still pouting companion obeyed mechanically, but before entering the eating establishment stopped dead on her track.

"Now listen, you mule-of-a-man, for hereby I grant you the last chance to make good on your promise the minute we'll get home. Got it? So let's have a good time. You're right it would be a pity to spoil our vacation with senseless disputes. Give me a kiss."

To my utter amazement the she-devil changed back to her everyday sunny self as abruptly as she switched earlier to anger, not unlike the storm in the dessert came and passed in quick succession. How could anyone alter moods so easily? I could never figure, but Philomela used to go through the same sort of morphing often enough, too. Oh well… what does an ordinary simpleton like myself know about the intractable soul of women?

THE FIRST LEG OF
JOURNEY HOMEWARD

The establishment we halted at looked as a typical *Hot Shop* restaurant on the Eastern Shore, before it went out of business. That it survived in Utah seemed natural in the state the Marriott family called home. Inside, a significantly warmer atmosphere than the chill outside welcomed customers through a host of uniformed, clean-cut, healthy buxom teenagers in hot pants, playing the roles of waitresses, hostesses or busgirls, while equally young boys efficiently acted as short order cooks behind the long counter.

To order burgers and fries seemed almost self-evident, and hot tea instead of coffee.

"Tell me what the hell happened to the crazy sizzling weather we endured for most of our trip? Could this unexpected chill herald the arrival of autumn in these parts?"

"Nah, the colder air is normal at higher altitudes. If not mistaken, this spot rises three thousand feet above sea level. The goose bumps on your arms tell me you have sensed the fresh crisp air the second we stepped out of the car."

"Yeah, it felt at last so wonderful filling my lungs."

"Don't worry, this weather will last all the way through the State of Colorado."

"Halleluiah! This is my type of climate! Forget the Southern states. I wonder why wasn't the country's capital established somewhere around here, in the middle of the continent?"

"Hmm, good question! The answer might be rather of historical than rational nature, I suppose. First, Colorado didn't exist when the capital got established, then again, little logic lies behind history and politics."

"Fine, fine, I get it, save your professorial remarks for later." I felt a gentle kick under the table. "Now better peel your bulging eyes off the sexy calves of these young waitresses, will you?"

"What calves, dear? Where? I see no such thing."

"I am sure you don't, and I am Marry Queen of Scots."

Huh! Didonna made a strong comeback to her genuine self. What a sudden change! Only the question persisted how long could the renewed sunny aspect of my concubine's mood last? Luckily I was free to ponder on the issue at liberty, as she went, so-to-speak, to the little girls room without bothering to wait for my answer.

Still under the spell of her admonition, my gaze slipped now reflex-like towards the pretty waitresses running back and forth in the dinning room. Unable to focus on a single best looking target among so many, I drew a tiny slurp of Coke through my straw, retrained my eyes indifferently on the large window framing in massive bluish mountains in the distance, and my thought flew anew to Philomela. I vividly recalled how she, too, used to tease me when young sexy women happened to freely and innocently flaunt their physical attributes in my proximity, allegedly attracting my attention.

Then I wandered perhaps all women resort to this game of annoying but benign pestering aimed against their men. Could this behavior be part and parcel of a natural defense mechanism or, on the contrary, a skewed way of indirectly complimenting male companions, especially when in little danger of actually gaining the attraction of other females in the given circumstance? Oh well, who can tell?

*

But no like incidents could have spoiled our mood that day even if we wanted. The scenery along route 15-to-70 through Utah became so enchanting as to overwhelm our puny little fighting spirits, confirming once more how natural grandeur might smear a healing balm on the worst sentimental wounds. Blue mountains, big sky, open roads can brighten even the most morose disposition. The air's freshness helped as well, as we eagerly filled our lungs just a few hours earlier burnt to a crisp in the desert heat. Our bodies and minds couldn't have enough of this miraculously invigorating oxygenation.

"I can easily imagine myself settled around here."

"Me too, however impossible that might be."

"How come? What is to hold us back?"

"A lot of things… perhaps our religion…"

"Now, this sounds really, really silly."

"So tell me are you ready to convert to Mormonism?"

"Why should I?"

"Just to belong and gain easier access to a better paid job, for instance."

"This sounds crazy, total nonsense. You lost your marbles. Why should a Mormon get a better job in this state?"

"Simply because in Utah Mormons are most influential, other folk are more or less tolerated, perhaps a little less welcomed than elsewhere."

"Hey buddy, Utah is in the United States, remember?"

"True, but haven't you noticed how all over this vast and rich United States immigrants tend to flock together? This is not New York, Los Angeles, Philadelphia, Baltimore or Washington DC. For Mormon eyes we might look just a tad too alien. To me they seem less friendly than other citizens. Of course they'll open up once joined to their creed, and ready to pay tidings. O course Mormons fit perfectly in the American religious landscape of diversity, but not quite like the rest. But I repeat this is just my own subjective opinion."

"Listen, how the hell can you so consistently come up with such cockamamie ideas? People are people, Mormon or otherwise."

"Maybe so. Allow me then to tell you a story about how I brushed against them some time ago in Europe."

"Alright, but it better be good, not another gassy emission of your overblown imagination."

So I went on to tell my friend how a group of young Mormons, aggressively proselytizing in the Traiskirchen refugee camp in Austria, accosted me years back by promising to speed up the process of our admission in the US, and then facilitate accessing good jobs, all in exchange of converting to their religion and practices. At the end of their pitch, the group presented me with the *Book of Mormon* –deemed by founder Joseph Smith Jun. as the *'the most correct book of any on earth'*, comparable only to the Bible. This statement alone seemed to me bombastic enough as not to take them at all seriously.

"Fine, fine, although quite ignorant about the book, I cannot buy your argument. It's impossible for me to imagine what could be so fundamentally different about their scripture in comparison to other similar religious texts?"

"Well, this is precisely the point I tried to impress on the group in response to their annoying insistence during subsequent days and weeks-- 'Why should I, a bona fide baptized Catholic, convert to another form of Christianity? Why decent people like you do not proselytize among non-Christians? For, even if you succeed in converting me to your religion, the number of Christians in the world will remain unchanged, won't they? I concluded"

"I can see some validity in your assertion", came my friend's retort, "on the other hand, aren't Mormons free to attract whoever wherever they wish, as anyone else?"

"Sure they are, and I accepted this right as matter of fact by harboring no ill feeling toward them until a few weeks later, when I found it almost impossible to shake them off. By then they had changed the tune, literally trying to impose on me all the worldly advantages I would gain by joining the faith. Pressured this hard, fed up with the insistence, I told them to bug off, and leave me be. In exasperation I compared them to Communist propagandists, who attempted luring the uncommitted to party membership by offering the same sort of material advantages in the Old Country of *budding Socialism.*"

"Ha, ha, ha... I imagine the tactic pissed them off enough as to leave you alone at last, tell me I am not right."

"You bet your sweet life my rebuff repelled them-- I never heard of them after that. Yet, the encounter left me a bit miffed about the Mormons."

"My, my, I never realized how many unhealed scars of Communism you still bear. Try to forget, why be paranoid about the past? It's over. Your present is what's important. Besides Mormonism is a religion, not a political ideology."

"So what, religion, ideology, political party, workers union, or whatnot... I hate to belong. Period. But you're right the Communist experience might have marked me, to leave me suspicious vis-à-vis any monolithic, secretive associations. In this sense I must plead guilty."

"Come on, my friend, try to be reasonable. Don't allow one bad personal experience interfere with your innate bent toward objectivity. Individuals may often act as bad apples, in spite of their religion's teaching. So let the issue be forever settled. And if this helps, I no longer wish to live in Utah-- it is a promise, ha, ha, ha... Is this good enough for you?"

"Fine, poke fun at me. Maybe it's crazy, but having grown up behind the Curtain makes me still cringe, when anything, or anybody is asking for my unquestioned submission, okay?"

"Hey, can I still count on your loving devotion?"

"Please, Didonna..." but then I turned my head, and saw her as radiant as ever the distinguished, tastefully ironic lady I fell in love with years ago, miraculously resurrected from yesterday's petty, malevolently smoldering ashes. She's looked all play, no in-my- face-reproach of any sort in her expression.

Indeed, women may change as the weather when least expected. Then again, men can be, oh-so convincingly boring, and a lot more prosaic in their well-feigned fortitude, even when brilliantly clever.

At this point, my golden silence may have saved the day, and sheltered my ass from becoming too romantically mushy, or silly aggressive. But what definitely prevented the exchange from turning truly personal was the unexpected appearance of a canyon on the right side of the road. A huge, telluric deep crack in the ground visualized in the distance however fleetingly immaterial from the speeding vehicle.

"Look, the Grand Canyon! Let's go and check it out."

"Isn't the Grand Canyon in Arizona?" I wondered aloud somewhat hesitating, momentarily puzzled myself by the eerie, phantom-like flash up. "This must be something else, probably not worth the detour."

As to confirm my guess, one of those brown highway signs pointing out tourist attractions came in view, inviting the visitor to Bryce Canyon. Mystery solved, my self-confidence restored.

"Can we visit anyway?"

"No dear, this time we won't. But say you take the wheel for part of the night... and I might reconsider your request."

"No way buddy, I promise nothing of the sort, keep on driving. You do it well, and enjoy it, too. I know Bucephalos prefers you at the wheel." A feather-light assuring touch of her hand to mine on the shifter settled the issue.

A pleasant tranquility filled the cabin anew, as we exited in time to route-50, about to become interstate-70 toward Denver 150 miles farther down the road.

The scenery turned wilder by the minute, as Bucephalos cut its way among apparently unassailable mountains, deep gorges fallen steeply off both left and right, the roadway dauntingly laid down over ancient basalt formations by authentic American pioneers, evidently harder in spirit than even the rock they had to deal with.

How true! Americans are capable of successfully tackling unimaginably huge tasks-- slashing through mountains, bridging vast expanse of waters, boring technologically impossible tunnels, landing on the moon, or doing other similarly heroic feats unlike few people on the planet. It's nearly natural for their weaknesses to surface elsewhere, as possibly in handling the emotional aspects of person-to-person relations, a nation rather consistently cheering loudly for the *lucky winners*, the powerful, while showing unambiguous disdain for the weak, for the *losers*. The proverbially apple-pie-good-American fervently and religiously believes in the so-called *win-win* actions, whereby everyone shares enthusiastically in the success of the victorious emblematic *Superman*. What a grand delusion, in brazen disregard of facts and reason!

Though it must be admitted these same United States, a fairly young country and nation, not so long ago still engaged in unmitigated hand-to-hand combat against the untamed forces of nature, had precious little time to develop to what high-nosed Western Europeans call cultured sophistication, while secretly envious of the raw vitality their brethren in the New Word so abundantly possess.

This paradoxical relationship, between the war-worn old and the raw new, is unabashedly exploited by the self serving propaganda on either side of the Atlantic, a never-ending rivalry between fathers and sons, until one day, possibly in the not-too-distant future, both sides are to wake up together no longer truly the influent powers of the world. Too bad, because the Oriental model, presently so temptingly and eagerly imported on both shores of the Atlantic through the so-called free trade, might evolve to lesser than the *win-win*-scenarios some New World Order advocates blindly promise, while madly driven by the lure of profits to the exclusion of all else.

I itched to share these certainly controversial thoughts with my pretty mistress, but abstained wisely. Why spoil her obviously serene mood by senseless intellectual drills. The proud mountains will still pierce through the azure fabric of the sky, as the naïve children of the New World will persist in cutting them down to size as long as Mother Nature must be subdued at all cost, the Faustian Deal never doubted, the dream of becoming masters of the Universe never abandoned. '*The dream must never die!*' Fear nothing fellow Americans! Even the sly Devil may be cheated, as the soul remains indestructible in the unshakeable faith in God. This is after all America, *the Number One,*

The Exceptional! Show me the dreamer in The New World prepared to entertain the slightest doubts in this respect!

In the meantime, as the violet dusk poured over the mountains gradually fading from view, I became aware of our falling short in fulfilling the daily plan of reaching Denver before nightfall. This shortfall didn't look good at all, and I felt suddenly too tired for the long drive in the dark, on unknown, twisting mountain-roads. Perhaps the deceptively refreshing air of higher altitudes, the reduced oxygenation took its toll on my overtaxed body, yearning naturally for its share of sleep earlier than usually. Turned to inform about my precarious state for driving on, I saw my companion's pretty head bobbing, fighting hard not to doze off definitely in the netherworld. My natural pity had to be willfully defeated in order to shake my poor mate out of the dream world right then and there, even if a bit harshly. What choice did I have? A couple of sinful lovers on the verge of slumber, but running at sixty miles per hour between ravines and gorges along the foaming Colorado River, didn't strike me as the smartest course of action

"Hey sweetie, wake up!"

"What? What is it? Have we arrived?"

"No dear, we are not anywhere yet! Denver is much too far to be reached before midnight. This is bad because I am dead tired, and you don't look in much better shape either. It could be dangerous for any of us dozing off. Please attend to your duty as pilot seriously, and find the next locality on the map, that we may lay down our weary bones for the night within the safety of four walls, not under the open sky in the middle of nowhere."

"Yes Master, your wish is my command. Just a little patience, please try to be the good boy you so often are. Tell me where is it precisely are we right now?"

"Just past Grand Junction, on Interstate-70."

Then my properly reprimanded pretty pilot carefully unfolded the map under the flashlight—always in the glove compartment—and fell silent. Fortunately not for long, her scintillating voice came alive sooner than expected.

"What do you know about Aspen? Could that be a good spot for a night-over?"

"Don't tell me you haven't heard about the famous ski resort. Of course Aspen would be an excellent choice, even if a bit expensive. But vacancies at this late hour might be another story altogether. Anyway, it's worth a try. How far is it?"

"I say less than fifty miles."

And as to confirm her rough estimate, the sign pointing to Aspen came in the headlights-- *20 miles to next exit, another twenty on route 82.*

"Excellent, Lady Luck must work overtime."

A renewed push *of pedal to metal*, and Bucephalos responded eagerly with the proper throaty roar as I eased off shortly again, when hearing my stallion purr soon at a decent clip of 75 miles per hour.

"Hey, what about the police?"

"Come on darling, don't be pessimistic. Everything will be fine."

"Oh-boy, silence is my name. I don't care, the ticket will go on your record, not mine."

"Don't you worry about that."

At that very minute my usual skepticism receded miraculously way in the background, my poorly oxygenated brain suggesting subconsciously, perhaps falsely, that there was nothing to fear. My star must have watched extremely hard over from above, making sure I did no wrong. This sort of magic moment can happen to anyone every now and then, and my mate intuited the moment's uniqueness, signaled immediately by a gentle touch to my hand rested calmly on the shifter. All of a sudden knew I still loved the woman, and she loved me. The logical corollary hit smack across my forehead: two people in love can't be hurt. A new type of electricity charged the sharp ozone-filled air --complimentary gift of the evergreens, suddenly breathing new vigor all around.

Bucephalos must have loved the combusting gift of over-oxygenation as well, as it swiftly pushed forward our bodies even faster, approaching the perilous speed of 80 miles per hour. Life seemed fantastic, almost a thrill.

The exit to Aspen came up fast. Even by the reduced speed permitted on side roads, we rolled triumphantly in Aspen's Main Avenue at nine thirty sharp. As chance has it for the bold, we stopped soon in the parking lot of a small but elegant, well-lit motel, located smack in the middle of town. There it glowed the red vacancy sign bright above the entrance. To top it, the vacancy turned out as the last available, a relatively inexpensive room --ours for the night. I paid the bill without a second thought. My mistress watched a bit dumbfounded my eagerness to open the billfold, my act probably seeming to her somewhat unnatural, to say the least.

Upstairs, in the rather smallish, tastefully elegant room, we disrobed quickly, shared a bottle of beer, set to watch the evening news, but fell quickly asleep in each other's arms not even attempting to make love. Nirvana enveloped our entwined souls, glossing over the kind of sensuality reserved for novices, I mused not for the matured in affection. 'Could it be' I mumbled to myself fleetingly before falling asleep 'that we behaved by then as any time-tested, well-seasoned married couple?'

*

The morning greeted Aspen sunny, crisp, cool and dry, as days begin often in the mountains. After having ravenously consumed a substantial eggs-bacon-and-pancake breakfast, washed down by coffee at the restaurant on the ground floor, we ventured outside to take in, even if on the go, the atmosphere of the famously posh mountain resort.

The pointers of time nearly touched the 10 o'clock mark. Mostly deliverymen, and their vehicles on the street, besides them groups of pedestrians marched strangely in the same direction, clad in colorful ski outfits, blades on their backs, seemingly out of whack for the promise of a typical dog-day in mid July.

"Were are these people headed bundled up like that?" my friend asked, obvious puzzlement in her voice.

"There is one way to find out, let's follow them."

And that's precisely we did. We needed not go far. Two blocks later, the small colorful crowd turned left to a side street, and the mystery cleared instantly. Together with the other pedestrians, we stepped on the platform of Aspen's ski lift, ferrying people to the summit.

"What about a ride up the mountain side?"

"Sure, I thought you never asked."

Two tickets promptly purchased, and minutes later we commenced the climb toward the peek, dressed, unlike the others, only in shorts, sleeveless blouse and shirt, sandaled feet dangling in the cold air, thirty feet above ground. It didn't take long to see why our fellow travelers wore cozy, warm ski outfits. The green mountainside at the base soon turned snow-covered-white, the temperature fell precipitously degree-by-degree each elevation foot higher we climbed. Fortunately, the summer sun came down warm enough to ameliorate the chilly sting to the exposed flesh, as to never become truly unbearable.

Besides, the trip took less than thirty minutes, plenty of time for the exposed limbs to grow huge goose bumps. This little bit of pain endured made us, however, that much happier the minute we sat down in the cozy glass-enclosed coffee shop-- a large open terrace in front of it. The view off this vantage took our breath away. But after absorbing the splendor for a minute or two-- a viewing dose amply sufficient for our frozen limbs, even for the proper mention in our contemplated memoirs--, we wisely opted for the inside, for two cups of steaming coffee, next to fresh croissants. This sort of warming up couldn't have been that bad of an idea, in view of our having to repeat the trip downward under the same conditions, even if temperature-wise in a reversed sequence.

At this point, the proverbial American ingenuity must be given some well deserved kudos, as it was precisely this sense of practicality that produced here--as elsewhere on the continent-- the adjacent familiar eatery, the souvenir shop, filled by run-of-the mill knick-knacks, mostly made in China-- Aspen-logo-decorated-t-shirts, and surprisingly, a sort of transparent throwaway nylon mantles for dumb people like us, unprepared for the occasional snow falls, often enough possible during the trip downward. Two such protective coveralls got promptly purchased in wise preparation, before having to brave the mountainside chill anew.

Under such protection, the trip downward proved uneventful, although it's worthy to mention that we arrived at the motel a couple of hours later than move-out-time, but luckily only minutes before the cleaning staff had to enter the room. My usually pedantic forethought might have helped a bit too, as I made sure to deposit the luggage by the door outside before leaving the premises, an act that possibly saved our sorry pecuniary foundation from the harsh penalty of paying for an extra day. By the same token, this could have been equally the result of the cute solicitous female receptionist's courtesy, which my jealousy-prone mistress fortunately couldn't see, as she decided to wait in the car. What a lucky break!

In this fashion concluded our totally unplanned adventure in Aspen, successfully all the way from beginning to end. Even retracing our way back to route-70 occurred in a jiffy, smoother than ever before. By now Lady Luck must have subscribed to helping us full time. Denver being less than an hour away, I remarked, perhaps more than a little boastfully.

"Didn't I say last night everything would be all right?"

"Yeah, so what's the big deal?"

About ready to snap back a nasty little retort, but as I turned, and caught her blue eyes smiling in mischief, and lips puckered to blow a light kiss, I had to smile. What else than to respond in kind, while reining in Bucephalos at the maximum legally allowed speed? Then out of the blue I remembered someone's confession about getting fined pretty badly in Colorado, whereby police didn't tolerate, allegedly, even a measly mile above speed limit.

We rolled triumphantly in Denver around three thirty in the afternoon.

ACROSS THE HIGH
ROCKIES PLATEAU

Some say *'The-Mile-High-City'* had been settled on a geographically ideal spot. This is fact. Between snow-capped mountains in the background to the West, and the high plateau of Kansas, and Nebraska to the East, Denver reputedly enjoys, aside from the most pristine air in the country, as little rain as San Diego and as much sunshine as Miami. At the point the four virtually divided squares of the United States align to their north-south, east-west axes, the region's past or present abundance of gold, silver and other mineral resources should have rendered the capital of Colorado by necessity into a natural corporate business hub. Strangely, this did not quite happen.

Apparently, the Wild West atmosphere pervasive during the *Gold Rush* favored the rugged colorful individualism of small adventurers more than the cold emotionless calculating objectives of big corporate business. Consequently, a plethora of smaller enterprises flourished naturally in Denver, such as brewing, manufacture of mining machinery, printing and, lately, software development, to render the mile high city into a place whereby both making money, and recreation activities flourish side by side.

*

But a fact must be stated clearly from the outset that such an important capital as Denver still offers the tourist a plethora of cultural objectives, such as fine museums, the famous Center for the Performing Arts, as well as the city's busy heart at the Larimer Square, with its chic boutiques set in a well-mimicked atmospherics-filled Victorian neighborhood. But even as the glass-and-steel petrodollar skyscrapers, or the golden dome of Colorado State Capitol may compare favorably to any such structures elsewhere, we decided, wisely or unwisely, to more or less skip the town, mainly for two reasons. Once, because our first impressions did not happen to be too good by sheer chance of the novice-- as we drove mostly through boring, uninteresting sort of run-down red brick neighborhoods--, and second, due to the previous day's side trip to Aspen our plans had to be rectified accordingly, just for getting back on the original track before the always fast approaching nightfall. Yet we enjoyed our rushed transit for two-to-three hours by properly appreciating the grand sub alpine land on the way eastward, punctuated by numerous magnificent villas in quaint little suburban towns, probably as charming as any in Switzerland or New Zealand. For some wholly unexplainable reasons, I imagined the Coloradoans in these parts to be the same rugged type mountaineers, although seldom seen, and then often in teams of rafters on the white foaming river, flowing alongside the road in alternation either on the right or left.

As this segment of our journey came to end fairly fast as all pleasant things in life usually do, willy-nilly we resigned to the belief to have made a good enough trade-off by skipping many of Denver's probably well-deserving attractions. As it turned out, the splendid scenery on the way out and down proved an ample reward instead, a visual thrill surely unavailable, had it been hidden under the dark veil of the always-approaching night. Some gains, some looses.

When the encroaching night drowned even the last sublime vistas of sub alpine valleys in blue ink to render everything gradually invisible, and since Bucephalos had to cut again a tunnel by its own lights through an increasingly denser black wall, our conversation first slackened, soon to cease altogether. On my right I overheard my friend's breathing slow down, a clear indication she dozed off, wafting away in the dream world. Her attitude, to selfishly abandon me to my own devices whenever her assistance I needed most, initially hurt my feelings, but then gradually mollified and turned inward, to listen to my own reverie, similarly dangerous, equally pleasant. Let's not forget, Bucephalos kept darting ahead on the apparently endless road at sixty miles an hour.

Some indefinite time later, I felt myself turned into a dot of light streaking comet-like through the indigo colored space. Out of this fathomless darkness, Philomela's image surged to my mind again to somberly ask.

'Why, my life-long spouse, did you have to betray me like this? Couldn't you at least have chosen a prettier, younger female for your conjugal treason?'

What a strange question! Although totally clueless, I repeated it mechanically in my mind over and over in dumb moroseness. 'Indeed, why didn't I go for a younger lover?'

Seconds, perhaps minutes later, I stole another peek to my right, as if I could've gotten an answer out of my sleeping concubine. Fat chance! Her crumpled, tired body twisted into a pretzel, her lifeless heavy head, and tussled hairdo fallen way-side, the steady stream of gurgling hisses escaping her slightly open mouth compelled my gaze to return instantly back to the darkness of the road ahead.

'So, why haven't I aimed for a younger female? Isn't this the usual choice of males going through middle age crises? Could my behavior have revealed just the opposite, that I wasn't undergoing a crisis at all? If not the proverbial middle age syndrome, what the heck happened to me?'

In a blink, the truth hit flash-in-the-eyes. 'I didn't go for the proverbial younger feminine lure, although plenty available for the prowling male at any age, mostly because I must have been afraid, worried about the possible failure, a hit my arrogant, all too-knowing, never-wrong ego could ill afford. My, my, this oversized ego of mine—couldn't have been somehow too cowardly for taking any such risks? So, why not prey on a hard working immigrant mom, having to care for a young boy without the benefit of his father in a strange new land? This must have been precisely what I did, consciously or not. A deep resounding silence suddenly wrapped chilling over my tortured mind, inescapably sucked in the maelstrom of a most unfathomable black hole, while the fading image of a sadly smiling Philomela's visage vaguely persisted as a diminishing echo on the wavy indigo backdrop.

I do not remember what exactly followed, what happened during the next two, three, maybe even four hours of monotonous drive in the dark. Only Good God Almighty could have protected two strangely intertwined migrant outcast lovers from disaster, Didonna's and my fate bound in sin, both totally or partially asleep in the same vehicle, speeding on the perfectly straight highway seemingly unopposed by anything under the stars. It had been a huge 18-wheeler that finally snatched me off this perilously long wandering in the dream world, as the behemoth passed on the opposite lane, causing poor little Bucephalos to jerk and shudder in the whirlwind created, as our suddenly shook-up, deeply frightened souls came abruptly back to senses.

"What happened? How far to our destination?"

"What destination, have you picked any? By the way, did you have a good sleep, because I couldn't?"

"Hey buddy, showing your petty nastiness again, right? You know I didn't doze off on purpose. Why didn't you wake me up if you needed help so badly? What time it is?"

"I don't know, maybe an hour or two before dawn. What does it matter? The truth is I can barely keep my eyes open. If I do not stop driving now, the worst could happen any minute. Maybe you want to take the wheel, yes?"

"No, I am not up to it. Honestly. Please understand. Just pull on the shoulder, and have a short refreshing little nap. Why don't you do that, sweetheart?"

However this wasn't to be. At that very minute I caught the glimpse of a tiny light, the very first in a long long time, alluringly twinkling now in the distance.

"Look, can you see that light? It must be a community surely to have a motel. Perhaps it's worthwhile to push it for a couple more minutes. What do you say? Is it a go?"

"Sure, darling, your choice is mine as always."

What a lucky guess. The distant light turned at long last into a solitary incandescent bulb hang precariously in a rickety fixture by the entrance of a motel, apparently for tired truckers. However no such sign visible, no pointers whatsoever other than the whitewashed, blank plywood board nailed on the door above the window cut in it. As we approached, dense masses of huge trucks contoured barely visible roundabout the large surrounding parking lot. Some had engines idling softly, probably for powering the air-conditioning or refrigeration units.

"This is a truck stop all right. I wonder if we can find a room at this late hour."

"I rather wish we don't, this place feels so spooky. Do we really need to overnight here?"

"What's our choice?"

"Please drive on for a few more miles, and maybe we'll hit the community this truck stop belongs to. The town must surely have a real motel."

"And what if there is no town nearby? Are you willing to risk it? By the way, can I guess that you're ready to take the wheel? Remember my driving ability is about to crash any minute into a dead, concrete wall."

"No, this can't be true, the cool fresh air must have recharged your batteries by now. Don't you see? Come on, I promise to stay awake and talk to you non-stop. You can do it. I know you can. Just don't make me drive, please, darling, don't be so cruel."

Indeed, she could have been right-- the night felt incredible, the air soft and velvety, the moonless sky filled by myriad stars gradually rendering the darkness less and less opaque. I looked around and caught fleeting glimmers, reflected randomly off the shinny fenders of some dormant trucks. Suddenly, what to my friend seemed spooky to me looked uncannily tranquil. As she guessed the fog in my mind cleared. I no longer felt quite so dead tired. Moreover, my improved reasoning kept whispering even more reasons for staying put, for not risking a drive in my surely ephemeral state, which might have been induced momentarily not only by the fresh air, but by the play of devil himself, always in his preferred element at some tricky hours of night. Consequently, my answer to my concubine's pleading might have been a bit harsh, and perhaps a little louder than necessary.

"Listen, woman, this time I will not budge, we will stay right here for the rest of the night. Period." Then, taking the ensuing silence as a sign of approval, I stepped out and approached the window cut in the door. But after attempted to peek inside, to my disappointment, my eyes met only with deep soft darkness. The reception office appeared devoid of any human presence.

'What a curiously neglected business is this, nobody on duty meeting or greeting customers? Hmm… very strange.' I mused on the way back to the vehicle.

"Please, darling, let's drive away. I don't like it here-- it feels ominous."

"Ominous or not, we won't go anywhere. Maybe I should try to knock."

It is exactly what I did next, in brash disregard of my mate's request. I returned to the window, and knocked once, twice, trice, every time more forcefully, but nothing happened.

The office appeared unattended-- nobody answered my increasingly louder knocks.

"That's it. We will have to spend what's left of the night in the vehicle, under the stars. It should be a lot safer than driving on dead tired as I am. You'll see how a few hours of sleep in the seats pushed down will do wonders, then at dawn, we may be on our way again. Why risk an accident? So, what do you say?"

She didn't bother to oblige, although I could see clearly from her pouting my decision wasn't at all to her liking. Yet she proceeded to adjust her seat, simply turned to the right, her arched back and round bottom presented in obviously ostentatious response. Then she ceased to move, pretending to have fallen instantly asleep. Perhaps she did so in earnest, as even her breath seemed to have stopped. I will never know. For the moment, though, I had to accept the situation as it was, turned my back to mirror hers, and soon enough let myself too, stolen away in the welcoming arms of the always-gentle Father Sleep, in the liquid world of forgetfulness-- no memory, no more problems.

However the realm of obliterated awareness has not turned into an abode for my nearly mortified soul as expected because I dreamed. As soon my eyelids just barely closed shut, and I've landed in a motion picture-like sequence, rushing image to image almost uninterruptedly, one more twisted than the other, my puffed up, uncannily light body hovering tethered to a barge, above the river meandering across my hometown as a greenish serpent never seen before, between inexistent shores, elaborately ornate buildings, gothic churches and redoubtable castles inhabited by yellowish-brown, quite repulsive reptilian humanoids with large bulging eyes. Amidst these constantly milling cold-blooded hellish creatures, from time to time, I glimpsed the lit-up but sadly ethereal face of Philomela, as she repeatedly pleaded and implored our infantile, angelically innocent-looking daughter Camellia: 'Did you really have to go to *Tra-La-La* land with that awful character Mark? Couldn't you find a better man for a husband? Why didn't you talk about your choice to daddy first? Why haven't you asked for his permission or blessing?"

Next heartbeat the images scattered as flocks of crows scared away by gunshots, broken black shards of glass flying in all directions, to finally melt into a crystal ball above my grandmother's ancient, weather-battered corner house in my home-town's inner city neighborhood. But my dream didn't come to an end, only became foggier, continuing on and on, and on along similarly twisted patterns, much longer than the generally accepted thirty-seconds-period deemed by the science of psychology to last during rapid eye movements. The convoluted stream of images kept incessantly floating past *ad infinitum*, up to the very heartbeat I'd been torn off the gruesome world by the harsh sound of Diesel engines, revved up to pull their loads in preparation to exiting the truck stop.

My eyes popped open. The darkness of night nearly dissipated, replaced by the dim glimmer of the impending dawn my watch confirmed as well. My concubine's body had not moved, still turned to a pretzel on her right side the same way I saw her a few hours earlier. The last evanescent rags of my dream wafted to smoke in the same breath, leaving only a vague, ashy aftertaste in my parched mouth. I felt the terrible need to have a sip of coffee-- miraculously, the enticing aroma of this good-morning-call permeated the air, all of a sudden tingling my olfactory sense in earnest, beyond any hallucination.

The air felt crisp and cool, in spite of the bluish smoke belched generously off the departing trucks' exhaust pipes. For the inveterate smoker lighting a cigarette seemed to be in perfect natural order, to fight fire with fire, without causing any significant additional harm to this beautiful beginning of a summer day, somewhere on the high plateau of American Midwest. The first tastiest of smokes exhaled off my lungs, and I absentmindedly performed a quick scan around the horizon, only to see us encircled by an ocean of wheat and corn fields, the truck stop an island in the midst of it.

But then another scent hit my nostrils, that of the infinitely vast space, its existence in all probability not detected as acutely anywhere in the world, with the possible exception of the Russian steppes.

The Romanian *Lebensraum* is small in comparison, its odor much too delicate for penetrating through the rich perfume of flowers, the freshly cut hay, or the ozone emanation of dark evergreen forests.

As the novelty of the crushing space bore itself ever deeper into my slowly awakening awareness, I realized the island we happened to spend the night was only a tiny speck of land somewhere within a much larger area, commonly called the grain belt, the food basket of America, and to a degree, of the planet. Oh what a boringly beautiful country this was in its nearly limitless agricultural grandeur!

In the same flicker of time, as I intuitively tried to fathom the paradoxical contrast between the scene's monotony and splendor, my weary bones felt the need of a good stretch, not unlike a perplexed dog when confronted by something greater than its ability to understand. Then I promptly forgot the whole thing-- my glance fell on the building I couldn't enter hours earlier, and the uniquely enticing aroma of coffee that woke me up a minute earlier got its own, quite banal explanation.

A silvery food truck —so familiar to most Americans-- was parked and open for business in front of the rather smallish rickety building. A long queue of truckers waited patiently for their turns to buy doughnuts and coffee, in order to properly energize before setting their rigs back on the road.

Another peek inside Bucephalos's cabin and, as my somewhat estranged female companion appeared still unmoved in her embryonic position, I decided to fetch coffee and doughnuts for us both, as a perfect morning goodwill gesture. Whether she feigned to sleep, or just continued to express her disaffection, I decided, perhaps wisely, not to find out the truth, in the hope of relegating her childish attitude to the wastebasket of forgotten emotional details, as an insignificant momentary annoyance often disturbing the harmony between couples during too many years of cohabitation.

But as the afterglow of my weird dream lingered somewhere in my mind's recesses, the woman's actual presence before my eyes that morning appeared for the first time not much more than an accident destiny must have brought about for some concrete reasons. The need to study, penetrate and understand my motivations became all of a sudden imperative, the situation simply no longer to be taken for granted. Nothing in the Universe can be without explanation, my love for this woman had to have some validity as well, I surmised. The time came at last to take charge of my fate, for figuring out exactly where I stood before attempting another step forward, for sharing equally and fairly with all parties involved the plan for the morrow, where to go next, **who with whom**.

Musing and chewing quietly on these somewhat murky thoughts on the way to the food truck, I resolved firmly not to hurt any party willfully ever again, not to repeat the needless cruelty shown to Philomela, as on the day I abandoned her mercilessly to wriggle in pain on the basement's cold concrete floor during our last senseless conjugal confrontation. My newly discovered attitude proved exhilarating, my conscience liberated instantly, the inveterate pessimist meticulously pushed to the remotest corner of my nature, the new optimist finally brought forward to a new reality not only rationally, but emotionally as well. At least this was the catharsis I imagined to have happened that banal minute on my way to fetch coffee and doughnuts. Big revelations may often occur in quite trivial circumstances!

About to find out there wasn't any motel within the perimeter of the truck stop, and that we spent the night in the vehicle as everyone else around --even if less comfortably than the truckers in their better appointed cabins--, my self-confidence got a little extra boost, my lately weltering ego received another well-deserved shot in the arm.

Inside the building I tried to enter last night only a large whitewashed waiting room, in it tables and chairs for sheltering truckers during inclement weather-- adjacent to this space a few coin-operated shower cabins. 'Didonna will like this', I mused intent on letting her know about the opportunity, and invite her to a hot morning shower following our coffee–and–doughnut breakfast, as the best way to refresh, to sweeten our soured moods, incurred perhaps by the curtailed night sleep in the car.

The idea must have struck the right chord because she agreed on the spot, even blew me a tiny kiss, her earlier pouting attitude evaporated in thin air to my utter surprise, as if to say 'You see, my love, unlike you I seldom hold a grudge.'

What she actually said sounded rather like a question.

"But I hope it didn't cross your loony mind to let me shower alone, surrounded by so many strange men?"

"How should I do a thing like that? Of course we will shower together. Don't worry I won't leave you naked in the proximity of any strange males, even if separated by the solidest of concrete walls. I wouldn't expose the woman I love to such a disgusting humiliation."

"Okay-okay, cut the crap. I hope the idea never even occurred to you. Then it is settled shower we will together. My dear boy, prepare to have your neck wringed if I am somehow to find out you thought otherwise." She sounded matter of fact, dead panning in the best possible fashion, while busily searching in the luggage for a change of underwear. "Do you want to change your underpants, or prefer to stay in your own juice a bit longer?"

"Come on now, no need to be obnoxious, a male is human too, remember?"

"Oh I am always thrilled to learn new facts about the creature. Let's go. Lead the way as the solid man you claim to be!"

It appeared my girlfriend fell back within her old deprecating self, although something in her tone betrayed a bit of change. I couldn't pinpoint precisely in what way, but her new attitude engendered in my mind a vaguely darker sense about our relationship. All the same, my apprehension could have been only a reflection, an echo of my own resolution of minutes earlier? I will never know, even though as I rifled through my thoughts for a fleeting but well-defined instant I became aware of a strong, strange novel foreboding that permeated my entire being.

In the dingy but spartanly clean concrete shower cabin, we undressed with peremptory shamelessness, as a pair of equally sexless individuals prepared only to cleanse bodies, and taking care to avoid the slightest hint of sensuality. This gender neutrality should have lasted quite a while, as long as we only tried to make the cheap soap bar foam on our wet skin, and could have continued so without any untoward effect had not my showering companion said on the best feigned tone of indifference.

"Would you wash my back? I will return the favor."

What a perfectly innocent proposal, was it not for the involuntary response it elicited, exacerbated progressively as I tried to fight it. Unfortunately, nature preordained males to respond in peculiarly predictable way, too familiar for the opposite sex not to take advantage of it as a weakness.

"Hey, buddy, something tells me you're happy to touch my derriere."

She mischievously paraphrased Mae West's famous line, as she turned around to reciprocate by smearing soap, first on my chest, then letting her slippery fingers run circles lower and lower on my sensitized abdomen, ever more eagerly producing goose bumps in the wake of the subversive touches.

"Aha, there you go again my dear little hungry, greedy boy. I think you might want something only I can give now, isn't it my little masculine monster? Come on, beg for it, let me be your Circe, as you turn into the little horny pig you actually are deep down in your core, and I will grant your wish right here on the spot."

"Right here, right now, what if someone sees us?" My voice turned unmistakably hoarse, a bit snarled by saliva.

"Don't be silly, no one is interested. It's too early in the morning, and the folks are now rather preoccupied by their guts, not their sex drives. Don't you know this, my always smart-alecky stud?"

"Okay, okay, baby, you win, I am ready."

"No, no, sweetheart, this time we won't do it your way, only I will be the doer. You know cunning beautiful Circe must be always in charge, unlike the masculine victim she never fails to turns into a little piglet."

And this is precisely what the wicked woman did to my flesh progressively overexcited to a frenzy-- she went on, and on, and on to relentlessly smearing foamy soap all over and around my sensitized zones in smaller and smaller circles, before closing in on her target, willfully disallowing any possible return before my sorry ending against her wet abdomen, suddenly pressed to my own in the tightest embrace I ever lived through. "Oh you, devilishly naughty woman!"

"Good job, little piggy, you behaved well, but not a word to spoil my victory, just let me plant a smooch on the pretty little snout, barely visible under your wet moustache. Don't guys and gals in love deserve to kiss after curtain fall?"

And we kissed, and kissed, and kissed nearly to choking, as her fingers continued running up and down my slippery spine, my hands busy over hers, helped along by the shower spray turned up full-force to a rinsing, refreshing cold torrent of evil purging, soul purifying *aqua vitae*. 'Am I owning my life, or life is the owner? Master, slave, or both-- what am I?'

*

Driving along the next segment of our track homeward proved more than monotonous. The highway, straight as only a giant could have build guided by a ruler, ran mostly among seemingly endless cornfields. Interspersed here and there in this vast vegetal ocean, squeaky working oil rigs brought to surface the precious black gold today's energy hungry society demands in ever larger amounts-- some say, to the ecologic detriment of the planet.

Here I must confess my own sinful complicity, as I enjoyed my vehicle as anybody unwilling to give it up for some illusionary benefit future generations might incur, in flagrant contradiction to my often vehemently critical, but (obviously) hypocritical attitude--so typical for most so-called progressive individuals, pretending altruistically interested in saving the word essentially through talking, but seldom behaving in tune with their own advise. Words are cheap, acting properly much harder!

Similarly vague random thoughts popped in and out of my head, as my partner in sin withdrew to silence, fallen in her own thoughts, basking perhaps in her own rediscovered feminine power, in the afterglow of the unique sensual demonstration she made in the shower, her blue gaze indifferently piercing through space beyond even the distant horizon.

From the truck stop eastward, route-70 didn't pass for a long time nearby any small or large town. Then at last came Junction City we never bothered to enter, except in a tiny *Safeway* grocery store located in total isolation somewhere by its proximity. Good enough! It was all we needed for replenishing our food and beverage supplies. Only two beat-up pickup trucks parked on the narrow gravel strip, which ran about a hundred yards left and right, in front of the one-winged glass entrance door.

"Are we lucky or what? Can you imagine the long lines at the cash register in this little dump? Judging by these lonely pickup trucks, we must surely be the only customers this early morning. The question is will we find all we want inside, beside the proud owners of these vehicles?"

"Back to your old facetious self, right? I am sure the store is stocked with all we need. After all, it belongs to the famous *Safeway* supermarket chain, does it not?"

"Yeah, so it appears, but I bet that this particular joint will hardly resemble the markets either in Arizona or Maryland, in spite of showing off the well-known *Safeway* logo above the entrance."

Both our opinions proved partially correct. Inside not a single customer to keep busy the two young female employees, trying hard to be as courteous as possible, although reservedly suspicious after hearing my obviously foreign accent.

"I bet no Romanian words hit these two nice country gals' eardrums ever before. But don't you worry, we look reassuringly Caucasian, especially you with your blond hair and blue eyes. This might relax them enough to act guardedly polite, even if a bit confused."

"My, my, there you go again with your analytical nonsense! Let me prove it how wrong you are. Let me do the talking." And so she did, even before getting my benevolent nod of acquiescence.

It took at least three attempts for her words to get through, but as she remained undaunted, they must have had sufficient time to establish no criminal intention on our part, and willing to lead us to a large, open-top refrigerated box, containing the items on our shopping list-- ham, bologna, cheese, and Wonder bread loafs, stacks of beverages-- unfortunately only *Safeway* brand Cola, next to some generic cans of orangeade.

"Good enough, these will tie us over until Kansas City."

"May we have a few tomatoes and green peppers as well? I timidly asked the gal that neatly fit our loot in a couple brown paper bags.

"Sure, sir, we have some canned varieties, but I strongly recommend you get fresh tomatoes and green peppers at the local produce stands in town. Around here, folk don't buy this stuff in grocery stores."

"How far to town?"

"Not very far, maybe a little over thirty minutes drive."

Right then it dawned these decent-looking young women, probably living in farmhouses built out here as far and in between as larger cities on the East Coast, might be judging distance quite differently than we did. So, I concluded my inquiry by politely thanking for their kindness, and pretty soon Bucephalos happily gobbled up unopposed the miles eastward on the wide-open freeway.

"I am so glad you asked about produce-- it would be nice to get some fresh tomatoes, peppers and fruit in town."

"Come on, woman, come to your senses. Why be irrational, and waste an hour and a half detouring in and out of town just for tomatoes? The trip ahead of us is long, and I'm set on reaching St. Louis before nightfall."

"Then why the rigmarole of questions, as you had no interest in the gals' advise anyway?"

"Is it really so bad being polite? Didn't you notice how scared the poor souls acted initially?"

"Of course, of course, for a second I forgot who you are. However I wonder whether you behaved as the same well mannered gentleman had the two pretty chicks been young studs instead."

"Are you saying the damsels were pretty? I didn't notice."

"Sure you didn't, and my name is *Candie-Bamby*, the little blond bimbo."

"Oh for the love of God, what's wrong with you again? A few hours ago I was about to believe you had outgrown your crazy jealousy outbursts. How foolish can I be?"

"Shut up, man, shut up. Will you take us in town, or not?"

"No, I won't, period. Please don't push it!"

"Okay, okay, I won't, but tell me how come it is always only what you want? Can't I have it my way, at least once in a while?"

To this flagrantly unfair accusation I was about to cast back a willfully furious glance, but as I met my complaining mate's innocent, wide open, obviously questioning blue eyes, I suddenly wised up, to leave the issue alone, in the hope of bringing the confrontation to a better end later, or maybe forgetting it altogether. Time can often place a welcome damper even on the silliest domestic clashes, I thought, remembering my earlier resolve to appease.

So there we ran anew slightly at odds with one another, somewhere between Junction City and Topeka Kansas-- possibly the most boring stretch on route-70 eastward--, a couple of lovers ever more frequently split by apparently minor, but mutually irritating issues any psychiatrist worth his salt --even some common-sense persons-- might see as symptoms of deeper fundamental misalignments, neither of us ready to accept yet as unadulterated truth working full time against the very grain of our sinful relationship.

Willy-nilly, within this super-monotonous context, enhanced by the smoothly purring motor of brave Bucephalos, it didn't take long for either of us to fall back in our own recurring reveries about the recent, or a more distant past. It became obvious that my ruffled-feather-friend's silence was hiding graver matters than the usual overblown reactions to minor nuisances, attitudes I unfortunately began to view as punishments she administered with increased frequency, whenever feeling unfairly wronged either by my words or behavior. This progressive aggravation I pondered upon more and more could herald nothing good. Yet still inclined to resolving peacefully the latest bad blood between us, I chose to cast in her directions a few persistent friendly glances, honestly intent on sparking reconciliation. This time my goodwill hit a wall of cold stone. She kept on sulking, never turned her head as if forever ostentatiously locked in bad mood.

'All right, dear, be that way' I thought in frustration, but feeling almost pity for her, or conversely, perhaps helplessly sorry for myself, for my inability to ever overcome magnanimously some minor obstacles raised by banal female obstinacy. All of a sudden, I turned bloody enraged, about to smash my head against the dashboard in response, but by nature disinclined to violence, resigned to my fate equally fast, and slowly faded away in my own habitual mental wanderings.

Philomela's dramatically admonishing question to Camellia came to fore again in my mind: 'Why, my flesh of my flesh sweet daughter, didn't you go for daddy Dorel's permission to marry the bum Mark?' 'Why, why, why?' I yelled silently back, and the answer ensued almost in the same heartbeat-- 'Show me the parent ever able to stop a daughter in love from stumbling into a catastrophic marriage!'

*

Next I recalled the sunny day that befell me nine months after our initial settling in Washington DC. On my way home earlier than usually from work, I came across Camellia in the company of her latest girl-chum Debby, both skipping school, roaming the streets of Georgetown, ostentatiously smoking cigarettes –who knows, perhaps something worse—that is brazenly behaving in-your-face-badly, totally unbecoming for pupils their age. Naturally I reprimanded Camellia on the spot in obvious disregard for the humiliation I might have caused her in front of a friend. What else should I've done?

Both Philomela and I, fresh resident aliens had to work hard to make ends meet, to pay for the food, shelter and clothing, moreover for our darling daughter's education --allegedly a quintessential prerequisite for a better future than she could have ever looked forward to back home in the Old Country, at the time still in tight grip of Communism. Well, well, so many good intentions gone to hell! Fortunately, it took only another short mental silence for my sidestepping this dilemma, for my conveniently taking refuge in placing the blame on others, as usually.

What the heck for did I listen to Mr. George, Philomela's uncle? Based on his own hellish experience with his run-away-from-home-daughter, he advised for placing Camellia in an expensive private Catholic primary school we could ill afford, and that only by partially sacrificing our own welfare at the worst possible initial times. How was I to guess the humiliations Camellia had to endure among her *preppy* classmates, looking down their noses at the poor immigrant girl barely speaking English, and never possessing the half dollar for buying lunch at the cafeteria, as all other kids did? How was I to figure out this American common place? Back home in Romania kids went to school with lunches wrapped in old, greasy newspaper sheets --no cafeterias on the premises.

Did anyone ever bother to inform the newly arrived immigrant about such trifle details? I yelled in my mind, increasingly upset. Only one questions obsessively persisted in red letters before me, one that many overly benevolent American neighbors unfailingly addressed us newcomers *'How do you like our country?'* To me this sounded as if the apple-pie-sweet locals were a bit unsure about their great country's goodness, apparently in need of repeated reinforcements for silencing their own doubts. Rightly or wrongly, I often wondered about this paradox.

One afternoon I have been invited to a parent-teacher meeting, to face the music the benign pious nuns reserved for my ears about Camellia not paying attention in class, under-performing in math, disturbing teaching in general, or excelling through other disruptive acts of wicked behavior day-in-and-out of classes.

Crimson with embarrassment, I reacted instantly with the promise to clip the culprit's hair short, to have the vain little creature locked up in her room, and thusly force upon her the extra time needed for homework, intent on allowing her think less about standing out as a troublemaker --as most above-average-kids often do when unable to shine on the side of good.

"Oh no, Mister Corbea," the abhorrent nuns retorted instantly, "this is not Romania, such humiliating methods had been rendered long ago unacceptable in America."

Furthermore, I have been advised to practicing patience, allow the good sisters to grant Camellia increased attention --if I agreed--, to have her singled out this way, as for me to keep in contact and monitor, teachers and parents together, our daughter's progress, prognosticated for sure to occur sooner or later.

I politely thanked the competent nun-educators for their goodwill and patience, although not before assuring them that Camellia, whom

I claimed to know a little better, will be taking advantage of this splendid benevolence to the detriment of her behavior, to render one-day in the future recovery impossible without resorting to drastic means.

It has not been my fate to prove the benign Catholic nuns wrong, as next year we moved to Maryland, Camellia transferred to a public school, where her downslide continued unabated, precisely as I predicted. Contrary to expectations of the most advanced American pedagogic methods, one day, an ultra-efficient, self-confident school principal-- pushed at last to the end of his patience-- had thrown our daughter out of school for good, bluntly advising her placement in an institution for troubled teenagers—naturally for the kid's very benefit.

This never happened. In spite of this, she finally had earned a somewhat stunted high school diploma a few years later in a more generous public school in Aspen Hill, Montgomery County, proving once more the adage that nothing is impossible in Land of the Free!

Soon after the memorable day Camellia met Mark, a well-to-do local family's handsome, but spoiled-rotten scion. This most probably happened during the *mandatory* celebratory prom-- apparently no self-respecting high school absolvent can live without in the United States. To make the story short, she married the guy one year later, of all places in jail, following a bargain with a lenient judge, inclined to give the bum another chance in exchange for tying the knot, and thusly be spared years of incarceration for selling fake drugs in Washington DC.

Following this über-surrealistic marriage, the happily married couple promptly moved to Los Angeles, the city of all dreams, purportedly for studying at some rather liberally oriented colleges-- Camellia to become a psychiatric nurse, and Mark a lawyer. How nice!

Miraculously enough, Camellia proved a bit more successful amongst the two, landing even a few jobs via *Kelly Girls*, until one day dear hubby Mark mercilessly and curtly ended the marriage, and kicked the young wife out of the *happy* conjugal home.

Mark's brutal change of heart must be searched for in Potomac, Maryland, the place the *expeditive* fellow's affluent parents lived.

Evidently sickened of being abused to no foreseeable end or good, the loving well-to-do mama and papa stopped covering the tuition fees for their profligate son, at the same time with cutting off the monthly allotment sent for the couple's daily living needs for several years in vain. Suddenly in a bind, the always resourceful Mark willy-nilly had to bring an end to his grand ambition of becoming the successful attorney -- sworn to defending the downtrodden and the oppressed --, forced again to taking to his old habit of peddling nearly illegal stuff, this time on the streets of Los Angeles. Wasn't Mark a proverbial embodiment of the enterprising Yankee spirit, or what? He told me once how unbelievably easy is to earn a buck anywhere in a big US town!"

For some reason I never figured out why the rejected wife didn't go along with this new-old formula, choosing instead a prompt return to the *hated parental nest*, to fit unknowingly in the latest behavioral pattern of many unsuccessful young, too hastily ran away from home. This is how it became incumbent my new mission of rescue, for good old dad to pick her up one day at Dulles airport. Unbelievably as this sounds, I nearly failed to recognize my pretty Camellia, as she looked not unlike an emaciate Auschwitz survivor.

'Dearest little apple of my eye, what the hell have you done to yourself? Why didn't you ask for help?' I raged in foolish desperation, deep within my horrified mind

*

"What, what, what are you mumbling about? Didonna's blues, her searing hot gaze fixed on my temple, as I began pounding the steering wheel, nearly bending it out of shape.

"Stop it, Dorel! Don't try to kill us," she shrieked, white with fury and fright.

Luckily, the road momentarily deserted allowed Buchepalos to swerve dangerously, but unharmed across the lanes. "What the hell is wrong with you, are you sick in the head? What's going on under that thick skull of yours?"

"Sorry, dear, I don't know what came over me... thanks for waking me up!" I answered sheepishly at first, quite self-conscious of my guilt. "It won't happen again. You see now why my insistence on your talking, particularly while driving on a monotonously straight road as this, through endless green-yellow corn fields."

"Okay, okay, I got the message, and better keep a watchful eye on you. Don't worry, you convinced me plenty. Only don't tell me you were thinking about good old Philomela again."

"No, about Camellia, and my failure to help her growing up successful in The New World-- perhaps too big and complex even for adults of stronger character build."

"What a waste of time! You've done all you could by giving her a chance. The rest was up to her. But don't mind my saying she's the nastiest little bitch I've ever seen. No one could help such a child. I had the dubious privilege to witness her talking back to Philomela once or twice. You know there is not much love lost between your wife and myself, but a daughter shouldn't ever treat a mom this badly. Had I used such words against my mother, dad would have beaten the living crap out of me, pardon my French."

"Sure, I believe it, but was your dad living in America?"

"O come on, there you go again with your excuses. America has nothing to do with it. The thing is my mom and dad had a good marriage."

"And what's this suppose to mean?"

"Absolutely nothing. Forget I said it."

"No, I can't forget. By the way, I overheard Alex too, talking back to you more than a few times in a manner I never dared address my mother."

"Yeah, yeah, but you see he is a boy. A good father might still do wonders for his education. What do you think I need you for?"

"Wait a second, now you seem to contradict yourself."

"No, I do not. A girl needs a loving mother, a boy a stern father."

"Fantastic! Then I infer you would accept Camellia joining us for a while, right? You might provide her the proper motivation until she'll find the right path, precisely as I'm expected to help along Alex in resolving his issues with life? What do you say? Is this a deal?"

"No way, definitely not! She's too far-gone on the wild side. I don't need your wife's bad seed to influence Alex. No, no, no Camellia in my household."

"Hey, this is unfair. Camellia's fate is not indifferent to me."

"Baloney, your attitude as a father did prove otherwise. This is obvious."

"Alright, then let me ponder a bit more on this, at least until we get back home. Okay?"

"Didn't we agree to these terms already?"

I only nodded, and the conversation dropped off to nothing. Yet, each and every time the periods of self-induced restraints turned ever more awkward, they gained nearly ominous overtones as well. Conversely, as the moments occurred with increased frequency, the well-intended efforts at overcoming the widening split on the meaning of our relationship became harder to feign.

Gradually I realized how our differences became more confusing while growing in complexity, hopelessly frustrating nearly all attempts at sound thinking. Slowly but surely, the gravest sort of doubts bubbled up again and again from the backwaters of my mind-- 'What if I didn't size up Didonna objectively at all as the perfect soul mate, the woman of my ideals? What if I imagined her alluring qualities only in compensation for the ills foolishly assigned to my less than satisfying marriage? Again, what if, what if?'

As my questions seldom received clear-cut answers, at the constant speed of 70-miles per hour my chances amounted to far less, the advantage of getting minute by minute closer to home came to rest by default within the promise of a solution to be derived off our mutually agreed pact of non-aggression. '*To be, or not to be*?' flashed Hamlet's famous question through my jumbled thoughts, to remind that not all problems could be acceptably reasoned to a conclusion without resorting to the simple choice of a '*YES* or *NO*'. Yes, yes, the human mind is surely less capable for finding adequate solutions than purported, even less when attempting to predict the future. However straightforward this simple truth sounds, in the end even the proudest analyst must bow before it in humble submission. There you have it I threw in the towel.

Precisely how long this latest interval of our dourly supercharged silence lasted I can't say, only knew when it ended, this time as we left behind the beltway around Kansas City, and as its downtown melted into the southern horizon.

"Dorel, please exit anywhere you can, if you don't want my bladder to burst open all over the upholstery of your car. Do me the favor as fast as you can."

"Okay I will, but why didn't you speak up earlier? Can't you wait just a bit longer? Soon we'll be in St. Louis, today's planned objective."

"How long should I wait?"

"Ten, fifteen minutes at most."

"I'll try."

With this our exchange dropped off again as I, out of the blue, began to imagine the last long stretch of our drive home. 'How will your patience survive the test then, my dear beloved mistress?'

Secretly amused by the thought, I smiled, resolved on the spot to forcing upon myself, in unusual optimism, the pleasure of the few remaining days of our vacation together, and leave the worries for after the time we had crossed the Grand Mississippi River again, this time eastward.

THE JEWEL CITY
of ST. LOUIS

Somewhere about the uppermost northwestern corner of St Louis, route-70 cuts trough a neighborhood the traffic signs pinpoint as Maryland Heights.

"How funny this is," I came alive breaking perhaps the longest silence settled in the cabin during our cross-continental trip thus far. "Look, apparently we are back in Maryland. Even the next exit south points to route-270, only over here leads to downtown St. Louis, unlike its namesake that takes the motorist toward Washington DC."

"What, what? Did you say anything?" so Didonna startled up, brutally extricated off her reverie." I am sorry, would you repeat what you said?"

At this point I would have paid a great deal to pick my friend's mind, to find out where she had wondered mentally, what she pondered on so far gone as not to register my question at all. Was she faking her startle, or it was myself the usual idiot trying to find explanations where there wasn't any? However I kept my cool, and rephrased my observation in a tone of absolute neutrality.

"The next exit warns about route-270 south, which I surmise cuts through Maryland Heights toward downtown St. Louis. What I find funny is the similarity of topographic names. By the way, it is high time you take seriously your role as the pilot of this ship, to find out whether I am right about my hunch. But hurry up, it is only a few miles before we must choose the right direction."

"Yes captain, just tell me where precisely are we right now?"

"Somewhere in Missouri on route-70, fast approaching St. Louis."

My thusly shaken up pilot set to work, unfolded the map, and quickly confirmed my suspicions. In fact she had ample time for the task, as I felt impulsively compelled to a sudden halt at a roadside information booth spotted on the way. Lucky, lucky travelers we've been again -- as it has been this spot where we picked up a generous voucher that granted three nights at the luxurious *Adam's Mark* Hotel in St. Louis, at half the regular price. How often may commoners like us fall upon such a pleasant break?

So Bucephalos galloped happily south, first on highway-270, then 64 trough a residential neighborhood isolated by high sound barriers, exited on 8th street, detoured around the large Busch Stadium, to arrive smack in front of the City Hall. Is there a better place to land in St. Louis?

The world-famous Gateway Arch glistened before our wide open eyes, the full majesty of its 630 feet of steel and concrete splendor daringly touching the sky on the left bank of the mighty Mississippi river. What a view!

I took a peek at my watch-- seven o'clock in the evening. The city lights just began to twinkle on slowly, as so many stars in the bluish, hazy crepuscule.

Surprise, surprise, although the voucher for the *Adam's Mark* hotel had indeed cut the price for the room in half, it wasn't cheap either. But, since we arrived at the final great destination in our cross-continental adventure, contrary to my often-derided thriftiness, I found a bit more money in the purse than expected for my mood to turn uncommonly generous.

"Are you about to kick the bucket without bequeathing anything to your heirs, or what?"

"You hit the nail right on the head, what else can I say?" I retorted maliciously narrowing my eyes in a sardonic smile straight into her sky-blues, just to caustically acknowledge her fine sense humor, but not a smidgen more. By now dimly aware that the hot phase of our love affair must have drawn to a close, I chose not to object too harshly, resigned to accepting our relationship as settled in a passionless track, of the sort typically reserved for the rather weather-beaten married couples, only rarely for hot, illicit lovers. Must all romantic affairs end up in this sorry state? I mused silently in the backdrop.

For the very first time in my life, an unknown blue-blooded gentleman awoke in me, happy to let the valet drive Bucephalos to a secret stable, and the bellboy carry the luggage to the room high up the building. All the same, it came hard to hide our jaw-dropping awe when suddenly faced by the magnificent Eero Saarinen's arch, mesmerized by the unforgettable picture, framed in by the wide window looking far out across the river. The bellboy, properly trained for overlooking such embarrassingly poor customer behavior, accepted his tip with the usual aplomb, dutifully thanked us, and promptly left the room.

At this point in my narration, I beg the reader to forgive my not touching the superlatives details of this grand hotel, its strategic location, elegant business façade, marbled halls and corridors, the crystal chandeliers, De Luigi's prancing horse in the well-lit atrium, the various restaurants and bars, the cavernous conference rooms, and so on and so forth, deserving all the poetic epithets others might surely describe better than I ever could. But because the above marvelous wonders, in my opinion, represent rather exceptional frivolities rarely available for folk of our modest condition, at least I had to mention the list, even if only *en passant*. Why depict in more depth such posh accoutrements matter-of-factly associated with the daily life of privileged few, but mostly prohibited fruit for the likes of our ilk, not born with a silver spoon in the mouth? Is it really indelicate, envious, or in bad taste to point out the exception rather than the rule?

*

The *spirit* alive in St. Louis for a little over 200 years I guess is not much to brag about from a European's perspective. However short this life-span might be, Americans know that in these two centuries a number of cities in the New World could boast about more achievements than many their counterparts across the ocean accumulated during millennia. This appears to be true for St. Louis as well. It's not an accident that Charles Lindbergh so tellingly baptized his airplane *The Spirit of St. Louis.*

From its modest beginnings as a fur-trading outpost near the confluence of Missouri and the Mississippi rivers, the successive waves of French, Spanish and German immigrants transformed St. Louis during a few generations into an important manufacturing base, presently ranging from aircraft to various mundane industries, among them the Anheuser Bush beer brand of world renown.

Naturally, I didn't have any inkling of St. Louis history, had I not read one of the pamphlets my companion dutifully picked up at the information center earlier. Ample time for the task, as she, super thrilled by the hotel's fantastic opulence at every nook and cranny, chose to retreat in the bathroom, not long after the bellboy draw the door shot behind him.

"This is like a fairytale," I heard her exclaim over excitedly as she probably prepared to step in the marble tub, to feel at least as *Venus de Milo* reborn, this time around, out of fragrant pink bubble, not off sea foam. "I guess you won't mind my relishing this vain pleasure alone, will you, sweetheart?"

"Don't be silly. Enjoy the luxury so long as you can. I'll be the happier for it. Have fun!"

And then the bathroom door closed, to allow my mistress whatever she wanted to do by herself, as in a wild dream come true. Although taken aback a bit by my lover's childish exuberance, frankly I didn't mind it either, happy myself to enjoy some time stretched out alone on the bed cover, to sort through the day's events and, eventually, trough the numerous pamphlets selling the City of St. Louis to visitors.

*

What struck my fancy as more important than the vaguely boring statistics was the obvious imprimatur left on the place by the first settlers, namely the French, to a large degree responsible for founding several other cities along the Mississippi river in the *Louisiana Territories,* as the huge span of land was known before Napoleon sold it to the incipient Union. What I am trying to timidly suggest under this *imprimatur* might be the so-called mentality of *joie de vivre,* obviously thriving in French settlements more than elsewhere, even if only reluctantly admitted by the puritanically inclined *WASPs.* Here I must admit to being a little partial to this zest for life's pleasures, now a days so disdainfully reproached even to modern French citizenry by simplistic, or possibly envious immature Yankee conservative defenders of the *American Way* that assigns precious little to the meaning of existence other than profit and productive efficiency.

Interestingly, this impression of French influence, well pointed out in the pamphlets as being common along the Mississippi River, was to augment my own subjective bent on the matter during the next two days of our sojourn in St. Louis, after we will have visited numerous magnificent churches and cathedrals-- belonging mostly to the Catholic flock, rarely the Protestant believers.

Dear reader, please forgive my surely exaggerated, obviously biased views on the role the Catholic French played in a large part of the former *Louisiana Territory*. But as the saying goes, in America the stupidly subjective must enjoy the same rights as the objectively smart. Isn't this wonderful?

Moreover, at this point a feel compelled to invite politely the reader to select the category best suited for the particular characters, to sort out at last whom to favor in this tale of forbidden love, the one or the other, the male or the female, either to praise or curse, but in the end forgive, as Christ the Lord has been teaching us all without fail forever and ever. Amen. 'Oh, well…'—by the same token, allow me hereby to forcefully reaffirm the same reader's right to object-- 'hey you, all-too-smart-author, why not mind your own business, and give us a break! Let us be truly the ones to decide when, and who to forgive or condemn! No need for your pushy intervention!'

*

Later that evening, as we decided to take the tour of down town, I shared my observations with my partner who, refreshed and radiating with renewed Venusians beauty, opted -- instead of my insipid philosophic considerations-- for one of the many popular jazz-bars the city is famous for. Yet I persisted to ramble on, as obstinately, stupidly, and annoyingly as the best Smart-Alec may too often do.

"You see, to assign human beings solely the motive of production and profit smacks me almost as a Marxist idea, what do you think about this idea, sweetie?"

"So what you tell me is you'd rather live without working, isn't it?"

"Oh no, dear lady, how could you arrive to such a conclusion? Working for a living is necessary and decent, but for the *crown of creation* to live for work is ungodly. I hope you can see the difference between the need to decent survival and the vice of hoarding."

"I am not sure I do. But I know a person ought to be self-reliant before expecting God's, or anyone else's help. However let me ask why must you always play the role of the *savvy idiot*? Why constantly play the dumb? Just to provoke, or are you the real moronic *McCoy*? Wouldn't it be nicer now to notice the beauty of this city, how civilized down town is, unlike in Washington or Baltimore, both pretty iffy after nightfall? This is what I see now. *Comprende, amigo*? So shut your clap, and find the jazz place I want. I feel sexy hot, and in need to dance. Why not stop all nonsense at once, would you?"

Instead of payback with a similar coin, I miraculously wised up, and did indeed clam up, to save the night by peremptorily swallowing my obviously wounded pride. Why fish for further abuse? Lately, sparks flew between us with increased frequency for the slightest disagreements. But— a new and huge *but*-- my darling mistress couldn't stop my conscience from gaining more new ground. Perhaps for the first time I asked myself with absolute clarity, even if silently what is it I have in common with this woman, after all? Could this something be enough for spending our lives together?

It didn't take long to find the much-desired jazz club, in spite of strolling through downtown, instead of driving. As in New Orleans, in St. Louis the center of town appeared pretty safe at night, probably more so than in some of the outlying suburbs, populated by the usual ghetto proletariat. This fact was to be reconfirmed on my way out the city a couple of days later, when cutting through some pretty rough neighborhoods.

As for the unusually mellow night, it has been a real delight to dissolve in the crowd by milling up and down the wide, modern, elegant, well-lit streets. Music leaked out of everywhere, the syncopated rhythmic of ragtime, the sad tunes of blues, or velvet notes of modern jazz.

Instead of reminding once again my partner suddenly turned romantic how right I've been in my earlier disrespectfully rejected philosophic observations, the hurt male in me chose magnanimity, the comfortable retreat to a fantasy-like island of queasy-rational inner prevarication, as the spark of love had almost died, not unlike the nice weather feigns calmness before turning stormy. In truth no such definitive conclusions solidified as yet in my jumbled thoughts, except that the air had to be somehow cleared between us at last, for finding out precisely where we stood, what we wanted from one another, how much of our past should be allowed to intrude in our future. In my own particularly convoluted way I might have been preparing, perhaps even scheming subconsciously for the discussion programmed for after our arrival back home whether to divorce, and take a serious financial hit, or continue the illicit affair until all negatives will have burned out naturally, one way or another.

As for the time being, we chose to dance the night away, against my strong initial reluctance, and in spite of my usually bumbled stepping talent under duress. But my mistress implored so sweetly, although well aware of my awkwardness on the dance floor. Pressed tightly against me, she made sure to invade my nostrils with the familiar Channel-number-5 scent, amplified by her body heat, succeeding to turn me on again as if all was fine and dandy between us. As always, the weak helpless Venus gained the upper hand over the allegedly much stronger Mars.

A couple hours of dancing and a few drinks later, just as dawn began to smear a bit of pink rouge on the eastern sky we found ourselves strolling arm in arm as in the best of times. Then the crisp cool air in my face brought back the stark reality, made me sharply aware of the farce, my soul drowned in a heaviest sort of lethargy, physically and emotionally more and more exhausted by each and every step nearer to the hotel. Should this lethal deflation have been foretelling a disaster in the making? I couldn't figure, as much in the dark then as am still today about those minutes. A moron is a moron. What I recall, though, is how menacing the impeding future suddenly loomed over my head, how acutely the oft-recurring self-pity hurt, how obviously unfair and unjust destiny's choice seemed for mistreating me forever so badly.

By the time the luxuriously silky bed came to caress my spent flesh in its soft embrace, the first thin rays of sun penetrated timidly through the dark drapes covering the windows. I turned reflex like to the other side, against the glaring light, ready to fade away in the deepest, heaviest slumber ever longed for in my earthly life. This was exactly when Didonna's hot breath hit the nape of my neck. For the first time in our years of togetherness, her sensual overture caused my body to cringe in slight disgust.

"Come on big boy, don't go to sleep. Please, not yet. Turn around to face me," and she began pulling on my arm, nearly forcing me obey.

"Not now dear, not now, I beg you, unless you aim to kill me. Good night."

She withdrew her hand, turned slowly her back, without as much as a whisper. "Oh, I exhaled an incipient sigh fast cut in half, as I sunk lead-like in the waters of all enveloping nothingness quicker than able to count two sheep.

When I opened eyes around noon, my concubine was up, dressed and ready to go, not a hint of leftover moodiness evident in her attitude.

"Come on, old buddy, get up, you want to sleep forever? Life is short. We have many sites to visit today."

This didn't sound like the woman rejected last night at all. "What the hell is going on?" I wondered, "Something is amiss," but willfully ignoring my apprehensions, washed, shaved and dressed as the ever-disoriented recruit under the sergeant's merciless eyes.

"Okay, let's go and take in St. Louis, but not before having a bite. I am hungry as a wolf."

"Fine, there is a McDonald a couple of blocks away from the hotel. *Avanti!*"

The strange thing is I've never known my discriminating girl to favor the famous fast food chain, other than occasionally getting a coke, or an ice cream cone. Myself would have preferred something more substantial, but as the cheapskate in me came easily to the fore, I readily accepted the suggestion, happy not to pile more debt to my bank-credit by having brunch in a full service restaurant.

A half an hour, and two *Big Macs* later, we stood ready for the day's touristy adventure. Yet this was to occur quite unlike our plan had called for.

Although we made the first moves right, all that followed turned out as in *one of those proverbial days,* when nothing goes as intended. The switch for the unexpected clicked on as soon as we exited the iconic Gateway Arch, erected right smack in middle of *Jefferson National Expansion Memorial Park*-- I guess a must for any tourist worthy of the definition, regardless of how culturally insensitive.

Indeed, the statistics all-too impressive, although today --two decades later--, what I remember is a little vague, such as when, how and why the project got commissioned, or how expensive it was. Strangely, aside from the monument's height being equal to the 630 feet between the leg-posts on the ground, mostly some trivial details stuck, among those the number of passengers accommodated in the trams, or how tiny the windows were on the top, looking as far as 30 miles deep into the truly breathtaking landscape on a clear day. Well, one more hurray for the *infallible* human memory and intellect!

About to walk back in town, to visit one by one some pre-selected well-deserving objectives, by a twist of destiny, or misreading directions on the map, we ended up on Walnut Street, at The Basilica of St Louis The King.

'Please, let's step in. I wish to light a candle for the souls of my dead. Don't you want to do the same for yours, Dorel?"

"Sure, but don't forget you are Orthodox, are you not?"

"Yes I am, so what? Don't we all pray to the same God? Then again, what are you complaining about? You are Catholic, are you not?"

"Indeed, so I am. So allow me the privilege to take the lead."

"Oh shut up, and open the door for me. By the way, can you still remember how to sign for the cross?"

"No dear, I expect a good Orthodox like you to teach me."

"Don't worry, I will. For a couple of years I have been enrolled at *Pitari Mosi* in Bucharest. What catholic school did you attend?"

"Fine, you convinced me." And I pushed the heavy door open, gesturing theatrically for her to step in.

The church received two earthlings in search of paradise lost in the cacophony of modernity, in the mysterious abode of a cool serene, quiet velvety tranquility, not unlike the ancestral womb of Universe accepts mortals longing for a return to their origin on the last day of their lives.

Suddenly the noisy bustling, hot burning materialistic world of outside receded to nothingness, replaced by the sad, suffering but infinitely benevolent Christ looking down mercifully on us from the cross bathed in sacred light, silently reminding how puny indeed our problems were in the wider context of a short life, and infinite death-- *to be, or not to be?*

Perhaps the question hadn't flashed on the screen of my mind as it logically should have, and I guess it didn't blip for pious Didonna either, although she lit a couple of candles for the dead. Following her motions, I fell almost reflex-like into regurgitating tired thoughts about the virtues of Old Europe, spontaneously and miraculously transported across the ocean, although physically sheltered under the high vaults of this catholic church so wonderfully replicated in St. Louis. Whether my impression reflected some historic truths, or only the peculiarity of a silly powerless puny man unable to sever his umbilical cord sufficiently as to maintain his independence outside the ancestral mother country, I am not sure. Whether I became a failed adventurer in the wake of my escape, or just another phony political refugee, remained equally unclear to me up to this day.

On the other side of the coin, my mistress apparently belonged to the category of free spirited adventurers, naturally at home everywhere, equally close to God in a Catholic or Orthodox Church. Only a daring character like hers could have left behind a child on the dim promise of a later reunion. A new rhetoric dilemma arose in my mind at the same heartbeat, whether two such diametrically opposed individuals-- an authentic adventurer and an ultra-cautious machinating tedious plotter-- can share their lives together in earnest? Ah, so many insufferable questions begging in vain for answers!

As one inadvertent misstep leads to another so did our plan to take in the mandatory tourist objectives of St. Louis got smashed to bits. Perhaps it has not been in the destiny of Union Station, Grant's Farm, The Arena, The Botanical Garden, or the Cervantes Convention Center to have us as visitors. Not even the romantic tour contemplated on a paddle wheel steamer had the power to lure us up and down the river Mark Twain loved so much. Too bad, because a train once lost can never be caught again, precisely as the ancient Greek philosopher said *it is impossible to step in the same river twice.* Such simple wisdom made me often wonder whether our affair could have had a different end were we committed to our initial plans. Obviously, by doing whatever we did, both our good or bad choices got similarly obliterated, locked away forever in an implacable mystery, the impossibility of being in two places at the same time. Much too often destiny seems to intervene with such devilish tricks of natural law in the lives of mortals! Can there be any sort of viable alternative, or defense against this sort of tricky paradoxes?

Before completing the tour in the grand Basilica of St. Louis the King, my friend, faithful to her habit of collecting pamphlets as souvenirs to be reviewed later on memory lane, collected a bunch from the piles strategically displayed on shelves by the exit. One of these invited the willing and curious faithful to other famous catholic churches in the city, among them the Cathedral Basilica of St. Louis, the Eparchy of Our Lady of Lebanon, the Epiphany of Our Lord Parish, the Holy Family Seminary Alumni, the Immaculate Heart of Mary Parish, the Jesuits of the Missouri Province, to mention just a few, all in walking proximity. Indeed, much the world of French Catholic America seemed to have a presence in St. Louis!

"Listen, dear, I have a proposal. Please don't say no before hearing me out!"

Although this sort of cautious approach usually spelled trouble, it was only fair to give my friend the chance to speak.

"Okay, out with it, I am all-ears. Just don't ask for something I obviously can't do."

"Come on, don't be facetious, did I ever ask you for such a thing?" Then she handed the pamphlet inviting the believer to the catholic churches listed above.

"I saw these too. The number of catholic parishes in St. Louis is impressive all right, so what about it?"

"You see all we planned originally were the sort of sites existent elsewhere too; buildings, monuments, parks, and so on. Why not try a different approach, go instead through as many churches as possible in the interval of time left this beautiful afternoon? You know this detour can reconfirm your views about the French influence along the Mississippi. So, what do you say?"

No doubt the proposal took me by surprise, and although suspicions lingered in my mind with respect to a hidden purpose behind my friend's change of heart, I had no good reason to reject it outright.

"Fine, darling, fine, your proposal makes sense. But I must warn you this will require a lot of walking. Are you prepared?"

"I don't have to. The hotel is just around the corner, go and fetch the car. I will wait for you in the nice coolness of the church. You can be back in fifteen minutes or so. Do this for me, please."

I hesitated a bit, but then, unable to figure anything diabolic in her request, I conformed, as a good boy ought to do. On my way to the hotel, however hard I tried to find faults with my friend's proposal, to my chagrin couldn't see any. Oh well, I remembered it's not easy for a man to navigate the waters of feminine thinking!

My friend guessed right it took a little over ten minutes to drive back to the church. She was waiting outside. And this is how the day came to end, instead of going through six or seven well advertised popular tourist sites, we visited an equal number of magnificent catholic churches, in my opinion rivaling, a few even surpassing many in the Old World.

By the time of our arrival at the Immaculate Heart of Mary Parish --of special interest to Didonna, allegedly protected by the Virgin Mother more than by Christ the Son, the evening service had begun, hindering somewhat the progress of our tour.

"Come, let's sit in the pew, and follow the service. When was the last time you bowed your head in the House of God?"

"Fine, why not pray a little? Every now and again, a small dose of piousness couldn't hurt."

"Right, even sinners like you might benefit from it occasionally."

"Hey lady, don't forget we are all sinners…" I began to whisper back as we sat down, but she cut me off sooner than I could finish the sentence.

"Hush, no more talking. I need to listen," and she kneeled, hands clasped in prayer.

There was nothing left but to conform, keep all thoughts to myself. Initially reluctant to follow suite by kneeling next to her, I took one of the available bibles in hand, opened it and pretended to read. I feigned this not as the atheist I wasn't at all, but because the letters in the dark were only barely visible, and the reverberating organ cut in often loudly enough to render me mute to the core, thoroughly voided of any distracting thoughts. What could I then do other than bowing my head, and take to praying as well? But I did it secretly, as Christ advised. What my unusually faith-filled mistress begged Holly Mother Mary for I can't guess, as for my prayer had been simple, naïve, concise, and mainly of my own wording: 'Oh Mighty Lord, help me see the way forward clearly, bless me with Thy Wisdom, and spare us all from suffering and hurting one another ever again.'

At this precise point, the ceremony called for the congregation to rise. We complied instantly, stood up, heads bowed, and as the priest delivered his blessing while liberally spreading the penetrating scent of smoking myrrh in the air, I felt my girlfriend's hand taking mine in a tight squeeze.

"We can leave now if you wish" she whispered in haste, "but please grant me another little favor before we do. I beg you."

Without further ado she took the initiative, dragged me out of the row of benches, to my surprise, not to the exit, but sideways, to an alcove dedicated to Holly Virgin Mary, the patron saint of the church. Once under the beautifully serene image of Virgin Mother Mary looking down from the golden-framed icon, she reached for my hand again, and said in a voice over suffused by emotion:

"Dorel my love, marry me now, under the blessing of Virgin Mary."

The suddenness of her request took my breath away. Given no time at all to prevaricate, my answer ensued fast, and brutally clear cut.

"No way, dear, I won't do that now. I am not yet divorced."

"Don't be ridiculous, this isn't official, just a bit of secret make-believe contracting between us. Please play along if you love me."

"My answer is still no. Be so good and stop this perilous, silly game right now."

"Okay, okay, I will if it bothers you that much. But tell me did you marry Philomela religiously?"

"What's this question supposed to mean? You know I didn't."

"Well then let me inform you that in The Eyes Of God you're not even married."

"This is preposterous. My answer is still no. Let's go," and quite unlike me I've torn myself away violently to head straight for the exit, never bothering to make sure my ruffled up mistress followed. She did, what else could she have done?

Outside the air stagnated unpleasantly warm and sticky. A dark violet band of haze painted high above the western horizon allowed a humongous orange-tinged-setting-sun's ember globe glow muted through it, as the city prepared for the night by switching on its own lights one by one. Whether my imagination played a trick following my concubine's weird proposal in the church, or nature choose to go along in sympathy with my vague disgust, the presence of the approaching night's bloody Valkyries on the ominous sky didn't seem to promise anything less for us than a huge impending battle, possibly doom. In preparation for this sorry, realistic eventuality I resorted to a strategy of forestalling and appeasement.

Predictably, on the way back to hotel, my evidently hurt dame displayed her usual glum silence, which I dared interrupt with a proposal of armistice only inside the brightly lit atrium, as we passed by a certain high-class restaurant, habitually avoided until then on the account of my puny sense of thriftiness. The idea struck as lightening-- why not enter? Whatever direction our fate might take, this unique occasion of splurging I figured to have few chances to repeat. So I spoke up.

"Listen, St. Louis is the last important objective on our itinerary. What do you say about spending the evening celebrating our entire adventure by dining for once in style, right here in this splendid restaurant? Is this a good enough proposal, or what?"

To my utter astonishment the reaction came with lightening promptness, no trace whatsoever of the earlier hurt, either in tone or attitude.

"This sure is a wonderful idea at last. But let's first wash up and dress accordingly, to make this a truly special evening."

"Fantastic!" I concluded, recalling again the adage about women's similarity to weather.

It took less than half an hour for our return, and march --heads high, arm in arm--, into the well-lit, luxury restaurant's dinning hall; my lithe mistress wrapped in a simple but elegant, decently low cut red evening gown toped by a string of bluish pearls, I literally stuffed in a white pair of trousers assorted to a dark blue blazer and red silk tie, to display the perfect pair, in best imitation of some trendy uppity socialite puppets in love. Isn't it strange how often the glitter of falseness can appear more credible and authentic than the stark naked truth?

During that unforgettable night I surpassed myself by showing woefully little restraint in opening my valet, although by now even for the most naive reader the gesture should seem a little tardy, as our game of love skirted dangerously near the final curtain fall. It's hard to say whether I acted totally unaware of the dire financial consequences my generosity entailed for the ensuing months, or even years. But if this was somehow fated to be the last act of our bitter comedy, I decided, in untypical grandiloquence, to perform in style, perhaps unforgettably for my sweetheart—at the time about to morph into my foe. Ah, what a born loser won't do for saving appearances when already too late! Too bad I never contemplated acting this grand while the going was good. So much for the psychological intricacies of the mentally brilliant, but emotionally handicapped!

To sum up, I staged on purpose the last tableau of our jut across America as the best-fit prologue for the serious discussions, preordained to ensue at home on the future of our sordid love affair, and on the fate of those directly or indirectly affected. Why are most similarly ill-conceived stories prone to self-destructing by their very nature?

But before attempting to answer such an obviously rhetoric question, let me return to the dinning hall. On that festive evening extended late into the night, we made sure to reach with perfectly sweet abandon for the silliest extravagant luxuries, so often only dreamed by folk of rather modest condition, generally of poorer taste than is worthy for the authentic connoisseurs. And such high-class sophisticates we were clearly not. Oh vanity, petty vanity!

Following some fancy, crusty cheesy *or d'oeuvres* (doesn't this sound better in French?) my naturally luxury-inclined accomplice-in-love went for the lobster tail in butter sauce, and I, following in step, ordered oysters Rockefeller on a bed of fragrant rice, choices seldom wholeheartedly agreeable for the untrained palates, particularly at first trial. To ameliorate the slight disappointment that ensued naturally, the wine-option veered in similar immodesty for the sophisticated *Veuve Clicquot Brut* champagne, almost funnily as bubbly on the tongue as the best, but dearest ginger ale we ever drank, were it just a bit sweeter. What else to expect off folk used to feta cheese, raw tomatoes and green onion for appetizers, stuffed cabbage and polenta or, suckling pig roasted in a pit, for truly festive occasions?

In spite of these tragicomic disappointments vis-à-vis the so-called finer things in life, we enjoyed the celebratory *once-in-a-life-time-splurge* in impeccably feigned good mood, alongside the gracious ultra solicitous service and, for the grand finale, hours of playfully rhythmic jazz tunes, increasingly mellower as the night progressed amid sips of *Courvoisier* brandy, overindulgently inhaled out of properly hand-warmed snifters. Long live credit cards! Live now pay later!

Few minutes before the hour struck midnight, the band dutifully performed the concluding number, then quickly left the stage, to return the dinning hall to the usual hum and hush late drinking customers usually cause. A bit dazed by the alcohol in my blood, I began to contemplate quitting the bash, having already paid the bill --*nota benne*-- for the first time in my life without bothering to check the addition on the credit card receipt. Precisely then the thunderbolt hit out of the blue!

"Listen Dorel, how much money we have left in our common purse?"

"I don't know, maybe three hundred dollars. Why do you ask?"

"Because I want to fly to Washington in the morning. I wonder whether my share can cover the ticket's price?"

"What are you talking about? There are only three or four days before we'll be home anyway? You're not serious, are you?"

"This time I am deadly serious. Now I know for sure you'll never divorce Philomela. Frankly, there is no point in my enduring this situation any longer. I must leave immediately, regardless of how idiotic my decision seems to you. Don't worry I will pay you back whatever I can't cover now."

The abrupt change in my concubine's approach sounded so unbelievably absurd as to render me speechless for the fairly long ensuing interval. This unwonted nasty turn didn't fit at all in the next chapter of our affair, as **I** imagined the script. After all, didn't she promise a final discussion, for sorting out one-way or another our difficulties, whether it remained anything salvageable or fixable in our life together? Why did she strike now, when my optimism was gaining at last some ground over my natural skepticism, divorce or no divorce? What could have made my mistress suddenly so impatient as to opt for the terminal solution with such ferocious brutality? Perfectly stunned, as the fervent believer in passivity must have secretly still hoped for the usual procrastination, to result eventually in a compromise, in the best negotiated outcome without causing the unnecessary suffering the unintended side effects of haste might inflict upon all of us.

To make absolutely sure, I cast another furtive glance on the suddenly reborn woman, in the hopeless hope of catching the slightest sign of wavering in her countenance. Nothing. On the contrary, my eyes met her unflinching stone-cold blues, patiently and calmly awaiting my long delayed response. In a flash I figured then why she fit so much better in The New World than I did. As the shocking discovery sunk in it succeeded to engender in my heart the most painful resignation and darkest melancholy. I had to summon all my strength just to barely feign my presence. It took a while to hear myself deliver my own line, in the softest, gentlest calmest voice ever mustered.

"Okay then, let's go to the reception desk right now. I am sure someone there will assist in getting you a ticket to Washington."

Indeed, information about daily flights readily available at all times, including the schedule of the free-airport-shuttles, a courtesy service provided by most luxury hotels. However the issue of finding a cheap ticket for next day shuttle in full summer season proved to be a different story altogether.

Yet, the impeccably solicitous concierge picked up the phone immediately, and after relating the offers a travel agent advanced at the other end of the line, Didonna herself realized the near impossibility of purchasing an economy class ticket, perhaps any seat against any cost, forget our derisory pecuniary reserves. Even so, the properly trained clerk went on to explain with unflinching professional patience that solutions existed, as for instance, at the airport in the morning, waiting in line for a last minute cancellation, sometimes quite conveniently re-offered for sale regardless of class. As he conveyed the option, I noticed a vaguely ironic smile fleetingly pass across the man's freshly shaved face.

Obviously, the waiting variant seemed much too risky, while the luck of catching a discounted first class seat utterly improbable. Then overcome by an uncharacteristically gallant mood, I offered to charge the damned first class ticket against my own credit. To my estranged friend's merit, she rejected my generosity outright, either out of pride, or might have remembered her earlier promise to pay me back later. I will never find out why. As we debated the alternatives in Romanian, thus denying the concierge's understanding, he still must have guessed enough to attempt a timid intervention probably out of pity, and suggest a solution unlikely to have ever presented for his regular customers.

"Without intending to be presumptuous, I wonder whether the lady might not wish to travel by *Greyhound*? Buses leave every half hour to destinations all over the United States. The fares are quite affordable for most pockets. In the meantime, for you folks I dare suggest another restful night with us, then in the morning drive to the Union Station, just a few blocks away."

Guessing maliciously the underlying motivation of the hotel employee's seemingly innocent proposal, I was about to brush it straight off offended, but Didonna proved a blink faster.

"I am perfectly okay to travel by bus." Then to the clerk, "Do you have any idea how much the fare to Washington DC could cost?"

"Probably less than a Benjamin Franklin."

"What about the trip's duration?"

"I say should take no more than eleven-to-twelve hours."

"Thank you. -- This is perfect. I might even have a bit of pocket-change leftover, sufficient to buy me lunch on the way. Let's go, we'll have to get up early in the morning." And she took my arm, as if all was fine and dandy between us.

This was my old girlfriend alright, plain and simple, partially justifying my obsession for orbiting her brilliantly burning sun-- the helpless inert planet taken hostage by an overpowering gravity, not unlike the young boy is attracted to his mother. Will I ever grow up?

Back in the room, lights turned off quickly, absent even the slightest sensual innuendos, so often attempted in the past for removing at night snags that endangered smooth navigation on the waters of cohabitation during the day. Sex can frequently work as wonderful medicine for healing minor rifts between lovers, but not always. That night we instinctively chose to spend possibly the last hours of our togetherness without pretending to fix what no longer seemed viable anyway. All the same, it had not been easy to ignore the light of extinguished love haunting the old, burned-out emotions (to approximate what the greatest Romanian poet so beautifully put to words). It took all my willpower to resist the pitfall of the basest romantic groveling, so sweet to country music aficionados. To my amazement I survived the sensual gauntlet with my pride largely intact, in spite of lying in the same bed with the woman subconsciously deemed still most desirable off all known to me. But my heroic feat exacted a price-- I couldn't touch eyelid to eyelid even for a measly minute. Fortunately, the hours until wake-up time remained few, regardless how long the ticking seconds seemed.

About what has been going through my newly alienated bed-partner's mind I could have hardly guessed, as she became dead motionless the instant her back turned against me, a position never changed till the morning. Palpably apprehensive about our last night together, I tried pitifully the compensating strategy of committing indelibly to memory the woman's well-known, sensually curvaceous silhouette contoured vaguely against the faint light filtering in through the windows. To my delight I succeeded in definitely etching in my mind the unique moment, when the first glimmer of dawn peeked through the curtains, and outlined sharply for the last time the known deliciously sinuous lines before my eyes. This visual memento I hoped to keep me warm during the cold days of loneliness surely coming my way. The always love-thirsty soul might feed on such emotionally pregnant images for a lifetime, as the conventional wisdom claims!

Nothing out of the ordinary occurred thereafter, to render the morning more dramatic than already was. We took to our hygiene and dressing routines somberly machinelike, talking little, fully aware of the impending final curtain drop. First ready to go, I resorted to watching in sad amusement the meticulous manner the surprisingly alien female set aside a few of my clothing items, inadvertently mixed in her suitcase. How strangely may humans caught in the web of obvious distress pay attention to minutia!

Once the task completed, including the mandatory glance in the mirror, accompanied by the unavoidable feminine touch to the always-rebellious hair lock, she said:

"I'm ready. Can you help me carry my suitcase? It got quite heavy."

"Of course. Let's go."

In the elevator, I squeezed in a suggestion.

"If you want breakfast now is the time. It's included in the price. We never took advantage of it by getting up too late."

"How many minutes can I spare?"

"Quite a few, and some more. It's not yet seven o'clock. If we arrive at the station fifteen minutes before eight, I think that will be just right."

The buffet spread, impressive as in all great hotels, prompted a well-disciplined, cool-headed Didonna to take ravenous advantage of it. Obviously aware of the long day ahead, she prepared for a late lunch, and save some money this way too. What an irony, to emulate my thriftiness now, when no longer having to please me, I mused sadly.

*

At the bus station, the usual hustle and bustle of a crowd totally unlike the sort left behind in the hotel. Randomly assembled people of all colors, shades, ages, attire and odors, men and women probably unfamiliar with *Oysters Rockefeller,* or *Veuve Clicquot Champagne* milled here equally alive, in search of happiness or unhappiness, similarly to their affluent brethren above them, different mostly in style, not substance. Didonna blended in much better among these folk than in the society of the opulent few, unlike myself, strangely uneasy and foreign in both worlds. At this point I feel compelled to ask whether anyone –common folk, or philosopher—should find objective fault, or merit in the so-called class-differences? Is there any truth in the fatalism of belongingness?

Before stepping in the bus ready for departure, my former mistress reemerged somehow, when turned around for the last farewell second.

"Good buy, Dorel. I hope you'll find happiness, if not with your wife maybe with some other woman. Though I doubt it, not because you're evil. On the contrary, you're quite monstrously benign. Take care of yourself."

"You too, Didonna. Have a pleasant trip!"

This way concluded my cohabitation in sin for about ten years, very much like in a regular marriage, had I divorced Philomela. Perhaps my thoughts could, or should have found a way out in words of a more properly phrased farewell, had the bus-door not slammed shut in my face in the driest of a clap, before the diesel clatter and roar choked all else in noise and smoke, both constant attributes of my life's motor as well.

IN PLACE OF EPILOGUE

On the way back to hotel, a huge wave of long forgotten loneliness hit me right in the breastbone, to make me wallow in abject self-pity nearly to the point of bursting in tears. For some minutes my life literally ended, my world crumbled to smoldering ruins. Darkness moved in the heart, the need to pretend otherwise no longer present. Then something strange happened. Slowly, out of this sinking, mute despair emerged a pimple-speckled, skinny boy, the estranged, solitary teenager of many years ago, the same sissy little Dorel, for years on end utterly incapable to befriend any girl --some the more I failed to attract the more I longed for. By her sudden act of disappearing, on that morning Didonna somehow re-ignited in my core the basic inferiority complex I thought forever buried. But this sorry image of myself in the rearview mirror came soon thereafter face to face with the experience of today's mature man, for whom, in this light, a cool-headed analysis became suddenly feasible. It is exactly what I, the well-versed verbal escape artist, resorted to.

After twenty years of tedious marriage to Philomela –officially still valid—, to the same woman who chose me probably out of pity in the wake of my burn-up on the pyre of a most romantic and passionately searing first-love to Adriana, this time around it remained little alive off the ill-fitting adolescent, regardless of how low I felt, how brutal the shock of rejection suffered in my just ended ungraciously illicit affair. All along my dull journey to middle age, life still served me a few lessons. As for instance, when in our perilous crossing the boundary between worlds of opposite political and economic ideologies, I learned to be numbed, adapted to novel fears as that of facing the business ends of two *Ak-47s*—pointed by a Soviet captain and his subordinate, patrolling the Czechoslovak border in 1968. Later on, following a few foul, sordid stints with easy women of different races, by surviving in jobs and through adventures never knew existed, I accumulated the experience and information my country brethrens could have hardly gained by sticking faithfully steadfast to the Motherland. A bit more iron dust fortified willy-nilly my timid sissy-boy Dorel's bloodstream than I started out with. What I reckon is that these worldly lessons, powerful as they were, might have robbed the comparison to my teenager period some of its validity. Adding life experience to the equation must count for something, is it not?

So let me try to rephrase the description of my emotions on that morning.

It could very well be that what I felt was nothing more than the frustration easily attributable to a defeated party, particularly as victory could have been equally mine, had I not vacillated so stupidly in the process by endlessly scheming to the very end, in spite of the danger of never arriving at a timely decision. Actions weigh heavier in balance than words, and daring Didonna acted. Pitifully, I didn't.

Yet our faulty relation had survived on life-support for quite a good while already, before the split actually occurred. Who the hell I am to complain, what does it matter who reached the land of damnation first? The truth is the truth. It is the only thing that matters

I concluded, regaining gradually my breath, much of calm, and my old removed, prevaricating sense of survival.

The way things evolved lately, my love affair was doomed to fail anyway, given its sinful nature. Even if the punctuation period might have been placed earlier than expected by me, not by her, why fret in vain? 'Essentially life is still good' I proclaimed in false victory over my self on the way back to *Adams Mark*. Maybe life was fine indeed, yet it held another unpleasant surprise in reserve just around the corner-- the hotel bill, which I had to face, this time, alone.

After I squared it --astronomically higher than promised in the voucher, not to mention parking fees, taxes and gratuities--, the new reality abruptly re-ignited my perennial sense of doom and gloom. But as I took refuge quickly in the well worn adage that life is short, my anger dissipated equally fast, to become nearly a liberating exhilaration the minute I launched Bucephalos back on the asphalt, my body and persona ready to race freshly inebriated on a misplaced highway of reckless optimism and abandon toward home in good Old Maryland.

Refusing adamantly to dwell objectively on my abject defeat in battling a funky sort of love, I elected instead to weave new plans, quite predictably by trying to rekindle old, worn-out sentimental circumstances. My thoughts flew back to Philomela, my sick imagination dreaming about fixing all I spoiled, in the hope of living happily ever after with her as if nothing disturbed our decade-long togetherness, in the falsely sunny conviction that familiarity must be stronger than any separation. This belief fermented in my subconscious so conveniently as to remind of the long tired dictum *women by definition opt for family ties more than for the particular men in their lives.* Why would Philomela be different in this sense?

Ruminating on these marvelously wishful but uplifting thoughts, I went totally gaga, to the point of not paying full attention to the road, to the numerous warnings and indications to be watched carefully for navigating correctly to one's destination. For the first time, without the benefit of a pilot at my side, I must have missed a few exits, and when finally weaned off the syrupy sweet comedy of my surrealist fantasies for regaining a bit of sanity, Bucephalos, instead of heading eastward on route-70, has been speeding already for over three hours southward on route-64.

Getting off the highway became unavoidable, if wanted to adjust my itinerary accordingly. My stomach began grumbling coincidentally at the same time, the flesh reinforcing once more the need for a halt. But returning to St Louis for correcting my error would have been absurd at this point. Consequently, Louisville replaced Indianapolis as the next objective. Good enough, I thought the choice a whole lot easier than finding happiness between two women. How hilarious, ha, ha, ha!

So my mood continued unabated on the path of optimism in spite of my just derailed love affair. Since in all bad is advisable to look for the good, I encouraged myself with well-imagined bravery going as far as postponing lunch. Two-to-three hours later, I reckoned both machine and human could be alimented somewhere in the proximity of Louisville, Bucephalos with gas and oil, I with a juicy burger, fries and coke. Life suddenly appeared worth living even without the perennial female domestic partner. This was precisely what I concluded before setting my way back on the highway.

Indeed, around one thirty in the afternoon, the promise of life on the new shores of optimism got fulfilled at least on the physical level-- for Bucephalos at an Exxon station, for me in a McDonald, feeding points strategically in close proximity to one another at the outskirts of Louisville. The oh-so-often boring America, as it may appear sometimes, is always comfortable in spite of its young age and super humongous size.

Inside McDonald an elderly gentleman approached, and asked for permission to sit at my table, as the place was crowded. Habitually disinclined to chitchat with strangers, but given the circumstance I had to be polite.

"No problem, please have a seat."

"Thank you" then the usual "Where are you from, if I may ask?"

"From Washington DC," retorted quickly, remembering the Texas border agent's advise.

"No, no, not that. Where you came originally from?"

Well, I thought the fellow is insistent, so I remained vague.

"From Europe."

"What part?"

By now well engaged in the game, I went along willy-nilly.

"Guess!"

"I don't know. Judging by your slight accent, you might be from Scandinavia, Lithuania or Estonia."

"Close, but no cigar."

"Hungary?"

"Very good, but not quite."

"I give up."

"Okay, I am from Romania."

"Ah" the man exclaimed, neutrally enough not to get my suspicions raised. "So then, what brings you to this neck of the woods?"

"Touristy curiosity. Say, what can I visit around here in a few hours time?"

"Not much-- but wait a minute. Did you hear about Lincoln's Boyhood Home?"

"A little here and there. Is it far away?"

"No, let me give you directions."

As it turned out, the site was near enough to merit the 30-mile-detour south on route-65, toward Elizabethtown. I thanked the man, and forty minutes later drove in the Visitor Center in Hodgenville, Kentucky. At two thirty in the afternoon, I could have easily afforded ninety minutes for the visit, as the center closed at four. Good enough, I thought, and parked.

I won't go into describing the center that covered quite a sizable area, deservedly suited in all respects for one of the most important presidents of the United States, although details about Abraham Lincoln could be researched elsewhere too, out of infinitely well-documented sources. All the same, I can't just peremptorily gloss over my impressions, considering how deeply the place affected me emotionally, particularly on that momentous day of my defeat. I found it hard to avoid comparing the indescribably modest log cabin in the woods, without having it juxtaposed to the incontestable greatness of its former inhabitant's childhood. So it was true no matter what humble birth a person might be handicapped with, destiny, persistence and hard work can propel him (or her) to the highest peeks of historical glory, in America perhaps more frequently than elsewhere. 'Wow! This is uniquely fantastic! Then what am I perennially complaining about, what is my suffering compared to such greatness? Not much, indeed.'

But wait a minute, the coin might have another face as well, my self-torturing, joy-robbing sense of prevarication interfered promptly as always, preventing me from seeing reality in unadulterated purity, unaffected by my damned habitual inclination to analytical deconstructing. Instead of dwelling on how Lincoln's greatness happened to grow out of absolute insignificance, instead of using his example as an inspiration, my idiotic intellect reminded sadly rather of the man's tragic end. Lincoln died assassinated, my soul yelled out in reflexively unfurled furry, **'the man got himself killed'** for fighting on the side of good, for breaking asunder the chains of slavery, for giving back to so many the dignity all human beings deserve, as the thirteen-to-fifteenth amendments to the American Constitution nobly has been proclaiming ever since. And what has been Lincoln's reward for his goodness? **Death**! The same death Christ received for declaring all men equally children of God, the same death Gandhi the Mahatma was paid for valuing Muslims and Hindus humanly alike, the same death Martin Luther King gained for having the similar dream of reaching the mountaintop of equality, the same death too many great men were slain for sacrificing themselves on behalf of their fellow brothers and sisters. Amen.

Is it then so illogical to ask whether a person's destiny assigned at birth can be truly overcome? Is the transgression of shaking off one's lot allowed without incurring a severe punishment? Why good deeds must always beget pain as payback? Silence! Silence! Silence! Deep within my perplexed mind, through my chaotically stirred-up emotions, the intellect kept ruminating on these paradoxes, trying to throw light into the darkness of a modest motel room late at night somewhere in Elizabethville.

But before succeeding to shut my eyes asleep, the vacuum-like silence had to be penetrated by the never failing personal noise, by the eternal issue of the self, in the end the sole mirror to be confronted at last, either in pity, self adulation, sheer indifference, malicious impulse, or grossest egotism. So then, what does this mirror reflect about me? Where do I fit in the equation? Is it possible for fate to have designated either one separately, Didonna, or Philomela as my only true partner in life, but not both? By the same token, was the present new, or the old fated to be my real country? How will I then have to atone for my transgressions, for my dare to altering such possibly preordained outcomes? Where should my allegiance go, to God, country, family? Stop, stop, and stop, intervened Morpheus mercifully, before switching my lights off at last. Oh Nirvana, welcome Nirvana!

But, early in the morning, as Bucephalos set out on the long, final stretch homeward, strangely enough I felt no longer bothered by previous night's tortured senseless philosophical considerations. Under the spotless blue sky, the bright, blinding sunlight burned off yesterday's bad dreams, out of my memory bank, as they never were. God acted merciful indeed by endowing humans with forgetfulness!

But, before getting home we --that is Bucephalos and I-- had to night over once more, somewhere near Charles Town, West Virginia. I could have continued straight on without a halt, had not elected to arrive at dawn, reckoning morning to be the best time to start a working day, as well as a new life. By prolonging even by a few measly minutes my woefully derailed adventure, I could enjoy one more night for weaving wonderfully luminous plans, to remake in my sick imagination my marriage to Philomela, to help Camellia out of her youthful wanderings in the wilderness, to fully toss my earthly transgressions in the fire of a new rising sun of blissfully renewed happiness. There must always be a way to redemption somewhere, I argued.

*

It was a little before nine o'clock in the morning when I pushed the key in, to unlock the door of our town home in Damascus. Then

I noticed the large cardboard box cast in the bushes by the stairs, a note stuck on it.

'The package contains your things left at my place. I hope you'll find everything all right. Sorry to leave the box like this. Nobody answered the bell, Didonna.'

Inside, another note on the kitchen table:

'I went to California. Mark wants me back. Looks like mother moved out. I didn't see her mug lately. Will call you soon, love Camellia.'

Huh, I sighed, what an auspicious scenario for a new beginning! It looks like I will have to work harder than imagined for reversing the unfriendly tide. Yet, the job must be done. But let's first wash off all the dirt accumulated during the last ten years on my stupid head. So march in the shower old Dorel, and then call the office to announce your return. You must proceed methodically. The thought had barely time to take shape, when a knock on the door forced my performing a quick about face.

"Are you Mr. Doru Constantin Corbea?" The question came from a female police officer, actually a sheriff, her function guessed off the cruiser parked in front of the house.

"Yes indeed, I am Doru Constantin Corbea!"

"Excellent. Sir, hereby you are officially served with the summons to your divorce from wife Philomela Corbea. Please sign above this line. Then, "Thank you Mr. Corbea, I am really sorry. Goodbye."

All of a sudden sixteen tons of granite boulders fell on my head, as my dreams crashed against the hard ground of reality in the same heartbeat. My knees turned jelly soft. I had to sit. For more than a few minutes could do nothing but read and re-read the summons, which in light of my latest optimistic resolution didn't make any sense whatsoever.

Finally my composure recovered enough to remember that I was about to shower only minutes earlier. Unable to stand in the stall as usually, my near-lethal weakness forced my lying down under the coldest stream of nerve-numbing water. Even so it took a long, long time to regain the minimum strength, to look life in the face as it was, not as I wishfully imagined it during the last couple of days. Then a miraculously electrifying glimmer of light rekindled in my almost dead soul like out of nowhere. I must show the summons to Didonna, and who knows... --hope springs eternal!

The minutes and hours until the evening hours ticked away painfully slow. I had little choice in the matter, couldn't rush as my ex-mistress surely returned to her regular work schedule. Finally around seven thirty in the evening, she opened the door following my impatiently impetuous knocks.

"Here, read this," and I handed her the summons.

It took her only a glance to turn crimson red in the face, and to yell out in the sharpest, bitchiest voice ever.

"Go to hell!"

Then she slammed the door right in my face.

***

"That's it?"

"Yes Mr. Manta, not an iota more."

"What happened at the divorce proceedings?"

"I don't have the faintest. The judge ruled in my absence."

"So you lost everything, isn't it?"

"Well, about half of all possessions, and thanks to God the right to an acceptably good retirement had been granted to me as well. Out of this I can presently afford renting the modest room you see, as well as paying for my daily bread, so to speak."

"Did you at least try fighting for a larger share of the pie?"

"Why bother? Too many things changed during the past two decades for a born loser to plan for anything in this New World Order."

"What's the New World Order has to do with your story?"

"Well, hasn't lately our planet engaged on a path of selfdestruction?"

"What, what are you talking about?"

"Oh nothing at all, absolutely nothing, you must know by now how I like to ramble on senselessly. Forget what I said!"

"What about Philomela, what happened to her?'

"She retired some years ago, then sold the house in Damascus, and moved to California. She must be still living there with her brother we helped immigrate in the US at the end of the seventies.

"And Didonna, how did she fare?"

"I can't say for sure. Never seen her again. The rumor goes she brought over a niece from Romania. Folks say she needs all the help she can get, for her articulations got afflicted by a crippling sort of rheumatoid arthritis"

THE END.